Gash took one last look around.

He saw the kid had wandered off a ways but was still within sight. No reason they shouldn't go back. Evening was coming, and the TJs would be calling it a day by the time they reached the lake. Gash was already thinking about lighting up and enveloping himself in peaceful blue haze.

He motioned to Cayenne, turned downhill, and called to Eamon, "Come on, kid, we're going back down." He had only gone a half-dozen paces when the turtle yelled.

"There's something here!"

"What is it?"

"Come here and look."

"He's probably found a shiny pebble or something," Cayenne mocked.

"It's a—" Eamon didn't finish.

Gash didn't know what it was, but something had the turtle excited. There was even a hint of fright in his voice. He guessed he'd have to trudge on over and see what it was.

He smelled it before he saw it. It was a human hand and part of an arm, poking out from under the scrap of on forest floor.

ALSO BY BRUCE GOLDEN

Better than Chocolate
Dancing with the Velvet Lizard (2010)

EVERGREEN

BRUCE GOLDEN

ZUMAYA OTHERWORLDS   AUSTIN TX

2009

EVERGREEN
© 2009 by Bruce Golden
ISBN 978-1-934841-32-7

Cover art © Daniele Serra
Cover design © Valerie Tibbs

Zumaya Otherworlds and the griffon logo are trademarks of Zumaya Publications LLC, Austin TX. Look for us online at http://www.zumayapublications.com.

Library of Congress Cataloging-in-Publication Data

Golden, Bruce, 1952-
Evergreen / Bruce Golden.
    p. cm.
ISBN 978-1-934841-32-7 (alk. paper)
I. Title.
PS3607.O452E84 2009
813'.6--dc22

                    2009004424

For Savannah

The oaks and the pines, and their brethren of the wood, have seen so many suns rise and set, so many seasons come and go, and so many generations pass into silence, that we may well wonder what "the story of the trees" would be to us if they had tongues to tell it, or we ears fine enough to understand.

— *Author Unknown*

1

Darkness veiled the walls of the dusty catacomb, toying with ancient superstitions and a newly-realized sense of claustrophobia. Jimiyu took a deep breath to calm himself. The air was stagnant, stifling. They were so deep within the labyrinth of alcoves and stairwells, he wasn't sure he could find his way out. The candles that lit their way provided little illumination, and he couldn't help but wonder why, after so many centuries, no one had installed electric lights. Or, even better, why they hadn't moved all these documents out of this hellish tomb and into the abbey's main library.

It's not my place to criticize, he chided himself. I'm here to assist Dr. Nikira, not to ask irrelevant questions.

He stood by as the taller man hunched across an oversized tome laid upon a rough stone slab, squinting as he searched through page after time-worn page, seeking answers to questions Jimiyu only half understood.

Even when they were boys together in Kenya, his friend Talib had always questioned everything, had always taken the lead, and Jimiyu had followed. Until the day Talib bade farewell to the tribal lands of the Kikuyu, left Jimiyu standing there, waving goodbye, and traveled across the ocean to continue his studies on another continent. Many years later, when they were reunited, Talib had become Dr. Nikira, noted theologian and psychologist, but Jimiyu was still just Jimiyu. Now, even in Jimiyu's thoughts, his friend was Dr. Nikira.

No longer in awe of his old friend's many accomplishments, what Jimiyu felt now was concern. The work was taking its toll. Nikira wasn't eating or sleeping nearly enough, and Jimiyu worried that all this research under such poor lighting might leave his friend blind. Even though they were the same age, the lines in Nikira's face, the gray in the goatee he pulled at continually, made him seem much older.

But there was nothing Jimiyu could do. The man was obsessed with finding some obscure reference that would support his theory, some corroborating bit of evidence that would silence the resounding disdain of ex-colleagues that Jimiyu knew haunted him.

Such is the destiny of men who try to understand the mysteries of God, thought Jimiyu. If you ascend too close to the heavens, the brightness is bound to burn you. That's what Nikira was trying to do. The scholarly former priest believed with all his heart that he knew something about God no one else did. He believed in it so much his insistence resulted in his banishment from the church. Even so, he had many followers—many who had come to share his beliefs. Jimiyu was not one of them. He served his friend out of loyalty, not because of any overwhelming spiritual convictions.

"Nothing," Nikira said, closing the massive volume he had been laboring over. He vented a sigh of exhaustion as he straightened up. Jimiyu heard the cracking of his old friend's bones. "Perhaps it's *all* been for nothing."

Jimiyu didn't respond. Nikira had a habit of talking to himself, even when others were around.

"Jimi?" Nikira turned as if to look for him.

"I'm here."

"I don't know anymore, Jimi. I just don't know."

"You don't know what?"

"I don't know if faith alone is enough. When does a man say, *Give me more, give me a sign, show me proof?*"

"You're just tired, Doctor. You need rest."

"Skepticism is like a disease, Jimi. And educated skepticism—that is a rampant plague. It infects with the ravages of doubt."

"Come, let's go up to the abbey and get something to eat."

Nikira seemed only just now to see him standing there in the gloom.

He started back up the chiseled stone steps, and Jimiyu followed, extinguishing the trail of candles as they went. They wound up and around and across, yet Nikira never hesitated. Unerringly, he guided them out of the gloomy abyss.

Until now, Jimiyu's prime concern had been Nikira's physical health. The weariness he'd heard in his friend's voice spoke of a damaged spirit. He knew what Nikira needed. He needed to free himself from his obsession—to find other goals, other reasons to live. That was why Jimiyu had invited Chanya to join them. Her feelings for Nikira, unrequited as they were, might yet draw him out. Maybe she...

A bright light struck them from above. A silhouette stood in the doorway at the top of the stairs. The slender build and waving arm told him it was Vincent Boorman, the young heir to the Boorman fortune and one of Nikira's "true believers." It had been more than a week since they'd last seen him, and Jimiyu had wondered if maybe he'd lost interest in Nikira's cause and gotten wrapped up in some more trendy crusade.

As they drew closer, Jimiyu saw unrestrained exhilaration on Vincent's face. Youthful as he was, Vincent was given to bouts of frivolous enthusiasm, but Jimiyu liked him anyway. He was one of a growing number of new-generation disciples who thought of Nikira as a sort of contemporary prophet. He was also a scion of wealth and privilege. Jimiyu tried not to hold that against him.

"Dr. Nikira, it's the mega-zapper! Come on, hurry, I've got to show you. Wait until you scan this."

Nikira trudged upward, showing no sign of succumbing to Vincent's impatience. "Everything comes gradually, Vincent, and at its appointed hour."

"Dr. Nikira needs rest. Can't this wait, Vincent?"

"No, it can't. You'll see, Jimi. This is mega. It's hugando."

Nikira and Jimiyu made their way into the abbey's study, and Vincent shut the door behind them.

"Sit down, Doctor," Jimiyu insisted, gesturing toward a comfortable chair. Nikira didn't argue. He dropped into the chair as Vincent retrieved a case he'd placed on the table.

3

"All right, Vincent, what is it that's provoked you so?"

"This," he said, opening the case. "This is it."

He pulled out a rather unsightly chunk of wood about the size of a man's hand, three or four inches thick. One side was fairly flat, but the other appeared to be an uneven tangle of shorn roots, covered with a thin veneer of an amber-colored resin.

Nikira took it from him. "What is it, exactly?"

"It's an ancient artifact. It was just chance that I heard about it," said Vincent, the words rushing out of his mouth. "I scanned it last week, then bought it. I got some experts to analyze, ruminize, and speculize—you know, run some tests. Look at it, Doctor. *Look at it.*"

Nikira examined the object intently. Jimiyu saw the spark of interest in his eyes fan to flames the moment he saw what was carved into the flat side of the wood. It looked to Jimiyu like a rendering of tree—one whose limbs were alive with movement. He wasn't sure why, but it seemed familiar.

"It looks like..." Nikira hesitated, staring at the carving, almost as if he didn't believe what he was about to say. "It looks like the Tree of Life."

"I knew it!" exclaimed Vincent. "I knew it. I remembered it from your book—the picture in your book."

"Yes, yes," Nikira replied, still preoccupied with studying the artifact. "That illustration was part of a pictographic representation discovered among the relics of Sumeria."

"It's very interesting," Jimiyu interposed, "but Dr. Nikira needs to get something to eat now, and then—"

"Where was this found?" asked Nikira, ignoring Jimiyu's concern.

"That's the best part," Vincent gushed, a convulsive smile entrenched on his face. "It was found off-world. It came from another world, Doctor—*another world.*"

Vincent could hardly contain himself waiting for Nikira's reaction. Jimiyu was slow to realize the significance. His attention was directed at his friend.

The gaze Nikira focused on Vincent Boorman would have been frightful to Jimiyu if he hadn't noticed the creases in the exhausted man's face pulling taut, and the fatigue in his eyes evolving into wonder—metamorphosis in mere seconds.

"And scan this," Vincent continued unabated. "They measured its isotopes or something. What did they call it? I don't tally that stuff—mass spectrometry or whatever. They say it's more than forty-five thousand years old. Zapper, huh?"

Nikira stood, still holding the artifact. Vincent beamed from ear to ear.

"I don't understand," Jimiyu said. "What does it mean?"

Nikira seemed as if he were still in a state of rapture, so Vincent replied, "Don't you tally this, Jimi? It could mean that Dr. Nikira's hypothesis is true."

"*Cidade de Deus*," Nikira mumbled, as if to himself. Then, focusing on Vincent, he said, "I must go there, see for myself."

"Already cycling, Doctor. I knew you'd want to go, to find more evidence, so I've got my people setting it up. Even with all the credit I've got to spread around, it'll take some time to secure space on the next outbound ship and arrange everything."

"You would finance such an expedition?" Nikira asked, making no attempt to conceal the hopefulness in his voice.

"In for an artifact, in for a little anarchy and adventure," Vincent quipped. "Besides, what better output for the billions my father left me?"

It was all moving too fast for Jimiyu. What were they talking about? Leaving Earth? Mounting an expedition to another world?

Nikira ran his hand across his balding head and stared up at the ornate crucifix mounted on the wall. "God has shamed me," he said. "Rewarding me even as my faith began to lapse. Though I'm no longer worthy, he beckons me."

Nikira turned, and Jimiyu saw a different man standing before him. Different and yet the same—standing taller, fuller, more like the astute, confident man he had known so many years ago.

Nikira looked again at the artifact, cupping it in his hands as if it were as fragile as crystal and not something that had survived millennia.

"On what planet was this found?" he asked.

"One of those colonial worlds halfway across the galaxy," Vincent responded. "They call it Evergreen."

2

Stillness dominated the verdant mosaic. But for an intermittent breeze or the occasional aerobatic maneuvers of a busy arthropod, equanimity reigned. Beneath the needle-clustered sky spread a vast herbaceous expanse of nettle and clover, fern and tamarack. Endless processions of stolid boles stood guardian-like over the emerald vista as cable-thick creepers extended their leaves toward the light of the new day.

Sustained by neural proteins and chain-like phosphorous deposits, organic awareness disseminated from root crown to collective consciousness. Hydrolytic impulse streams converged and diverted, continually generating new communiqués. An ancient sapience simmered. Information was shared, commands were issued, procedures delegated.

The awareness was boundless, its concept of time quantified by eons. As its environs raced from life to death to life again, it contemplated, evaluated. Days to ponder a single thought, a decade to compel an action. Distress was assessed and codified seasonally. Deliberation was protracted. Once cognition determined a course of action, processes commenced. Responses were all-encompassing.

Even now, the panoplied consciousness was entrenched in extended contemplation. Anxiety relative to a rootless, encroaching fungus infected its being. The ever-accelerating invasion disturbed its sensory network, agitated its nutrient balance, provoked its core existence.

Threat.

Menace.

Survival was essential. All non-related matters were routed to secondary nodes. Neural messages bristled with multifarious data and conflicting deliberations. A determination was forthcoming.

3

Gash stepped back as the majestic giant teetered. Six tons poised on a splintered hinge, suspended, defiant of gravity, almost as if it refused to fall. But fall it did, with a ponderous sway, followed by a resounding, ground-shaking collision. The impact reverberated like a death rattle through the ranks of its fellows, followed by a moment of deceptive stillness. Then, like scavengers, the limbers moved in. They got right to work, dismembering, desecrating, indifferent to its noble heritage.

It was far from his first, and it wouldn't be his last, yet a surge of unexpected melancholy prompted Gash to offer a silent salute to the downed colossus. It had to be at least five hundred years old, yet he'd felled it in a relative blink of an eye. How quickly life could change. One instant you're presiding over the apex of your world, the next you're fodder for the mill.

Gash checked the power level of his saw. It was nearly drained. Before he could concern himself with his options, he heard the wrap-up whistle and realized it didn't matter. The sound inspired the limbers to work even faster, though that didn't prevent a pair of choker-setters pulling cable from chiding them to speed it up.

"Let's go, turtles, get the briar out of your britches and move it."

Gash took a seat on the stump that moments earlier had been so much more and leaned against the holding wood remnant. The sun had already dropped behind Bailey's Ridge, and in the twilight he saw a sky sprite dancing playfully across the horizon, fanning from violet to lavender to carmine and back again. He never tired of watching the dazzling auroras that frequented Evergreen's atmosphere. They were the gaudy crown jewels of a world so magnificent that, even after all his time here, Gash still found himself captivated by the simplicity of its beauty.

He took off his cap and wiped his sleeve across his forehead. From where he sat, he could see across the sloping treeline to the boundless, glassy expanse of Lake Washoe. When he turned his head and looked up through the haze, he caught a glimpse of the colossal grandeur of the Twin Tits. Snow Tree stood out on the face of the right-hand tit, a reminder of high-altitude winter come and gone. It was a world of breathtaking splendor, a tour de force of nature, a virgin paradise only recently encroached upon by mankind.

A madfly suddenly strafed his face, interrupting his reverie. Its frenzied flight path brought it round again, and he swatted it away with his cap before it could bite him. It spiraled to the forest floor, where it made the fateful choice to alight on a gum frond. Gash watched it wriggle to free itself. Its wings beat so desperately in its attempt to escape the frond's sticky grasp he could hear the frantic buzzing. Its efforts were in vain. An accumulation of mummified husks foreshadowed the futility of its endeavor.

There was no going back for the madfly, thought Gash, just as there was no going back for him. The choices we make are as irrevocable as our birth, as immutable as the very mountain he now rested on. You can clear-cut its face, but its summit still stands.

> You've got to do it, Paul. You've got to
> blow it now!"

An echo from the past. Memories that were more than a ghost, yet haunted just the same. Gash pulled off his work-frayed gloves and tossed them to the ground. He reached into his vest pocket and pulled out a pipe. He knew how to deal with unrelenting phantoms. A few hits was all it would take to render them into abstraction.

9

4

Amanda unfolded her long legs to find a more comfortable position. It was times like these, when she was trying to make the most of a small space, that she disparaged her ungainly limbs, recalling the word her father had used to describe her when she was a girl. "Gawky" he had said.

She moved slowly so as not to disturb the ursu, though her concern was more out of habit than anything. She'd been camped with this community for months now, and they'd grown accustomed to her presence—or at least tolerated her. Even now a pair of cubs wrestled on the forest floor not four yards away, while nearby a group of males groomed their thick coats and sniffed the air for estrus. She recorded a few more photos of the youngsters before putting her camera down.

For Amanda, this was paradise. This was where her soul resided. She ventured into the boisterous frontier civilization of Woodville as seldom as possible—only to restock her provisions and download her notes into a secure data file for transport. She reveled in the peaceful company and simple life of the ursu. They were extremely social animals, and she believed they were only an evolutionary gradation away from true sentience. She was far from proving it, but the concept excited her.

She had guessed as much upon her first contact with the species, but their large brain-to-body ratio wasn't the only sign of intelligence. Observation revealed they taught their young basic survival skills, created foraging groups and used simple tools for acquiring food and water. She equated their intellects with that of dolphins or gorillas, and found the ursu shared characteristics with both the orangutan and various species of North American bear. Hence her composite of the two to create a temporary designation for the species—*Pongoursus evergreeni*. Temporary only because she awaited official confirmation by her colleagues on Earth.

Now, however, she had a new theory, which she was trying to confirm by observation. Unlike men, and most species of apes, she'd determined the ursu had a highly developed sense of smell. She believed they had facial scent glands, much like certain kinds of squirrels, and that complex odor bouquets were used not only for mating and familial determination but in combination with their verbalized grunts for more intricate communication. Eventually, she hoped to isolate various scents and communicate with the ursu herself. It would take many months, possibly years of living in isolation with the creatures. However, to Amanda, it was less sacrifice than it was concession to her reclusive nature. Cloistered here in the wilds of Evergreen, light-years from Earth, miles away from even the nearest outpost, she felt serene, secure.

She organized her thoughts and entered her latest findings onto her Trans-Slate. When she was finished, she read over some of her earlier notes while waiting for the device to transcribe her latest hand-scrawled observations into legible fonts.

> The animals are distinguished by their bulky, disproportionate physiques, and the manner in which they squat when remaining motionless. Thus the origination of the derogatory term "squats," which the colonists use in reference to the species I have come to know as the ursu.
>
> Like a bear, they have wide shoulders, and thick rear legs with broad paws, possibly due to Evergreen's Earth-normal-plus gravity. Yet their forepaws, which are more streamlined than those in the rear, have the

opposable thumbs necessary to give them primate-like dexterity. This difference is more pronounced in females, who do more climbing. All the ursu, however, have long, orangutan-like arms that make them agile climbers, despite their bulk (estimate males weigh as much as 170 lbs., females a little more than half that). Unlike either bears or orangutans, they have long, prehensile tails they employ for climbing and to stabilize themselves once perched in a tree. Their sharp claws are used for both climbing and digging.

Their shaggy, rust-colored coats have shown no signs of shedding, despite the onset of warmer weather. Like a bear, they have long snouts and rounded ears, but their large gray eyes are more simian in appearance. However, they apparently don't see great distances, though they have acute senses of hearing and smell.

Unlike Earth primates, the ursu shape their environment. They live in large communities (I've counted close to eighty near my current camp), with the females and their young sleeping in the trees, in semipermanent nests. The males stay primarily on the ground, sleeping and taking refuge in crude shelters they construct out of stones and tree branches—another sign of their intelligence. This particular community of ursu has moved once during the three months I've been studying them. The move itself was less than a mile, and was, I theorize, prompted by the need to find richer foraging grounds.

The ursu have varied, seemingly indiscriminate eating habits. According to what

I've observed, they eat nuts, berries, grasses, lichen, certain plant leaves, insects, grubs, and fish when their foraging brings them across bodies of water containing aquatic life.

She made a few minor revisions then, satisfied, put away the Trans-Slate and pulled the cedar flute from her pack. A flicker of movement caught her attention before she started to play. She saw a small swarm of madflies hovering over a nearby mud hive. The warmer the weather, the more active the flies had become. She had some ideas concerning the flying insects, and the possibility they functioned as pollinators; but she'd been too busy studying the ursu to pursue those theories.

She raised the flute to her lips and began.

She wasn't what she considered an accomplished musician, but her tunes were passable—and soothing, she discovered, to the ursu. Her music also kept her company. It made her feel as if she weren't so alone, even when she was.

She was trying to master "Amazing Grace;" however, there was this one modulation that kept giving her trouble. Even so, the notes resounded melodiously through the trees—at least to her ears. There was a certain, haunting simplicity to the way the sound carried through the forest. There were even times when she thought she could hear the wind harmonizing with her.

5

The sensation crept up on her as opposed to overwhelming her. It began with the feeling of ants walking across her skin. First a few, then a swarm. It seemed as if her head were spinning, though the rest of her body remained stationary. The next thing she knew she was looking up through half-closed eyes at Luis.

"What happened?" she asked, trying to remember.

"It's all right, *mi querida*. You just fainted."

"I passed out?"

"Only for a few seconds. Remember, the captain warned us that when we emerged from the jump we might experience dizziness, queasiness."

"I had forgotten." Filamena tried to rise. Luis helped her into a sitting position on the bed. "Are you all right?"

"I experienced a brief loss of equilibrium. Nothing significant. Fortunately, I was near enough to catch you when you collapsed."

"Dear Luis, you're always there for me, aren't you?"

He smiled. "Yes, except when I'm—what's the word you use?—gallivanting around the world."

"It's your work that takes you away from me—I understand. You do always encourage me to join you."

He fixed the pillow behind her. "Yes, but I know you can spend only so much time watching me brush the dust from buried bones and piece together pottery shards. I'm sure you thought when you married me that gallivanting around the world with an archaeologist would be much more fun."

She *had* thought so, but she would never tell him that. "I do enjoy it...at times. I'm with you now, aren't I?"

"And I'm so glad you wanted to come."

"Who wouldn't want to visit a strange new world?"

"You didn't feel the same way when I went to Mars, and that was the most important dig of my career."

"I know. At the time, it just didn't seem that exciting. All those pictures of Mars you showed me looked so dreary." Of course, the pictures had had nothing to do with it. There had been another reason she hadn't gone to Mars. In a way, it was the reason she was with him now.

"You may find Evergreen's not all that strange or exciting either. I understand that it's very much like Earth—at least the parts of it which have been explored."

She slid her legs over the edge of the bed and grabbed his hand. "Then we'll be explorers together."

He patted her hand. "My dear, loyal Filamena."

She stiffened at the praise, yet refused to let shame consume her. "Are you really so surprised that I would come with you?" she asked.

"No, *mi querida*, I'm not. I'm more surprised that Maximo wanted to come. I can't believe he's as excited as you are about visiting an alien world. I think, maybe, he's trying to mend fences."

Filamena stood and walked to the compartment's mirror as Luis continued.

"Do you think he asked to come on this trip in order to get to know his father better? Maybe he's finally matured—forgiven me for not always being there for him."

"It's possible," Filamena said as she began brushing her hair. She had been as surprised as Luis that Max had asked to join them on this expedition. Yet she was afraid she knew the real reason he had come, and it wasn't to bond with his father. "You've been a good father to him, Luis. You have nothing to feel guilty about."

"You don't know how often I had to leave him in the care of others after his mother died. I was always so obsessed with my work. I convinced myself it was better to leave him at home. It wasn't until he was older that I knew I had lost him. Now he's a young man with no need of his father."

"You haven't lost him, Luis. He's here, isn't he?"

"Yes, that's true."

She watched in the mirror as her husband picked up his data pad, paused, and put it down again.

"I think I'll go see how he is."

"That's a good idea."

"Would you like to come with me?"

"No, no," she replied quickly, "I think it's best if you two spend as much time alone together as possible. I think I'll go for a walk—maybe down to the viewport to see what this Evergreen looks like."

"You won't be able to see much of it yet, dear," he said, opening the compartment door. "We're still weeks away. Remember how the captain explained we couldn't come out of the hyperspace jump too close to the sun's gravity well?"

"You know I don't understand all that."

He smiled that smile of his that contrasted his fleshy nose and thin lips. "I know you don't. I'll be back soon."

"Take your time."

He closed the door, and Filamena put down her brush. In the mirror, she could see her face was still flushed. Her reflection looked back at her, judgmental. She studied the minute worry lines in her face and knew that soon there would be many more.

As much as she hoped Max had come on this trip to make amends with his father, she knew in her heart it was wishful thinking. He was young and headstrong, and had obviously not listened to her. Either that, or he didn't believe her. There was nothing she could do about it now but pray her mistake didn't destroy all their lives.

Ritually, she checked her makeup, endeavoring at the same time to dismiss the strain of emotions that pulled at her. Composed, and finally satisfied with her appearance, she left the compartment and made her way down the corridor, passing only a single crewman, who was cleaning vomit off the deck. She guessed someone else had reacted poorly to "coming out of the jump," as they called it.

There was only one person standing at the viewport—a young man, tall, lean but wiry, with wavy brown hair and a doleful expression. He was probably only a few years younger than Max. The thought made her feel old—much older than thirty-four.

She'd seen this fellow when they first boarded the ship. She recalled how troubled his boyish face had looked. He was much too young to be so somber.

"Hello," she said, as cheerfully as she could manage.

He turned, and when he saw her he forced a brief smile. He had large, round gray-green eyes she found striking.

"Hi," he responded.

"Can you see anything?" she asked, stepping up to the viewport and looking out. It was so large she had to rein in the feeling she might fall out into space.

"Just the sun," he said, pointing at the largest object visible to them. "It's called Aurora—but you probably knew that."

"No, I didn't," she said, though she half-remembered Luis telling her.

"It's supposed to be brighter than our sun, but you can't tell from here."

Filamena searched the void. "Where's Evergreen?"

"I don't think we can see it yet."

"Oh, that's too bad," she said, feigning disappointment. She offered him her hand. "I'm Filamena."

He took it lightly, almost if it were a piece of china he was afraid might break. "Eamon," he replied.

"So, do you know how much farther we have to go, Eamon?"

"Not exactly. But I know how far we've come. Eighty parsecs, according to Captain Amidon, or, as the cabin pamphlet says, more than two hundred-sixty light-years."

Filamena shook her head. "I have no idea how far that is."

She was happy to see that made him smile. He responded, "Neither do I, really."

6

Amanda correlated her notes, transferred her photos to the file and added a brief summary of her latest findings. All the while the night desk company clerk ignored her. When she was finished she made a copy for transport to Earth, where her colleagues would, she was certain, rebuke her theories. She could hear them now. *You were sent to catalogue various species, not develop unsubstantiated theories on the possibility of sentient life.*

She didn't care. The university financed her study so she was obligated to share her research, but she wasn't concerned with their opinions.

She had planned her trek to Woodville to coincide with the arrival of the next ship so her most recent entries could be sent back. Shuttles from the *Heinlein* would begin landing tomorrow, so she'd finished just in time. She handed the file drive and her paperwork to the clerk, who accepted them, looking over the forms.

After careful inspection, he nodded and said, "We'll send this up with tomorrow's outgoing communications."

Amanda thanked him and left.

Her pack was loaded with all the provisions she could comfortably carry, and there was no reason not to head back to camp. Except that she had an unusual impulse to spend some time with other people.

For anyone else it would have been a normal response. After all, until she'd crossed the river she hadn't seen another human for...what? Five weeks? Six? It certainly wouldn't hurt her to mingle with humanity, such as it was, for a short while. Besides, it was past sundown, and she'd rather make the trip back at daybreak.

She'd already had something to eat at one of the local cafés, so there was really only one place to go--a place she'd been curious about. She'd heard some wild stories about it when she first arrived on Evergreen, but had never taken the time to see for herself. As a scientist, the very least she could do was base her opinions on empirical data instead of hearsay. At least, that was the excuse she gave herself.

So, she hitched up her pack and hiked the dirt road a short distance to Tahoe Tilley's. Even if she hadn't already been aware of its location, she wouldn't have had any trouble finding it. The noise alone was likely to draw customers from all around.

It was Funday by the local calendar, and that meant the timber jockeys were in town, venting a long week's-worth of steam.

Woodville had the look of a settlement right out of an old video about America's "Wild West." So much so that Amanda figured whoever designed the initial buildings did so on purpose. Whether it was it a matter of practicality or some private joke, she couldn't guess.

It wasn't a very large town—a few hundred people at most actually resided there. The majority of Evergreen's population lived outside the town—homesteading farmers, miners and, of course, the timber jockeys. For the most part, the people who lived and worked in Woodville served the needs of those in the outlying communities, or the needs of the company—which were practically the same thing. BMX was a big multi-national corporation back on Earth, but on Evergreen it was the *only* corporation. How it had managed to acquire exclusive rights, she had no idea. As she understood it, the company owned or leased almost everything in the colony, and managed it all with an iron fist. Or so she'd heard.

Only two streets served the town, crossing in its center. The shops and businesses were stationed along these main roads, while some living quarters, storage facilities, and the like branched off down lesser alleyways. The boardwalks along the front of the buildings were built up off the ground, and while the streets were level, they were unpaved.

Making her way down the dusty thoroughfare, it occurred to her that anyone seeing the town for the first time would know immediately how it got its name. Everything from buildings to bathtubs to the ungainly frames of its few solar-powered vehicles was constructed from Evergreen's most abundant natural resource—its giant redwood trees. At least she thought of them as redwoods. It wasn't her area of expertise, but from the little she'd studied them, Evergreen's redwoods seemed nearly identical in nature to the Earth species, *Sequoia sempervirens*, which got its name from a Cherokee Indian scholar and the Latin term meaning "always green." An odd combination, she'd always thought.

Mining operations had only recently begun on Evergreen, so most anything not made of the local wood had to be imported from Earth or other worlds. That included the red/violet neon lights ablaze with the moniker TAHOE TILLEY'S next to an improbably positioned, overly buxom female form. She gazed up at the display, thinking how out-of-place it was in this austere outpost of civilization.

Looking westward over the roof, Amanda saw fog in the distance, drifting in from the ocean. It was a good thing she hadn't tried to make the trek back to her camp tonight. As well as she knew the way, the often-thick Evergreen fog might have made it difficult.

She stepped up onto the boardwalk, ignoring the stares of a handful of timber jockeys gathered outside. The stench of smoke, sweat, and alcohol assailed her. She was used to the scent of the forest, the smell of the ursu. The reek of humanity was a foreign thing.

She straightened her khaki jacket and, after a moment's hesitation, approached the bulky saloon doors.

They were the kind of hinged doors she'd seen in the movies—more for show than anything. The real doors were pulled back and locked open, probably on a permanent basis--as she understood the place never closed.

She pushed through the doors, and a wall of frenetic sound enveloped her like a physical force. She hesitated again, but walked in, determined to see this adventure through.

The lower level was like some grand hall, a single large room crisscrossed by an irregular pattern of support beams rising up to a high ceiling. It was littered with a hodgepodge of chairs and tables—round, square, rectangular. There wasn't a whole lot of décor. Odds and ends of what looked like old lumberjack tools adorned the walls, as did some garish paintings of nudes. A threadbare rug embroidered with a medieval knight in armor served as a tapestry above the bar, which was packed shoulder-to-shoulder with standing customers. The area around the bar was relatively well-lit, but the rest of the place had a dark, cave-like ambience. If there were any windows, Amanda couldn't see them. She *could* see the muddy filth on the floor. What it consisted of she didn't even want to imagine.

Two sprawling staircases led to the second floor, one on each side of the room. The gaudy design of the carpet lining the risers was well-worn, but not as grubby as the place's lower level. The upper floor was terraced over the main room, and from that perch men and women leaned against the railing—talking, drinking, groping each other.

Among the many striking tableaus she encountered, the one to immediately catch her eye was a group of lumbermen who had commandeered the player-piano and were mocking the robot piano player as they sang along with boisterous gusto, if not entirely in tune. Not far away, more men were packed in tight around a gaming table where jeers and cheers erupted intermittently

Amanda took a seat at a small table in a dim corner and removed her pack. She was promptly greeted by a waitress whose unenthusiastic expression revealed as much as her outfit. She guessed by the way the woman was dressed that serving drinks wasn't the only service she provided.

"What can I get you?"

"I–I guess I'll have a beer."

"One beer," she repeated dryly, already sauntering away.

Relaxing in the relative safety of her corner table, Amanda looked around. There were some townies, a group of mining engineers she recognized because she'd arrived on Evergreen with them and timber jockeys, who made up the unruly majority. Most still wore hats even though they were inside. She gathered by the variety of headgear that they served both as protection from the sun and symbols of individuality. Like the stripes on a zebra, each timber jockey had his own markings. Most wore baseball-type caps of various colors and bearing various emblems, many with extended bills, but there was an assortment of Panamas, fedoras and cowboy hats as well. Some were more practical for protection from the sun than others.

Their bacchanalian pursuits were pretty much what she imagined, though she saw some things even her imagination wouldn't have allowed for. One woman four tables away, wearing a lot less than Amanda would need for minimal modesty, had both hands full of burgeoning genitalia, which she casually squeezed and stroked. The two fellows attached to her ministrations were engaged in a somewhat heated discussion but seemed otherwise unfazed. The woman appeared just as intent upon their conversation as she was with her handiwork.

The overtness of it surprised Amanda, but didn't shock her. She knew what went on upstairs, though she hadn't expected such outré escapades here, in full public view. When she realized she was staring, and that a rather warm feeling was creeping into her own loins, she looked away, nonchalantly, as though witnessing such sexual gratification was commonplace. Instead, she turned her attention to the fellows who were just finishing their bawdy, off-key rendition of "I've Been Workin' on the Railroad."

Gradually, she regained her composure, and when her beer arrived she paid for it with Evergreen scrip and quickly took a drink. It was bitter, and not like any beer she'd ever tasted on Earth. Whether it was better or worse, she couldn't say—she wasn't that much of a beer drinker.

She put the mug down, looked up, and her line-of-sight fell on an interesting fellow sitting alone just across from her. He caught her attention because he *was* alone, and because of the obtrusive scar that ran from his left eye across a broken nose and down his right cheek. It had been one nasty cut. Yet, regardless of the scar's grisly appearance, Amanda found the fellow handsome—if in a haggard sort of way.

He had close-cropped hair that was beginning to gray, and deep-set blue eyes that, despite herself, she found fascinating.

22

There was no particular spark of life in those eyes at the moment. In fact, the fellow looked downright maudlin, staring into his beer with more introspection than the brew deserved. Amanda was weighing the pros and cons of introducing herself when several of his compatriots showed up.

One of them, the runt of the litter, said to the others, loud enough to be heard over the din, "I'm going to find Sunny." Another newcomer waved him off, and they all sat at scar face's table.

Amanda recognized one of them but couldn't recall his name. He was an elderly fellow whose leathery face was as furrowed as plowed earth. His long, straight gray hair was held in place by a simple headband. He moved so sure-footed through the bar, with only a hand lightly placed on the arm of a companion, that Amanda wouldn't have known he was blind if she wasn't already familiar with the local legend.

Ford—she remembered now his name was Ford. Reputedly, he was the only remaining member of the group of Native Americans who originally colonized Evergreen. Of course, he must have been a child then. The stories of what had happened to those colonists were as varied as they were colorful, and likely, Amanda believed, embellished by the local Chamber of Commerce.

Sitting down with Ford were four others—timber jockeys by their look, though one, she realized belatedly, was a woman. She was dressed like the others, fairly tall, big-boned, and looked as strong as any man. She'd have to be for that kind of work, thought Amanda. Still, she'd never seen a female timber jockey before.

Something else caught her attention then. A tall man wearing a brocade vest embossed with gold thread was making his way through the saloon, slapping some patrons on the back, trading quips with others. He had a pencil-thin mustache, a tiny triangular patch of hair pointing down his tapered jaw and a single gold earring. It occurred to her he looked like a pirate.

Without any warning Amanda could discern, a fight broke out. Two men began trading punches, nearly toe-to-toe. The fancy pirate moved in without hesitation and pushed the combatants apart before they even realized he was there.

"None of that shit in here!" he snarled, and continued on his way. Amanda wondered how he could be so certain the fight wouldn't resume, but it didn't.

The fellow ambled from table to table, bellowing, "Drink up, you cocksuckers! Drink up!" He paused to converse with someone, then stepped up onto an empty chair and shouted so everyone in the place could hear him. "Shut up! Shut up and listen!" The intensity of the racket fell a few decibels, though not much. "Pussy's half-price for the next half-hour!"

A roar of approval thundered through the establishment, and Amanda wondered for a moment if the wooden rafters would hold. The brassy proprietor jumped down and pointed at the female timber jockey.

"That goes for you, too, Butch. Unless, of course, you prefer cock, in which case I can probably swing you a deal there, too."

The hard-looking woman cursed him in what sounded like another language, and added, "You kiss your mother with that mouth, Larimore?"

The proprietor laughed. "Hell, my mother could out-cuss any ten TJs, and then bounce their butts if they got sassy."

"Must have been quite a lady," said the older fellow next to Ford.

The proprietor grunted. "Wasn't much of a lady. She ran a honky-tonk that would make this place seem like a kindergarten class. Truckers called her Tahoe Tilley because her place was just above the lake near Emerald Bay."

"Isn't that sweet," taunted the burly woman. "You named this joint after your mother."

The proprietor dismissed her snide comment with a wave, as if she wasn't worth a comeback, and sauntered away, cajoling more customers.

Meanwhile, two of the men who'd just sat at the table said something to their companions Amanda couldn't hear, got up and hurried off. Amanda watched them go, then felt a hand on her shoulder. She turned and shrugged off the unwelcome paw.

"How much?"

Standing there, weaving visibly, was one of the mangier specimens of manhood she'd seen in the place. The fellow had a ragged beard, dirty clothes, and was so inebriated Amanda figured she could push him over with a finger.

"I said how much?" he slurred again.

"What are you talking about?"

"You know."

"Back off, Sanford." It was the scarred man, coming to her rescue. "The lady's not interested. Go find it somewhere else."

The drunk flashed a look at who had ordered him off but didn't reply. He held both hands up as if in surrender, almost losing his balance. Righting himself, he lurched off.

"He's as harmless as a broke-down plow horse, ma'am." It wasn't her mystery man who spoke, but the other fellow who sat with him. This guy was older, probably in his late forties, dark curly hair, small as timber jockeys went yet with the same compactly muscled frame most of them sported. He was hard-looking—not mean, but with a face chiseled by grit. "A woman sitting alone is kind of asking for attention in here. If you'd like to join us, you could avoid further such inconveniences."

Amanda considered the offer. "All right. I think I will," she said, getting up. "If it's okay with everyone."

The woman at the table nodded. The scarred man took another drink of his beer. The older fellow motioned her over and pushed out an empty chair for her.

Amanda sat, noticing, now that she was closer, the variety of tattoos. The scarred fellow had one on the inside of his big forearm. She couldn't see it all, but it looked like some kind of lightning bolt. His timber jockey friends, at least from what she saw of their exposed areas of flesh, had quite a bit of body art, too.

"I'm Eduardo—Eduardo Ramos," the dark-haired fellow said. "This old hombre here is Ford."

The sightless fellow held out his hand, and Amanda took it. "Ford Bennington Haverslaw, last of the mighty Washoe," he said. "Not that might makes right, you understand."

Ramos continued with his introductions as if he hadn't been interrupted. "And over there is Cayenne, and that's Gash."

"Dr. Amanda Rousch," she replied, realizing how formal she sounded. "It's nice to meet you all."

"I've seen you around, Doc," Ramos said, "but I don't think I've ever seen you in here."

"Please, just call me Amanda. No, you're right. This is my first time, though I've heard about the place."

25

"Surprised that didn't keep you away," he said with a chuckle.

"Oh, I figured I'd see what it was all about. Even the most monastic recluse needs a little human interaction once in a while."

"Is that what you are? A monk?" It was the one introduced as "Gash."

"Actually, I'm an exobiologist. I just live like a monk." Amanda smiled, but Gash didn't react. "I'm camped north of Vaughn's Valley. I've been studying a community of ursu—squats, you call them."

"Really?" Ramos seemed surprised. "Just you, by yourself, living with the squats? Sounds dangerous."

"They're not dangerous, I assure you."

"It's pretty far from civilization, though. You like living out there?"

"There are times I prefer the simplicity of nature to the complexities of human society. Civilization's not always what it pretends to be."

"Not much civilization around here anyway," Cayenne spoke up. "Woodville's about as raw as a town comes."

"To Woodville," Ramos said, lifting his mug, "and its lack of civilization."

Amanda joined them as they touched mugs in a toast.

Ramos wiped his lips with the back of his hand. "Well, I hope some of the shenanigans of our uncivilized men haven't shocked you, Doc—I mean, Amanda. They can be a pretty raunchy bunch when it comes time to cut loose. You have to understand their situation—how hard they work."

Amanda waved off his disclaimer. "It doesn't bother me. Men aren't all that complicated. Not anymore than your garden-variety houseplant." She noticed Cayenne laughed at this. "They drink as much as their stems will hold, and then point themselves in whatever direction the sunshine is warmest." She noticed even Gash smiled.

"So, too, are the tree spirits like men," Ford stated in a quasi-mystical tone. "The tree spirits eat and drink. They dance and sing the songs of the forest primeval. Listen. Can you hear them?" Ford cocked his head as if listening. "The tree spirits think, they hunt, they kill." The old man's tone changed from earnest to frivolous.

26

"At least, I think they do. I think they think. At least, I used to think so. They sure as hell drink, but do they actually dance? There's a thought worth thinking about."

Ramos tapped his finger against his head twice as if to let Amanda know he doubted Ford's lucidity. She nodded.

"Would you like to hear the story of the tree spirits?" Ford asked.

"Sure," Amanda replied.

As if it were a signal for him to leave, Gash stood. "Ford's quite the raconteur," he said to Amanda. "I'll be back," he added to no one in particular.

Gash wasn't a tall man, not much taller than Amanda, but he was muscle-thick. She furtively followed him with her eyes as she listened to Ford's tale.

"There was a young boy," Ford began, "who one day awoke from a terrible nightmare only to discover his village was deserted, his people all gone. His mother and father and all his friends had disappeared. He was so scared he fell down and cried. He was so sad that the sun itself wouldn't shine on him.

"When he stopped crying, he discovered he was in the dark and all alone. He clutched the medicine bundle his mother had put around his neck when he was just a baby and prayed to the tree spirits to protect him. And they did."

Gash had struck up a conversation with someone. The other fellow's back was to her, so Amanda couldn't see him.

"When he grew hungry the tree spirits brought him food. When he became thirsty, they guided him to the river. When he heard wild animals all around him, they sang their song to him. The song comforted him and kept the beasts away."

Gash appeared to complete a transaction of some sort with the fellow he was talking to and stuffed something in his pocket. The other fellow turned enough she could see he was rather scruffy-looking, and too scrawny to be a timber jockey.

"Years later, after he had grown and learned to feed himself and travel through the dark of the forest on his own, he was discovered by other people. They took him in and cared for him. And even though he could take care of himself, he let them, because he was lonely for his own kind. From that day on, the tree spirits no

27

longer sang to him—no longer watched out for him. But his world remained dark."

"It's a beautiful story," said Amanda when she was certain he was finished. "You make it sound so real."

"Think so?" Ford cocked his head toward her. "Then let me tell you about twenty acres of prime swamp I can sell you cheap."

"She's heard enough of your tall tales, Ford," Ramos said. "So, uh, Amanda, how long have you been on Evergreen?"

"Only about four months," Amanda replied. "What about you?"

"I'm one of the old-timers. Not like Ford, of course. He was born here. But I've been here eight years. I came to work here when they were just starting the logging operation. I was one of the first timber jocks—got sawdust in my blood now. Of course, that's not what I set out to do. I mean, I didn't leave Earth just to become a TJ."

"Why *did* you leave Earth?"

Amanda saw Ramos going back in his mind, reminiscing.

"I was young, dumb, full of fanciful ideas about outer space. I dreamed of adventures that would take me to alien cities, and into the arms of seductive, green-skinned women. So, I quit punching cattle and took the first outbound ship I could find. Of course, the joke was on me, because there aren't any alien cities, and all the women I've found are the same color as they are on Earth. Who would have thought that in all the galaxy we wouldn't find a single intelligent creature?"

"Just because they haven't found none yet, doesn't mean there ain't any intelligent aliens anywhere," Cayenne said, as if she still had hopes of such a discovery. "Look at what they found on Mars."

"It was an intriguing find, all right," said Amanda. "From what I hear, the jury's still out on whether the builders of those hives were intelligent or just instinctual."

Gash returned to his seat and took a drink. He'd overheard enough of their conversation to comment.

"Speaking on behalf of the one known intelligent species in the cosmos," he said, raising his mug in mock toast, "I say here's to something better."

He followed through with another drink of his beer. Amanda wasn't sure how to respond, so she continued with her previous thought.

"Cayenne's right, though. Man has only encountered a dozen or so inhabitable planets. It's still possible we may discover intelligence somewhere, sometime."

"I don't know," said Ramos, sitting back in his chair. "Got my doubts about that."

"Well, take the ursu, for instance. They show signs of intelligence."

"The what? Oh, you mean the squats?"

"Yes. They use crude tools, they have a loose tribal system, they build shelters..."

"Birds and beavers build shelters, too," Gash countered, "some pretty fancy. That doesn't make them intelligent."

"Actually, the nests of the ursu are quite similar in some ways to the lodges beavers build. As for intelligence, there are many ways it can be defined, many factors to consider. Just as there were many factors that resulted in man's own ascent into intellectual awareness. Standing upright and walking on two legs was actually the first evolutionary step between ape and *Homo sapiens*. The ursu are in that transition stage—sometimes walking on two legs, sometimes on all fours. In ten thousand years or even a thousand, who knows how they will evolve."

"By which time, no one will care," Gash muttered.

Ramos and Cayenne nodded in agreement. Amanda took another drink of her now-warm beer and studied Gash. She didn't know why, but he didn't seem like your typical timber jockey. Was it his restrained manner? The way he spoke? The words he used? "Raconteur" was not part of your characteristic timber jockey's vocabulary. She wasn't sure, but she felt there was something percolating underneath that scar and behind those blue eyes of his. Was it just her own loneliness talking? Was her attraction to this stranger strictly hormonal? Was she that susceptible to her own biology?

"So, Amanda, how'd you ever get the company to let you run free here on Evergreen?" Ramos asked. "Their set-up gives them exclusive mineral and timber rights, and management doesn't like to have scientists roaming around unchecked. I've never seen any except those that work for the company."

"I didn't have much to do with it," Amanda replied. "I know they weren't very receptive to the idea until an alumnus at the university where I work arranged it somehow. I guess she had some pull with someone."

"Must have been some hellacious pull to get them to bend their rules," said Cayenne. "They got more regulations than any five armies."

"Did you hear what the company's doing now?" Ramos asked no one in particular. "They want to change the vill's name. I hear Earthside they're already calling it 'Redwood Springs' or some such insipid burro's milk, trying to lasso investors and rich tourists."

"Woodville's not exactly glamorous-sounding," Cayenne said.

"Maybe not, but it's been Woodville since before the first wall was ever raised here, and that's the way it should stay. Hell, there's not even any *springs* hereabouts. Next thing you know, they'll be wanting to change Lake Washoe's name. What would you think of that, Ford?"

The blind man shrugged.

"It doesn't really matter what *they* call it, does it?" asked Gash. "The people who live here are still going to call it Woodville. And it'll always be Lake Washoe to us, right?"

Ramos took another drink of his beer. "You're probably right. It just sticks in my craw, that's all."

"So, are we going to eat or what?" Ford asked.

"I'm ready to put on the feedbag," Ramos replied. "How about it?"

Cayenne nodded. Gash was noncommittal.

"Doc Amanda, want to join us? Ford here is our bean master when we're working, so we get him a meal at the Pork Palace when we come to the vill, just so he'll know what proper food is like."

Ford sniffed indignantly and responded, "Sure, make fun of the blind old Injun."

"Thanks for the offer, Eduardo, but I'm a vegan."

"I thought you were from Earth."

"No," corrected Cayenne, "a vegan's some kind of a religious health thing."

"Neither, really," Amanda said. "It's more of a peaceful-co-existence-with-other-animals thing. I think of it as not eating anything with a face."

"That's, uh, interesting," Ramos replied, though the look on his face said much more about how queer he really thought it was.

"I've already eaten anyway, but thanks for the invitation."

"Will you go back to the forest?" Ford asked, concern in his voice

"Sure, early tomorrow."

"It's a dangerous undertaking, that," said Ford.

Amanda wasn't certain whether to take him seriously or not. She'd already noticed he had this way of twisting solemnity with satire.

"I want you to take something with you when you return to the domain of the tree spirits," he said. He pulled off a cord from around his neck and held it out to her. Attached to it was a small bag. "Take this as your guardian. It's my lucky medicine bundle. I've had it since I was a child. It protected me when the tree spirits sent the rest of my tribe to join their ancestors. And it smells good, too," he added with what Amanda could have sworn was a wink.

"I couldn't possibly take something like that, that you've had for so long," said Amanda.

"Tradition would have demanded I give it up long ago, had I any descendants to pass it on to," said Ford. "But, alas, my withered loins never produced offspring. You would do me great honor if you were to accept this as my *wa she shu e deh*—my spirit daughter."

"All right," Amanda said, taking the medicine bundle and placing its cord over her head. "What's in it?"

"Oh, the usual. Dried flower petals, mint leaves, Evergreen's version of garlic—an assortment of native weeds and herbs."

"Thank you very much, Mr. Haverslaw," Amanda said, extending her hand. Belatedly, she realized he couldn't see it and felt foolish. However, the old man reached out and took her hand as if he knew it was there. His age-roughed fingers caressed hers like they were reading Braille.

"Please, call me by the tribal name my grandfather gave me."

"What's that?"

"Ford, my dear, just Ford. It was a name endeared to my grandfather by his love for a metallic mustang, which he rode for decades, until the day he said goodbye to life's highway and ventured forth to meet his revered ancestors. That bond of man and machine was like no—"

"Sorry, but I've heard this one before," Gash said, interrupting what promised to be another long story. He got up. "Nice to meet you, Dr. Rousch. I'm sure we'll see you around." To his companions he said. "I'm going to yard-up Meanan and Porno Eddy. No doubt they're still upstairs somewhere. I guess I'll look for Farr, too."

"You'll never find Mousey," said Ramos. "He's sure to be shacked up with his girl, though how he can afford to keep her for himself till Riverday is more than I can savvy."

Gash shrugged. "We'll meet you over at the Pork Palace."

He walked away, and Amanda found herself contending with a sense of disappointment. She didn't know exactly why, or what she expected, but the feeling was there. It was silly. What did she think was going to happen? What did she *want* to happen?

7

ash shouldered through the crush of rowdies, thinking about Dr. Amanda Rousch. She was an interesting sort of woman, if somewhat of a plain Jane. From what little she'd said, he gathered they shared similar opinions about the state of mankind. He wouldn't mind talking with her again. She might be someone he could relate to, open up with. Not that he had anything more in mind than talking. He hadn't had any interest in that since...well, in a long time. Besides, she was a bit skinny for his taste.

He reached the main staircase and headed up. No doubt Meanan and Eddy would be deep into it by now. He wondered how many doors he was going to have to bang on if they didn't pop out soon. At the top of the stairs was a lavishly furnished hall-way—lavish for Woodville, anyway. It was a sort of staging area where selections were made, pairings confirmed, and connections heated up. He was surprised to find it empty—usually, there were at least a couple of Timber Tinas lounging around, waiting for customers. Then he remembered the half-price announcement. That explained why business was bopping.

He decided he'd wait a few minutes and see if the men appeared on their own before opening doors to hunt for them. He pulled out his recent purchase and began filling his pipe. He was about to light up when he heard a scream. It was clearly not the kind of scream you'd expect to hear in a bordello. It was a frantic outcry, a hysterical shriek of pain.

He stuffed the pipe back in his pocket and listened. He heard it again and ran to where it was coming from. He was surprised to discover the door to the room where the scream came from was locked. From past experience of hauling out TJs, he knew none of these pleasure rooms had locks. It was a safety measure.

He heard another screech and threw his shoulder into the door. It flew open in a shower of splintered wood.

Gash wasn't so much astonished by *what* he saw as *who*. One of the house girls was strung up, naked, on some contraption shaped like a double crucifix. She was face down, her back and buttocks streaked with whip marks. Wielding the whip was Administrator Oshima. The sight of Evergreen's chief bureaucrat and de facto governor left him momentarily stupefied. The administrator was so enthralled by her sadistic onslaught that even the cracking of the door hadn't broken the spell.

The whip struck again, and this time its target barely whimpered, as though she were only semi-conscious. The administrator had flung the whip over her shoulder for another strike when Gash grabbed her arm.

"That's enough!" he said, wrenching the whip from her grasp.

Oshima glared at him, her eyes irrational with hostility.

"What are you doing in here? Get out."

The tone of her voice carried the expectation of compliance. Nevertheless, Gash wasn't going anywhere.

"A rather aberrant hobby, don't you think, Administrator?" he said, tossing the whip across the room. "Or is *abhorrent* a better word?" He began untying the prostrate girl.

"Who are you?" she demanded. "How dare you break in here?"

"What's going on?" It was Shay Larimore, Tilley's proprietor, along with another of his girls. Gash had never had occasion to speak with the man, but knew who he was. Everyone knew who he was. He was the kind of fellow who stood out wherever he went.

"This...*person* barged in here," Oshima stated, regaining her composure. "You assured my privacy, Larimore."

Larimore assessed the situation with an experienced eye and smiled at Gash. "She's right, you know. You don't belong in here. Who are you?"

"Gash is the name. I came in because this girl was screaming bloody murder. Look at her."

"Pearl," Larimore said, addressing the girl, "did you get paid for what was done to you?"

Pearl, free from her bonds and rubbing her wrists, nodded her head.

"See, nothing to be alarmed about, Mr. Gash, just a simple business transaction. One in which both parties are satisfied. Shit, Pearl eats pain like candy, don't you, Pearl?"

"Why don't you and I go downstairs and I'll buy you—"

"It's just Gash, and I think Administrator Oshima's already gotten her money's worth. Wouldn't you agree, Administrator?"

Oshima didn't reply. She shot a look of disdain first at Gash, then Larimore, and stalked out without a word.

"Jelina, take Pearl and get her fixed up," Larimore directed.

The other girl did as she was told and led the quietly sobbing Pearl through the broken door. When the women were gone, Larimore turned to Gash.

"Gash, huh? I've heard mention of you."

"Oh? Why would that be?"

Larimore's middle finger played with the patch of hair on his chin. "Just casual conversation," he responded, shrugging.

"And what do you call this?" Gash said, gesturing toward the frame. "Just a little casual enterprise?"

He could tell Larimore took umbrage at this. He looked like he might stalk out. Instead, he replied, "I call it political leverage."

"Political what?"

"Let's just say this is a special room, where bad girls are seen *and* heard."

Gash didn't know what he was talking about. What did he mean "seen and heard"? Gash looked around. He didn't see anything unusual about the room, but the inference was there. Someone, or some*thing*, was watching this room.

"I have no idea what you're talking about," he said, turning to leave.

"No? Ask your friend Ramos, then," Larimore suggested, examining the busted door frame. "And go easy on the cocksucking construction next time, would you?"

35

Gash passed him as if he were part of the furnishings. "Yeah, I'll do that."

8

As the shuttle descended, Eamon got a spectacular view of his new home. His home for at least the next four years—the term of his enlistment. It didn't matter to him. He would have enlisted for a lifetime if he had to. He didn't expect to be allowed to leave anyway. Not after he did what he had to do.

The first thing he noticed about the planet was that it had no polar ice cap. Instead, the region was encompassed by a vast ocean. He remembered one of the ship's officers describing Evergreen as a world covered with forests and fresh-water seas. Indeed, all Eamon saw through the clouds during the descent were large expanses of indigo water and irregular land masses draped with greenery.

As beautiful as it was, he wasn't there to sightsee.

He wondered about the other passengers who had boarded the shuttle, and what their business was on Evergreen. He'd only talked at length with one of them, the beautiful lady with the raven hair who reminded him of his mother, but neither of them had discussed the reasons for their journey. It was just as well. He would have hated to lie to her. He wasn't sure why she reminded him of his mother. They didn't look that much alike, though she was probably about the same age his mother was when she...

Eamon didn't want to remember that right now. But he didn't want to forget it, either, and the incessant struggle twisted his insides. He reached to his neck and pulled up the thick silver chain that hung there. He groped for the medallion as the g-forces pushed him back into his seat. He felt the shuttle begin to level off, and the farther they dropped the heavier he felt. He could barely move his arm. He was told he'd feel his weight more on Evergreen. He hoped it wouldn't be this bad when they landed.

❧ ❧ ❧

The landing itself turned out to be so smooth, Eamon almost fell asleep. He no longer felt as if he were being pushed back into his seat, though his muscles were lethargic. Between the fatigue and the excitement of disembarking on a new world, he couldn't tell if he felt heavier or not. Still, by the time he got to the local customs office he felt the need to rest.

Yet it didn't appear he'd be sitting down anytime soon. Compared to any transit station on Earth, security here seemed rather lax. However, that didn't mean there wasn't bureaucracy. There was a commotion up ahead of him. Someone had run afoul of some local official. The dispute involved a caged animal. Eamon couldn't get a good look at the beast from where he was, but the animal's owner was definitely upset.

As the discussion ensued, Eamon noticed one member of their party surreptitiously moving an item of uninspected baggage past the customs man. He was an odd-looking fellow with big winged eyebrows that accentuated his protruding, bug-like eyes. He wore what Eamon recognized as an Atlanta Braves baseball cap. He casually placed the small satchel with the baggage that had already been cleared.

Eamon didn't know what he was trying to get away with, and he didn't really care. Though he was anxious to see this new world, all he wanted right then was to find a place to sit. He suddenly felt very tired, like he was carrying a burden he couldn't put down.

9

"The animal will have to remain in quarantine for at least a week."

"A week! That's ridiculous. Look, I've got all the documentation. See, he's licensed, fully inoculated, and—"

"I'm sorry, but those are the regulations. You can have all the documentation in the world. It doesn't matter. All animals are quarantined upon arrival."

"What kind of an asinine policy is that? I'll tell you..."

Jimiyu listened as McCroy continued his tirade, berating the customs official without much effect.

Lyle McCroy, along with his associate, one Jesper Scurlock, had been hired by Vincent to lead their expedition. Vincent told them McCroy was an experienced tracker and hunter, and would be invaluable once they began their trek. Be that as it may, Jimiyu wasn't sure he cared for McCroy's brusque manner. He'd only encountered him a few times, but had gotten the impression he was a rather rude fellow. Still, he hadn't been hired for his diplomacy. It was his job to guide the expedition through whatever wilderness they encountered.

Disregarding the ongoing dispute about McCroy's big cat momentarily, Jimiyu wondered where that wilderness was. If it hadn't been for the long weeks in space, he would have thought he was still on Earth. The land looked the same, the topography was unremarkable. The trees and other vegetation he saw beyond the landing field certainly appeared Earth-like. He even saw what looked like cultivated orchards in the distance.

The people were just people, not unusual at all, though he thought it odd they all seemed to be wearing hats—all different kinds of hats. Then he remembered the warnings they'd been given about the planet's intense ultraviolet radiation, and it didn't seem odd at all.

Still, he didn't feel like he was on an alien world. He felt the heaviness of his body, but the change was slight, as if he were overly tired. The hue of the sunlight did appear strange, though he wasn't sure why. When he first learned they were going to travel to another planet, he'd envisioned exotic aberrations, strange creatures, queer natives. Instead, he found only a quaint, rustic quality in the architecture and a small-town informality that reminded him of his village in Kenya.

"Isn't the air sweet?" Chanya asked, as if trying to distance herself from McCroy's ravings.

"Sweet?"

"It tastes so clean. It's invigorating."

Jimiyu took a deep breath. He hadn't noticed before, but it did seem very pure. "I guess it is."

"...this isn't some farm cow. This 'animal,' as you call it, is worth more than you make in a year," McCroy ranted at the customs man. "Thor is the ultimate in genetic breeding, a hybrid Siberian lynx crossbred with the best attributes of a South American jaguar and an Afghani leopard. He's a highly-trained tracker and sentry, and..."

Indeed, it was beautiful animal, and reminded Jimiyu of some of the great cats of Africa. Yet it was different, too. It had exaggerated hind legs, thorny ears crowned by black tufts and a rich, faintly spotted golden-brown coat of fur suited for cooler climes. It must have weighed more than a hundred pounds—all of it muscle. However, what struck Jimiyu most about it was the throaty noise it made. Its growl sounded like a saw rasping across coarse wood.

The exchange between McCroy and the official grew heated, and Dr. Nikira stepped in to soothe both parties. He tried to forge a compromise, but the customs official was hesitant to bypass his protocol. Meanwhile, McCroy acted reluctant to leave the animal at all.

Just when it seemed the official might call for help, Professor Escobedo, who stood at the rear of the party with his wife and son, spoke up.

"Look at that. How odd."

Jimiyu did look, and saw that a delegation of sorts had arrived in a peculiar conveyance that, outwardly at least, was constructed primarily of wood. As the professor said, it *was* an odd-looking vehicle.

The delegation, as it turned out, actually consisted of only one official. The other three held back, apparently subordinates. On further observation, they seemed more bodyguards. Jimiyu noticed they were dressed uniformly in dark-gray jumpsuits and boxy headgear. Each carried a baton-like instrument as long as their forearms. Jimiyu had seen police on Earth use similar "shock sticks" for riot control and suspect subjugation.

The official in charge, an Asian woman whose age was difficult for Jimiyu to determine, walked right up to Dr. Nikira as if she knew him. She wore a business-like beige suit and a broad-brimmed hat that drooped so as to nearly cover her face.

"Dr. Nikira, I'm Chief Administrator Hiromi Oshima." She reached out, and they shook hands. "I want to welcome you and your party to Evergreen."

Jimiyu noticed Chanya move possessively closer to Nikira when the handshake lingered. He saw that Administrator Oshima noticed it, too, and fleetingly eyed Chanya.

"Thank you, Administrator," replied Nikira. "I didn't expect a welcome. How did you know?"

"We're not quite the isolated outpost you might think, Doctor. Word of your expedition has preceded you. I understand it's quite a *cause célèbre* in some circles."

Nikira accepted the compliment with a slight nod. "If so, they're very small circles, I can assure you."

"I'd love to hear more about your expedition, and your theories." Jimiyu thought he heard a hint of derision in her tone. "I would be delighted if you and your party were to join me for dinner tonight."

"Thank you, Administrator." Nikira spared a glance to his companions. "On behalf of us all, I thank you. We accept your invitation."

"Good, good. I look forward to meeting you all then," replied Oshima, turning back to her vehicle.

"Administrator, there seems to be a minor problem concerning a special animal we've brought with us. Something about an extended quarantine. Such would unreasonably delay our expedition. I was hoping there might be a compromise we could come to."

"I'll look into it, Doctor. I'm sure we can accommodate you," she said, settling in her seat. "By the way, you'll find your timepieces won't be of any use here on Evergreen."

Jimiyu glanced down at his wristwatch. It appeared to be working.

"Our days are shorter than Earth's. However, we usually eat around sundown. Anyone can direct you to my residence." She ordered the driver of her vehicle to proceed and called out, "Until later, then."

The wooden vehicle departed in the same, nearly silent fashion it had arrived. Chanya edged close to Jimiyu and whispered in Kiswahili, "I don't like that woman."

"Which woman? The archeologist's wife?" Jimiyu asked, even though he knew the answer.

"No, that other woman," Chanya said earnestly. "The chief administrator."

"Why don't you like her?" he said, still using their native tongue.

"I don't know." Chanya continued to whisper, shaking her head. "There's something about her I don't like."

"You're imagining things," Jimiyu replied. He hoped that convincing Nikira to bring Chanya with them on the expedition hadn't been a mistake. He still believed she could be good for Nikira...especially if this grand expedition ended in failure.

10

amon was told to wait with two other men who'd gotten off the shuttle. He hoped it wouldn't be long, because he didn't like the looks of them. One was missing some teeth and wore an incessant scowl. The other sat playing with a large pocketknife, picking his fingernails with it and staring at Eamon. Neither looked like someone he wanted to run across in the dark. But, except for some discontented grumbling by the scowler, at least they were silent.

They'd been waiting almost an hour when a short, stocky guy maybe twice Eamon's age approached them. He wore a distressed straw hat with a leather cord band and a brim that curled upward at the sides. His arms, at least the parts Eamon could see where the sleeves of his worn denim jacket were rolled back, were covered in tattoos. He stopped in front of them and tilted the hat back from his eyes.

"You my new turtles?"

"Who you calling a turtle?" growled the fellow with the frown. He stood threateningly, but the old guy pushed him back onto the bench with one hand as easily as if he'd been a child.

"Cool your spurs, Charlie Nobody. You get up when I say you get up. And you, put that toy away."

The fellow with the knife stared at him momentarily, taking his measure, then folded up the blade and put it back in his pocket.

The old guy looked at Eamon but didn't say anything.

"The name's not Charlie," responded the frowner, making no attempt to conceal his belligerence.

"You're Charlie if I say you're Charlie."

The old guy waited, ready for his authority to be challenged, almost daring it. Instead, the newly christened Charlie Nobody asked in a still surly tone, "Who are you?"

"Ramos, North Lake honcho—that's boss-man to you turtles. North Lake, don't forget it. That's your outfit."

"What you mean—turtles?"

"Until you lay low your first sixty-footer, you're a turtle. Now, grab your gear and follow me."

He didn't wait for them, but started down the road at a brisk pace. Eamon hurried to retrieve his duffle and catch up.

"I'm taking you down to the flop," he told them without looking back to see if they were following. "You can bunk there on credit. Just stay out of trouble, keep away from the west end of town—that's off-limits to timber jocks," he said as though the restriction were a personal insult, and punctuated the statement by spitting. "After that, I don't care if you spend the night painting your noses or doing the fandango, as long as you're at the river dock come sunup. Don't make me round you up."

"What time is sunup?" Eamon asked.

Ramos looked over his shoulder but didn't slow his pace. "There's only two times for a timber jockey—day and night, light and dark. If it's light, you're working. Anyone can tell you where the dock is. Be there when the sun comes up. The flops have alarms to wake you."

Eamon had other questions but decided not to ask. He was having a hard time just keeping up with Ramos in spite of the man's age and shorter legs. He hitched up the duffle for better leverage on his back and, as he did, looked up. There, he saw one of the most beautiful sights of his short life.

The sky was awash with an array of color. It was as if someone had spilled various hues of paint into a pond and the colors were spreading haphazardly. It was so amazing that he blinked to be certain he wasn't seeing things.

"What's that? In the sky."

Ramos didn't even look up. "Sky sprite. You'll get used to them."

"Sky sprite? It's incredible."

"Reminds me—you turtles use some of that Evergreen scrip you were given, go down to Lizzie's General Store, tell her I sent you, and buy yourselves a hat. Make sure you keep yourselves covered when you're outside. We'll get you some UV screen when you get to the dock. Sun's a lot meaner than on Earth. It can cause some nasty burns."

Eamon remembered the warning all the passengers had been given about the ultraviolet radiation, though he still wasn't exactly sure what it was. He wondered if it had anything to do with the luminous bands of color wavering across the sky. The majestic brilliance of the display made him feel very small.

11

"Sure, I remember that. It was a long time ago, though," the store owner said confidently. "You came all the way from Earth to ask me about that?"

Jimiyu, Chanya and Vincent stood patiently by as Dr. Nikira questioned the woman.

"Yes," replied Nikira. "Please tell us what you know about it."

The woman was puzzled they should care so much about an old wood carving. She sighed indifferently.

"All I know is that Harley came in here one day, said he'd found it somewhere east of Hokan Pass, and wanted to know if I'd trade him for it. We both figured it must have been carved by one of the original Washoe who settled up that way, 'cause it looked pretty old. I guessed I could sell it as a curio, so I traded him for it. Somebody from Earthside bought it. Don't know who he was. Didn't get much for it, though. If you're here asking about it, it must be worth more than I thought."

"Who is this 'Harley' who found it?"

"Happy Harley," the store owner said, going back to cleaning her counter. "He's kind of a local character, if you know what I mean."

"Where can we find him?"

"He's not likely to be around today. You can probably find him at the dock come sunup on Riverday. He'll be trying to drum up some last-minute business."

"What *is* his business?" asked Vincent.

"He deals in happy smoke. Got the market pretty well cornered. Spends most of his time off in the woods looking for his makings."

"When is Riverday?" Nikira asked.

"Tomorrow. So, this old chunk of wood, it was carved by the Washoe, right?"

Nikira was already turning away, apparently lost in thought.

"Thanks for the input, Ms. Lizzie," Vincent said. "Our guide will cycle in late-time to buy our supplies."

The foursome headed for the door.

"That thing is worth a lot more than I got for it, isn't it?" the store owner called out as they were leaving. Jimiyu saw that neither Nikira nor Vincent were disposed to reply, so he simply said "Thank you" in response to her question.

They followed Nikira up the dirt road, though Jimiyu had no idea where they were going. He wanted to suggest they go back to the inn where they'd taken lodging and rest. He was a simple schoolteacher, not used to the exertion required to move around on this world. His legs already ached. It was as if with each step he was slogging through a swamp. Yet Nikira moved normally, walking briskly as if the weight of this new world was nothing he could concern himself with.

"What next, Doctor?" wondered Vincent.

"I don't want to wait until tomorrow if we don't have to," he replied. "We'll see if anyone else knows where we might find this Harley person. Jimi, you and Chanya go up that way. Vincent and I will take the other direction." Jimiyu saw a brief look of disappointment cross Chanya's face. "Ask anyone you see if they know where this Harley might be. However, let's not mention the artifact. We don't want to rouse too much curiosity."

Jimiyu nodded, and he and Chanya headed up the road in their designated direction. He half-expected her to complain about being paired with him, yet she remained silent.

She looked odd—she had all day. He soon realized it was because he'd never seen her wear pants before. She was outfitted as all four of them had been, in dark olive-green khakis. Chanya looked especially queer, her shapely form blunted by the baggy androgynous fashion. Such clothing might be appropriate for tramping through the wild, but it was too militaristic for Jimiyu. It reminded him of the time, decades ago, when Chanya had come to Talib's rescue.

He and Talib were maybe sixteen, Chanya must have been only eleven or twelve. She had always been an impertinent little girl, and was particularly audacious when it came to her feelings for Talib. It was no secret she was infatuated with the older boy. She was always following him around.

One day, a truck carrying a group of soldiers stopped to rest. A few of them—not much older than he and Talib—had grown up in the village. Even then they'd teased Talib because he was such a serious student, because he was always reading some book. They swaggered through the village, emboldened by their uniforms and their guns, and came across Talib, sitting in his favorite spot under the weeping tree, reading. First, they mocked him, and then they took his book. They belittled his efforts to get it back, tossing it from one to the other.

That's when Chanya blustered in. She berated the soldiers with the acerbic tongue of an angry grandmother. At first, they laughed at her. Then, they noticed how many villagers were watching. It wasn't long before the shame of being taken to task by this little girl ruined their fun. They gave Talib his book back and retreated, grumbling and arguing with each other.

Jimiyu remembered Talib's chagrin with being treated so, and how Chanya had soothed him by telling him to disregard the ignorant bullies. She was such a little spitfire that Talib forgot his embarrassment and laughed.

Now, so many years later, she was still following him around, still looking out for him—at least when he'd let her.

"Do you think he deliberately avoids being with me?" she said unexpectedly, still looking straight ahead. "Or does he just not see me?"

Chanya seldom made any reference to her feelings, but Jimiyu knew them well. He was certain there must have been other men in her life at some time, though he had no firsthand knowledge of such relationships. What he did know was that she was always there for Nikira, always hoping. Even now, he heard the quiet despair in her voice.

"I'm certain he sees you, Chanya. But who can say what goes through the mind of a man like Talib. I know that right now, he is consumed with this quest. He has not been the same man since Vincent showed him the artifact."

"I wish he had never seen it," Chanya said with unexpected vehemence.

"His soul cries out for resolution," replied Jimiyu. "I think...I think he had to find this artifact. I think he needed this expedition, the way a bird needs to fly...the way a cheetah needs to run. We can only hope that, regardless of what he encounters, he finds what he is looking for."

"And what is it that he's looking for, exactly, Jimi?"

"His faith."

12

She had been using a variety of scents, rather haphazardly, to sample and catalog the reactions of the ursu, and found it interesting that the smell of lilac seemed to invoke fear in the creatures. Cinnamon she discovered to be a powerful aphrodisiac. The smell of it excited one male to such an extreme he accosted the nearest ursu, another male, until warned off by a series of threatening grunts. Amanda decided she'd been lucky he hadn't gone after her, and put the cinnamon away.

Despite her chance discoveries regarding scent, she was disappointed. What she needed was a proper setup, the right equipment. She would never get close to even a rudimentary basis for communication with the ursu if she proceeded like this. Such communication would require the classification of hundreds of scent patterns. It was very likely the ursu naturally produced scents she could never duplicate. At least, not without some sophisticated equipment she knew she could never convince her department heads to send her.

She was finalizing her notes on the subject when a madfly, possibly drawn by one of the scents she'd been using, began harassing her. She flailed at it and missed. It flew off, and in watching it withdraw Amanda spotted a small swarm nearby.

The swarming habits of the insects had always intrigued her, so she decided to follow them as best she could. After only a short distance she lost sight of the swarm among a tall patch of ivory-colored aurora blossoms—flowers she'd named after Evergreen's sun because of their resemblance to earthly sunflowers. She pushed apart the blossoms, and the swarm reappeared. She stepped back so as not to be engulfed, and the swarm continued on its way. Its circuitous flight path allowed her to stay close enough to follow it.

Eventually, dozens of yards from her camp, the swarm dissipated. The flies flew off, each in its own direction, as if suddenly developing individual missions. It was curious. Then one of flies bit her neck and flew off before she could brush it away. She watched as it buzzed around her head then dropped to the forest floor. It landed on thorny vine as thick as her arm. The vine curled serpent-like up and about a young redwood.

Looking around, Amanda noticed many of the trees in this particular area were draped with the vines. The creepers trailed from one tree to the next, the network of intersecting lines creating a helter-skelter webbing across the forest floor. They were so entangled she couldn't tell where one vine began and another ended.

She hadn't come across any such twining plant on Evergreen before. Unlike many Earth varieties, which were stick-like, almost dead-looking, this tracheophyte was bright green and nearly as leafy as ivy. She wondered, because of the way it was attached to the tree, whether or not it was a symbiont, or possibly even a parasitical organism. Botany, however, was not her strong suit. She'd make a note of it as she had other new species and leave the detailed study to those more qualified.

She bent down where the madfly had landed, and the little medicine bundle the old man had given her plopped out of her open shirt. She tucked it back inside and searched for the madfly. A tree lizard scampered out of her way. She'd seen many of the tiny reptiles. They were chestnut brown in color, their skin the texture of rough bark, and were rarely more than three inches long. Normally, they clung to tree trunks, dining on worms and other small bugs they found there, not unlike their Earth cousins.

She kept looking and finally spotted the madfly at the base of one of the vine's leaves. It was engaged in a frenzied, almost comical dance around the stem.

Amanda found it a curious action. Was this the pollination she'd theorized? She saw no sign of any pollen-like substance that might be exchanged, yet there had to be some biological rationale for such activity. Was it like the declaration of the honeybee dance inside the hive? If so, for whom was the message of this dance intended? She needed to get one of the madflies under her microscope, check it for pollen residue that might not be visible to the naked eye.

Amanda took out one of her small sample containers and captured the madfly. Inside its glass prison, it buzzed angrily. Such was her nature that she experienced a fleeting moment of regret over the insect's fate. Amanda didn't like killing any creature, even one as simple as a madfly. She returned the container to her vest pocket and proceeded back to camp.

13

Content disrupted. Liaison incomplete. Chemo-synthesizers respond. Impulses sent through bacterial network. Neurons discharged. Phototropic nodes construe variations of shadow. Extraneous motion perceived. Interpretation—messenger has been rendered inactive. Perceptions conveyed to root crown. Evaluations contemplated. Distress relayed.

Speed of the interloper germinates anxiety. Defense necessary. Appendages unfurled. Reaching out, seeking, traversing. No tactual evidence. No trace of invader.

Disruptions ongoing. Response vital. Contemplation resumes. Resources allocated. Energy diverted. Systematic measures and countermeasures delineated.

14

It was a grand table, oblong in shape, massive in both size and bulk, constructed of immaculately varnished redwood and edged with ornate carvings. The settings were lavish and formal, with silver candlesticks, matching silver silk table linens and golden daffodil floral arrangements.

The room itself gave the impression of being the interior of some medieval castle with its open-beamed ceiling and bulky redwood doors inlaid with spiraling wrought iron. More candles inset in the walls created a florid glow about the table.

Filamena appreciated the ambience, which she thought of as European. She admired the ornate dinnerware as the introductions proceeded around the table. Their hostess, Administrator Oshima, sat at one end, enthusiastically learning the names of each of her guests. One name she repeated as if trying to recall where she'd heard it before.

"Boorman...The same Boorman who patented Solaric? Was that your father?"

"My grandfather," responded Vincent Boorman. "He developed it."

"I understand then how you could afford to finance such an expedition. On Evergreen, Solaric provides most of our energy. You could say we're fairly dependent on the fabric for our power needs. Our mining operations, being relatively new, have yet to produce any supplemental sources."

"What do you do during extended periods of overcast?" It was Luis who offered the question. The seating arrangement had placed him next to the captain of the *Heinlein*, who sat at the end of the table opposite the administrator. Much to Filamena's chagrin, Max had been assigned the chair next to hers.

"Our storage cells provide us with all the power we need, Professor. We aren't so backward as to be at the mercy of the weather. Of course, logging operations are shut down when it rains particularly hard—strictly a safety measure. However, our seasons are very mild, so we don't really have a winter as such—at least not at this elevation. Why is that again, Captain?"

"There's almost no tilt to the planet's axis," responded the space cruiser's commander. "Thus, only slight seasonal changes. Evergreen's spin is different from Earth's, too. The days pass more quickly—twenty-one-point-five hours, though they've established a local calendar with an eight-day week, and—"

"Thank you, Captain," interrupted the administrator. "We don't want to overburden our guests with a lot of statistical trivia, now, do we?"

"I tally your timber is used by some other, more barren colonial worlds," Boorman said. "Captain Amidon says he'll be taking a load back with him."

"Not just timber," said the captain. "Evergreen's farms produce a surplus that helps feed those colonies as well."

"Does Earth import any of the timber?"

"Too costly, for the most part," said Captain Amidon. "Earth is content to continue using the same synthetics they've been using since the anti-deforestation movement. Once in a while some ultra-rich type will put in a special order for prime lumber so he can have something specially made, but most of the timber is shipped to nearby planets."

Oshima flipped her hand disdainfully. "Lumber and wood by-products have their uses, but our geologists assure us this world is rich in mineral deposits—iron, magnesium, sulfur, copper, zinc. Those will be the ultimate source of the planet's wealth."

"If the colonials let you collect," Captain Amidon said slyly, trying to egg a response from the administrator.

"Yes," she said, glaring at him as if he'd committed an infraction of good taste, "we do have a few independent-minded colonists who don't like the idea of exporting their raw materials. However, they don't comprehend the economic realities that have made their colonization possible.

"Evergreen was first settled more than seventy years ago, but it's been a prime colony for less than a decade—coinciding with when our company first began to take an interest. There's actually been very little exploration or detailed mapping outside the immediate surrounds of Redwood Spring, because the area is so rich in timber and minerals. Of course, we'll get to it eventually.

"For now, the influx of farmers, tradesmen and homesteaders continues to increase. Redwood Springs is expanding its horizons daily, and that expansion has been made possible by the financial support of our company. GMX was the only company willing to take a chance on investing in this backwater planet. Naturally, we expect a return on our investment."

"Redwood Springs?" asked Filamena. "I thought I heard someone call the town Woodville."

"An obstinate colloquialism sustained only by some of the more unstable elements of the local population, I assure you, Mrs. Escobedo."

"Actually, it's Ms. Policaro."

"Oh? I thought—"

"Please excuse the confusion, Administrator," spoke up Luis. "My wife is a modern woman." Filamena heard the distaste in the way he said *modern*. "She insists upon using her maiden name rather than mine." He stared at her, but it was an old point of contention so she ignored him.

"Well, then, you're somewhat like our little town of Redwood Springs, aren't you? Two names, two assertions for the same beautiful thing."

Filamena nodded in acceptance of the compliment.

"You have to understand," Captain Amidon said, continuing the aborted conversation, "that many of those who chose to homestead here—the 'unstable elements' Administrator Oshima refers to—have, shall we say, questionable backgrounds. Why, the largest single contingent, the timber jockeys, consists primarily of debtors

56

and convicts. I'm sure you've all heard about Earth's off-planet indentured workers program that was started to reduce prison overcrowding. That's where eighty-five percent of Evergreen's population comes from. It's the same thing they did with Australia a few hundred years back."

"Come now, Captain," disputed Oshima, "eighty-five percent? It's actually closer to sixty."

Captain Amidon shrugged as if the difference were meaningless.

Two servants appeared and began clearing away the soup bowls, replacing them with small salads. Filamena was surprised to find she recognized most of the ingredients. Part of her was relieved, but another part was disappointed not to be faced with a more exotic collection of produce.

"What's this I've scanned about a gigantic lake monster?" asked Boorman.

Captain Amidon laughed.

The administrator smiled and said, "Officially, it's a mystery. Certain sightings have been reported, and so on and such. Unofficially, company publicists have revived the legend of 'the monster of a thousand arms' handed down by the members of a Native American tribe who were Evergreen's first settlers. They hope it will encourage tourism. I have my doubts."

"Administrator, what are those incredible lights I saw in the sky?"

Filamena wasn't surprised to hear Max, always the artist, bring up the subject of the lights. She had already seen him trying to capture the essence of the celestial display on his Imaginator.

"Those are our auroras. Beautiful, aren't they?"

"Yes, yes, they are. I've seen pictures of the aurora borealis on Earth, but I don't remember what causes them. Are your auroras similar?"

"I'd better let Captain Amidon answer that. Would you share you expertise with the young man, Captain?"

"I'd be happy to," the captain said, wiping dressing from the corner of his mouth. "The auroras over Evergreen are similar in the sense they have the same cause and effect, but ours are much more prevalent. The sun in this system, which you've probably already guessed gets its name from those auroras, is brighter than Sol. It's an F7 class star, not only brighter, but more active. It's that activity, in the form of solar flares, that sends streams of charged particles hurtling toward Evergreen. The planet's unusually strong magnetic field traps the particles, creating the auroras.

"You've been warned about the ultraviolet radiation, which can be especially harmful. Even though Evergreen's O-two levels are slightly higher, creating a thicker ozone layer, and that it's somewhat farther from its sun than Earth is, the radiant..."

The more detailed the captain became, the more scientific jargon he used, the less Filamena paid attention. Instead, she used the time to ponder what she'd observed about her dinner companions.

The captain she'd seen plenty of on the ship. He was a nice enough fellow, if a bit of a bore. To his left was a beautiful black woman. Filamena couldn't decide if she was younger or older than herself. There was, however, something about her quiet manner, her restraint, that spoke of maturity. She didn't recall her entire name—Chanya something—but she did notice the way the woman looked at Dr. Nikira...and Administrator Oshima. Her feelings for the doctor were as transparent to Filamena as if her heart were made of glass. She was obviously annoyed Nikira had been seated at the other end of the table, next to the administrator, who was lavishing most of her attention on the esteemed doctor in a manner just short of flirtatious.

Dr. Nikira himself seemed as oblivious to the coquetry as he was to Chanya's jealousy. He sat fully upright, almost stiff, as if his shoulders were pinned to the chair, his clothing simple but tight-fitting.

Two other members of their party had chosen not to join them, but the places set for them remained. Filamena couldn't say she was sorry. There was something in the manner of their two guides she found disquieting—especially the small one with the bad teeth and bulging eyes. Maybe she was just being elitist, letting appearance prejudice her. Still, she didn't like the way the fellow looked at her.

The remaining two at the table were Dr. Nikira's assistant, whose African name eluded her, and Vincent Boorman. He struck

58

her as a rich kid used to getting his own way, though pleasant enough once you waded through the slang. She'd seen plenty like him during her time on the Riviera, when she was much younger and the men swarmed to her like bees to honey.

She'd first met Boorman when he convinced Luis to accept his offer to join the expedition. He seemed too young to be organizing much of anything. Apparently, though, he had the capital to back his eagerness. It didn't take much to convince Luis, though—the sum Boorman offered made the decision an easy one. She knew Luis wouldn't have turned down the opportunity even if he had to pay his own way.

"...why Evergreen has no polar ice caps." The captain finished his prolonged spiel and took a breath. When it looked like he might continue, Oshima spoke up to change the subject.

"As I mentioned previously, Doctor, the general aspects of your quest have preceded you, but not the specifics. Tell me all about it, please, about the nature of your theories and this artifact you say was found here on Evergreen."

Dr. Nikira stroked his goatee. He looked somewhat uncomfortable with the request but resigned to answering his hostess's query.

"It isn't easy to encapsulate a lifetime of research and matters of subjective faith into a concise, comprehensible declaration," Nikira stated, almost as if it were a disclaimer. "That being said, what I believe, what I have come to believe, is that Earth was not God's primary creation. I believe He divined his first miracles on another world, and that He is not just an omnipotent spirit, but a being of immense energy. I believe it is on this other world, this provenance of God, that His power was honed, and that He only then created the Earth."

Oshima tried to conceal it, but Filamena saw she was taken aback. It was the first, too, that Filamena had heard about Dr. Nikira's beliefs. She was no theologian, but she knew the Catholic priests of her childhood would have taken issue with his theories.

"Are you saying you believe God to be a physical being like you and me?"

"Not like you and me at all." Nikira's words ran together as if rushing to correct her. "What form He actually takes I can't say.

Though it is written that man was made in God's image, it could be He takes many forms. But energy does have its own physicality. What I'm saying, what I believe, is that this energy of God is not simply spiritual, it's measurable. Vast but not infinite."

"Well," Oshima said, "no wonder you created such a stir within your own church, Doctor. Anglican, isn't it? Or should I put that in the past tense? I understand they excommunicated you. The first such excommunication since the same-sex marriage clashes of the early 21st century. Is that true?"

"Yes," replied Nikira. "The church, I'm afraid, has become nothing more than a bureaucracy, more interested in international politics and global finance than matters divine. I joined the church as a young man because I believed in something purer. It was my dissatisfaction with what I saw as the defilement of my beliefs that encouraged my forays into other areas of study." His voice trailed off as if he were tired.

Something Max was doing caught Filamena's eye. He was furtively sketching on a piece of paper. She wanted to tell him it was rude, but didn't dare once she saw what he was drawing. His pen was capturing, in astonishing detail, the features of her own face.

"Tell me, Doctor, does the priesthood still practice self-flagellation?" Oshima asked with a wanton gleam in her eye.

Filamena's attention went straight to the African woman, who made no attempt to repress a scowl.

Nikira's lack of response appeared to irritate the administrator. As though to spur a reaction from him, she said, "I understand some members of the media have referred to you as 'Moses,' saying you're trying to lead your people to the Promised Land."

She smiled as if it were a joke, but no one laughed. Instead, Nikira's assistant sprang to his defense.

"Dr. Nikira has spent years combing hundreds of religious and historical texts," he stated, as though responding to an insult, "from the earliest works of the Egyptians, Greeks and Hebrews to the Assyrians. He's found evidence to support his theories even among the ancient writings of the Sumerians."

"Impressive," Oshima said flatly, eyeing Dr. Nikira and ignoring his assistant, "but not surprising from a man with Ph.Ds in philosophy, theology and psychology. Tell me about the artifact,

Doctor. How does it fit into your theories? What was so fascinating that it brought you to Evergreen?"

Nikira motioned to his assistant, who lifted the satchel Filamena had noticed he carried with him at all times. "Many of the ancient texts Jimiyu made reference to describe the existence of a Tree of Life. And it's not only in bygone Mediterranean cultures that such references are found. Similar beliefs are scattered throughout Asiatic and Native American lore. Even Nordic myth has its Yggdrasil.

"The most pertinent ancient writings describe the tree as blossoming in the provenance of God."

From the satchel, the assistant pulled out a piece of wood, flat on one side, jagged roots extruding from the other. He passed it to Nikira, who handed it to the administrator.

"Some of the texts include illustrations of a tree. They are all almost identical. Each shows a tree whose boughs are apparently alive with movement. Each looks very much like what you see carved into that artifact."

Oshima examined the chunk of wood, unimpressed. She handed it to Boorman, who passed it on to Filamena.

"So, someone on Evergreen carved something similar. I don't see what the big deal is."

"It's been determined that this artifact is more than forty-five thousand years old—how much older isn't certain," Nikira said, and waited for a reaction.

The administrator didn't disappoint. "That's not possible. Evergreen was discovered less than a hundred years ago. Humans didn't set foot on..."

The administrator didn't bother to finish. Nikira nodded, somewhat smugly Filamena thought.

"Exactly," he said.

Filamena turned the artifact over in her hands. It felt smooth, despite the apparent rough edges of the roots. It had a glossy sheen, a slick yellow-tinted glaze of some sort. She spoke up without meaning to.

"What's this finish on it?"

"It's tree resin, dear," Luis answered. Of course—he'd probably examined the artifact before they left Earth. "Trees secrete it to heal wounds, and sometimes as a form of defense."

"And what, exactly, is *your* specialty, Professor Escobedo?" Oshima asked.

"I'm an archaeologist."

"Professor Escobedo discovered the ruins on Mars," Captain Amidon added enthusiastically.

"Well, my research team made the discovery, yes."

That was her unpretentious Luis. Not even wanting to take credit for his greatest achievement.

"Surely, you don't expect to find anything like that on Evergreen, Professor?"

"We won't know, Señora, until we look."

"So, what is it you hope to find with this little expedition, Doctor?"

Nikira hesitated before answering, but his reply was confident. "I believe I will find *Cidade de Deus*...the City of God."

15

amon found a seat on a polished wooden stool at one of the bars and ordered a beer. He didn't even like beer, but that's what everyone else was drinking. Given the raucous nature of the place, he had quickly decided it was better to fit in, not that he would ever have been mistaken for one of the burly rowdies he found himself elbow-to-elbow with. He was certain he stood out like a puppy in a pit bull arena.

It wasn't like any bar or nightclub he'd ever been in. Not that he'd been in that many, but this place was like something out of a vid about the 19th century Wild West. It was dirty, smelly, and had all the appropriate props. He did, however, see one thing he liked. Several things, actually, that he couldn't take his eyes off.

There were girls everywhere—some serving drinks, some dancing, all wearing very little. They looked like they were having fun, taking part in games of chance, engaging patrons in conversation and other, lewder activities. One of the girls strolled by him and smiled. She stopped and looked at him. He looked back. She was older than he was—how much older he couldn't tell—but she was pretty. No, he decided, not pretty so much as sexy. She was vaguely Asian, with almond eyes and creamy skin. Her ebony hair hung past her shoulders.

"New in town?" she asked.

Eamon nodded. He guessed he looked as out-of-place as he felt.

"I'm Sunny. What's your name?"

"Eamon."

"Eamon—that's an unusual name. You want to come upstairs with me, Eamon?" She smiled immodestly. "That's where the real fun is."

Eamon had never...He'd never been propositioned so bluntly before. He was caught so unaware he was mute. She took his silence for rejection.

"All right, honey," she said. "If you change your mind, I'll be around."

She sauntered away, Eamon staring at her lithe figure as she went. He wanted to follow her. He thought about what he was missing, then caught himself. He wasn't there to play around, as much as he was tempted. He was there to look for a face. A face he hoped to recognize, despite the years that had muddied his memory.

After a time, he discovered, all the faces began to blend together. Any one of them could have been the man he was looking for.

During his search, he noticed the pair from the shuttle he'd seen acting suspicious at customs. They were sitting at one of the tables. The smaller man, the one with the bug-eyes, was chatting up a barmaid, unsuccessfully, it seemed. Either that, or they were negotiating and his offer came up short. The other man just nursed his drink and observed.

Eamon's beer arrived, and he paid for it with the strange currency he'd been provided as an advance aboard the ship. He'd never used cash before, though he was aware of its historical significance. The paper money looked like something from one of his childhood games.

He took a sip of the beer, and its ultra-bitter taste incited a reflex reaction. He jerked back and spat it out. As he did, he bumped into another patron, turned quickly to apologize and splashed more of his drink onto both them.

He looked up. Eamon was tall, yet this guy towered over him and was twice as broad. It appeared he'd just soaked the biggest bruiser in the place.

He stared up into a blue-veined potato-nose and a pair of dark, penetrating eyes. The intensity of the fellow's stare was emphasized by a no-nonsense burr haircut that squared off the shape of his head.

"Why, you irreverent little heathen," he swore.

He grabbed Eamon's shirt in a catcher's-mitt fist and thrust an enormous blade in front of his face. Behind the glint of steel, adorning the giant's bony jaw, was a crucifix tattoo.

"Cleanliness is next to godliness, you little rat turd. I am His paladin, and I will render your guts unto the light in His name."

"I'm s-sorry," Eamon sputtered. "I...I..."

"Now you seek sanctuary in the face of His wrath," he bellowed, lowering the knife between Eamon's legs. "When the sword of righteousness imperils your manhood, you'll cry His name for certain." He stuck his face so close his acrid breath made Eamon gag. He whispered menacingly, "Cry His name, boy."

Scared beyond rational thought, Eamon had no idea what this enraged hulk was talking about. All he knew was that the flat of the blade was pressed against his balls.

"Boy, I told you to—"

"Don't do it, Kruto."

Out of the corner of his eye, Eamon saw a man who was much shorter than his assailant, though just as muscular. A jagged scar branded the fellow's face.

"Don't do it," his would-be defender repeated, as if in warning. Then, in a more genial tone: "As a favor to me."

The beast named Kruto relaxed his grip and looked at the newcomer.

"He's a turtle," said the newcomer. "He's not worth your time."

"I'm going to castrate him and deliver his genitals unto God."

"Can't you see he's just a kid? He probably hasn't even had a chance to use them yet."

That provoked a chorus of laughter from the behemoth's compatriots, though the panic that coursed through Eamon prevented him from seeing the humor. Even so, he was relieved when the laughter led to encouragements of leniency from his assailant's companions, and he felt the knife slide out from between his legs. He exhaled the breath he'd been holding.

Kruto flashed a gap-toothed smile at the newcomer. "Okay, Gash. As a favor to you. His will be done."

He released his hold on Eamon's shirt and turned back to his drinking buddies as if nothing of any significance had happened. Eamon's benefactor looked him over as if trying to decide if his intervention had been worth it.

"You'll live longer if next time you don't pick a fight with the meanest psychopath on the planet," he said, and walked away before Eamon could explain what happened.

Eamon eased away from the bar. Now that the little episode had ended, no one was paying any attention to him. Still, he felt embarrassed. He decided he'd had enough excitement for one night. He just wished he'd had a chance to thank the fellow who'd come between him and a radical circumcision.

He looked around, but didn't see where he'd gone. He decided to get out while he could.

16

It had been a foolish thing to do. He had no business, no right butting in where he wasn't invited. He could have ended up gutted like a trout, painting a blood trail out Tilley's doors. Worse yet, he could have gotten the kid killed.

But that's what he did, wasn't it? He got people killed. Hadn't he learned his lesson? It didn't matter what your intentions were. All that mattered was the result.

> *There's no time. That tank's going to explode. It'll depressurize the entire station. You've got to blow the transfer chamber hatch now!*

The voice in his head cut through the din as clearly as his memory of that day. No matter how he tried to bury it, dilute it with happy smoke, wash it away with rot gut, it never dissipated. It would never leave him.

Gash guzzled his beer and pushed back in his chair until it pressed against the wall. He checked to make sure the kid was gone. He was. Good. A kid like that didn't belong here in the first place. He wondered what cruel joke of fate had led him to Evergreen.

Sitting there, staring across the room at nothing in particular, he watched a pair of marshals walk into the bar. They brandished their shock sticks like credentials. Their faces said they were looking for trouble.

Trouble was likely what they were going to get. Marshals didn't usually come into Tilley's. They kept the peace on the streets but let Shay Larimore police his own place. These two had to be new to Woodville; otherwise, they wouldn't have come strolling into a ruck of drunken TJs.

They hadn't taken five steps inside before they got what they were asking for. Someone called out something they took exception to. They wheeled around, sticks at the ready, looking for the insolent transgressor. Their reaction only incited more derisive catcalls. They weren't sure which way to turn. It looked to Gash as if they only now realized they were surrounded by a surly multitude.

Before the matter could escalate, Shay Larimore swooped in and put himself between the marshals and the timber jocks they had targeted. What Larimore told them Gash couldn't hear, but the man was insistent, though smiling the whole time as if it were a game. What manner of logic or graft he cajoled them with, Gash could only guess, but he figured fear played a part because in less time than it took for them to stir up trouble, the marshals withdrew.

Larimore went about his business, exchanging insults with a number of his customers, and then approached Kruto. He said something and walked away. The fanatic crank followed him. They sat at an empty table, away from any others, and began what looked to Gash to be a serious discussion.

Larimore did most of the talking, but that was to be expected. Kruto listened intently, apparently agreeable to whatever the whoremaster was telling him. That's when the scenario took an even more bizarre turn, from Gash's perspective.

Ramos walked up to their table, said something and sat down. Kruto was part of Ramos' outfit, but as far as Gash knew, he never had anything to do with Larimore—never so much as spoke to him. Yet there the three of them were, looking for all the world like chummy co-conspirators.

Then he remembered. *Ask your friend Ramos,* Larimore had told him. What was it that was going on between them? Did it have something to do with Administrator Oshima, and what he'd seen the night before?

Gash looked away. It didn't matter. It wasn't his business. He took another drink and contemplated taking a couple of hits from his pipe.

17

Eamon reached the dock as daylight crept over the distant
mountains. The sun had yet to make its entrance, but the last
shreds of fog were dissipating in anticipation of its arrival. He saw
the morning's crowning sky sprite dance across one summit, trailing luminous streamers of green and yellow, before fading wraithlike into the dawn.

He was caught staring, and was almost bowled over by two
lugs hauling a hefty sack with the word *RICE* printed on it.

"Watch it!" barked one as Eamon scooted aside.

The wharf extended a good fifty yards, and was already bus-
tling with activity. Men were loading various sacks and boxes onto
bloated canoes—Eamon didn't know what else to call the vessels.
They were designed like canoes he'd seen pictures of, though instead of fiberglass they were wood—each apparently hollowed out
from a single gigantic tree. They were big and bulky, not at all how
he pictured a canoe, though they still tapered to a point both front
and back. A few had already pulled away from the dock and were
headed downstream. He counted fifteen men to a boat, along with
a hefty load of supplies. Half the occupants had paddles out, but
the current was so strong they were guiding the vessels more than
propelling them.

Not for the first time since he arrived on Evergreen, Eamon felt
out of place. The rough-looking sorts engaged in loading the boats,

like those he'd seen in the saloon, were not like anyone he'd ever been around. He couldn't shake the apprehension that he didn't belong.

When he'd signed the indenture contract he hadn't had any idea what he was getting into. He only knew he was signing up for logging work. They didn't care that he had no experience. They said they'd train him. All he knew, all he cared about, was that it would get him to Evergreen.

Now, though, he was full of trepidation. He didn't know how he was going to fit in with these gruff, burly men. His mother would have said it was because he was immature. She liked to use that word, especially whenever he got into trouble. She'd used it the last time they'd spoken. He'd gotten into trouble and then...

Eamon remembered why he was here—not that it was ever far from his thoughts—and steeled himself to do whatever had to be done. Nothing else mattered. Certainly not his nervousness.

"Quit mooning over there, Mousey. It's time to say goodbye. Grab that line, Meanan. Eddy, Cayenne, help Chaltraw and Nishi finish loading."

The booming voice belonged to Ramos, the fellow who'd given him his rough introduction to Evergreen. His outfit's honcho was directing operations on the dock, though it seemed to Eamon everyone was familiar with what needed to be done. The one referred to as "Mousey" was busy kissing some woman. She was a touch taller and somewhat older than the diminutive fellow, who appeared too rapt to let go of her.

"I said now, Farr!"

The little guy said his final goodbye, kissed the woman once more and hustled to help with the loading. Eamon saw her face. It was the same woman he'd spoken to in the bar.

"You, Pretty Boy, lend a hand."

"Me?" Eamon asked, though Ramos looked right at him.

"Yes, you, turtle. Where are your friends?"

"My friends?"

"The two who came in with you."

"They're not my friends."

"Well, grab those cases of canned goods and find a place for them."

71

Eamon put down his duffle and did as he was told.

"Gash, show Pretty Boy where to put those."

Gash turned out to be his benefactor from the night before. He hadn't noticed him at first, but now Eamon nodded in acknowledgment. The man with the scar simply directed him to a half-empty boat.

"Put those in there," he said, going about his own work.

Eamon complied, and about the time he'd finished loading the stack of canned goods, he saw Charlie Nobody and Mr. Knife strolling up to the dock with their duffles. Unlike Eamon, they hadn't bothered to get hats.

Ramos cut short their dopey grins with a crisp stare.

"What don't you two savvy about sunup?"

They looked at each other real stupid-like, which Eamon figured they were.

"Get your gear and butts in a boat," Ramos ordered. "I'll deal with you later. "All right, everybody pipe down!" He shouted to be heard across the dock's expanse, and waited for quiet. "I've got an official notification from the company."

The announcement was met by a chorus of derisive snorts and muttered complaints.

"Shut up and listen! I'm going to give you the short version. I'll post it later if any of you jailhouse lawyers want to read the legal lingo for yourselves. Basically, it cites safety concerns, blah blah blah blah, then goes on to say that 'alcoholic beverages and psychoactive substances of any kind will no longer be allowed in specified areas, including Lake Washoe and the surrounding timber region.' That means no hooch, no happy smoke in TJ City."

"Yeah, right," said someone, and his sarcasm was met by laughter.

"Okay, okay," Ramos said. "It goes on, there's more blah blah blah, and it finishes with 'violators will be subject to censure deemed appropriate by the administrator, including deduction of credit for time served.'"

There was more grumbling, as well as some graphic descriptions of what would be done to any company official who tried to enforce the regulation.

"Anyway, you've been warned, for all the good it will do." Ramos stuffed the paper in his pocket, and Eamon heard the shift in his tone as he called out, "Let's go, North Lake! Move it out! Cayenne, you wait for Ford and his pot rustlers. Make sure they don't slow-poke."

Members of the North Lake outfit hustled to find places in the dugout canoes. Eamon grabbed his duffle and did likewise, only to find himself face-to-face with the unpleasant giant who had threatened to castrate him the night before. But the fellow called Kruto didn't give him a second look. Even though chance seated them next to each other, the truculent behemoth offered no sign of recognition. Eamon didn't press his luck. He grabbed a paddle and tried to imitate the others.

The sun had edged high enough Eamon could see it peeking over the mountaintops. In the full light of day, he realized the water was a queer reddish-brown color. It looked like someone had stirred a pot of blood and sand.

The thought of blood reminded him of the goliath next to him. Kruto had the middle seat, which he had surely commandeered knowing he wouldn't have to man a paddle. Instead, he closed his eyes and pulled his floppy camouflage hat down over his face.

The fellow sitting on the opposite side looked almost as young as Eamon, and seemed relatively harmless. So, Eamon motioned at the river and said to him, hoping for an explanation, "The water sure is red."

"That's why they call it Rust River" came the curt reply that failed to satisfy Eamon's curiosity.

Their journey downriver took them past some beautiful terrain. Most of the land on either side was hilly, and densely wooded. Eamon didn't think he'd ever seen so many shades of green. It was such a wilderness he half-expected to see strange creatures at every bend. Yet he didn't see a single animal—not even a bird.

The current was so strong the initial leg of their voyage required little effort, though Eamon thought he'd hate to try and make the return trip, fighting that current for what must be several miles. Despite its muddy tint, he saw that in some spots the water was shallow. There were a few instances where he was afraid the dugout was going to run aground on the rocks he saw beneath them. Indeed, a couple times he heard the bottom scrape against some protrusion or another.

As they got closer to their objective, whatever that was, he observed that the river widened and grew deeper. Its rusty color took on a darker, more natural tint.

He was plunging his paddle into the water, intent upon seeing what its depths might contain, when he glanced up and saw before them an immense expanse of water. He feathered his paddle and stared. It was enormous—a vast sea of limpid glass. From Eamon's stunned vantage, it seemed a great ocean.

Without warning, Kruto jerked and cried out as if awoken from a nightmare. He clutched the big knife sheathed in his boot and sat up, looking around him. As suddenly as he'd started, he relaxed. He caught Eamon staring at him, and his face contorted into a snarl. Eamon quickly looked away, thrust his paddle into the river and pulled.

"All right, TJs," called Ramos from a nearby boat. "Put your backs into it. Lady Washoe's waiting for her nose hairs to be trimmed."

With renewed vigor, paddles bit into the water and the dugouts gathered momentum. Eamon strained to stay in rhythm with the others but had difficulty keeping up. After only a few minutes, his arms felt like stone weights. He heard someone begin to sing, and he tried to concentrate on the words to take his mind off how exhausted he was becoming.

> I've been working in the timber
> All the live long day.
> I've been working in the timber
> Just to piss the time away.

As he struggled with his fatigue, he heard other voices join in, until it seemed each dugout crew was trying to outdo the other.

> Can't you hear the cable skidding?
> Rise up so early in the morn.
> Don't you hear the honcho shouting,
> Tina, blow that horn.
> Tina, won't you blow
> Tina, won't you blow
> Tina, won't you blow my ho-o-orn?

74

Tina, won't you blow
Tina, won't you blow
Tina, won't you blow my horn?

Even if he'd known the song, Eamon couldn't have sung along—he was breathing too hard. He wondered how the rest managed it. Still, he was getting into the rhythm. He found staying with the beat made the paddling that much easier. He felt each stroke matching the cadence of the song.

Someone's in the timber with Tina.
Someone's in the timber I see-ee-ee-ee.
Someone's in the timber with Tina,
Humping on that old pussy.

18

It was not a large river, but when Jimiyu, Nikira, and their guide, McCroy, came to it, they stopped and marveled at its color. It reminded Jimiyu of the story of Moses, and how God gave him the power to turn the Nile into a river of blood. Ironic, he thought, considering the "Moses" tag that had been facetiously attached to Dr. Nikira.

"It's redder than the Colorado after the sixty-three quake," said McCroy.

Standing there, looking at the rushing waters, Nikira said, more to himself than to his companions, "'There is a river whose streams make glad the City of God, the holy place where the Most High dwells.'"

They moved down the dock but found few people to question.

"Excuse me," Nikira said to the first two men they encountered.

Belatedly, Jimiyu realized the younger of the two was a woman. From behind, her stout legs and broad shoulders had misled him. The older man with her, Jimiyu realized, was blind.

"Pardon the intrusion. Could you tell us where we might find a man named Harley?"

"Happy Harley," Jimiyu added.

"Who wants to know?" the woman replied in a tone that was less than friendly.

"I'm Dr. Talib Nikira, and these are my two associates. We're about to mount an expedition into the wilds of Evergreen, and we need Mr. Harley to point us in the proper direction."

"You're going into the deep woods?" she said, looking them over as if taking their measure. "I don't think you want to do that. Tell them, Ford. Tell them about how the forest is haunted."

"*Haunted* is such a naive word, like something out of a child's tale," the blind man said, scratching his pocked nose. "There is nothing childish about the spirits who inhabit the forest. They are more than myth, yet they cannot be seen. They are as old as the world itself, neither mortal nor immortal. Their power, their intellect, is beyond our understanding. If you believe in that sort of thing."

The woman chuckled and the old man let a brief smile cross his heretofore serious face. Jimiyu didn't know if the man was warning them or having a laugh at their expense.

"What's that in your hand?"

The beefy woman pointed at the artifact Jimiyu held. He held it up to show her, but before he could explain its significance, she said, "Looks like Snow Tree, the old tit tattoo."

"What?" Nikira asked, his interest aroused. "What do you mean?"

"It looks a little like Snow Tree," she repeated. "You can't see it from here. It's over that ridge, on the other side of the lake, miles away even from there, wouldn't you say, Ford?"

"Many, many miles," the old man agreed.

"Anyway," she went on, "that's where the Twin Tits stand."

"The Twin Tits?" McCroy asked, amused.

"The two biggest mountains hereabouts. There must be some kind of canyon where the sun don't shine on the right Tit, cause when the rest of the snow melts off the face, it leaves white markings kind of like this," she said, pointing at the design on the artifact. "Snow Tree."

Nikira looked at McCroy. "Could that be where he found it?"

McCroy shrugged, his close-set eyes noncommittal.

"Found what?" the woman asked.

"This artifact," Jimiyu replied. "That's why we're looking for Happy Harley. We want to know where he found this."

"He didn't find it on the Tits, I can tell you that," she said.

"How do you know?" asked Nikira.

"No one has ever traveled that far," spoke up the old man, pulling at his long grey hair. "No man has ever ventured even to the base of those mountains."

"Are you certain?"

His disdainful expression was the only reply he offered.

"So, where's this Harley guy?" McCroy asked gruffly.

"Don't know," said the woman, returning to the task they'd interrupted. "He was here earlier. I haven't seen him since. Probably in the vill somewhere."

"Thanks a lot," McCroy said, with little sincerity. To Nikira and Jimiyu: "Let's track down this Harley and get the show on the road, huh?"

Nikira nodded.

"It's a small burg. I say I go down one side, you two take the other, and we keep going until we find him."

"All right," Nikira agreed.

They separated, Jimiyu following Nikira as usual.

His old friend still seemed energized, yet Jimiyu was concerned. It wasn't anything in particular that worried him. Nothing major, just little things—slight deviations in Nikira's mood, undefinable moments, abstractions with no common rationale, glimpses of a man he didn't recognize. Most of the time Jimiyu simply attributed it to his imagination. Nikira was, after all, a complex man, and the complexities of his character were not always easily understood by someone used to the elementary queries of rural schoolhouse students.

"What happens..." Jimiyu began, then hesitated. "...if you don't find what you're looking for, Talib?"

By invoking his first name, Jimiyu had broached their public relationship for a more personal one he rarely called upon anymore.

Nikira looked at him with an expression of mutual respect Jimiyu seldom saw.

"I know what you're thinking, Brother. You're worried if I'm wrong, if I fail to locate the provenance of God, I'll become irrational, that obsession will blind me to the reality of failure." He paused, pulling at the little hairs of his goatee. Jimiyu could almost see the gears shifting in his head. "Remember when we were boys, and we had to undergo the traditional rite of passage—cross miles of savannah without food or water?"

Jimiyu nodded.

"I was afraid I would fail then."

"You? You were never afraid of anything—even as a boy."

"But I was, Jimi. I was terribly afraid of failing—of failing my father, my family, our tribe. I carried that fear with me when I left Kenya to attend Cambridge, and even later when I studied at the Vatican. The fear of failure clung to me like a foul odor until I found my faith.

"Faith, Jimi, that's the rock I've anchored myself to all these years. Faith, and the intellectual capacity to comprehend both the logic and illogic of it."

His velvet voice lulled Jimiyu into a rapt audience. Goose bumps erupted down his arms, as they often did when he became entranced by Nikira's speech.

"You might think that logic is the antithesis of faith, but I have spent my life coalescing the two into a single, unifying ideal. That's why we're here, Jimi. That's why I have to know the truth, even if the truth means failure.

"But I don't let myself think about failure. Before we embarked on this journey, doubt had begun to weaken me. I must bear the guilt for that lapse. I won't allow myself to doubt again. Doubt and faith were not meant to coexist. We won't fail."

Jimiyu didn't know about faith and logic. He wasn't even certain what "coalescing" meant. He did, however, know Nikira. And, despite his friend's vague assurances, he had an idea what failure would do to him.

19

She observed the trio of cubs rollicking for almost an hour. They'd come close enough for her to touch, and their parents didn't seemed to mind. They were growing more used to Amanda's presence every day. Maybe they had even accepted her as part of the community, though she admitted to herself that might be too much to hope for.

The more she watched the cubs, the more amazed she was at how much they were like human children. What was interesting was how much their play imitated the actions of the adults: the way they tried to stand on two legs and groom each other; their play-fighting, complete with immature grunts and growls; the way they circled each other in comedic imitation of the ursu mating dance.

While two of the cubs wrestled, the third decided to examine Amanda more closely. It approached slowly, cautiously, sniffing the air for any hint of danger. But, childlike, it soon put aside its concerns and began pawing playfully at her arm. Amanda giggled at the ticklish touch. She adjusted her sitting position to see it better. She wished she had a big ball to see how they'd play with it.

The cub stood on its hind legs and steadied itself against her; it was still learning to walk on two legs. It reached up and pawed at her hat. She took it off and put it on the ground next to the cub.

The cub seemed unsure. It looked at the sweatstained khaki hat and then back at her hair. It wanted the hat, but first it wanted to sniff her hair.

Either it didn't like what it smelled or it decided to pounce on the hat before it got away. The cub dropped down on the hat, but in doing so, it scratched Amanda's arm.

It was an accident. The ursu had long, sharp, non-retractable claws. The claws of one paw caught in the material of Amanda's shirt and poked through, scratching her when the animal moved.

The cub's attention was now focused on the hat, and its two playmates saw it had something of interest. They ambled over as Amanda checked her arm. The scratch wasn't deep, but she knew she had to be careful about infection. No studies had been done on what kinds of bacterial agents existed on Evergreen, so she made a point of being cautious.

She poured some water from her canteen over the cut to irrigate it, used a tube of disinfectant and pulled out her container of aloe vera gel. She found the natural salve's healing properties useful for many things, from minor burns to gum inflammation. She rubbed some on her scratch as she watched the cubs fight over her hat. She decided she'd better retrieve it before they tore it to shreds.

Suddenly, all three cubs squatted on their haunches, smelling the air. Amanda looked around. She didn't see anything. Though the cubs showed no signs of moving, they'd become alert, almost rigid.

Abruptly, several adult ursu hurtled towards her. They were agitated, growling. Three of them whisked up the cubs and moved them back. The others stood a few feet from Amanda and sniffed the air. They seemed confused.

Amanda had been too startled by their sudden onrush to even move. Their charge frightened her. She wondered what it was that alarmed them so. They'd come straight to their young as if...

She looked at the open jar of aloe vera. Could it be the smell of the salve set them off? She screwed on the plastic lid, rolled down her sleeve and wrapped a towel around the shirt where she'd applied the gel. The ursu continued to sniff the air but appeared to calm somewhat. Gradually, they moved off, away from her. Either they'd determined there was no real danger, or the scent that had alarmed them had dissipated. Almost as quickly as it had been disrupted, the community returned to its normal routine.

Amanda was certain it must have been her salve that disturbed them. It was possible the aloe smell was consistent with the scent the ursu young gave off when they were in danger. It was another lucky accident of discovery, though she realized she'd been lucky in another way. They could have assumed she was the source of the danger.

Still, what intrigued her most was how the ursu, or at least those within in range of the scent, had reacted. The idea of something jeopardizing their young had aroused the community as a whole. It had reacted with no particular concern as to whose offspring the cubs were. That told Amanda volumes about the nature of the ursu, and what they might be capable of.

20

The lake was endless from Eamon's perspective, extending to the horizon and beyond, its farthest shore left to the imagination. More stunning were the trees on the hills surrounding it. Even from this distance, he saw how enormous they were. Thousands of them, packed crown-to-crown like a massive army ready to march on command.

The green blanket of forest led his gaze upward to a distant range of sawtooth mountains that extended across almost the entire field of his vision. Two mammoth peaks rose above the rest, though how far away they stood, he couldn't begin to guess. Their summits were still snow-covered, despite the warmth of the air.

He realized, when Ramos called for a break from their paddling, that he was exhausted. He rested his weary arms and soaked in the scenic wonder. He reached for the medallion around his neck, as he habitually did to assure himself it was still there. He pulled it out, but his tired fingers fumbled with it.

"Don't drop anything out here," said a fellow behind him. "Something goes overboard, it's gone. It's as deep as two thousand feet in places."

Eamon nodded in response and tried to peer into the depths of the water. It was dark, impenetrable and subtly terrifying. He'd never been much of a swimmer, and the idea of plunging into those alien waters made him shiver. Who knew what kinds of creatures inhabited that murky world?

"Are there any fish?"

"Sure, the cooks go fishing all the time. Sometimes they—"

"Fishing?" The sleeping giant next to Eamon roused as if someone had said the magic word. "I went fishing once," he said, pushing his hat out of his face and sitting up. He stared at Eamon with intense dark eyes, but still no sign he recalled their encounter the night before. "I went fishing in the Euphrates. We had this prisoner, a heathen who wouldn't talk. He wouldn't tell us where his fellow vermin were hiding, so I started cutting off pieces of him. Just little pieces you know—a fingertip here, a slice of thigh there—nothing he'd really miss...not at first. We sat him there and made him watch while we used those pieces to go fishing."

Eamon gaped, transfixed, afraid to turn away, afraid not to, afraid to say or do anything that might set him off.

"So, did you catch you anything, Kruto?" asked the fellow behind Eamon.

"Nah. I don't think there were any fish left in that godforsaken river." He smiled, as if remembering. "But we caught ourselves some vermin later that day."

Kruto pulled his hat over his eyes again and slumped down as if returning to his nap. Eamon looked away and suppressed a shiver. Gash was right. This was definitely someone he wanted to avoid.

When the current began turning their boats, Ramos called out, "All right, lay to, TJs. We're almost home."

Eamon took up his paddle again only to discover his arms had grown wooden. The respite had only served to stiffen them. Nonetheless, he fought through the stiffness, and it wasn't long before the strokes of his paddle synched back into rhythm with the others.

As they drew closer to their destination, Eamon saw what looked like a floating city. Scores of boats, large and small, most surmounted by dreary, ramshackle structures, all conjoined as a single entity. He saw a number of men sitting round the fringes of the flotilla, apparently fishing. Looking landward, he saw bare patches in the timberline, stumps and broken ground, balding parcels of sallow brown infringing on the lush, green curtain, moving grimly upward from the lake like an encroaching infection.

He wondered at the scope of it all. He considered how fate had brought him to this place, at this time. He considered and then dismissed it. It was too much to comprehend. His youth didn't provide him with any perspective from which to grasp the moment. But he didn't need to understand it. He only needed to focus on his objective. He only needed one thing.

21

Filamena decided to accept Administrator Oshima's invitation from the previous night to visit her private garden—a botanical sanctuary enclosed by ivy-covered walls adjoining the administrator's residence. It turned out to be a lovely little flower garden—lush, fertile, teeming with blossoms both familiar and exotic. Most of the varieties she recognized from Earth. The others she assumed were native to Evergreen, though the well-manicured flowerbeds certainly presented a different face of the planet than she'd witnessed thus far.

What she'd seen of the township bordered on barbarous. She'd known it was a frontier world; however, she wasn't truly prepared for the lack of civilization she encountered, the crudeness of the facilities. Unpaved roads, no web, no broadcasts of any sort, no environmental controls, and drinking water that came straight from the plumbing. Not to mention the impoliteness of some of the people.

Yet the tranquility of the garden was more a refuge from her own anxiety than from the rough-hewn nature of the locals. She wanted to get away from the other members of the expedition, especially Luis and Max, to be where she could think without distraction.

She had managed to avoid Max for most of the journey, and had taken measures to assure they would never be alone together-

She knew she couldn't avoid him forever. Not any more than she could evade her feelings—her own culpability.

She reached out and touched a single vermillion petal, feeling its velvety softness between her fingers. She felt a chill and pulled her hand away. An irrational notion swept through her. She was overcome by the impression the flowers were looking at her, watching her.

As quickly as it consumed her she dismissed the sensation as emotions run rampant. She couldn't let her feelings get the better of her. She had to maintain her poise.

She saw something move behind the blossoms. It was a small spider—at least it looked enough like a spider for her to think of it that way. It had only six legs—six fat, stubby legs that barely held up its knobby body as it skittered across the ground. She was thinking how funny-looking it was when footsteps prompted her to look up. She almost didn't have to. She knew who would be standing there. She was resigned to it.

"I figured I would find you here," said Max. He didn't wait to gauge her response. He came straight to her with the impulsiveness that marked him.

Filamena turned away from him, just enough to signify her rebuff. "I came here because I wanted to be alone," she said.

Max hesitated, running his fingers through his thick, dark hair as if suddenly uncertain. The duck-tail wave of his coif fell neatly back into place. An idea registered on his face, and he pulled out his Imaginator.

"Let me draw you, here, in this garden. It will be a beau—"

"*É pazzo di te!*"

Max smiled. "I love it when you speak Italian."

"Max, what are doing here?"

"I came to find you. I knew when you heard about this garden that you'd—"

"No, Max, I mean what are you doing *here*, on this world, on this expedition? I told you it was over. I told you we couldn't do this anymore. I thought you understood."

"I do understand, Mena," he replied, putting the art pad back into his jacket. "I understand how much I love you. I understand I'm not going to let you throw away what we have just because you're married to my father."

Filamena exhaled a hiss of impatience. "What do we have, Max? We don't have anything. Two weeks of passion that never should have happened—that I should never have *let* happen."

Max gently took hold of her arms. "You can't blame yourself. We have nothing to feel ashamed of."

"But I do feel shame, Max. The worst kind of shame." She looked into his eyes for some kind of understanding of her plight, but all she saw was single-mindedness. "Don't you realize what we've done? What I've done? I'm a *puttana*. I've betrayed your father in the worst way possible."

She saw a fleeting look of guilt cross his face. He wasn't totally immune to their ignominy after all. He stood there as if he didn't know what to say next. Without warning, he grabbed her and kissed her.

Filamena's first impulse was to resist. She was prepared to. She knew she must, but somehow when his lips pressed against hers, and she felt the embrace of his arms, his lean body pressing against hers, she gave in to the moment. It had been so long since Luis had kissed her like this—like she needed to be kissed. If only he had been more passionate, more attentive. If only he wasn't the kind of man who was so immersed in his work. If only he had not gone to Mars and left her alone with Max.

Yet Luis didn't deserve all the blame. She should have gone to Mars with him. He had wanted her to. She shouldn't have given in to the carnal desires that consumed her.

She broke from the kiss and pushed Max to arm's length.

"You have to tell him, Mena. You have to tell him the truth. Tell him how you feel about me so we can be together."

"That's not going to happen, Max. I'm not going to leave your father."

"But I love you."

"You don't even know what love is. The only thing you feel is the heat of infatuation. You'll get over it. You'll get over me."

"No, I won't," he responded resolutely, looking at her with an intensity that made her uncomfortable.

When she didn't respond, he pulled out a small pocket knife, bent down and cut one of the ruby roses. He offered it to her. Instead of taking it, she turned away. For a ponderous moment, silence separated them. Then, an angry voice with a decidedly Jamaican accent swept the heavy stillness aside.

"What you doing, mon? I can't believe what you do." An old, ebony-skinned man, the gardener by his outfit, came at them, poking the air while glaring at Max. "You don't cut me roses, mon. No, no, you don't cut me roses."

Max looked properly chastised. "I'm...I'm sorry. I was just going to give it to the lady."

The gardener threw his hands back behind his head in a gesture of frustration. "I don't care, mon. You still don't cut me roses. Me roses is like me little children. You don't cut little children, do you?"

"I'm sorry. I didn't mean to hurt them."

"Well, don't do it again. Don't cut me roses anymore."

"Since I've already cut it, is it all right if I give it to the pretty lady?" Max asked, as if he wasn't sure what to do with the damaging evidence still in his hand.

The gardener frowned, contemplated a moment and responded, "Sure, sure. Go ahead. But don't cut me roses anymore, mon."

"I promise."

Max held out the rose to Filamena. She decided to take it to avoid irritating the old fellow further. As she did, a thorn on the stem pricked her forefinger. It was a tiny wound, marked by the bloom of a single crimson dot. She sucked at it out of reflex, looked at Max briefly, and then left him standing there.

22

"Yeah, I remember this."

They'd finally tracked down the enigmatic Happy Harley. However, he was not as lucid and informative as they'd hoped. He held the artifact, looking at it as if he could barely focus. Jimiyu could tell the man was under the influence. Under the influence of what, he couldn't say. It didn't take him long to see, and smell, that the fellow's hygienic practices were also in serious need of reformation.

"It was a long time ago. A year maybe? Yeah, something like that. I think I traded it for a bag of cookies and a really cool pipe. Lost the pipe somewhere, though. Lost a ring once, too. Can't ever remember where I put anything," he rambled. "I found some nifty rocks you might like, too. Let's see, where'd I put those? Got to remember to get some more cookies, and some—"

"Where did you find it?" Nikira interrupted when it seemed the fellow would go on and on.

"This? Yeah, I found it."

"*Where*, Mr. Harley?"

"It's not Mr. Harley, just Harley," he said, emphasizing the point. "Just plain old Harley. They call me Happy, too, but—"

"Can you tell us where you found it or not?" McCroy said, the nostrils of his flat nose flaring with impatience.

"Sure, sure." Harley thought for a moment, looking to Jimiyu as if he didn't remember at all. "I found that carving east of Pickle Peak, past the old Washoe settlement. I remember because I was out there—I mean *way* out there—looking for shrooms, you know, for my makings. You've got to dry them and then mix just the right amount with buds from..." He paused, looking slyly up at them as if they'd been trying to trick him. "But I can't tell you all my secrets, can I? Not unless you were to pay for them." He looked hopefully at them then continued. "Anyway, I don't usually go out that far. I remember finding that thing after I got lost out there. It was odd-looking, so I put it in my pack. I thought I'd never find my way out. If it wasn't for my lucky acorn...I tell you, you don't want to go deep in those woods when you're stoned. No, sir. That's a reeeeaally bad vibe."

"Could you take us to where you found this?" Nikira said, retrieving the artifact.

For a moment, Harley looked as if he'd floated off to another reality.

Jimiyu spoke up. "We'll pay you for your time if you take us there."

"Pay me?" he said, dazed and somewhat confused. "You got any cookies?"

"Yeah, yeah" grunted McCroy. "Can you show us where you found it or not?"

"Sure, sure, I can take there. But it's a long ways out there—several days, at least. When do you want to go?"

"Immediately," said Nikira.

"Okay, yeah...uh, just let me take a little nap first. Then I'll be ready to go."

"We'll leave tomorrow morning," Nikira replied. "Will everything be ready, Mr. McCroy?"

"We'll be ready," answered McCroy, lifting his hat to run his fingers through his hair. "Though I doubt he'll be." He nodded at Harley, who had started to wander away. "You're not really going to follow him, are you, Doctor? He couldn't find his own balls with a searchlight."

Nikira ignored the crude reference, responding with assurance. "Even if he can't take us to the exact location, Mr. McCroy, I'm sure he can point us in the right direction. Then I have no doubt your estimable skills will lead us the rest of the way."

"Yeah, sure," McCroy responded with a grudging laugh.

"Jimi, retrieve our friend before he wanders off and gets lost again," Nikira said, pointing at Harley. "Secure him a room next to ours so we'll know where he is in the morning."

Jimiyu nodded obediently, though the idea of nursemaiding the scraggly tramp was about as appealing as marching off into unknown terrain on an alien planet. Still, maybe he could coerce the fellow into taking a bath.

23

The lumbermen—timber jockeys, Eamon had learned they called themselves—wasted no time getting to work. As soon as the dugouts were beached, they headed for the tubs of UV screen and smeared it on their arms, hands and faces. When they were properly "greased up," they collected their tools and set off without further direction, each to his own task. Eamon, unsure of what to do, wandered over to ask the bull-like fellow they called Gash. Before he could even ask his question, the honcho began pairing up the newcomers with experienced men.

"Gash, you show Pretty Boy there the ropes," said Ramos.

His new mentor frowned but didn't say anything.

"I never got a chance to thank you," said Eamon.

Gash didn't respond. He picked up a pair of thick gloves and tossed them to Eamon.

"Thank me by putting those on."

He complied, and Gash showed him how to strap cleats to his boots. When they were secure, he followed Gash to the tool stacks, where they passed the collections of power saws, wedges and axes, instead taking away a variety of steel attachments and cable Gash called rigging. Then, he led up the slope of a hill through the clear-cut into an area so thick with giant trees the mantle of needled branches kept the sunlight at bay.

Eamon quickly discovered how hard, and how dangerous, the work was.

There was much to learn—the terminology alone confused him for days. He felt for a time like he was back in school, a recollection that didn't serve him well. Each time he felt like he was getting the hang of it, the nerve-jarring crash of another evergreen giant or the roar of an engaged power saw would rattle his concentration. It was hours before he grew accustomed to the disconcerting sounds.

Their task, it turned out, was skidding—hauling the felled trees after they'd been topped and limbed. The logs were too enormous to be moved by men, so they had to rig them with cables thick as Eamon's arm and link the cables to the strawline drum of the nearest yarder, all the while checking the guylines to make sure the machine was firmly stabilized. He had to work quickly, and get out of the way even quicker. And while he was trying to avoid getting a foot smashed or a hand crushed, he had to watch out for the logs—make certain they didn't splinter against other trees or stumps as they were hauled along the broken ground. He was dragging a length of heavy cable through a bramble patch at one point when it snagged. He wrenched it loose after several tugs and staggered on. He jerked and hauled the unwieldy cable until he thought his arms would wrench out of their sockets.

Gash didn't say much, but when he did it was with a resounding voice that matched his imposing physical presence. Even when he'd make some offhand comment Eamon took as dark timber jockey humor, he didn't smile.

Despite a healthy dose of caution, Eamon found himself whip-slapped by loose lines several times before the end of the workday. By then, the magnificent forest he'd regarded with awe so short a time ago wasn't so magnificent anymore. It had become an arena of potentially crippling hazards and debilitating fatigue. His body was crisscrossed with welts and scratches. He had never questioned his resolve so much as he did that first day on the timberline.

When a screeching whistle echoed through the trees, Gash told him, "We break for lunch."

Eamon caught his breath and tried to relax. He felt Evergreen's pull weighing him down. He leaned back against a stump and started to sit.

"If you stop moving you're going to stiffen up," Gash said nonchalantly as he headed downhill. "Don't worry, you'll get used to it."

Right now, Eamon wasn't much of a believer. His muscles ached so badly, he couldn't tell where one sore spot began and another ended. Despite his gloves, he could feel the beginnings of blisters. A voice inside him said *Quit, don't even try anymore.* He'd given in to that voice in the past—many times. He was where he was now, in part, because of that voice. The reminder of the self-indulgent adolescent he used to be only fired his determination. He wouldn't quit. He wouldn't give up until he'd done what he'd come here to do.

24

Jimiyu didn't learn that a portion of their trip would be via the river until the night before their departure. He'd been dreading it ever since—obsessing over his fear of water. Now, as he stood on the dock at the river's edge, his feet had grown roots and refused to move.

He pulled at the chin strap that held his straw hat in place. He had never learned to swim. Growing up on the arid plans of Kenya, there had never been a need to. He looked at the little boats they were supposed to load their packs onto. They were mere slivers, whose design seemed less than stable.

"Can't we use the bigger boats?" he asked no one in particular. There were several much larger craft tied to the dock farther down. They were much more stable-looking than the two precarious vessels they'd chartered.

No one bothered to answer him, and the loading proceeded.

"The river is a very strange color," said Chanya. "It looks almost like blood."

Jimiyu had seen the bizarre river water before. He didn't need the reminder. Now he had to deal with flimsy boats *and* gruesome waters.

"I was talking to one of the local miners about that," offered Professor Escobedo. "There's an extremely high iron content in the soil upriver where they've established one of their mining operations. It's the iron sediment that causes the reddish-brown color."

"The Washoe used to call it the 'River of Tears,'" said Happy Harley, whom Jimiyu discovered wasn't so happy when he'd been forced out of bed at daybreak.

"Why is that?" Chanya asked.

Harley shrugged. "I don't know. Some old legend, I guess. But you have to give legends their due. Otherwise, it's bad luck."

Jimiyu decided to take his mind off the river, and looked around at his fellow travelers. Assigned to the first boat at McCroy's direction were Nikira, Chanya, Vincent, and their native guide, Harley, along with McCroy. From the beginning of their journey, he'd thought them an odd group to be thrust together.

Jimiyu had already formed an opinion about their expedition's overseer. McCroy was coarse, abrupt and oblivious to the fact he was simply a man for hire. He acted as if he were some sort of military officer and this was his campaign. As a child, Jimiyu had learned to be suspicious of the military mentality, and he didn't like McCroy, or the disrespectful way he often spoke to Dr. Nikira.

McCroy had designated Jimiyu to ride in the second boat, which included the archaeologist, Professor Escobedo, his son and his wife, a woman whose beauty Jimiyu couldn't help but admire. From her alluring almond eyes to the tiny mole that marked her jawline to the swell of breasts beneath her shirt, she was Venus incarnate. Her appeal was defined as much by the stately way she carried herself as by the femininity of her figure.

She was quite a contrast to her husband, a plump, somewhat clumsy though genial fellow. Jimiyu guessed she was not the mother of the professor's son, simply because she seemed closer in age to the boy than the father. However, cosmetic transformation being what it was, she could have been old enough to be his own mother and he wouldn't know it.

"Let's move it, Waka." It was McCroy's associate, one Jesper Scurlock, who'd been assigned to his boat. The man spoke with a drawl that emphasized each vowel and, Jimiyu thought, unnecessarily exposed his yellowed teeth.

"My name is Obwaka—*Mr.* Obwaka. Or Jimiyu, if you prefer."

"Oh, yeah? Sorry," he replied in a manner that made Jimiyu doubt his sincerity.

"My brother doesn't like the water," spoke up Nikira, with the closest thing to a smile Jimiyu had seen on his face in months.

"Well, don't you worry at all, Mr. Jimiyu," Scurlock said, grinning to reveal the full scope of his dental discoloration. "I've never lost a customer yet. I'll take right good care of you. You won't get so much as a drop on you."

"Speaking of water," Nikira said to McCroy," are we going to be able to carry enough for our journey?"

McCroy shook his head—a bit condescendingly, thought Jimiyu. "On an expedition like this, the average person is going to need more than ten pounds of water a day. We can't haul that much. I asked around. As I expected, there are plenty of mountain streams up these hills. We'll use purification tablets and fill our canteens as we go."

"Look up there." The professor's son directed everyone's attention to the sky over the distant mountain range. The sight was indeed impressive. A cloud formation had billowed into the shape of a giant column, extending level as a tabletop at its summit. Its patterned whirls gave it a sense of movement, almost as if it were a living entity. It conjured the notion of great power.

"An anvil cloud," said Professor Escobedo. "Probably means rain."

"It hasn't rained in a while," added Harley.

"It's all right, Mr. Jimiyu," Scurlock teased. "It's too far off to get us wet."

Jimiyu didn't care for his patronizing tone. "Just Jimiyu will do fine."

"Let's go, let's move it," McCroy commanded, his hand resting on the hilt of the machete he'd tucked into his oversized belt. "We haven't got time to stand around and chitchat. Let's get this junket in gear. Come on, load up and get in."

He knelt next to his big cat and stroked its back. The animal, leashed to a dock cleat, responded affectionately to his touch. McCroy untied it.

"In the boat," he directed with a wave of his hand, and the cat jumped in. Harley, who'd already seated himself, almost fell backwards trying to avoid the animal. He looked at it as if he were prepared to dive overboard at a moment's notice.

Jimiyu was the last to leave the firm footing of the dock for the rocking instability of his designated canoe. There was only one reason he could bring himself to do it—his own stubborn sense of loyalty. He wasn't about to let Nikira go off without him.

They proceeded downriver, McCroy and Scurlock steering from the rear position of their respective canoes. Each of the others was given a paddle to use, but based on his own awkward attempts, Jimiyu was certain the river current was doing most of the work.

The woodland vegetation on either side was so dense he couldn't see much beyond the riverbanks. Both sides inclined upward to varying degrees, and all he saw were trees and more trees. He was more surprised by what he didn't see. He hadn't spotted a single bird or other living creature.

Then, just as he was thinking how barren it seemed, he spied a furry creature at the water's edge. It looked like a stout, short-eared rabbit. His first impression was that it was a rotund little thing, a veritable lump of fat. A second glance convinced him the ripples under that fur were pure muscle.

It was strange little beast. It made him wonder if there were any fish in the river, and how strange *they* might be. He decided not to dwell on what might live in those murky depths. Still, the thought was in his mind, and he was primed for panic when his paddle struck something.

"What was that? I touched something."

"It's a shallow river. Probably just rocks," Scurlock said, his thick hairy brows arching as he grinned maliciously. "They won't bite much."

Jimiyu ignored him. He didn't know what the stylized *A* on Scurlock's cap stood for, but he had a few suggestions.

He was beginning to settle into the boat and feel more at ease when they came to an area of rapids. The disturbance was sudden. The river rushed along with single-minded strength, conveying them with its urgency. McCroy yelled for them to store their paddles and let the current carry them. It was a rough, but unexpectedly exhilarating ride, with McCroy and Scurlock guiding the two boats, keeping them midstream. When the rapids subsided, they began to paddle again. Soon, he heard Harley calling out, directing them to the right bank. They'd been on the river only a few miles by Jimiyu's estimation.

As soon as the lead canoe hit the shore, the exotic cat bounded out and onto land. McCroy ordered everyone out of the boats, and Jimiyu discovered there was no way to avoid stepping in the water. He slogged through it ankle-deep, taking his pack so he wouldn't have to go back for it.

The professor's wife was having some difficulty lifting her pack. Both her husband and his son moved to help. The son gave way to the father, choosing instead to take hold of her hand and lead her out of the river.

Vincent, a slight fellow, was also having trouble with his pack. He grunted, lifting it onto his back.

"What's the input, gold bricks?"

Scurlock laughed as if at some private joke, and McCroy responded, "Fifteen days' rations. I figured that was about all this group could carry."

"How many radios did you bring?" asked Professor Escobedo.

"No radios," replied McCroy. "They're no good on Evergreen. Too much interference from solar winds and the planet's magnetic field. Which reminds me—everyone be sure and use plenty of that UV screen you've been given. Word is you'll slow-cook if you don't."

"Wait a minute, you mean we have no way to contact anyone in town?" the professor's wife inquired, containing her alarm.

"Believe me, ma'am, you're safer out here with us than you are in that town," McCroy replied.

Jimiyu found his reasoning less than reassuring.

He noticed Nikira had strolled off, away from the riverbank to the edge of the forest. He stood there a moment before turning back to the others.

"Look around you," he said. "Look at the splendor of it, the magnificence of creation. See what God has wrought."

"It's so like Earth," Professor Escobedo added. "At least, the wilderness refuges that remain."

McCroy swung his pack onto his back. "Let's get these boats ashore, or we'll be swimming back," he called out. "Jesper, break out the scatterguns."

"What guns?" asked Nikira.

"These babies," said Scurlock, hoisting a pair of short-barreled shotguns and handing one to McCroy.

Nikira responded sternly. "We were told that no firearms were allowed on Evergreen. How did you manage to—"

"I slipped 'em by the customs man slick as swamp slime," Scurlock boasted.

Nikira ignored him and addressed McCroy. "I have no intention of violating local laws."

"Then don't. Me, I'm not traipsing off into unknown country with nothing more than Jesper's ugly mug to protect me," McCroy said, loading his weapon. "Just think of it as a necessary precaution."

Nikira didn't press the issue, though he looked as if he had more to say on the subject. Instead, he joined in the effort to beach the canoes. Once the boats were secure and everyone had donned their packs, McCroy called the cat to his side.

"Thor, heel!"

The animal obeyed then promptly sneezed.

"Hearing a cat sneeze is a good omen," said Harley, nodding. "A good way to start a journey."

"Then let's get it started." McCroy gestured at Harley. "Lead the way."

Harley scanned the woods briefly and started off in a direction Jimiyu hoped wasn't as random as it looked.

25

Amanda backed off a few feet from where she had been observing. An uncommon dispute had broken out over mating territoriality. Since the ursu, unlike most species of bear but like orangutans, were not monogamous, such conflicts were rare. From her previous observations, Amanda had classified the ursu as basically nonviolent. Except for a few minor spats concerning the distribution of food, she'd seen little hostility among the members of the community.

Now, however, the rancorous vocalizations of two confrontational males had stirred the entire community. The females and their young retreated to the treetops—including the female who had initially aroused the attention of the two suitors. From what Amanda could tell, a dominant male had momentarily moved away from the female, possibly to bring her a gift of food. When he returned, a younger male was attempting to mount the female in question.

Now they were face-to-face, growling and grunting to a degree Amanda had not witnessed before. Part of her wanted to interfere, distract the combatants before they came to blows—if indeed that's what was about to happen. But she told herself she couldn't. She was here to learn about the ursu, not to try and conform them to her notion of proper behavior.

In the midst of her observations, a small swarm of madflies descended upon her. She swatted at them until they moved on. The insects had become more bothersome lately. She didn't know if the increased activity had been brought on by seasonal changes or some other factor.

As she chased away the madflies, she noticed an odd odor permeating the air. It wasn't the flies, though. It had to be emanating from the two males. They were communicating their anger, each warning off the other. It was unusual for her to detect ursu scents, but this one was powerful. Still, she couldn't identify what, if anything, the smell reminded her of.

The older male grunted and turned away, his long, matted hair trailing across the ground. Amanda thought perhaps he was ending the confrontation. Instead, he snatched up a broken tree limb, turned and smacked the younger male across the side of the head. More stunned by the unexpected blow than injured, the younger one retreated. His withdrawal precipitated what Amanda interpreted as a victory growl from the older male.

The implications of this encounter disturbed her. She'd never seen an ursu make use of a weapon. Of course, she'd seen very little conflict at all. Was it typical, or had she witnessed the first such incident? She'd seen the ursu make use of crude tools for gathering food, yet nothing like this. Was this evidence of their intellectual development—another step up the evolutionary ladder? It was a chilling idea—that an urge for violent action might be a precursor of higher learning. Still, she couldn't deny how similar it was to the belligerent pattern of man's own evolutionary ascension.

Troubled as she was, Amanda diligently made note of her observations, as well as her impressions. When she finished, she felt the need for a walk—maybe even a bath. It could have been her imagination, but she thought she could still smell the ursu's combative scent on her.

She collected a towel and her flute, and hiked off toward the stream she used. It was possible she had begun to empathize too much with the ursu. She had grown to like them so much, she'd taken the clash personally, finding the behavior at odds with her own nonviolent nature. She reminded herself she needed to remain objective. The cold water would refresh her, clear her head.

26

You had to concentrate on what you were doing, pay attention to what was going on all around you if you didn't want to end up flatter than one of Ford's rubbery flapjacks. A timber jockey with an attention deficit disorder either cured himself quick or learned what he could do with less than a full complement of working limbs.

For Gash, it was asylum, blessed refuge. He reveled in the fact that his mind was kept as busy as his body. Distraction was good. Distraction kept him going.

However, now he had this turtle to babysit. He had to keep him from crippling himself and somehow turn him into a timber jock. Though it kept him fully engaged, he didn't care for the responsibility. He didn't ever want to be responsible for anyone else again. He almost went to Ramos to tell him to find someone else to play nursemaid, but he knew what Ramos would say. Besides, this kid Eamon looked like he'd need all the help he could get.

He *was* a kid—fresh out of some private school by his looks—soft wavy hair and big round eyes in awe of everything. Not a callus on his hands, not an ounce of street smarts in his head. Both would change soon. How he'd ended up here, Gash couldn't imagine. He didn't want to. But now that the kid was here—now that he'd been assigned to him—Gash figured the least he could do was keep him alive and in one piece.

"Look, pay attention. I'm going to show you how to do this and then you're going to do it on your own."

"I'm looking," Eamon replied.

"You've got to learn to read the trees. When you pick your tree, you look for the longest ground. That's where you're going to drop it. You want to find the best ground you can, so it doesn't splinter on another tree or a stump when it comes down. A splintered log isn't worth much.

"Then you undercut right about here, on the side you want it to fall. Not too deep—about halfway in. You go to the opposite side and make the backcut about three inches above the undercut. That leaves a strip of holding wood between the two cuts that acts like a hinge when it falls. All the while, you're checking the lean, making sure it's going to come down where you want it to. If the lean's not right, you knock a wedge into the backcut to direct the fall. Get it?"

The turtle nodded his head.

"All right, let's see. Grab your axe and go to."

"Why can't I use one of those power saws?"

"Baby steps, turtle, baby steps. The chains are used for big timber, not this little fifty-footer you've got here. We've only got so many solar packs. We've got to conserve. So you just start swinging that blade, and we'll see how big your bite is."

Gash stood back as Eamon began chopping away. The kid's technique was rough, but that was to be expected. It would smooth out on its own when fatigue kicked in. Fortunately, he was a tall, wiry kid. Those long arms of his would muscle-up soon enough, after the timber and Evergreen's pull had their way with him.

Gash hadn't been much different himself when he first arrived. A little shorter, a little heavier, and much older. However, the years of hauling timber had made him bull-thick and tougher than a Pork Palace steak. How many years had it been now? How many years since...

> *"...we've got a problem with a pressure equalization valve in the transfer chamber airlock."*
>
> *"You sure it's not just air bubbles in the coolant line?"*

"Not likely."

"All right, tell the shuttle commander to back off until we find the problem."

"He's not going to like it."

"Too bad."

"Okay, you're the duty engineer...Shuttle commander confirms a hold on docking procedures. I won't..."

"Gash!"

The sound of his name brought him back.

"Gash!" It was Cayenne, coming up the hill from the lake.

"What's up?"

"Ramos wants you and me to scout new ground. Apparently, those company cocksuckers want to move the operation up to higher elevations."

"Still plenty of good wood down here."

"I'm just the messenger," she said, shrugging. "Ramos says to go up about four hundred yards or so."

"Shit, that's quite a hike up these hills."

"Don't I know it."

"What about the turtle?" Gash asked, pointing at Eamon, now chopping his backcut.

"I don't know," answered Cayenne. "If he's still attached at the hip, I guess we take him with us."

They watched Eamon hack away for a little while.

"Come on, Pretty Boy, knock that toothpick down!" Cayenne heckled.

Eamon gave the tree another dozen whacks. It began to teeter.

"I think it's going to fall," he blurted.

"Well, call it, boy," said Cayenne.

"What do I call it?"

Gash throttled a laugh as Cayenne stared at him, incredulous.

"Didn't you teach this turtle anything?" To Eamon she said, "Timber, boy, call timber."

"Timber," Eamon called out weakly as the tree began its slow-motion descent.

"Shit, call it out like you got a pair, boy! *Tim-berrrr!*" she yelled.

Gash stood next to the exasperated TJ and watched the tree's downward slide, each inch, each foot augmenting its velocity exponentially.

Exponentially. Funny, the words that wandered into your mind when you weren't paying attention—old, forgotten words. There was a time when he could have calculated the tree's acceleration in his head. He still could, he guessed, if he wanted. But the numbers were only numbers now, the calculations pointless extrapolation. The tree would fall. It would descend violently to the ground, be stripped of its useless limbs and hauled off for purposes still to be determined. That was the only thing he needed to know. That was the totality of what he needed to be concerned with now.

The tree collided with the ground, crushing its weaker branches beneath it and kicking up a cloud of dust and dead needles.

"When you call out 'timber,' boy, it's a fucking warning!" Cayenne was still ranting. "You do it so everyone will know to get the fuck out of the way."

The turtle stood there like he didn't know what to do with this pit bull of a woman chewing on him.

Gash came to his rescue. "Let's go, Cayenne. Come on, kid, we're going for a hike."

❦ ❦ ❦

The higher they traipsed, the denser the forest canopy became. Little sunlight intruded into this shaded domain, but Gash knew that would change. When the timber jocks swept through here the sun would stream in like molten gold, recasting the face of the terrain for decades to come.

Alerted to the unexpected intrusion, a pair of pudge rabbits ran for deeper cover, and dozens of dwarf tree lizards scampered across bark that was dappled with gray-green moss. There were more of the tiny reptiles than he'd seen at lower elevations.

He held back a moment and turned to his left while Cayenne and Eamon kept going. He'd spotted an odd patch of growth around one old giant and wanted to examine it. He hadn't seen anything quite like it before, and guessed it might be something that only grew this high up.

When he got closer, he saw it wasn't as odd as it looked. Just a grouping of vines that had curled around the base of the trunk.

With his eyes adjusting to the light in the pale shadows, he saw several other trees with the same kind of vines strung around their trunks, some climbing higher than others. He bent down over one of the vines and fingered a fat thorn. He'd tell Ramos to pass the word. They'd have to be careful around those. They looked like they were sharp enough, sturdy enough, to pierce even timber gloves.

Cayenne and the turtle were way ahead of him and starting to spread out. He didn't want the turtle to get lost, so he halted their march.

"Hold up there." He caught up with them. "We've gone four hundred yards, wouldn't you say, Cayenne?"

"If you say so," she responded.

"Looks to me like there's plenty of good timber up this way, not that there's a bare acre anywhere up here. Mostly clear ground, not too many boulders, brush isn't too bad, either—though it's a mighty steep slope. Even so, I don't see any reason they can't move up here if that's what they want. What do you think?"

Cayenne shrugged.

Gash took one last look around. He saw the kid had wandered off a ways but was still within sight. No reason they shouldn't go back. Evening was coming, and the TJs would be calling it a day by the time they reached the lake. Gash was already thinking about lighting up and enveloping himself in peaceful blue haze.

He motioned to Cayenne, turned downhill, and called to Eamon, "Come on, kid, we're going back down." He had only gone a half-dozen paces when the turtle yelled.

"There's something here!"

"What is it?"

"Come here and look."

"He's probably found a shiny pebble or something," Cayenne mocked.

"It's a—" Eamon didn't finish.

Gash didn't know what it was, but something had the turtle excited. There was even a hint of fright in his voice. He guessed he'd have to trudge on over and see what it was.

He smelled it before he saw it. It was a human hand and part of an arm, poking out from under the scrap of on forest floor.

"Jesus," said Cayenne, covering her mouth and nose.

Gash brushed away the thin blanket of dirt and needles, enough to reveal there was an entire body. At least, what was left of it. It had been there for some time—weeks, he guessed—not quite buried and fit snugly into a depression around the base of a sapling like so much mulch.

"What's that on the shoulder?" asked Eamon.

"It looks like...it's a tattoo," Gash said. He could barely make out the illustration—a T-shaped tree being split open by a jagged, J-shaped streak of lightning. Most of the dyed skin had decomposed. "It's a TJ bolt."

"It's Conklin," Cayenne stated flatly.

"How do you know? There must be fifty TJs with that same tattoo." Gash had one himself.

"Look under the tree." Cayenne brushed the black, nutrient-rich soil from the dead arm. "You can still see two of the three Cs—Conklin's initials. I remember, 'cause when he got drunk one night he was telling us his real name—Charles Chester or some such shit. But I remember the three Cs. Besides, they never found his body. It has to be him."

"What happened to him?" Eamon asked, his face turned away from the rotting remains.

"Drowned," answered Cayenne, "about a month ago. Somebody saw him fall in, drunk as usual, but they never did find his body."

"If it's Conklin," Gash said, standing, "then how the hell did he get all the way up here?"

27

I t was such a beautiful animal—its flared facial ruff flamboyant, distinct; its white ears curled outward and topped by sharp black tufts; its coat sleek, golden; its muted rosette spotting almost imperceptible in the late-evening gloom. So luxurious was its fur that Filamena couldn't resist touching it. Even tied to a leash, lying down, it evoked images of speed and grace.

She approached it gingerly but without fear. She'd always loved cats and, as a little girl, had fed the strays of her town whenever she could. She couldn't have a cat now—Luis was allergic and refused to medicate himself.

Filamena reached to pet the animal on the head. It wasn't asleep, but its drooping eyelids gave it that calm, drowsy appearance cats get.

"Better be careful." The voice startled her. It was McCroy. "He may just decide to snack on ladyfingers."

She hesitated. The cat's amber eyes were alert now. The presence of its master altered its disposition from restful to ready. She extended her hand and gently stroked the back of its head. The beast acknowledged the touch with an affectionate lift of its chin.

"He likes you," said McCroy. "He doesn't like everyone. He barely tolerates Jesper."

"Your associate?"

He nodded.

"What's his name?"

"Thor—god of thunder and lightning. He's fast and he's power-ful."

"Why do you keep him tied up?"

"I don't, usually. But as well-trained as he is, it's his nature to wander at night, to hunt. Back home, I let him—he always comes back. I want to make sure he's here when we move out in the morning."

"I'd think you'd worry about him getting hurt by something out there. It's a strange world."

McCroy grunted skeptically. "It's more likely he might hurt 'something out there.'"

"Is it true, what you told the customs agent?" Filamena asked, still petting the cat. "That he's some kind of hy—what did you call it?"

"Hybrid. A genetic mix of species, artificially bred."

"What for? Why change an animal that's already so beautiful?"

McCroy moved closer. The cat's reactions enabled Filamena to fully appreciate the bond between man and beast. It sat up on its haunches, waiting patiently, its stubby tail twitching, its eyes never wavering from him.

"It has nothing to do with appearances. The idea is to take the best attributes from various species. Thor is primarily Siberian lynx—a smart breed, easy to train. But, because of the genetic ma-nipulation, he can also climb like an Afghani leopard and hunt like a jaguar." McCroy bent down to the animal, and they butted heads in a sort of rubbing motion. "That's his way of showing affection."

She'd had little interaction with the expedition's guide before now, and had formed an opinion of him based on stock stereo-types. Now she saw him in a new light. At least he seemed much more personable around the cat. His sand- blond hair was almost a match for the animal's coat, and she would have considered him somewhat handsome if not for his mottled skin and a nose that looked as if it had been flattened by an injury.

"So, what are you doing on this expedition, Mr. McCroy?"

"I don't let beautiful women call me 'Mr. McCroy,'" he said, smiling, his close-set green eyes narrowing so she wasn't certain whether he were flirting or not. "Especially not ones who've made friends with Thor. Call me Lyle."

"You flatter me, but I'm not sure my husband would appreciate the familiarity, Mr. McCroy."

He shrugged and pulled out some kind of treat he fed to the cat.

"So, why *did* you come to Evergreen?" Filamena pursued, her curiosity aroused by the man's contradictory nature. "Is it just another job?"

"You make it sound like there are a lot of jobs like this. There's not much call for a great white hunter these days."

"Is that what you are? A hunter?" Filamena said, disapprovingly.

"I don't kill animals, if that's what you mean. I got fed up leading hunting safaris a long time ago. No, mostly I guide geological parties into remote areas, like parts of the Congo, or timber mining teams into the Amazon. When they want someone who knows the terrain, the local customs, they hire me.

"You could call me a frontiersman, if you prefer. That's what I was, a frontiersman stuck on a world with few frontiers...at least until young Mr. Boorman approached me with the idea of this expedition. I thought it was a joke at first, but one look at my credit account and I decided who was I to stand in the way of a quest for Shangri-la?"

"You don't sound like you have much faith in Dr. Nikira's theories."

"Sister, I don't have faith in anything, except maybe Thor here. That doesn't mean I don't hope we find something worth looking for. What that is may not be exactly what our heretic priest has in mind, but one man's folly may be another's fortune."

Filamena wasn't sure what he meant. His tone said he was hinting at something. "You expect to find some kind of treasure?"

"I didn't say that," he answered abruptly. "But if I can help Moses lead his people to the Promised Land, who knows what there'll be in it for me."

A dodgy grin grew on his lips and spread into a smile. But the smile vanished, replaced by stern vigilance when a noise from the brush alerted him as well as the big cat. Filamena heard it, too.

McCroy pulled a knife from his boot and moved silently toward the continuing rustle. She followed him, and could tell Thor wanted to. However, the animal kept its place, its ears moving like sensors.

What they discovered was their local guide, standing in the brush, lighting a pipe. McCroy put away his knife and grabbed the pipe from the fellow's lips.

"Hey! What are you doing? That's my lucky pipe."

"What are you doing, Harley?" McCroy sneered. "Getting stoned?"

"Yeah, so what? It's what I do, man."

McCroy stared at him with loathing. "Don't you think you're having enough trouble showing us the way?"

"I'll be straight by morning," he protested, trying to stand his ground, summoning up what little courage he seemed to possess. "Hey, man, I can just leave and go back to the vill if that's what you want."

McCroy glared at him, snorted in disgust and tossed the pipe back at him. Harley fumbled the catch. He was bent down in the dark trying to find it when Filamena followed McCroy out of the brush and back to the anxious cat. McCroy petted the animal reassuringly, and it calmed.

"So, what are *you* doing here, on this expedition?" asked McCroy, as if their conversation had never been interrupted.

It wasn't an outlandish question, but Filamena hesitated, then replied, "I would think that would be obvious. I'm here with my husband." She looked at him. His expression was hard to read. Maybe there was nothing there *to* read. "Speaking of my husband, I'd better get back to him. It was nice speaking with you, Mr. McCroy."

❧❧❧

He didn't look at her as she moved off toward the camp. His attention remained focused on his pet.

"Yeah, a pleasure," he said.

28

Aurora kissed the mountaintops, its gentle descent casting a fiery pall over Bailey's Ridge. A rogue thunderhead dispersed in a spray of florid pinks and oranges as sunset transformed the snowcaps of the Twin Tits into a crimson bra. Even the sky sprites had ceased their frolic and faded, as if in deference to the magnificent display.

Gash swore the sunsets of Evergreen were more beautiful than any he'd seen on Earth. Then again, it had been so many years since he'd been on his home world, let alone taken the time to look at a sunset there. As a kid, he'd watched many a sunset from where he'd played in the sand along Mission Beach. Each day, when the fiery ball descended into the water, he'd stop whatever he was doing to watch the last little sliver disappear beneath the horizon.

He doubted he'd ever see the sun go down over the Pacific again.

At times, he allowed himself to imagine how, someday, when his indenture was paid, he would homestead on Evergreen. More often his future didn't extend past the next sunrise. His only plan was to get himself through another night by the assistance of a bitter bottle or the peaceful lobotomy of happy smoke illusions. His only hope was that this night, this one time, the nightmares would pass him by.

Ramos called for an early wrap, and all around him TJs streamed toward the lake, a hot meal and the end of another long day. Shoulders slumped, arms hung like leaden jerk-wires and weary legs shuffled the crew zombie-like down the slopes. Gash looked round at the toll they'd taken on Evergreen that day. Discarded limbs and decapitated stumps attested to the carnage of their efficiency. If only he could clear-cut his conscience the way timber jockeys decimated an expanse of wildwood. He might as easily waltz with a hurricane.

He joined the exodus of TJs and soon enough smelled the brew of another one of Ford's culinary concoctions. He got in line and spotted his delegated protégé collapsed next to a boulder, as if too tired to even eat. Gash recalled his first few days on Evergreen. He'd been just like that. The boy was going through the worst of it now. He'd adjust soon.

"Eamon," he called. "Let's go. Get up. Get yourself something to eat."

Eamon looked like he'd rather sit, but he struggled to his feet and queued up behind Gash.

"Pretty Boy," called out Ramos, "you've got first watch tonight."

"First what?"

"Fire watch. Bravo Tower. Gash will show you where to go."

Ramos moved on without further explanation, but some TJs overheard and couldn't resist a little taunting.

"Turtle's going to Bravo Tower."

"Watch out for the ghost, turtle."

"Beware the ghost of Bravo Tower."

"What ghost? What are they talking about?" Eamon asked, turning to Gash.

"It's nothing. Ignore them."

But good old Meanan wasn't going to let an opportunity to needle a turtle go by.

"Nobody's told you about the ghost of Bravo Tower? They say it happened six, maybe seven years ago, when they used to leave someone out in that tower for days at a time. This one TJ—nobody remembers his name—went stir crazy out there. They found him strung up in the wiring—hung himself, he did. Now, at night, you

115

can hear him singing work songs and laughing. Some say they've even seen him."

Gash didn't bother to look back to see if the kid was taking the old tale to heart. The story had been passed on to every turtle who'd been assigned fire watch since he'd been there. He was as certain now as when he'd first heard it that the entire account was a myth. Something some bored timber jock made up a long time ago to relieve the monotony. Either way, it never fazed him. He had his own ghosts.

Kruto was ahead of them in the chuck line, right behind Mousey Farr. Compared to Farr, Kruto was a colossus. Playfully he set his tray atop the smaller TJ's head. Farr took it in good humor, but then, what else could he do?

Kruto moved up the line opposite Ford, who stood next to one of his assistant cooks, arms folded against his chest as if overseeing the portions being ladled out. The volatile behemoth stopped, frowned at the food that was slopped onto his tray and sniffed it. His head slowly rose, and his edgy stare focused on Ford. Blind as he was, Ford seemed to stare right back.

Gash had gotten used to seeing the old man act as if he had some kind of sixth sense—as if he could, indeed, see. There were times when Ford moved around with such poise Gash forgot he was sightless. The nature and veracity of his blindness was a matter of ongoing dispute among the timber jocks.

"May God forgive you for whatever you've put into this profane stew," Kruto said with the earnestness of a monk.

Gash steeled himself, ready to jump in if he had to. One never knew how Kruto was going to act or react. Even as he braced to intervene, he censured himself for the impulse. Let someone else get in the middle of it this time.

His anticipation of trouble proved false. Ford responded to the fiercely pious Russian by saying, "It's leprechaun stew. It's good for you."

Several TJs laughed, but Kruto simply contorted his face into a painful grimace and moved on.

"Aren't you mixing your mythos there, Ford?" Gash asked. "Since when did the Washoe go in for leprechauns?"

Ford shrugged. "I can't help it if the little bastards like my cooking."

116

More laughter was punctuated by Porno Eddy, who said, "Ford, you're the first Irish Indian I ever met."

"We come in all shapes, sizes and brand names," Ford replied.

Gash and Eamon moved on down the chow line, stopping to get some bread. Gash usually ate by himself, but with his turtle in tow, he decided to join a group huddled over their suppers on a patch of grassy ground near the lake. It was a group he was comfortable with—Cayenne, Ramos, Meanan, Eddy and a few others. They were the ones he associated with—when he felt like associating at all.

Half were busy eating, the other half were arguing about the remains Eamon had stumbled across the day before. It had become the mystery du jour.

"I say some squats drug it up there," offered Meanan.

"Why would they do that?" Cayenne wondered.

Meanan shrugged. "How else could it have gotten so high in the timber?"

Cayenne shook her head. "It doesn't make any sense."

"Well, it was definitely Conklin," said Ramos. "The company identified his DNA. Cause of death was drowning, so it was an accident, as far as they're concerned."

"There are no accidents."

Gash recognized the voice and looked over his shoulder.

"Accidents are only acts of fate that man can't explain," Ford added. "Fate holds the strings, and men, like marionettes, dance as they're directed."

"What's that, Ford," asked Eddy, "an old Indian saying?"

"Nah, someone read it in a fortune cookie last week at the Dizzy Dragon."

Laughter erupted, and even Gash had to smile.

"Tell us one of your stories, Ford," called out Meanan.

"Something new. Something we haven't heard before," said Eddy.

"Pretty boy here hasn't heard *any* of them," Meanan said, motioning at Eamon.

Gash could tell by the kid's expression he didn't care for his TJ moniker, but he kept his mouth shut. He was learning.

Ford turned his attention to Eamon, like he knew right where he was sitting.

"I'll tell you a story," he began earnestly. "I'll tell you about the legend of Dat-So-La-Lee, a woman of the Washoe who lived on Earth nearly two centuries ago.

"Now, Dat-So-La-Lee wasn't a beautiful woman. To describe her in the kindest of terms would be to call her overly voluptuous. Still, her husband was an extremely jealous man, known to fly into a rage if another man's gaze fell upon his wife. His possessive nature ate away at him until he was nothing but a tempest of suspicion. He became convinced that Dat-So-La-Lee was cuckolding him."

"Cuck-what?" interrupted Cayenne. "What the fuck is that?"

"That's exactly what it is," Ford responded. "Dat-So-La-Lee's husband thought she was fucking someone else. He conceived of several suspects in his mind, and soon came to believe they were all taking turns dallying with his wife whenever he was gone hunting or fishing.

"One day he returned early from his hunt and discovered the smell of bear grease on his wife. At the time, bear grease was only used for two things. The women used it for cooking. The men rubbed it all over their skin before entering the sweat lodge. Dat-So-La-Lee was a lousy cook, so the other women kept her away from the pots. Therefore, her husband was certain she had been in the arms of another man—very likely many men. He grabbed his knife and his axe, and he went on a rampage, killing and maiming many Washoe braves before he was brought down by several well-directed arrows.

"It was a black day for the Washoe nation. The spirit of mourning lived with the tribe for years, and the story was handed down from generation to generation, though the name of Dat-So-La-Lee's husband was never again repeated."

Ford fell silent and turned his blind eyes from Eamon.

Sensing the old man's story had ended, but not totally satisfied, Eamon said, "Well, was she?"

"Was she what?" inquired Ford, and Gash could see him reeling the turtle in.

"Was she fucking around with other men in the tribe?" asked Eamon.

"No," Ford said, "she wasn't. It turned out she was actually engaged in an adulterous affair with a grizzly bear of some ill repute.

After her husband was killed, Dat-So-La-Lee ran off with the bear, and was never heard from again."

Eamon's jaw dropped. In a matter of seconds, his expression ran the gamut from deadly serious to astonishment to I've-been-had. The collected timber jockeys howled with laughter, and Gash joined in. It felt good.

Ford, having wrapped his tale and looking as serious as when he began it, wandered off, back toward his field kitchen. The TJs continued to razz Eamon over his gullibility.

Gash noticed Ramos had walked off mid-story, and now he spotted him moving along the shoreline. There was nothing down that way, so naturally he wondered what Ramos was doing. He squinted to see through the waning twilight.

Across the lake, the old steamer used for towing logs approached the shore. Of course the *Sir Real* didn't run on steam anymore—Gash didn't know if it still could. Like all the engines and power tools on Evergreen, it had been retrofitted with Solaric, and would run as long as the fabric covering its wheelhouse and other exposed areas kept its batteries charged.

The ship was on an unusual heading, rounding the western corner of TJ City. The flotilla bobbed irregularly but gently in the evening wind. The ship was apparently moving towards the same point as the camp honcho.

"Why'd they come here?" asked Eamon.

While Gash's attention was elsewhere, the gathered TJs had become embroiled in a discussion of Evergreen's original settlers. Each one wanted to pass on his version of the tale to the turtle. It was a time-honored tradition, like telling scary stories around the campfire. Seniority gave Cayenne the floor.

"The way Ford tells it," she said, "their native land had become a tourist attraction, overrun by gamblers and ski bunnies who polluted the air and water. When they heard about Evergreen, it sounded like the wilderness sanctuary they were looking for. They wanted to return to the old ways. So, the tribe, or most of it anyway, pooled its resources, sold its tribal lands and emigrated."

The *Sir Real* pulled as close to shore as it could and dropped anchor. Gash saw Ramos standing talking with Kruto, who'd hauled a small canoe down to the water's edge. What were they doing?

119

"...built a settlement, east of where Woodville stands now, across the river."

"So, if Ford is the last of his tribe, what happened to them?" Eamon wondered aloud.

Cayenne went on. "No one knows for sure, except Ford, and that's one story he won't tell."

"I heard disease wiped them out," said Eddy, as if it were gospel.

"That's one version." Cayenne sounded as if it wasn't the one she favored. "Another says there was tribal in-fighting, and that many died in the violence, while the survivors gave up and returned to Earth on the next ship."

Gash had heard the all the theories concerning the Washoe before. He was more interested in what Ramos was up to. The veteran TJ and the mildly psychotic Boris Krutonov, an odd-pairing at best, were paddling out to the big boat. The captain of the *Sir Real*, along with two other men, waited on board for them. One of the men Gash recognized as a long-time homesteader, a spokesman of sorts for Evergreen's southern farming community. From the look of his work uniform, the other man was a miner. What they were doing on the lake, Gash had no idea. Miners and farmers never got out this way. He wondered what business they could possibly have with Ramos.

"I heard they pulled a Jonestown and all drank poison," Meanan said.

"That's bull," Cayenne said with a sneer. "That never happened."

"You don't know," replied Meanan. "It could have. It makes the most sense. How else did Ford end up all by himself, a little blind kid wandering in the woods when they found him?"

"Was he always blind?" Eamon asked. "I mean, was he born that way?"

Cayenne shook her head. "No, I've heard him say he could see things just fine when he was boy. No, something happened to him about the same time his people disappeared. He won't say what, though. He won't talk about it."

"I heard the doctor in the vill says there's nothing wrong with his eyes, that he should be able to see just fine," added Meanan.

120

"The doc says his blindness is just, what do they call it—psycho-matic?"

"Psychosomatic," Eddy corrected.

Meanan nodded. "Yeah. It's all in his head."

"I don't believe that for a second," said Cayenne. "If he could see, he would see. That's stupid."

Gash looked out over the lake. A rolling bank of fog swept down Bailey's Ridge and across Zephyr Cove. He could almost see it move, like an approaching apparition. Soon it would pull its misty shroud over them all.

Ramos and Kruto boarded the *Sir Real* and shook hands with the three men waiting aft for them. The captain motioned, and everyone followed him inside the wheelhouse, out of sight.

As much as he told himself it was none of his business, Gash couldn't help but speculate on what they were up to. He couldn't imagine what the quintet could possibly have in common. It was some kind of intrigue, no doubt. The idea reminded him of the cryptic exchange he'd had with the proprietor of Tilley's. *Ask your friend Ramos*, he'd said. Maybe he would. Then again, why get involved at all?

29

It was a long hike up to Bravo Tower, uphill all the way, but the trail was plainly marked and he had a lantern to light his way through the fog and the gloom. Beyond the protective halo of light, the dark was complete, a wall of murk where only dim shapes loomed. Eamon told himself he wasn't scared, just wary. Though wary of what, he didn't know. He had no idea what was in these woods. Maybe some of Ford's leprechauns.

He didn't believe half the stories the timber jocks told, but there was that body he'd found high in the timber where it had no business being. Meanan said the squats must have drug it up there. He'd heard the squats described as big hairy creatures that lived in the forest, but he had yet to see one. He didn't want to see one.

Before he'd penetrated the darkness far enough to see the tower, Chaltraw spotted his light from above.

"You're late! Get up here, I'm starving!"

Bravo Tower loomed above him in the night. He guessed it must be at least 80 feet high. An affixed wooden ladder ran up one side of the supports all the way to the catwalk, where he saw the TJ on watch. Eamon hooked the lantern to his belt and started climbing. Dew had settled on the rungs so he took care to get a firm footing and a good grip. He noticed, too, that the underbelly of the tower and its supports were coated with spider webs. He tried not to dwell on them as he clambered up the ladder.

"Let's go, Mr. Slow!" Chaltraw ranted. Then, as Eamon neared the catwalk, he recognized him. "Oh, it's you. Come on, turtle, get your butt in gear."

Eamon crawled onto the catwalk, stood and was struck by a sudden wave of vertigo. He steadied himself on the railing and avoided looking down.

"You been on fire watch before, turtle?"

"No," Eamon replied, the brief dizziness fading.

"Well, turn that damn light off, and keep it off. You can't see nothing out there if your light's on." Chaltraw opened the door to what was basically an eight-by-eight box inset with framed glass to give a 360-degree view. He pointed at a handset connected to some wiring. "That's your land line. If you see anything that looks like a fire, you call in. Otherwise, you just keep a watch out until your relief arrives. Got it?"

"But I can't see everything from here."

"You can see enough. If you can't see it, it's not your area, so don't worry. Alpha Tower's manned up on Bailey's Ridge, and from Charlie Tower they can see across to Zephyr Cove. You just worry about staying awake and keeping your eyes peeled up here."

Chaltraw didn't wait for anymore questions. He was back out the door and moving down the ladder before Eamon could even think to ask when his relief would arrive. Then again, he figured it didn't really matter. One place was as good as another. Just more time to pass until he got his chance.

He peered out the south-facing window. Now that he was above the fog, he hoped to see more of the auroras, but there was no sign of any. The only light came from the stars. There were hundreds of stars—many more than he'd ever seen on Earth. Still, the galaxy's nightlight revealed little more than patches of fog, an endless sea of treetops and the glimmer of Lake Washoe.

The lake was more immense than he'd guessed. Even from here, he couldn't see the entire reservoir. He moved from window to window, but the view from each was much the same, though looking out to the west and the north he could see mountains that dwarfed even his high vantage point.

123

In little time, he grew bored. From the boredom, his imagination sprang full-bodied. The stillness, the utter quiet of his surroundings began to play tricks with his mind. He started feeling as though *he* were being watched. Soon, every grim tree was glaring at him, every star in the inky night was another reproachful eye.

It had nothing to do with the so-called "Ghost of Bravo Tower." He didn't believe in ghosts. He didn't care if it *were* true, if a timber jockey had really killed himself inside this tower. Ghosts were make-believe, like fairies and leprechauns. He knew no ghost could haunt him as much as his own regrets.

Those were real. Like vitriolic gremlins, they gnawed at him, seeking escape. Most of the time, he managed to confine them, turn them inward. Now the silence, the sheath of darkness around the tower, freed those demons, emboldened them, gave them shape and substance.

Before long, the floodgates of his mind opened, and he was swamped by jumbled recollections. It was so few years ago, yet it seemed like another lifetime—like he'd been an entirely different person.

At the time, he'd thought it was a big joke, a challenge, a way to thumb his nose at the authority he so despised—a way to get attention. Pulling it off turned out to be easier than he'd thought. Then again, it had also been easy for them to trace his handiwork back to him.

He could have denied it. He could have said it must have been someone else. But who else would have hacked into the school's record system only to improve *his* grades? Besides, he didn't want to deny it. He hadn't wanted to admit it to himself, never thought of it that way until now, but he'd *wanted* to get caught. Why else would he have done it? He didn't care about his grades, or care what anyone else thought of them.

Still, he hadn't thought his little incursion into the restricted files was such a big deal. The academy's director thought otherwise. She told him it was the final straw, that this time he was going to be expelled. She told him they had informed his mother, and that she would be coming to get him.

He didn't care. He was glad his mother would have to come get him. He resented that she had what he thought of as a glamorous job, full of adventure, while he was stuck in a miserable boarding school. He'd always been in one school or another. It wasn't the first time he'd gotten into trouble, and there was nothing to make him think it would be the last.

But it was. It was the last time his mother would be sent for. The last time she'd ever come to get him out of trouble.

30

It was hot, but Jimiyu didn't mind the heat. It reminded him very much of his homeland. Compared to many of the cold, damp places he'd followed Nikira to, the warmth of Evergreen was inviting.

However the terrain was nothing like the endless plains of Kenya. If their party wasn't going up a hill, which it was most of the time, it was going down, often fighting through dense scrub and thorny brambles. Four days out, and the going had only gotten more arduous. Initially, he'd been awed by the giant redwoods. Now, his muscles aching, Jimiyu no longer had the energy to expend in admiration of the often formidable inhabitants of this woodland. They had ceased to be great silent titans, standing sentry over the verdant hills and valleys. They'd become nothing more than impediments, gnarled-rooted obstacles to climb over, thick-trunked barriers that forced them to alter course.

To make matters worse, Jimiyu was having trouble keeping up. He kept losing his footing on the downward slopes, while his pack made the uphill climbs a challenge. He was falling back from the lead.

Nikira, meanwhile, had no problem staying in step with McCroy and his big cat. Jimiyu knew why. He knew what compelled Nikira, what motivation enabled him to ignore fatigue.

Jimiyu wished his own motivation was as strong. Even Chanya had managed to stay up with Nikira, but then Jimiyu knew her motivation as well.

The only one having more trouble than Jimiyu was Professor Escobedo's wife. It was apparent she was no more used to such extended physical exertion than he was. One look at her delicate white sun hat with its stylishly banked brim told him she was used to more refined environs—not at all a pioneer type. She kept falling behind, pausing to rest while the others moved on, despite the complaints of Mr. Scurlock, whom McCroy had assigned to bring up the rear.

Today, as he had on the previous day, her husband dropped back to help her. Already the weight of her pack had been reduced to almost nothing—before the first day had ended, the professor and his son had divided what they could of her provisions between them. Still she couldn't keep up.

It wasn't for lack of effort. He saw the determination on her face. She didn't like being the weak link, and was doing her utmost to keep pace. For his own part, Jimiyu was grateful for the extra rest breaks they took to accommodate her.

McCroy, however, was anything *but* grateful. He was frustrated by all the delays, and visibly aggravated by the seemingly erratic route their guide was taking. He continually questioned Harley about their direction, and didn't seem mollified by the answers he got.

They climbed a particular steep foothill, crossed over and headed down into a narrow valley. Before they reached the valley floor, Jimiyu spied a tiny stream running through it. The sight spurred him on. He couldn't wait to splash some cool water over his head.

McCroy's cat reached the water first and, unlike the big cats Jimiyu was familiar with, didn't seem to mind standing midstream to quench its thirst. It was lapping at the water when a teeming black cloud emerged from the thicket on the opposite side of the stream. The cloud accelerated, diverting downward and falling on the cat.

The animal was transfixed for only a moment, its stubby tail twitching. It quickly turned and raced back the way it had come.

The cloud followed it right to its master, and before they realized what was happening, McCroy, Harley, Nikira and Chanya were enveloped by what Jimiyu could now see was a swarm of flying insects.

They flailed ineffectively at the frenzied bugs. Chanya shrieked. Vincent and the professor's son, Max, were in the path of the swarm and fell to the ground, covering their heads with their arms. Suddenly, the winged menace unaccountably veered off as abruptly as it had appeared and vanished into the forest.

McCroy bent down to soothe his ruffled pet.

"What were they?" Chanya asked, her tone still near-hysteric.

"Madflies," Harley answered, "though I've never seen them act like that. Nasty when they're riled. Usually, they only swarm around their hives. There must be one near here."

"Let's get going before they come back," McCroy commanded, moving on. Jimiyu noticed the big cat stayed close to him. It was still wary, glancing about with a feline look of disapproval.

Professor Escobedo, his wife and Spurlock had caught up by then, and each member of the expedition paused briefly at the stream to cool off and fill their canteens after McCroy okayed the water using a sampling device Jimiyu was unfamiliar with.

They trudged on for another hour, maybe two—Jimiyu found his sense of time was addled by exhaustion. All he could do was stare at his feet, concentrating on placing one foot after the other. He needed to stop. He needed to rest, to eat. He didn't want to seem like a weakling, but he decided he needed to say something. Surely the others must feel the same.

Before he could formulate what he considered a logical argument, McCroy called a halt. Jimiyu was surprised to see their dauntless leader plop to the ground. His expression spoke more of annoyance than fatigue. He stared hard at Happy Harley, who now looked less than happy.

"Just where the fuck are you taking us?" McCroy asked, leaving no doubt as to his disposition.

"Where you wanted to go," Harley mumbled. Jimiyu couldn't tell if it was a statement or a question.

Nikira had fallen back with Jimiyu. When they reached McCroy and Harley he asked, "What's wrong? Why are we stopping?"

"This fungus-head doesn't know where in the bloody blue blazes he's going. Do you?"

Jimiyu could tell McCroy was trying to keep his anger in check, but that it wouldn't take much for him to go off.

Harley scratched his head and responded weakly, "Sure...I think so. I mean, I thought I did. Yeah, I'm sure this must—"

McCroy was on his feet in an instant, and before Jimiyu could flinch he'd grabbed Harley by his shirt and slammed him up against a tree. Just as quickly, his cat was at his side, as if waiting for Harley to make an aggressive move.

"Owww!" Harley shrieked as his head bounced off the abrasive bark.

"You waste of space. I should gut you for maggot meat right here."

"Mr. McCroy!" Nikira moved as if to intervene, but stopped when the big cat turned its head and snarled. "McCroy! Release him!"

"He's taken us in a big semi-circle," McCroy replied, still holding on to the startled Harley.

"How do you know?" asked Nikira.

"Because I'm not stupid. A compass might not work on this planet, but the sun sets in the same place every day. I know which way we've come. At first I thought maybe we were going round-about for some reason. The farther we went, the less reason I could see. Now I'm sure."

"Let him go," Nikira said, and this time McCroy complied, though he kept his face right up in Harley's. "What makes you so sure now?"

"Take a look over this slope. Unless there are two big red rivers on this planet, we're headed in the wrong direction. Well, are there?"

Harley shook his head, and eased away from McCroy to join Nikira and Jimiyu on the rise. Below, Jimiyu saw the serpentine crawl of a large river. Its water looked even redder from a distance than it had up close. He figured it was the way the sun was hitting it.

Harley stared down at the river with a puzzled look and scratched his head again. "How did we get here?"

McCroy made a noise of disgust and started back the way they'd come.

"Jesper, set up camp here. I'm going to have to backtrack and...what's that?" He stopped abruptly, as if listening.

"What's what?" wondered Scurlock.

By then, Jimiyu was listening, too. It was very faint, very distant, but after a moment he was certain he heard it. Where, exactly, it was coming from he couldn't tell; he'd noticed before how sounds seemed to carry through the trees and echo along valley walls. It wasn't like Kenya at all, where only the wind could carry a sound. Here, the terrain had a way of deceiving you.

Though he couldn't ascertain where it was coming from, he realized right away what it was. It was soft, melodic music.

31

Despite the dearth of new discoveries, Amanda was glad she'd taken this hike. It was good to get away from the ursu for a while, and explore new areas of Evergreen.

She had hoped to find several new species to catalog as part of her biologic survey of the planet, but so far she'd only come across one. She first noticed it from a distance because of its odd color.

Within a wide expanse of forest ground cover bearing the typical camouflage shades, she spotted the strange patch of growth immediately. They were unusual plants, gray as parched bones, with no real leaves, but stalks patterned like lace coral. She'd seen similar vegetation on Earth. Except for the aurora blossoms and a couple of other smaller flowers, it was the only flora she'd discovered on this world that wasn't some variation of green.

She noted her observations, took a sample for further study and decided she'd come far enough to take a break. She'd pulled off the small pack she used for day trips and found her flute. Eyes closed for concentration, she began to play.

She was pleased with what she heard. It seemed she'd finally mastered that one passage that had given her so much trouble. The melodic line moved smoothly from one transition to another, becoming almost ethereal. She imagined herself adrift in the tree-tops, not flying so much as floating, accompanied by three-dimensional clefs and staves, portly flat notes and strident little sharps, all drifting alongside her, lifting her.

When she came to the end, she sustained the last note longer than usual, punctuating her little personal triumph. She opened her eyes and there, sitting not six feet away from her was a huge cat. She didn't know whether to run or sit perfectly still. She chose the latter more from fear than reason.

She was so startled by the creature's sudden appearance, it took her a moment to calm herself. After her heart stopped stuttering and she caught her breath, she realized the animal was familiar in many ways. The realization eased her immediate terror, though she had no clue as to the beast's intentions.

It was a beautiful creature with a magnificent tawny coat—certainly not like anything she'd encountered on Evergreen before. It must have been drawn out of the deep woods by her music. It sat on its haunches, staring at her but showing no sign of aggression. So, Amanda decided to play more and see how it reacted. She moved the flute slowly to her lips.

The moment the music began, the animal's ears turned and its head tilted in a familiar feline way. Its dark-yellow eyes locked onto the flute. It was definitely intrigued by the sound.

As she played, she heard something in the woods behind her. Someone was singing, and the sound was getting closer. A timber jockey out here? She was afraid the big cat would attack whoever it was, so she kept playing, hoping the music would soothe it.

> Amazing grace, how sweet the sound
> That saved a wretch like me.
> I once was lost, but now am found,
> Was blind, but now I see.

A man stepped into view. One look at him told her that her first guess was wrong. He wasn't a timber jockey, that was certain. He had on a stylish but stained gray canvas bush hat and carried what looked like a gun. She realized it was, indeed, a weapon. What surprised her even more than the gun was that the cat got up and sauntered to the man's side.

Amanda stopped playing.

"He's always liked music," the fellow said, patting the animal's head. "Sorry if he startled you."

132

She stood. "Who are you?" She tried not to sound impolite.

"I guess I startled you, too. Lyle McCroy. This is Thor. And you are?"

"Amanda Rousch—Dr. Amanda Rousch."

"Are you lost, Doctor?"

"No, I'm not lost. I'm here studying species native to Evergreen. I'm an exobiologist. What are *you* doing here? I didn't expect to see anyone this far out from Woodville."

"I'm ramroding a little junket. The rest of the expedition is back that way about fifty yards. We heard your music, and I came to check it out."

"What kind of junket?"

McCroy took off his hat and wiped the sweat from his forehead with the back of his hand. "Some holy Joe is looking for his Grail."

"What?"

"Dr. Talib Nikira. Ever hear of him? Well, he stirred up enough dust to make the news back on Earth. You know, wackjob of the moment." McCroy paused to see if she was with him. She was—kind of. "He's a former priest with some oddball theories. So odd I guess his brethren kicked him out. He thinks he's going to find his god out here somewhere, or at least evidence of him."

"If he's such a wackjob, why are you out here with him?"

"Money talks, you know?" McCroy replied stone-faced, yet Amanda saw a spark in his active green eyes that spoke of something else. "Coin of the realm and such. I guess I'd better be getting back to them, if you're all right here, Doctor."

"I'm fine," she said, then added quickly, "Mind if I go with you? I'd like to meet this Dr. Nikira."

McCroy shrugged. "No skin off my nose."

She thought it a curious choice of expressions, considering the man's face was blemished with splotches that looked as if the skin had been peeled in spots. She dismissed the thought as unkind and picked up her pack.

"Thor, heel," he called, already on the move, and the big cat darted alongside him.

"That's a very unusual feline. He looks like some type of lynx, but not one I'm familiar with."

"You know your cats, Doctor," McCroy said without turning around. "He's a genetic hybrid—primarily Siberian lynx."

"Oh."

"You don't approve?"

"I don't disapprove," responded Amanda. "I just respect natural selection more than I do human breeding programs."

"I don't know anything about that, but I can tell you Thor is a special animal. He's smarter than any dog I've ever had, and quick as a cobra."

"He's certainly a beautiful animal," she said, not wanting to foster any negativity.

"That he is, but don't let that fool you. He's not some cute kitty. He's a predator, Doctor, and no human breeding's going to change that."

"Please, call me Amanda. I'm not that big with titles."

He half-turned, looking at her with an expression that was part smirk, part curiosity. In profile she noticed his flat nose more than she had before.

"All right, Amanda." He turned his attention back to the trail. "An interesting choice of music you were playing back there," he said as they walked.

"You mean 'Amazing Grace?' I'm not really much of a musician. I just picked it because I thought it might be easy to learn."

"Are you familiar with the song's history?"

"No. What about it?"

"It was written back in the nineteenth century by a former slave ship captain turned clergyman and anti-slavery proselytizer. The ironic thing is, after he wrote, he went blind."

"I guess it is ironic, considering the lyrics. And how is it you know this?

"I do read, Doctor—I mean Amanda."

They didn't go far before they came to a small clearing where a rudimentary encampment had been set up. The people there—ten by Amanda's count, including McCroy—looked exhausted. Most were resting, a few eating.

Her attention was drawn to a tall black man with a perfectly-trimmed goatee. She knew right away he must be the former priest McCroy had spoken of. It was more than the African-sounding name, it was the assurance he exuded as he approached her.

"Dr. Talib Nikira," McCroy said by way of introduction, "Dr. Amanda...Rousch, was it?"

"Yes," replied Amanda. "Good to meet you, Dr. Nikira, though I must say I'm surprised to find your group out here."

"As I am to come across someone else in this wilderness," said Nikira in such a resonant voice she could easily picture him speaking from a pulpit.

"I'm an exobiologist, Doctor. I'm out here as part of my field study. However, I understand your reason for coming to Evergreen is more spiritual than scientific."

Nikira glanced at McCroy. He was occupied with feeding his cat.

"You might be surprised, Dr. Rousch. I believe the line between the two isn't as rigid as many think. What I hope to discover could change mankind's beliefs forever."

"A formidable ambition," said Amanda.

"Not *ambition*, Dr. Rousch," Nikira replied. "I'm not an ambitious man. I only seek the truth." He smiled. "And I'm afraid the truth right now is that we're lost." He turned to look at McCroy. "Unless you were successful, Mr. McCroy."

"Only in confirming I was right about the direction we've been traveling."

"And you asked me if *I* was lost?" Amanda jibed.

"I'm not lost," responded McCroy. "I know exactly where I *am*. I just don't know where we're *going*. It's Happy Harley here who's lost."

He jerked his thumb at a disheveled fellow Amanda had seen before. She recognized him from Woodville. He stepped forward and said, "I know which way to go now."

"Yes," Nikira said, "Harley tells me he has his bearings now."

"Yeah," McCroy muttered, "that's about as likely as a snowstorm in the Sahara."

"No, I remember now," Harley assured them. "We just have to go up Vaughn's Valley to Hokan Pass." He pointed down the slope they were on. "That'll lead us right to the old Washoe settlement."

Amanda remembered where she'd seen him now. He was the one that timber jockey named Gash had bought something from in Tahoe Tilley's.

"That's right," Amanda spoke up. "Except Vaughn's Valley is a little more over that way." She motioned to correct his direction.

"Are you familiar with that area, Doctor?" asked Nikira.

"Well, I've never gone as far as Hokan Pass, but I know where it is. Is that where you're going—to the old Washoe settlement?"

"The place we're going is farther east than that," said Harley, "on the other side of Pickle Peak."

"Pickle Peak? Oh, yes, the TJs have another, somewhat cruder name for it. That's quite a ways."

"Would you considering guiding us, Dr. Rousch?" Nikira asked.

"As I said, I've never been past Vaughn's Valley. I don't know if I would be much help." Amanda thought about it for a moment. "I would, however, like to explore that region, see if there are additional ursu communities farther in from the lake. If you don't mind, I could join your little expedition, though I didn't bring much in the way of provisions."

"I'm certain we have enough to share, Doctor," said Nikira, obviously delighted. "Between you and Harley here, we should be able to find our way, don't you think, Mr. McCroy?"

McCroy shrugged, not looking entirely confident. "If you say so."

"Well, Dr. Rousch," Nikira said, taking her hand, "let me introduce you to the rest of our party."

32

Like an enormous assortment of puzzle pieces, the flotilla that was TJ City spread out across the north side of the lake. Junks, garishly-painted hoys, fringed-topped lighters, dilapidated houseboats, tented barges—all separate yet connected by bobbing planks and thick, braided ropes, a giant raft of a community. Gash thought it an apropos residence for the timber jockeys—rugged, outcast individuals all, yet linked by a brotherhood of sweat and blood.

He'd been watching the sky sprites transform the heavens into their own private kaleidoscope. From his vantage point on the periphery of the floating burg, he could see the myriad colors play across the tops of the boats. He enjoyed a few more minutes of the exhibition, of the peaceful solitude, before slipping off the roof and ducking inside the flatboat's shelter.

As he did, a dark cloud enveloped him and streamed inside. Eamon was sitting where Gash had left him. The younger TJ began swinging ineffectively at the cloud all around him. Gash calmly pulled his shirt collar over his head, tucked his face down and waited. The insect swarm was gone almost as quickly as it had appeared.

"What was that?" Eamon asked, scratching at the bites on his hands and arms.

"Madflies. They're thicker than usual this season."

"They're not poisonous or anything, are they?"

"Just pests. The itching will fade...if you don't scratch."

Eamon promptly ceased digging at his skin. Gash quelled a chuckle.

The turtle, as a matter of course, had ended up bunking aboard his boat—not that it was really his. It was the company's, like almost everything else on Evergreen. He'd snatched the chance at the tiny floating shack when it became vacant years ago. He'd hoped its size would offer him solitude but knew it wouldn't last forever. No one had private quarters. He was lucky to have been left alone as long as he had. Then again, he could have done worse than Eamon.

He wondered about the kid. He wasn't your typical indentured jocko with a past that would shame a grifter. From his boyishly handsome face to his quiet demeanor, he just didn't fit the mold. His large round eyes only enhanced the innocent puppy-dog look that branded him. But wondering was different from inquiring.

There was one thing Gash had noticed—or at least thought he did. It was probably what drew him to Eamon. The kid had this hidden pain. What it was, he couldn't guess, and didn't care to know. He had his own pain to deal with.

Out of the relative silence, a scream resounded from outside like a gunshot. The outburst was followed by muffled sobbing. Gash answered the look on Eamon's face.

"That's Kruto. He has nightmares—combat flashbacks most likely. He's got demons that would daunt the devil. That's why you never know what he's going to do."

Gash pulled out his cache and his pipe. It was a rough-hewn, bowed thing, about a foot long, with enough kinks in it to give it a serpentine look. He'd made it from the slender limb of a redwood he'd felled himself. He filled the notch that served as a bowl and lit it. He took a long hit, resting back again the shelter wall. He felt the genial vapors meandering through him, his body compliant, beckoning the familiar calm. He offered the pipe to Eamon.

"No, thanks," Eamon responded with a wave of his hand.

"There's a bottle of home-brewed TJ juice in that cupboard, if you want," said Gash, taking another hit.

Eamon shook his head. He looked at Gash with an expression that was part pity, part repugnance. Gash ignored him. What did a baby-faced turtle know, anyway?

"How long have you been here—on Evergreen?"

"Four, five years," said Gash, exhaling. "It's hard to keep track. The years are different here. Hell, even the number of hours in a day is different, so what measure can you use?"

Eamon nodded. "How'd you get that scar?"

The question surprised Gash. Most people tried to pretend they didn't see it. This brash kid was either overly inquisitive, or rude to a fault. Either one could get him in trouble.

"Rigging snapped, and I got chain-slapped. Broke my nose and gave me something to remember it by. I was just a turtle then, like you, but I didn't have anyone riding my ass."

"Is that why you're always nagging me about everything I do?"

"Nagging? Is that what you think it is?" Gash snorted. "You think I like babysitting you? I'm just doing my job, kid. The honcho gave you to me, so I've got to keep you in one piece."

"When I enlisted, I didn't think cutting down trees would be so involved, so dangerous."

Gash had just put the pipe to his lips. He pulled it away and said incredulously, "You *enlisted*? Nobody just enlists in this outfit. Not unless they're trying to hide from something or someone."

Eamon turned his face away. Was he embarrassed? Was he thinking back?

"I've got my reasons," he said, and Gash heard the resolve in his voice.

"Well, it's none of my business, but I'd advise you not to tell any of these other mutton-heads. They'll think you're crazier than Kruto if they know you enlisted. Everyone here is a criminal serving a sentence, or indentured, or running away from something even worse."

"Why are you here?" Eamon asked as if he were inquiring about the time of day.

Gash stared at him, long and hard. "You never ask a jocko that question," he said, his tone making it obvious even to the turtle that such a query was a serious breach of TJ protocol.

"Then how do you know nobody here enlisted?"

Gash got up. "I just know, okay?" he said, and went outside.

He clicked his lighter and held it up to the pipe. Another hit of passivity coursed through him. Another memory cell expired. Yet even as it did it left behind trace residue no narcotic could cleanse.

This court finds Paul Brandon not guilty.

Not guilty? Not guilty didn't change anything. It didn't change the way he felt. It didn't change the expressions on the blanched faces that followed him out of the courtroom. It didn't stop the nightmares, or the accusing voice that whispered with malice in his ear. Not guilty? Guilt sucked at his marrow. How could he be not guilty when guilt was the only thing he had to hold on to? Guilt was what kept him going.

He looked up at the languishing aurora. His gaze followed the fading lightworks but his thoughts focused on the irony that had brought him to this point and place in time. Irony had tracked him down and had its way with him, long after his criminal trial was over. As if his ignominy wasn't enough, he was hauled into civil court and found liable for damages. Damages? Out of what law book do you get the calculations to determine such damages? How many zeros does it take to appease a conscience?

He remembered being incensed that someone could put a price on such a thing. Yet he also remembered welcoming the verdict. It fell on him like a hallelujah from above—vindication for his guilt.

33

Amanda watched the aurora dance across the sky, a swirling curtain of light made more brilliant by the darkness. Conjured from a palette of icy blues and greens, it was so iridescent it never held a single hue long enough to properly describe. She thought of the auroras as iconoclasts, always changing, always evolving, never satisfied with the status quo. In an odd way, they comforted her.

"'When the sun had set and darkness had fallen, a smoking firepot with a blazing torch appeared.'"

Amanda heard the voice behind her and looked to see Dr. Nikira. He wore a full-length cloak to ward off the chill of the night, and the garb gave him a much more priest-like aura than he'd had earlier. Without his straw hat, she saw he was balding.

"Shakespeare?" she inquired.

Nikira walked up next to her. "Genesis." He gazed up into the sky. "A wondrous display, is it not?"

She nodded. "The locals call them sky sprites."

"I'm sure the idea provides as much comfort as the light. I've noticed that, when they fade away, the nights here are very dark."

"Evergreen has no moon."

"Ah, yes. That would account for it. There are, however, a great many more stars visible here than on Earth."

"It seems so, anyway."

They stared at the heavens in silence for an empty moment.

"If you don't mind my asking," Amanda said, "what is it exactly you're looking for on Evergreen?"

Nikira sighed, as if explaining himself had become a burden. "Like anyone, Doctor, I'm looking for proof that what I believe in is true. Isn't that what we all want out of life—confirmation?"

"Yes," she replied in a tone of qualification. "Substantiation, corroboration, that's what I look for to validate my work. But I'm a scientist. My truth is based on verifying the facts, on scientific method. You, however, are a man of faith, aren't you?"

"Touché, Doctor. Yes, I've devoted most of my life to following the doctrines of my church. My faith in its teachings was second to no one's. Then, one day, I opened my eyes. Once I could see, I could no longer blind myself to the truth."

"What truth is that?"

Nikira placed his hands together over his nose and mouth as if praying—or thinking. Amanda waited. At first, she didn't believe he was going to answer.

"There is no way for me to adequately relay to you the years of personal tribulation and spiritual anguish I endured. Even if I could it would be of no interest. Suffice to say I found the core of the church lacking. Its policies had more to do with geopolitical intrigue than matters divine, its clergy obsessed with infighting, backbiting and public relations.

"As my faith waned, I threw myself into study. I discovered tomes I never knew existed, writings that suggested other possibilities. Each discovery led to another. I developed a thirst that couldn't be quenched, until I finally came to a conclusion independent of, and contrary to, the teachings of my own church."

Nikira paused, taking a breath as if the statement left him exhausted.

"And that conclusion was?" Amanda asked, intrigued now more than ever.

"I came to believe there must be something else—something more. That's why I'm here, on Evergreen. I believe that God is not just an omnipotent spirit, but a living being." Nikira watched for her reaction. "A being of immense energy."

142

She didn't react. Her expression didn't change, and she thought she saw a look of disappointment cross his face.

"So, that's what you meant about blurring the line between the spiritual and the scientific. Still, it doesn't seem like such a radical departure from what I know about Christianity."

"No, that alone was not. However, I also came to believe that the provenance of God was not Earth, or some heavenly dimension, but another world—a planetary body from where He created mankind, as well as other wonders of the universe. This place is referred to in the texts as the City of God."

"I can see why that might have stirred up quite a hornet's nest of opposition," Amanda said, nodding her head. "But aren't the stories of a City of God supposed to be apocryphal? Isn't it just a metaphor for heaven?"

"That's how Saint Augustine described it," Nikira agreed. "However, the research material available to him in the fifth century was limited."

She stood, stretching her legs. "So, what makes you think your City of God is here on Evergreen?"

Nikira pulled something from inside his cloak and handed it to her. She could barely make it out by the light of the still-flickering aurora. It was a chunk of root wood, flat on one side. She felt the smooth, glazed sheen that covered it.

"In my research, I came across several ancient renderings of what the texts referred to as the Tree of Life. Each of the illustrations was almost identical, even though discovered in cultures on opposite sides of the world, often centuries removed from one another. The same likeness is carved in that artifact you hold. It was found by our guide, Mr. Harley, deep in the wilds of Evergreen, and it has been determined to be more than forty-five thousand years old."

Amanda suddenly acquired new respect for the item in her hands, and handled it accordingly. She pulled out her penlight and examined it more closely. The thin glaze was some kind of amber coating, and beneath it, carved into the wood, was a design that was no doubt a tree of some sort, though a tree whose limbs seemed animate.

"Quite intriguing, I must admit," she said, still studying the artifact. "It reminds me of symbols I've seen representing Ninhursag, the Mother Earth of Sumerian myth."

"You're very well-read," acknowledged Nikira.

"Evolutionists also study creationist myths," she responded with a smile. "I believe the Sumerians considered Ninhursag the source of all life. Sometimes she's seen as a tree, other times as a more human figure, wearing a leafy crown and holding a branch to indicate fertility."

Nikira nodded. "The Sumerians also believed the first men grew from the earth in the manner of grass. In one telling, the heavens are removed from the earth in order to make room for the seeds of mankind to grow."

"A veritable garden of souls," joked Amanda. "Man as vegetable."

"Tell me, Doctor," he said, stroking his goatee, pulling at the tiny hairs, "do you believe God created man in his own likeness?"

"I don't believe in God at all, and even less in organized religion. The idea of a supreme being, omnipotent or otherwise, is too far from the realm of science for me."

Nikira looked as if it was the response he'd expected. "Tell me, then, Dr. Rousch, what *do* you believe in?"

She took a moment to think. It wasn't as transparent a question as it seemed.

"I believe in nonviolence, in the power of pacifism. I believe in the potential of creatures other than man to advance and achieve. I believe in living in harmony with your environment. More specifically, and more relevant to our immediate environs," she said with a gesture of her arm, "I believe the logging and mining operations man has forged ahead pell-mell with have already begun to upset the ecological balance of Evergreen."

She noticed the other two African members of their party approaching, but she continued.

"For instance, the cutting of timber around Lake Washoe is doing more than disfiguring the land and diminishing the forest. Those are just the obvious scars. Less obvious are the biochemical effects. When vegetation is removed from around a body of water, it increases the temperature of the water, as does the accruing erosion. This thermal pollution speeds the metabolic rate of aquatic organisms, leading to—"

"I'm sorry to interrupt, Doctor," said the man who had been introduced to her as Jimiyu, "but Dr. Nikira needs his rest."

"Jimi, you mother me like an old desert hen," Nikira said, almost smiling.

"I *was* going on a bit there," Amanda admitted.

"You are passionate about your beliefs," responded Nikira. "That is nothing that needs apology. Sometimes, belief can be a tenuous thing. Did you know, Dr. Rousch, that there are some peoples in my native Africa who consider the supernatural world far more real than this..." He held out both hands. "...this physical world, which they believe to be only a waking dream?"

"Please, Talib, you must get some sleep," said the woman. Amanda didn't recall her name, but she remembered noticing the way she looked at Nikira. There was a longing in her eyes that persuaded Amanda she wasn't his wife, or even his lover. She noticed, too, that Nikira seemed to disregard her, or at least pretended to.

"Yes, Chanya's right," said Jimiyu. "You need to sleep. Tomorrow will be another long day."

"All right, Brother, all right," Nikira relented. "Goodnight, Dr. Rousch. I'll see you in the morning."

Amanda couldn't tell if the last was a question or a statement.

"Good night, Dr. Nikira. Oh, you'd better take this back."

She handed him the artifact, and he passed it to Jimiyu. As the trio walked off, Amanda gave in to a puckish impulse and said aloud something she'd been thinking.

"Do you ever think, Dr. Nikira, that you might be looking for God in the wrong place?"

Nikira halted and turned to look at her.

"That maybe God is just inside us all?"

Even in the gloom, she could see Nikira smile. But he didn't reply. He walked away with his companions, leaving her to the night.

Once alone, she contemplated their conversation. The more she thought about it, the more Nikira seemed an enigma. There was no doubting his intelligence or, for that matter, the purity of his motives. Was he truly a man of vision, or simply a seeker blinded by obsession? And what about the other members of his band?

Jimiyu and the woman, Chanya, were obviously followers. Whether they followed out of shared beliefs, friendship or something else, she wasn't sure. Likewise, Vincent Boorman, though he seemed an odd companion to the others. A billionaire on a joyride of a quest, or was he a true believer?

She understood what Professor Escobedo was doing here. Like her, he was a scientist, looking for evidence of past civilizations. That he believed there was a chance of finding such evidence said something about both him and the charisma of Dr. Nikira. The professor's wife Filamena and his son, she assumed, were simply accompanying him on the journey. Yet there was something going on there—a strange distance among them, a barrier keeping them apart even as it drew them together. She wasn't normally one to pry into the affairs of others, but their obvious tension had aroused her curiosity.

Most intriguing of all was the artifact Nikira had shown her. She doubted it was as old as he claimed, but if the dating of it was authentic it would mean—

"Evening, Doctor."

She was so involved in contemplation the voice startled her.

"It's a right pretty night, isn't it?"

It was McCroy's associate, a weaselly-looking fellow with a bridgeless nose, stained teeth and eyes that bulged. As soon as she thought those things, Amanda reprimanded herself for being superficial. She was the last person to be judging someone by their outward appearance.

"It's Mr. Scurlock, isn't it?" she asked.

"Call me Jesper, ma'am." He doffed his cap in a show of politeness then, as if realizing he was staring at her, looked back up at the aurora.

"As many places as I've been, and I've been all over, I ain't never seen nothing like that. It's something else."

"Yes, I never tire of looking at them," Amanda said.

"Must be quite a pot of gold at the end of that rainbow," he said in a tone that left her wondering if he were serious.

When she looked down from the sky, he was staring at her again. It made her uncomfortable.

"Have you worked with Mr. McCroy for long?" she asked, hoping to deflect his gaze.

"Yeah, me and Lyle, we've been all over hell and gone and back again. We've seen some things, yep, we have. Why, I could tell you

146

stories—heck, I remember back once when we was in some bad trouble, surrounded on all sides by these Bolivian rebels. They wanted our guns, our boots and this woman geologist we had with us, if you know what I mean." He smirked as if to emphasize the point. "They was under the false illusion they had us. But we didn't lay down like dogs, no, ma'am. We circled right around them jungle boys, and they never even seen us. We was too smart for 'em," he boasted. "Their faces must've been cherry red when they found out we'd given 'em the slip."

Amanda had found his Southern drawl charming at first, but eventually, it seemed only to reinforce the stereotype she was trying to resist.

"I suppose this is another adventure for you," she said. "I mean, coming to Evergreen."

"Shit, no, if you'll pardon my vulgarity, ma'am," he said with all sincerity. "We're not here for no adventure. We're here for the treasure."

"Treasure?"

"That's right. Me and Lyle figure if this is really God's city, there must be big treasure—you know, gold, jewels, everything," he said, as if taking her into his confidence and hoping to impress her. "I bet I'll find something that would look mighty pretty on you."

"I didn't hear Dr. Nikira say anything about treasure hunting," she said, changing the subject.

"What he doesn't know won't hurt him."

"Jesper, go secure the supplies and stop bothering Dr. Rousch." It was McCroy. "Then get yourself some sleep, I'll be waking you for the watch in four hours."

"I ain't bothering no one," he said with what Amanda thought was a hint of rancor. Still, he complied with McCroy's orders. "'Night, Doctor," he said, retreating. "Nice talking with you."

"Goodnight"

"I hope he wasn't pestering you, Doctor. Jester tends to bluster."

Amanda noticed McCroy had reverted to calling her "Doctor," despite her request that he use her first name.

"Oh, he wasn't bothering me. I actually found Mr. Scurlock quite interesting. Especially what he had to say about hoping to find some kind of treasure."

McCroy laughed, but she thought it sounded forced.

"Jesper's always talking about treasure," he said. "I wouldn't get your hopes up."

"What about you?" she asked. "Are you hoping to find a divine hoard of gems and precious relics where we're going?"

He shrugged, stone-faced, then let a smile escape. "Doesn't hurt to look, does it?"

She was about to ask him what Nikira would think of his desecrating a spiritual quest with acts of plunder when McCroy's big cat trotted in from the darkness with something in its mouth. It was a huge lizard, at least three feet long from nose to tail, its skin the color and texture of a lime peel, its underbelly striated in various shades of lemon. It was either dead or playing so, and it had several wounds from the cat's teeth and claws. It was a new species—one she hadn't come across before.

The cat dropped the reptile at McCroy's feet.

"I hadn't let him out at night in a while, but I figured we were far enough from any human settlements now." McCroy made a point to stroke the animal as he examined his catch. "He likes to bring me gifts."

"Maybe he thinks you're hungry," said Amanda.

McCroy overturned the lizard with the toe of his boot. "Not that hungry."

"You know, you probably shouldn't let him eat it, either."

"I wouldn't worry about that. Thor eats just about anything. He's got a tough constitution.

"Maybe on Earth that's true," she replied, "but that reptile's biology is alien. You don't know how Thor's system might react to it. And I'm sure you know many reptiles on Earth excrete poisons as defensive measures."

He looked thoughtful. "Maybe you're right. I'd better not take any chances. He won't like it, though." He picked up the lizard by the tail, and the big cat looked at it expectantly, as if he wanted to play with it some more. "I'll get rid of it."

"Do you mind if I take a look at it first?"

McCroy's first reaction was surprise. "What do you...? Oh, that's right. You probably want to study it, cut it open."

"Nothing so thorough, I assure you. I *would* like to look it over, though, make some notes. I could name it 'Thor's Lizard,' or maybe 'Thorsaurian,' in honor of its discoverer."

McCroy smiled. "All right," he replied, tossing the lizard to the ground in front of her.

Thor wheeled and was about to pounce on it when McCroy called him back.

"Thor, heel!"

The animal cut short its leap and obeyed. It followed McCroy as he walked off, but glanced back longingly at its prey.

34

Placid garden hues belied the activity beneath and all around the smoldering, silent sea of life. From wraithlike ferns to the rich, fleshy leaves absorbing sunlight and moisture, root-node connections conveyed and confirmed cognition. Awareness ripened. An ancient had been mounted. A foreign entity inflicted carnage upon it with each stage of its ascent. Even now it stabbed and worried at its outer layer.
***

Incursion noted. Immediate response vital. Compliance with the root crown initiative vital. Assessment of the collective consciousness vital. Action forthcoming.
***

"Damn bugs! Get...get away!"
***

Infesting entity's vibrations absorbed through ancient. Frenetic activity signals distress.
***

"God damn swarm! Get off...get ahhhhh!"
***

Neural impulses transmit impact. Appendages extend and examine. Absorption cells respond to moisture. Warm, viscous. Infestation inert. Correction. Detect minimal, weakened movement.

***

"Ohhh..."

***

Confirmation. Infliction of trauma nullified. Newly synthesized directives instituted.

***

"Uhhh. Shit! I think I've broke both my legs. God damn it hurts! I'm going to have...what's that? What's that crawling on me? Shit! Get off me! Get off!"

***

Infestation acquired. Proceed with dispatch. Render nutrients for requisite germination.

***

"Let go. Let go of me! Help! Somebody help me!"

***

Chaotic vibrations. Desperation signaled. Infestation secured. Reactions, capabilities noted by root crown for further analysis.

35

By the time the sun burned away the chill of dawn, the expedition had already been on the trail for what seemed like hours to Filamena. They were making their way up a severe incline through chest-high brush that appeared impenetrable—though not to McCroy. The farther they traveled, the more use he was getting out of his machete. Like an unrestrained automaton, he hacked at the stubborn brush, carving out their path as he went. Filamena didn't know how he kept it up.

She found the hike exhausting. It was bad enough on even ground, trudging ahead, one foot after the other; climbing this hill was as hard as anything she'd ever had to do. Of course, she'd said that yesterday, and the day before. It wasn't the first time she'd regretted her decision to come along on this expedition.

Yet the more time she spent around Luis, the more she realized why she'd fallen in love with him. It wasn't his intelligence, or his blunted sense of humor, or his body, which had grown more portly over the years. She loved him because he was so caring. His constant concern for her along the trek reinforced what she already knew, deep in her heart—that he loved her. His preoccupation with his work might have taken its toll on their marriage, but he was still the same dear man who had charmed her. The same man who had whisked her away from the small town where she grew up, where the men were not nearly so respectful. If only she'd...

But life was full of if-onlys, wasn't it? Regrets didn't change anything. They just perched there on the corners of your mind, like crows on a clothesline, waiting, always there, always hovering.

When he reached the crest of the hill, McCroy called a halt, in part to wait for Filamena and the other trailing members of the group to catch up. She was envious of the American scientist, who seemed to have no trouble keeping pace with McCroy. Dr. Rousch was tall, though not particularly attractive. She didn't seem to care much about her appearance at all. She even had on an old wavy-brimmed hat that looked like something a gardener would wear. Yet she was vigorous, and obviously experienced with the hardships of outdoor life. Filamena admired her strength and independence.

"Well, which way now?" McCroy asked their guide.

Harley looked around, examining the terrain with a somewhat baffled expression.

"Don't tell me you're lost again."

"I'm not lost." Harley took off his hat and scratched his head. "I'm just trying to get my bearings, that's all. Look, there's Pickle Peak over there. That means the settlement should be off to our right somewhere."

Luis took Filamena's arm, helped her up the last few steps to the top and pulled off her pack. She saw the oddly shaped rock Harley was pointing at, though it seemed more phallic in shape than like any pickle she'd ever seen. Maybe that was just the *puttana* in her talking again.

"Off to our right somewhere—that's helpful. What about you, Dr. Rousch?" inquired McCroy. "Any idea which way this old settlement is from here?"

"All I know is that it's supposed to be at the end of Hokan Pass."

McCroy stabbed his machete into the ground at his feet and wiped the perspiration from his forehead. "Well, I'd say that pass ended when we started up the back of this bluff. We're—"

"Over here!" It was Max. He'd wandered away from the group and was waving them over. "It's down here!"

Max had behaved himself since their encounter in the garden. He had gone so far as to avoid even making eye contact with her. At least, that's how it seemed to her. Maybe he was angry, or maybe he was just trying to respect her wishes. Regardless, part of her found his behavior annoying, even though it's what she'd told him she wanted. There were times she still caught herself looking at him in a way she shouldn't be. Each time she chided herself for being so weak.

Filamena rubbed more of the protective lotion onto her arms and face as she joined those gathered around Max. At home she stayed out of the sun—she didn't even like to tan. It was bad for the skin.

She stood next to the other woman in their party, Chanya, and gazed downward. All she could see was a stream meandering through the canyon below. She wondered what everyone was looking at. She saw only trees and more of the same scrub they'd been hiking through for days. Then she spotted it through the treetops—a cabin of sorts.

"Let's get down there," said McCroy.

❧❧ ❧❧ ❧❧

As they approached the abandoned settlement, Filamena saw there were actually several structures made of various materials and in various states of disrepair. Some were prefabricated, others were constructed primarily of wood, stone and other natural materials. How large the settlement had once been was hard to determine. Most of it was overgrown with tangled vines and rampant clumps of wild brush. Spider webs studded small corners of the structures. She wondered if they'd been made by the same stumpy kind of spider she'd seen in the flower garden. There were no gardens here—no signs she could see that the land had ever been cultivated.

Under the matted grass, half-buried, she saw remnants of what she guessed was once a cooking pot of some sort. Otherwise, she saw little evidence that people once lived here.

Luis, of course, was fascinated. He saw the cooking pot, too, and began to gently unearth it. Next to him, Dr. Nikira closed his eyes and quietly uttered a prayer of some kind. Harley, meanwhile, was fixated on a large tree. Filamena couldn't tell what he was doing, but he was busy at it. Scurlock noticed him, too.

"What are you doing? What you got there?"

Harley half-turned so they could see he was carefully plucking apricot-colored sprouts from the tree bark.

"Shrooms. Big ones. Lady Luck's smiling today."

"What the hell are shrooms?" Scurlock asked.

"Shrooms are the prime ingredient, man. They're what—"

"What was that?" Suddenly, Scurlock's attention was jerked from Harley to something he saw across the encampment. "Did you see that?" He pulled the gun he carried from where it was lodged in his pack and brought it to bear. As if by conditioned reflex, McCroy did the same.

"What is it, Jesper? What did you see?"

"There, look!"

Filamena looked and saw what had alarmed Scurlock. Three or four large creatures scrambled out of one of the ramshackle cabins and disappeared into the trees. They were huge, hairy, reddish-brown things, thickset but not as tall as men. They were gone before she could get a good look, but Filamena thought they had tails as well.

McCroy's cat took off after them.

"Thor! Heel!"

The cat slowed and returned.

"There's more over there," shouted Scurlock, swiveling his weapon around as if to fire.

As quick as he was, the American woman was quicker. Two agile strides brought her up behind him, and in the instant before he fired, she knocked the barrel of his gun down. Filamena's hands flew to cover her ears much too late. The blast was deafening.

"You idiot!" screamed Dr. Rousch. "They're not going to hurt anyone. They're just ursu."

Scurlock scowled. Several more of the creatures fled in fright.

McCroy put his gun away, frowning. Filamena couldn't tell if his look was meant for Scurlock or Dr. Rousch.

"Well, it appears we've got the place to ourselves now," he said. "We'll stay here the night and start again in the morning. How far from here, Harley?"

Harley was just getting to his feet, having dived belly first when the shot sounded.

"Just a day or two."

McCroy snorted as if he'd believe it when he saw it.

Filamena noticed that the gunplay had barely disrupted Luis's digging. He'd found something else near the pot. He unearthed it and held it up. It was half-covered with dirt, and Filamena had no idea what it could be. It looked like a cracked gourd painted with faded designs.

Luis had his recorder out, and spoke into it as if nothing out of the ordinary had just happened. She recognized his look of preoccupation. For him, nothing but archaeological artifacts existed at that moment—not danger, not alien animals, not his son, not her.

Max recognized it, too. He tried to get her attention. When she ignored his nodding, he playfully undid the bright multi-colored band from around his straw hat and waved it at her, grinning. She didn't know what he had in mind, but she had an idea. She wasn't going to let herself fall again. She avoided his gaze and decided it would be best if she assisted Luis with whatever he was doing.

Young Boorman stood over Luis, staring at his find. "What is that thing, Professor?"

"I'm not certain. It looks as if it could be some kind of shaman's rattle."

"Zapper," replied Boorman. "You'll probably find all kinds of moldy oldies here."

"I don't see any signs of a graveyard, though," Luis said, as though thinking out loud. "I'll have to find it before we leave. It should be a treasure trove."

The idea sent shivers through Filamena. She pictured all sorts of gruesome discoveries.

Scurlock perked up. "Treasure?"

"Why would you want to scan a bone farm?" asked Boorman.

"Most Native American tribes buried their dead along with many of their possessions," replied Luis in what Filamena thought of as his lecture tone. "Such a find should—"

"There is no graveyard," Harley interjected.

Luis frowned. "What do you mean? I thought most of the tribe died out here."

"They did," said Harley. "At least, that's how the story goes. But no bodies were ever found."

36

His legs were getting used to tramping up and down the hills overlooking the lake. The first few days had left him so sore he'd felt like a cripple trying to get up in the morning. Now it was just tedium. He no longer paid attention to the view that initially had struck him as so awe-inspiring.

Simply making it through each grueling day, working sunup to sundown, took all the energy he had. By the end of each one there was nothing left in him—no vigor, no intensity, not an ounce of strength to pursue his only reason for being. He began to think his enlistment had been a mistake. Nearly all these men used assumed names, and the quick glimpse he'd gotten of the man he sought's face was so long ago his memory of it was no longer reliable. Yet each time the web of doubt closed in on him and began to constrict his resolve, he remembered his mother.

There had to be a way. There must be some kind of official record of legal names. He had to find a conduit to hack into the company's files. Computers were one thing he was good at. His finesse with a keyboard had gotten him into trouble at school more than once. As soon as he got the chance he would—

"Step it up, turtle. Quit your daydreaming, you're lagging."

Eamon despised the way they treated him. He kept his mouth shut, but each time they called him *turtle* or *kid* or *pretty boy* he steamed inside. Instead of boiling over, he simmered, channeling his cauldron of rage. The mockery only fueled his determination.

Gash was the only one who treated him with any respect. The only one who, despite his outwardly gruff nature, had been fair with him. He was a moody guy who frequently went off by himself, yet Eamon had come to appreciate his rough guidance. He'd even gotten used to the ugly scar that marred his face. What he wondered about were the scars underneath, the ones he couldn't see. The man had them—that was certain.

Eamon never had a father, and had stopped wishing for one by the time he was twelve. The previous night, though, he caught himself imagining that, if he'd ever had one, he'd want him to be something like the man who had befriended him on this alien world.

"I've found something!" someone called out far to Eamon's left.

He and Gash had been assigned to a search party sent out to find a missing TJ; they'd been combing the mountainside in vain for more than an hour. The search had been conducted in a wide semi-circle, and now they were returning to the edge of the timberline, several dozen yards north of where they'd begun.

Everyone converged on the man who'd made the discovery. He held a red hat.

"It's Macho Charlie's," he said, holding the hat up.

"Are you sure?" one of the others asked.

"Do you know anybody else who wore a St. Louis Cardinals cap?"

"That was Charlie's, all right."

"Is that blood on it?"

"That looks like blood there on those leaves."

"What do you think happened to him? He would have come down if he was hurt."

"What if he was dead?"

Eamon noticed Gash wasn't taking part in the speculation. He was bent down examining the ground near the blood-spattered leaves. He stepped up next to him and saw the marks on the ground.

"Dead or alive, it looks like he was dragged away," said Gash. "Look at how the ground's tore up going that way."

"Let's follow it," ordered the group leader. "Spread out, though, keep the line like before."

"Maybe the squats did it," offered one TJ.

"I never heard of a squat attacking anyone," said another.

"Maybe they didn't attack. Maybe they just found him there."

"That's crazy. Why would they drag him off?"

"Maybe they ate him."

The suggestion prompted loud laughter.

"Well, knowing Macho Charlie, I bet they found him tough to swallow."

That evoked more laughter.

Eamon failed to see the humor in it. The idea that some strange animals might have grabbed one of them struck him as horrifying.

Eventually, the drag marks terminated, and they spread out to conduct a thorough search of the surrounding area. They found nothing. It was nearly sunset when the fellow in charge called an end, and they all straggled down the mountain.

No more morbid theories were espoused. There was no more joking or laughter. There was barely any conversation at all. Eamon got the feeling the silence was a kind of unspoken agreement, acknowledging the missing man's likely death but not going so far as to toss the first shovelful of dirt on his coffin.

37

A damp mist hovered just above the ground at dawn, clinging to the forest floor like a shroud. Jimiyu was not a particularly superstitious man, but one look at the fog confirmed his feelings about the abandoned settlement. It was a ghost town, not a place for the living. They should never have spent the night there.

He didn't voice his feelings, yet he was glad when McCroy rousted everyone and got them off to an early start. It was the first time he'd looked forward to the daily trek. Everyone else seemed be in high spirits as well, likely because they knew there wasn't much further to go.

He was worried about Chanya, though. She was more withdrawn than usual. He was concerned because, the night before, he'd watched her enter the rustic shelter Nikira had chosen to be alone in. She had only been inside a few minutes when she left. The night was too black for him to see clearly, but there was no mistaking what he heard. She was crying. He had no trouble imagining the conversation that must have taken place.

The settlement behind them now, the misty vapor burned away by the rising sun, their objective almost within reach, Jimiyu felt optimistic. Until he saw the creatures.

At first, it was just a glimpse, so quick he wasn't sure what he saw. Then they were there again, and he was sure. The hairy brutes

Dr. Rousch referred to as ursu were watching them—following them on a parallel course through the trees.

He hurried to catch up with Dr. Rousch, who walked alongside McCroy.

"Doctor, do you see?" he said, pointing out the animals.

"Yes, they've been tagging along since we started out this morning. They're just curious. The ursu have an almost human curiosity. They'll probably tire of us soon and turn back."

"Ugly buggers, aren't they," said McCroy, smiling.

Dr. Rousch ignored the comment. "There's something about them, though. I can't tell what from this distance. I know their coloring is a little darker than the ursu I've been living with, but there's something else different. There's something about the way they move. I don't know what it is."

"Woman's intuition, Doctor?" inquired McCroy.

She frowned as if dismissing his question. "It's intuition if I'm right."

"But look at them," insisted Jimiyu. "Look at the way they stare at us. It's...it's more than curiosity. I know, I know—it sounds ridiculous. But it's as if they know something we don't."

"Yeah? Flowers turn toward the sun," responded McCroy. "That doesn't mean they're mapping the solar system."

Jimiyu ignored the sarcasm and kept an eye on the animals. Several times, the creatures disappeared, each time leading him to believe they'd given up as Dr. Rousch suggested, only to reappear again farther up the trail. Everyone in the expedition had noticed them by now, and no one seemed concerned, so eventually he paid them no more attention.

They were more than two hours into their hike through a relatively clear area when they came across a huge tree that had fallen across their path. It was long dead, its branches bare. Jimiyu wondered if it was a storm that had uprooted the giant, or just old age.

The quickest way around it was to the right, past its exposed roots. McCroy led the way, followed by Dr. Rousch, Vincent and Jimiyu. It was Vincent who first saw something unusual.

"Scan that," he said, looking down at the uneven ground under the exposed tree roots. "Looks like bones."

Jimiyu took a closer look as everyone gathered around. They certainly looked like bones to him. Apparently, they'd been unearthed when the tree fell. He wondered what kind of bones they were, and how long they'd been there.

Professor Escobedo knelt down over the remains, dug into the soil to extract a couple of pieces and examined them. "They're human," he stated matter-of-factly. "I'd say they're at least fifty years old. It doesn't look as if they've been gnawed on by carnivores, but they're really too old and too deteriorated for me to tell much without laboratory analysis. However, I'd like to study the—"

"We've got to keep moving, Professor," McCroy said. It was more command than suggestion. "This isn't what we're looking for."

"Yes, all right." The professor got up, wiped the dirt from his hands.

The professor's wife said, "I wonder who it was."

"Maybe one of the missing settlers," offered Dr. Rousch.

"Well, whoever it was," said McCroy, "is long-past caring about any of it. Let's get moving."

"Don't let your cat jump over the bones," said Harley.

McCroy glared. "What are you talking about?"

"If a cat jumps over a corpse it turns it into a vampire," Harley explained.

Dr. Rousch smiled as if it were a joke. "The cat or the corpse?"

"The corpse," replied Harley.

"Those bones won't be sucking any more blood," said McCroy, walking past.

His big cat followed him, apparently too close to the remains for their guide. Harley backed away and gestured with his hand, holding down his middle and ring fingers with his thumb and extending his index and little fingers towards the remains like a pair of horns.

"What's that supposed to mean?" asked Vincent.

"He makes the *mano cornuto* to keep away evil spirits," answered the professor's wife.

"I thought that had something to do with cuckolding," said Dr. Rousch.

The professor's wife responded flatly, "Yes, that too."

They followed McCroy, filing slowly around the remains. No one said anything else. Jimiyu sensed a pall had been cast over the group. He certainly felt it, even if no one else did.

162

Nikira, alone, didn't move. He stood where he was and closed his eyes, as if offering a silent prayer over the remains. When he opened them, he hitched up his pack and moved on. Jimiyu took a last look back at the bones and suppressed a shiver.

Some two hours and unknown miles later, after another appearance and disappearance of their ursu followers, McCroy called a halt. By then, everyone was exhausted and hungry. There was little conversation. Most stayed to themselves. After a few bites of rations he shared with his cat, McCroy leaned against a tree and tilted his hat over his eyes. The sleek animal curled up next to him.

Some of the others tried to nap, but Jimiyu didn't see anyone actually manage to fall asleep. His legs were tired, but he didn't feel much like sleep himself. He noticed Dr. Rousch stray off a ways, still within sight but far enough not to disturb anyone when she began playing her flute.

He had heard her play the night before. Now, drawn by the melody, he meandered over and sat next to her. He didn't interrupt, he just listened. He recognized the tune she played, but couldn't recall its name. He closed his eyes, concentrating on the music, and was almost lulled to sleep until she stopped abruptly.

"Do you hear that?" she asked.

At first he thought she meant the music, then realized she was listening to something else.

"You mean the wind?" he replied.

"I don't know, it sounded like more than the wind there for a moment. It's gone now," she said, but he could tell she was still listening. "Maybe it was just my music echoing from the trees."

"Maybe."

She put her flute away and leaned back on her elbows, surveying the forest.

"Is Dr. Nikira really your brother, or is that just a spiritual thing?" she asked, then added, "I heard him call you 'Brother.'"

"Actually, it's a tribal thing. We are Kikuyu. All men of the Kikuyu tribe are brothers."

"What part of Africa are you from?"

Foreigners always referred to Africa as if it were one place, one nation. Jimiyu resented such a perspective. He wasn't African. He wasn't even Kenyan, at least not in his thinking. He was Kikuyu.

"Kenya," he told her.

"And Chanya, too?"

"Yes, we all grew up in the same village."

"You must know Dr. Nikira very well, then."

Jimiyu bobbed his head in tacit agreement.

"Do you share his beliefs, his desire to find this City of God?"

He didn't want to tell her that Nikira's beliefs weren't his own, and that he thought the likelihood of them finding such a city about the same as their chances of coming upon a good restaurant in this forest.

"I am his friend," he said, as if it answered all her questions.

She must have sensed his reluctance, for she didn't pursue that line of inquiry. Instead, she asked, "Have you always...worked with Dr. Nikira?"

"No. For many years I was a schoolteacher for the younger children of my village. It was just a small school, but other children came from a nearby orphanage. I also helped out there when I could."

"That must have been rewarding. But you left that to work with Dr. Nikira?"

"The orphanage closed down, and a bigger school was built in Tambach. I was not qualified to teach there."

"Oh, I see."

Jimiyu couldn't tell if the expression on her face was compassion or admiration.

"I was wondering, is Jimiyu your first name, your given name or your family name?

He wasn't sure what she meant—given name, family name. "My name is Jimiyu Kinisu Obwaka. All Kikuyu male children are named for their grandfathers. While still young, all boys of about the same age are also given a tribal name they share. Dr. Nikira's name is Talib Kinisu Nikira. Kinisu is our given tribal name."

"And the girls?"

Jimiyu waved his hand as if the question had no meaning. "Female children are different."

"Oh. Very interesting."

He caught a hint of condescension in her response, as if a truly civilized people wouldn't treat its women differently. It was an attitude he was familiar with. Outsiders didn't understand.

"I'll tell you something I believe you'll find even more interesting, Doctor. It will tell you all you need to know about Dr. Nikira. His name, Talib, in our language means *to seek*. I can assure you of one thing, Doctor. No man could better fit his name."

38

isembarking from the *Sir Real*, Eamon followed Gash into the queue of timber jockeys. Despite the long line, he sensed a certain zest in their attitudes. Even the tone of their voices was different. There was a boisterous anticipation among them as they joked and teased and tussled almost playfully, like hyperactive children.

"Going to get me some tonight," howled one TJ. "Funday couldn't come soon enough."

"Came the same time it always does," responded another, to the laughter of bystanders.

"I can't wait to see Sunny." It was the little guy, Farr.

"You got to get off that same old Tina and try some fresh poontang, Mousey," said the timber jock behind Farr, poking him in the back.

"There ain't no such thing as fresh poontang at Tilley's," responded the fellow in front of Farr.

Everyone but Farr laughed. He frowned and replied, "Fuck you guys."

Everyone laughed again, and this time even Farr smiled.

Eamon sensed all the trash talk and carping was goodnatured. He'd seen timber jocks come to blows and then laugh about it afterwards. There was a spirit of camaraderie in the unrefined assemblage that went beyond the release that came with the week's end. Whether it was a bond forged by time or sweat he didn't know, but it was there—almost a tangible thing. A small part of him was envious. He wondered if he'd ever experience that feeling. Probably not. He doubted he'd be around that long.

For him, it had been an exhausting, mind-numbing several days. Nothing he had ever done approached the backbreaking, grueling labor required of the timber jockeys. Even so, he was left with the impression he hadn't even done his share. His constant battle with fatigue made it impossible to keep up with the others. Gash told him he'd get used to it—that he'd get better at it. He wasn't so sure. His body hadn't stopped aching since that first day. It seemed like a month had passed since then, instead of just their six-day work week.

As the line of TJs shuffled slowly up from the shore, Eamon spotted the top of the yarder. Unlike the smaller, mobile yarders mounted on sleds they used to haul the logs on the other side of the lake, this one was fixed, stabilized by permanent guylines. It was a mammoth tower, sixty, maybe seventy feet tall, with massive revolving drums at its base. Around the drums, thigh-thick cables coiled and uncoiled in squealing metallic shrieks and gnashing groans.

He hadn't seen this part of the operation before, but he'd learned enough to know that the rigging used to attach the huge cables to logs was made up of cinch lines—*chokers*, as some TJs called them. The mainline drum would grind into action, and the log would begin its ascent to the top of the rise, where the timber was released and the line routed round and down by the haulback drum. What he didn't know was what happened then.

He wondered why the logs were being cable-skidded uphill. He was even more curious when he saw each log carried a number of timber jockeys. Before he resolved to ask Gash about it, they'd reached the front of the queue.

He saw Meanan, Porno Eddy, Cayenne and a few others climb onto a log that was being rigged.

"Let's go," said Gash, and without further explanation sunk his grapples into the log and pulled himself up with ease. Eamon had wondered why Gash told him to bring his cleats and grapples. Now he knew. "Let's go! Come on, kid," Gash called impatiently.

"Come on, turtle," Cayenne mocked, "you can shit your britches later. Swank Summit here we come!"

Eamon clambered up, and Gash grabbed him by the collar to pull him the last few feet. Just as he gained his balance aboard the log, it jerked like a thing alive and began its grating ascent. By the time he felt secure enough he no longer thought he might slip off, they were halfway up the steep incline.

"Why are they hauling the logs up?" he asked Gash.

"You mean why did the chicken crawl up the side of the mountain?" Gash responded without turning around. "To fly down the other side, of course."

Eamon didn't know what he was talking about. "Wouldn't it be easier to move them by water?"

"Would be if you could. Rust River's too shallow in places for the *Sir Real*, and too strong. Against that current, the dugouts can't make it back to Woodville. Even in smaller canoes, you'd find it tough going."

"Then how do the logs get to town?" Before Gash could answer, something else occurred to him. "How do *we* get to town?"

Gash turned his head and smiled, his scar furrowing. "The same way," he replied. "The same way we get the dugouts back there."

He turned back around without elaborating, so Eamon shut up.

When the log they were riding reached level ground, the TJ's unhooked their grapples and jumped. Eamon did likewise, though wresting one of his grapples from the timber took him an extra tug. He hit the ground awkwardly, then followed Gash and the others to another staging area. There he saw the logs were being lifted by crane onto a chute that looked to him like an enormous rain gutter. The gutter image was reinforced by the water being pumped into the chute from a conduit that trailed back down to the lake.

The trough was mounted, on dense stilts, a good dozen feet off the ground, and designed so that it leaned into the natural slope on the other side of the summit. On each side of the near end of the trough was a catwalk. A handful of timber jockeys on each catwalk climbed onto the log just released from the crane and, on bent knees, thrust their boots back, chipping at the bark to embed their cleats into solid timber. Their legs fixed firmly, they thrust the hooks of their grapples into the wood in front of them.

Eamon watched Ramos climb up to the catwalk to a place where he could look down on everyone gathered below.

"All right, compadres, listen up!" he called over the din. "I've got an announcement to make. The company is—" A surly rumble of booing greeted the word *company*, but Ramos went on. "The company is threatening to make the vill off-limits to all timber jocks if there's a repeat of, shall I say, some of the more colorful incidents—I have a list here—that occurred last Funday."

That set off a symphony of hooting and hollering that overwhelmed the booing.

"Hey! Hey!" Ramos yelled to get their attention. "They're not kidding around. Go easy. Stay out of the west end and leave the citizens alone." He searched the pack of TJs and found the face he was looking for. "That goes for you especially, Cromartie. You let the administrator's gardener take care of the fertilizing, and you find another place to take a shit."

A raucous wave of laughter greeted the jibe. Ramos motioned to the fellow overseeing the operation, who checked the TJs mounted on the log in the chute and shouted "Set!" He waited a moment, and then pulled a lever that released the log. It started slowly enough, but as the incline increased so did its speed.

Eamon's jaw dropped, and he stood there, immobile, realizing for the first time how the timber, and the men, got to town. He watched as the log barreled down the flume, the TJs aboard it whooping and hollering like they were on an amusement park ride.

Gash noticed him standing there with his mouth open, came up behind Eamon and said, "Now you know how the timber jockeys got their name." As if reading Eamon's mind he added, "Don't worry, it scared the crap out of me the first time, too."

Eamon shook his head, still watching the rapidly vanishing log. "I'm not doing that."

"You are if you want to get to the vill," replied Gash sternly. "Just watch me and do what I do. You'll be fine. It's an eight-mile ride. Takes less than twenty minutes."

"Twenty minutes?"

"Yeah," said Gash, bending down to tighten one of his cleats, "it gets up to fifty miles per in some stretches."

"Come on, turtle," said Cayenne, heading for the catwalk ladder, "it's time to catch the TJ Express."

"Yeah," said Meanan, clapping him on the back, "maybe you'll catch a flamer, Pretty Boy."

Meanan and Cayenne started up the ladder, followed by Eddy.

"Let's go," ordered Gash, not looking back to see if Eamon followed.

Before he knew it, he was on the catwalk, bending down to crawl aboard the log and doing his best to kick away the loose bark and jam his cleats in to where they would hold. He slapped both of his grapples into the timber but felt awkward, and not at all secure.

Gash, dug in a few feet in front of him, offered some last-second advice.

"If there's a jam along the way, the lead rider will call it out and we'll jump. It doesn't happen too often, but if I say 'jump,' you'd better jump. Leave your grapples in so you don't gore yourself. Same goes at the end of the line. They'll retrieve them later. I'll give you a heads-up when we get close. We'll be unhooking and jumping staggered. I'll go left, you'll go right. They've got pads there, so it'll be a soft landing. Just don't kick yourself with your cleats."

Before Eamon could think to ask any questions he heard "Set!" and the log crawled forward. He squeezed his grapples even tighter and braced himself.

"Ye-hah! Tina, here I come!"

Eamon didn't know which one of the TJs aboard his log had yelled out, and he wasn't about to look up to see. His gaze fastened onto Gash's back. It wasn't until he felt the rush of air and the swerve of a turn that he dared a sidelong glance.

The terrain whipped by him at a speed he didn't want to contemplate. He felt exposed—vulnerable. One of his cleats kept losing its grip. He tried hard to dig it in, but the jarring sway of the swift-sliding log made it difficult.

At each slight angling of the flume the log slowed then regathered momentum, gradually regaining speed. It wasn't a smooth ride, but he hung on; and once his adrenalin-rush drained he calmed enough to where he thought he might begin to enjoy it. That was until he chanced a look ahead and saw the reservoir full of logs—and the end of the flume.

"Get ready!" Gash shouted against the onrushing wind. "When I jump left, you jump right!"

Eamon tensed up again. What if he froze? What if his cleats caught in the wood? What if he couldn't jump?

"Kick loose your cleats!"

Eamon did so, trusting his balance to grapples alone now. There was a bump. Somebody screamed. Then another piecing cry, and another. The shrieks sounded almost jubilant. In front of him, Eamon saw bodies propelled off to the left and right.

"Jump now!" shouted Gash, hurling himself off to left.

Eamon didn't hesitate, and he didn't look before he leaped.

39

hen are we going to rest?" asked someone behind her who was breathing hard.

"Yes, I think we should stop soon." Amanda recognized the second voice as belonging to Professor Escobedo.

It had been a long day. She estimated they had traveled more than a dozen miles, most of it uphill. As experienced a hiker as she was, she felt it in her legs. Even so, she was better off than almost everyone else in the expedition. Some of them looked like the walking dead when McCroy finally relented and they straggled into a clearing he'd selected.

Professor Escobedo and his son were practically carrying the professor's wife, and even the youngest member of their party, Vincent Boorman, collapsed in exhaustion. Only McCroy and Nikira looked as if they could go on, like they *wanted* to go on. An unlikely pair, she thought, the cynic and the true believer.

Harley was sprawled on the ground like a dead man, staring straight up through the trees. McCroy looked down at him and shook his head.

"How did you ever make it this far?"

"I took my time," Harley replied, still out of breath.

"Are you sure we're headed in the right direction?"

"I got you to the settlement, didn't I?"

"Blind luck, if you ask me."

"Better than no luck at all," said Harley as McCroy walked away.

Amanda reached into her pack to find something she could nibble on before they got around to building a fire and boiling some of their less-than-tasty condensed nutrients. Scurlock must have been watching her, because he came over, pulling something out of his own pack.

"Want some jerky, Doctor?"

The thing he held out to her looked like a piece of twisted, burnt cardboard.

"No, thanks, I'm a vegan."

"A what?"

"A vegan. I don't eat meat."

Scurlock looked at her like she was demented.

"The good doctor doesn't eat anything with a face," said McCroy, who was busy piling kindling. "Isn't that right, Doctor Rousch?" Amanda didn't bother to reply. McCroy looked at her with the hint of a grin and added, "You know, even broccoli screams when you rip it out of the ground."

Scurlock chuckled, and Amanda flashed a sarcastic smile McCroy's way. At the same time, she became aware of a growing argument between Professor Escobedo and his son.

It had started quietly, in English, and had somehow morphed to Spanish as it got louder. It wasn't a particularly heated discussion, but there was definite disagreement. She had no idea what they were talking about. It wasn't any of her business, so she took her ration bar and strolled away. She noted when the professor's wife intervened and cut the argument short.

Being so close to so many other people for so long only reminded Amanda how much she enjoyed her solitude. She found a spot to sit while she ate the bar and contemplated what she had seen in this virtually unexplored region of Evergreen. Thinking about it reminded her it had been a while since she'd recorded any of her observations. She finished the bland snack, pulled out her Trans-Slate and entered her most recent observations.

This morning we spotted what appeared
to be a large herd of hoofed mammals in the

distance. They were too far off for me to get a good look, but from my vantage it seemed as if they were shaggy, short-legged equines of some sort. I can't wait to return here for further study.

The deeper we travel into Evergreen's eastern wilderness, the greater the variety of trees and other vegetation we come across. Here the pseudo-redwood species that makes up the primary source of timber around Lake Washoe has given way to gnarled, thick-bodied, oak-like boles, and a type of tree with a massive canopy and enormous exposed root system that seems to be a variation of the Moreton Bay fig. These are the most striking of several new plant species I've seen.

(Note to self: Remember to recommend, once again, that a botanist be assigned to Evergreen as soon as permission can be obtained.)

As for the ursu who have followed us since we disturbed their community at the old settlement, they continue to pique my curiosity. Their existence tends to confirm my theory that there are thousands of ursu in the unexplored regions of Evergreen. However, there's something about them that is different from the ursu I've been living with closer to the lake. Whether it's just appearance, or the manner in which they observe us, I'm not certain. They do seem to vocalize more, though that might only be a product of their excitement and curiosity. I need to make closer observations, but so far, they won't let me approach. Probably because I'm traveling with such a large group.

I plan to return to this region to further study this community of ursu once the ex-

pedition ends and I restock provisions. Until
then, I will continue to—

"Excuse me, Doctor, I thought you might want some company."

It was Scurlock. He sat next to her—much too close for
Amanda's comfort.

"What you writing there? A love letter for someone back
home?"

"No," she replied, startled at the unexpectedly personal nature
of his question. "Just taking some notes. Part of my research."

"A smart, fine-looking woman like you probably has someone
back home waiting for her," he said, eyeing her in a way that added
to her discomfort.

Before she could recover from incredulity at his forwardness,
and tell him it wasn't really any of his business, he went on.

"I've got girls back home. Girls who'll be right anxious for me
to get back to them."

"That's, uh, very nice, Mr. Scur—"

"Call me, Jesper, ma'am. Please. All the girls do."

The way the words oozed out of his drawl made her cringe.

"You should hear how they call my name when I'm close to
them—I mean, *real* close." He scooted even closer to her. "Maybe
you and I could—"

Amanda was on her feet before he could finish. "I don't think
so, Mr. Scurlock," she said, and turned back towards the others.
She was so repulsed, she wanted to run, but she didn't.

40

Evergreen's immigrant farmers churned the soil, gouged out their irrigation channels and spread their chemical fertilizers. They sprayed pesticides, eradicated uncultivated growth and extracted their produce as it ripened from the ground. The land was fertile, the harvest bountiful. They prospered.

Yet below the wheatfields, the rice paddies and the orange groves, anxiety simmered. Aggression stirred. Unseen, unheard, unfelt beneath the passive meadows of vegetables and grain was an organism that needed no cultivation. An entity that sustained itself, propagating as needed, endowed with a cognizance extending from vestigial to transcendent. A presence but not an animal mind. A simplistic pattern of cells, yet a complex awareness. Its inner dialogue composed not of words, but of concepts, impressions, perceptions. It existed, and it was roused.

❧❧❧❧

Nutrient imbalance...infection...infestation. Incursion of alien root systems confirmed. No response detected to biochemical, bacterial entreaties. No communication. Non-conscious entity confirmed. Extirpation ongoing. Annihilation essential, inevitable. Augment nitrogen, phosphorous intake. Initiate protein, enzyme synthesis. Root crown confirms process. Need for additional or-

176

ganic awareness confirmed. Incursion widespread. Neural impulses extended to all nodes. Threat assessed. Containment necessary. Conflict imminent.

41

Eamon's equilibrium was still shaky when he arrived at the lumber mill. Everyone else was rushing off towards Woodville. He was lucky to be able to walk. Gash clapped him on the back and said, "You're a real timber jockey now." Maybe, but his legs were wobbly, and the adrenalin rush had left him exhausted. He found an out-of-the-way place inside the mill to lie down to recover from the wild ride and, before he knew it, had fallen asleep.

It was nearly sundown when he woke. The nerve-wracking ride, along with the strenuous week of labor, had taken more of a toll on him than he'd realized. He got up and walked the short distance to town.

Even at the edge of the "vill," as the TJs liked to call it, hard partying was in full rampage. One group of inebriated timber jockeys gathered below a rooftop ledge, daring a compatriot who stood on the ledge to jump. He did. Right on top of them. No one seemed seriously hurt, but there was much laughter and several exchanges of Evergreen currency, which led Eamon to believe it had been a sporting wager.

He moved farther into town, and as he neared Tahoe Tilley's he saw a couple—a TJ and one of the bar girls, he assumed—both naked from the waist down. They were going at it in the shadows near the back of the building. When he got closer he recognized the woman. It was Cayenne. He didn't know the guy who had her propped up against the wall.

That it was the gruff, masculine Cayenne shocked him more than the idea of what they were doing out in the open. He found the idea of her having sex a bit revolting, yet mesmerizing at the same time. She opened her eyes and looked right at him. Before he could pretend he wasn't staring, she smiled at him.

Eamon hurried on past, trying to shake the image from his mind. It shouldn't have been so strange, but it was. It was also stimulating. It tempted him to think about venturing into Tilley's and going upstairs with one of the girls. He'd heard plenty of talk about what went on there. The thought was exciting—even more so because he'd never been with a woman. Oh, he'd come close, but he'd never really done it. He'd never been in one place long enough when he was younger to even have a girlfriend. Later, he'd had other priorities.

He had other priorities now, too. He shouldn't go inside. He had to gain access to the company's data system. The information he needed was there. Once he was in, he was certain he could find what he needed. Skills that had gotten him into so much trouble before would come in handy now. All he needed was a portal.

Then again, maybe it was better to wait until later—until he was certain all the company's techs had finished work for the day. The more he thought about it, the more waiting a while seemed a good idea. He told himself it wouldn't hurt to go into Tilley's for just one drink. Maybe he'd even talk with one of the girls.

❧ ❧ ❧

Eamon sat by himself, though he recognized many of the timber jockeys gathered at various tables inside the bar. He was just passing time. He didn't want to get carried away and drink so much he couldn't do what he needed to. Maybe, he thought, he should try his hand at gambling. He wasn't familiar with any of the games he'd seen, but he was certain he could figure them out if he tried.

He saw Gash similarly sitting alone, but decided not to bother him. The man was probably tired of having Eamon in tow all the time. He saw Mousey Farr talking with the same woman he'd spoken to briefly his first night on Evergreen—the woman he'd seen Farr with at the dock. He remembered her name was Sunny, and

179

that she was the one Farr was always talking about. The one he called "my girl." Right now, though, they were arguing about something. As he watched, their discussion became more and more heated. The woman finally got up, as if to leave, and Farr grabbed her arm. She shook off his hand, said something Eamon couldn't hear and stalked off.

She crossed the room in his direction, and he saw her fasten her eyes onto him. Maybe she'd noticed him staring, or maybe he was just the first likely fellow she came across. Anyway, she came straight for him and sat uninvited at his table.

"Hi, there," she said gruffly, forcing a smile. "I'm Sunny. Hey, I remember you. I see you've made it through your first week."

He heard the restrained anger in her voice subsiding.

"Yeah, barely."

"You'll get used to it."

"That's what everybody says."

"Your name's Eamon, right? I'm good with names."

He nodded and glanced over at Farr. He'd been joined by several other timber jocks, who were trying to get his attention. But Farr was staring at Eamon, and his expression wasn't a friendly one.

Sunny followed his gaze and saw who he was looking at. "Ignore him," she said with a flip of her hand. "He thinks he owns me, but he doesn't."

"I thought that..." Eamon started and stopped.

"That I was his girlfriend?" she said derisively. "He likes to think so, but that's not the way it is. I mean, I like him—he's a nice enough guy most of the time, but it's not the way he thinks it is. I'm for rent, not for sale."

She paused and looked around at Farr herself. "I'll say this, for a little guy he's got a ton of nerve. You know what he wants? He wants me stay here and wait until he works off his term, so we can go back to Earth together. Ha!"

She made a sound that was part laugh, part grunt and all ridicule. Yet, despite this, Eamon thought he heard a hint of admiration buried beneath her words.

"Can you imagine that? I'm this close to getting out of here. I'm working my tail off to make it happen as soon as I can, and he wants me to wait. I can't wait for him. I can't wait for nobody. He may *never* get out from under. Do you know, hardly any timber jockeys ever leave this place, even if they work off their terms?"

Eamon shook his head, and she continued her rant.

"It's because most of them can't ever save up enough credit to pay their passage off Evergreen. They drink it away, gamble it away, whore it away." She hesitated a moment as if in thought, then went on. "And even the rare ones who can save some don't usually leave. They get caught up in the life. You know, hooked on the whole timber jockey mystique, like it was a religion or something."

As if suddenly realizing she'd been monopolizing the conversation, she sighed and forced another smile. "So, what about you? What's a kid like you doing here?"

"I'm not a kid," Eamon stated defensively.

"Sure you're not," she replied, as if to mollify him, though he thought she was being sarcastic. "You're a man. You're a man with a real good reason for being here, aren't you?"

"That's right." He took a drink of his beer. "Why are you...?" He stopped.

"What were you going to say?"

"Nothing. You probably don't want to tell me how you got here—on Evergreen, that is."

"You mean why am I a whore?"

"That's not what I—"

"Why is anybody here?" she said, swinging her arm about to indicate the patrons in general. "They've got sentences to fulfill, plea bargains to honor, debts to be paid. The women who work Tilley's are no different. This is just easier than scrubbing somebody's floors or hauling garbage—and more lucrative, too. We're working off our terms just like any timber jockey. Just like you are."

"That's not why I'm here," Eamon said.

"Oh? Then, why *are* you here?"

He hesitated, then decided there was no reason to hold back. "I'm looking for someone."

As if realizing it was a subject he wasn't going to elaborate on, Sunny said, "I'm looking for someone, too." She stared at him and smiled coyly. He was fixated by her exotic eyes. "I'm looking for someone to come upstairs with me. How about it, Eamon? I promise you'll have the time of your life. We'll both have fun, and I'll be one trick closer to getting out of here. How about it? Will you help a damsel in distress?"

Eamon realized his attempts at furtive glances had likely been only too obvious. The flesh exposed by her minimal outfit was smooth and supple. He wanted to go upstairs with her. He wanted to know what it was like to be with a woman before he...

He looked over to where Farr had been sitting. He was gone. The table where he'd been with the other TJs was empty. Where did he go? Eamon looked around. He didn't see him. Maybe his comrades had hustled him off somewhere. Maybe he'd even gone off with another one of the girls.

"Well?" asked Sunny. "Do you want to or not?"

"Sure, yeah, let's go."

42

Gash sat alone in a dark but not so quiet corner. There was no quiet to be had in Tilley's when the timber jocks were in town. That was all right, because the cacophony soon blended into a background buzz of white noise he could shut out. He raised his mug to his lips and took a drink. The beer was cool and bitter.

Left to himself, his thoughts often strayed. He was used to that. He'd gotten good at reining them in so they didn't stray too far—so they didn't wander outside the confines of Evergreen. At the moment, he was wondering about that exobiologist. He remembered her name: Amanda. He wondered whether she'd show up here again. He thought about the kid, Eamon, and wondered what had happened to him after he'd lost track of him at the mill.

He was also curious about Ramos. The old TJ had been acting strange lately. Nothing overt, nothing anyone else had probably noticed. But Gash had. Now he saw him standing across the way, talking with Shay Larimore. It wasn't a "hello, how you doing" conversation either. It was a serious discussion, long and involved. At one point, he saw Ramos point in his direction. Larimore followed the gesture with a glance. There appeared to be a disagreement. Larimore seemed to acquiesce and walked off. Ramos headed his way.

"Beer," Ramos told the barmaid, pausing in front of Gash's table. "Is this a private funeral or can anyone pull up a casket?"

Gash motioned indifferently for him to sit. Ramos did so without speaking, and they sat in silence until the honcho's beer arrived. Ramos sipped it and stared at Gash with a discerning gaze Gash thought seemed judgmental. He liked Ramos; he had since he first met him. In another place, another time, they might have been best of friends.

But this wasn't another time or another place, and circumstances weren't about to change.

Just as Gash was about to ask him what the hell he was looking at, Ramos spoke up.

"I had this pretty palomino once," he began enigmatically. "I really loved that horse. But she broke a leg real bad one day when we were out riding, and I had to shoot her. I loved that horse so much I buried her, because I didn't want to leave her to the buzzards." Ramos took another sip of his beer. "Do you know how big a hole you have to dig to bury a horse?"

He took another drink but remained quiet, just staring into his beer. About the time Gash was going to say something about horses in general, Ramos picked up where he'd left off.

"Afterwards, I fretted that maybe if I'd taken a different trail, or ridden her easier, she might not have broke that leg. I was young, and didn't know any better, so I stewed on it and worried over it until my brain started fraying like an old rope.

"Yeah, I sure did miss that horse. But I knew, as much as I missed her, it wouldn't do me any good to go back and dig her up."

You didn't have to be an astrophysicist to get his point, though Gash didn't particularly care for being preached at.

Was he so obvious? Was he wearing his conscience on his sleeve? He'd known Ramos for years now, and the man had never said a thing. Why now? As an intervention, it was a bit belated.

He took another drink, wiped his mouth and said, by way of changing the subject, "So, what's going on between you and Slick?"

Ramos's eyes narrowed, staring at him. "I thought you were the don't-want-to-get-involved type."

"You're right. Forget I asked. I don't want to know."

Ramos kept looking at him, and Gash got the feeling he was trying to come to a decision. They sat there, nursing their beers, for a few minutes.

Meanwhile, Gash noticed Eamon across the room, one of the Tinas nestled up next to him. He recognized her right away and looked around for Farr. He spotted Mousey not four tables away, watching the pair, apparently sulking. Some other jocks were trying to distract him, but he didn't seem to be going for it.

That Eamon kid sure was a magnet for trouble. This time though, the kid was going to have to handle it himself. He was a man now, a timber jock, whether he liked it or not. And a man had to suffer the consequences of his own actions. Gash knew that better than anyone.

"What do you know about the independence movement?" Ramos asked out of nowhere.

Was that what all the skulking was about? Gash had heard talk—the usual TJ scuttlebutt—but he knew better than to put any credence in that. He'd dismissed the notion as the grousing of a few homesteaders. But if Ramos was involved, and Larimore...

"Not a thing," he answered. "You know, just rumors."

"It's not a rumor, it's real. There's a bunch of mavericks in cahoots that's dead-set on declaring independence."

"Independence from who?"

"From Earth," said Ramos. "From the company."

He had always thought of Ramos as a reliable if simple fellow. He was a good man to work for—tough but fair. Now Gash wondered if the TJ honcho understood the scope of what he was suggesting.

"And you're part of this little cabal?"

Ramos nodded.

"So, why tell me?"

"We're getting together for a little palaver," said Ramos. "I want you to come."

Gash made a noise that was half scoff, half chuckle, but it sounded unconvincing even to him.

"Remember me? The don't-want-to-get-involved type?"

"All I'm asking is that you listen," Ramos said, "just listen. You know me, Gash. I'm not one for sucking down burro's milk. Just listen. We may not be as loco as you think."

Gash shrugged as if to say *Why not?* He took another drink.

Ramos did likewise, stood and motioned for Gash to follow him. Gash glanced at Eamon as he pushed back from the table.

The kid was still talking with Sunny, but Farr and the other TJs were gone. Maybe they'd finally hauled him off somewhere.

He followed Ramos through Tilley's, past a rowdy bunch of TJs who were in the middle of a drunken chorus of "Big Boss Man."

...got me working, boss man,
Working 'round the clock.
I want me a drink of water,
You won't let me stop.
You big boss man,
Can you hear me when I call?
Oh, you ain't so big,
You just tall, that's all...

Ramos led him to the back of the honky-tonk where, not surprisingly, Kruto, arms folded across his chest, stood outside a closed door. The brute eyed Gash with cool calculation but didn't say a thing when Ramos opened the door and they entered the room.

Conversation ceased, and every set of eyeballs focused on Gash. He was the newcomer, and he understood their suspicion. He figured there were about twenty people in the room, a real mix of Evergreen's population. There were townies, like Larimore and Ms. Lizzie from the general store, homesteaders from Evergreen's farm community, a livestock rancher, a few timber jocks—he recognized Lenny Chaltraw and Sam Nishikawa—some miners, even Captain Clemens of the *Sir Real*. One of Larimore's whores was there, too. He remembered Larimore had called her Jelina. Whether she was part of the grand conspiracy or simply window dressing, he couldn't guess.

The door opened, and a man he recognized as a local carpenter walked in, followed by Kruto, who shut the door and stood, arms folded once again.

As if this signaled the beginning of the meeting, discussion ensued, becoming heated at times. To Gash, it sounded like one long litany of complaints, impractical suggestions and arguments for argument's sake. Everyone had a different beef, either with the company or with one of the other factions. Larimore informally chaired the meeting, but for the most part he let the give-and-take run its course without interference, listening as he fingered the triangular patch of hair on his chin.

The current speaker, a farmer by the look of him, seemed to be one of the more rational voices.

"...cost everything I owned to bring my family here, and now I got to pay the company's levy as well? As it is, we pay premium prices for every little thing we import—"

"And the prices keep going up!"

Several voices shouted in agreement with the interruption, but the speaker continued unabated.

"...and yet the prices we get for our surplus harvest, food the company makes a profit on shipping to barren colonies, has been fixed for the five years I've been farming here."

"I say we stop buying, and we stop selling," spoke up another farmer. "Whatever we can't use ourselves we store, we bottle, we can. We won't starve, that's for sure."

"But the company has the mines, and the logging operation. They own all the rights."

"Then we have to stop mining, and stop cutting timber," said Captain Clemens. "It has to be all or nothing."

"If there's a real plan," said one of the miners, "and everyone agrees, the miners will be with you. Most of us got hornswoggled on the deal when we signed up."

Gash knew the kind of labor contract the miners signed to come to Evergreen made them only slightly less subservient than the indentured TJs. Most of them had agreed to it because they had little else going for them. Apparently, that didn't matter to them now.

After the miner spoke up, most eyes turned to Ramos. He studied at the floor, either thinking or maybe shy. When he looked up he was smiling.

"I figure most of the timber jocks are up for good fight," he said.

"That's right!" Chaltraw shouted in agreement.

More discussion ensued, getting raucous at times. Everyone agreed they didn't care for the way the company's marshals acted as the ultimate purveyors of law and order. But the biggest grievance, the one shared by all concerned, was the taxes imposed by the company. It even put a damper on the credit earned by the timber jocks.

GMX charged exorbitant fees to bring colonists to Evergreen, and all transactions were taxed to support what there was in the way of a local bureaucracy. Apparently, the company had decided to put even more of the financial burden on the colonists—three-fold more—and they weren't having it.

"What about a declaration of independence?" asked the carpenter. "Don't we need something like that?"

"Jelina here has been working on writing something," Larimore said, gesturing towards her. "Any of you cocksuckers with literary aspirations can work with her on it if you want."

That led to a number of shouted suggestions for such a document, some more pragmatic than others. Eventually, Larimore prevailed over the noise and steered the debate to more practical matters.

Gash watched Ramos. The old-timer said very little, yet seemed to go along with the general attitude. He wondered how much Ramos, how much any of them, knew about the rigors of revolution.

The talk continued, until Larimore waved his arms to get their attention.

"We are agreed, then?" he said. It was half question, half statement. "We have to stick together, regardless of what petty differences we may have. And when the time comes, you're all going to have to convince your own people. For now, just gauge their temperature. See where their thinking's at. This..." He swept his arm to encompass everyone in the room. "...remains just between us for now. No one knows unless it becomes absolutely necessary. Until then, encourage resentment of the company, let tempers chafe."

"For how long?" asked one of the miners.

"Not long. The first step is self-reliance. We have to be certain we have the food and materiel necessary to support ourselves. Because the first thing those cocksuckers are going to do is cut us off. We have to be ready to hold out indefinitely."

Heads nodded in agreement, and one of the farmers chimed in, "We already provide all of the produce and fresh meat on Evergreen. What we don't have we can live without."

There was a clamor of assent salted with bravado.

"You're going to have to be prepared to fight as well," said Larimore above the noise. "The company's not going to just give in. We've got to be ready to meet violence with violence."

It was as if he'd thrown a bucket of cold water over the room, but Gash knew he was right. GMX wasn't about to let this ragtag group of colonials take over what they'd invested so much in. Not to mention what the bureaucrats on Earth would have to say about it.

The hush was broken by Kruto, who slammed his fist into his open palm and proclaimed, "God be with us!"

Several ideas pertaining to forming a militia were bandied about, and other assorted details debated. When the discussions began breaking into smaller groups, Ramos turned to Gash.

"Well, what do you think?"

"I think there's going to be trouble."

Ramos shrugged. "You can't break a horse unless you're ready to take a fall."

"Why you, Ramos? Why this?"

Ramos considered before answering. "Evergreen's my home. At least, I've been here long enough to think of it that way. The company's pushing too hard—making up too many new rules. No man's going to tell me what to do in my own home."

Larimore came over, but before he could say a word, Gash spoke up.

"You had a camera on Oshima that night, didn't you? You recorded her. It was all part of this, wasn't it? Some kind of blackmail scheme."

"As I said, political leverage."

"You can call it whatever you want, it's still blackmail."

Larimore got a look of righteous indignation. "For independence, I'll blackmail, steal, kill, whatever it takes."

One look at him, hearing the resolve in his voice, Gash was sure he would. What he wasn't so sure of was whether the saloon keeper truly cared spit about liberty, or if it was all just about business.

"So, will this independence extend to your girls, like Jelina there, or are they still going to be your chattel?"

"They're not any different than you timber jockeys," Larimore said indignantly. "They're just paying their debts, making the same choices women have been making for centuries. They can find some kind of grunt work or they can sell their pussies. Jelina had a choice—she made it. Your TJ friend, Cayenne, she had that choice. She went another way. You had a choice, too, didn't you?"

Gash turned away. He had nothing to say—no reply to counter Larimore's logic, as warped as it was. The man was right about one thing, though. Everyone made their own choices...and had to live with them.

"We've all got pasts we're running away from, don't we?" added Larimore.

What did he mean by that? Gash looked at Ramos. Did he know? No, he couldn't know.

"So, why invite me to this shindig? What do you want me for?"

"I told Shay and some of the others how you were an engineer," said Ramos. "We figured your savvy could come in handy."

"Sorry. I wish you the best of luck with your little rebellion, I really do. But I'm not interested."

"A lot of people are counting on you, amigo."

"That's as good a reason as any why I should stay away."

He looked at Larimore.

The tavern owner didn't appear surprised, much less disappointed. He shrugged and said as he turned away, "Yeah, well you can only dance between the raindrops for so long."

A colorful metaphor, thought Gash, but *shit storm* is more apropos for what you have in mind. It was going to come down. It was going to pour. There was nothing he could do about that. But when it started coming down on him, Gash didn't want to be mired by obligation.

He made for the door. Kruto stood in his way. For a moment, Gash considered they might not trust him to keep their secret. He looked back at Ramos and Larimore. The whoremaster nodded and Kruto stepped aside. Gash got out while the getting was good.

He left Tilley's and headed for the flophouse. On the way, he pulled out his pipe, filled it and lit up. He inhaled and began thinking about the would-be insurgents. Most of them weren't hard, desperate men, by any means. He wondered if they had it in them.

Would they be able to do what was necessary when the time came? When grizzled destiny looked them in the eyes and held them accountable. His feelings wavered from ridicule to pity to admiration.

He wondered if they truly had any idea what they were doing. Did they realize what they were playing at? The danger, the possible repercussions? Did they have any chance to succeed? Well, at least they were standing up for themselves. They were doing something. Who was he to criticize? All he wanted to do was get stoned.

43

She was so tired from the day's journey she should have fallen asleep immediately. Instead, her mind was as active as her muscles were sore. Filamena lay next to Luis inside their small tent, her arm draped over him. She knew by his breathing noises he was sound asleep. Otherwise, everything was quiet.

Yet the stillness only exacerbated her unrest. She opened her eyes. She wanted to sleep, but the harder she tried the more her mind wandered.

Max was out there somewhere, lying in his tent. Being around him so much, seeing him day after day, walking next to him along the trails reminded her of the physical attraction they shared. The more she tried not to think about it, the more it wasn't possible. Even now, she could slip out of her tent and go to him, feel his strong young arms around her, taste his kisses. She knew she'd have no trouble sleeping then.

It was fantasy. She wasn't going anywhere. Better it had remained a fantasy and she'd never given in to temptation. Yes, she was attracted to Max, but that physical attraction was all they shared. That, and a certain distance from Luis. Beyond that, she and Max had little in common. His unrestrained infatuation proved that.

It also proved she'd been a foolish girl. No, she didn't even have that excuse. She wasn't a girl anymore. She'd been a foolish old woman, looking for love in the arms of a younger man—the wrong man.

She snuggled closer to her husband, holding him tight. He stirred only slightly.

She had been reminded of something else on this journey. She'd been reminded how much she loved Luis. For all his flaws, he was a good man, an honorable, decent man who truly cared for her. Though he was often too preoccupied with his work to show it, he adored her, trusted her. She'd violated that trust in the worst possible way.

Part of her wanted to tell him, to confess her scarlet sins the way she had been raised to confess her sins to the Church. She no longer considered herself a religious woman, but the idea of absolution, of washing away her guilt and starting anew, was alluring. The temptation to relieve herself of the burden she carried was enormous. But it was selfish. What would such a confession do to Luis? She knew her husband. It would destroy him. It would destroy *them*—their marriage, Luis's fragile relationship with his son. In the end, no one would be better for it. The guilt was hers, and she'd have to bear it.

Filamena closed her eyes. Best not to think about it—not now. She tried to empty her mind. She had to get some sleep, or she'd never be able to keep up with the others tomorrow.

44

A night spent in the embrace of happy-smoke dreams left Gash groggy and morose long after he woke. He was still weaning himself from the lethargy, and waiting for his breakfast to arrive, when an agitated homesteader entered the little café and ordered coffee.

"You look like shit, Earl," said the café owner as he poured a cup.

"I've been up all night. Some kind of damn animals eating my crops. The hell of it is, they're doing it from underground, chewing up the roots just enough to kill them. We looked all night and never did catch one of the varmints."

"You say from underground?"

"That's what I said. And I'm not the only one. They hit Andrews and Gutierrez the day before. Same thing—ate the roots right off them. Must be some kind of underground rodent we've never seen before."

"Maybe it's worms," offered someone else.

"It's not worms," asserted the farmer, "I know what worm damage looks like. These things tore the roots and didn't leave no trace. I'm going to tell the company about it, see if they got some kind of traps or repellant or something."

"Shit, the company won't do a damn thing," said another patron. "They'll sit on their asses as usual."

"They got to do something," the farmer groused. "If they don't, it could ruin us. Then what would Oshima eat?"

"Hell, they'd just ship in some fancy food from Earth for her."

The farmer dismissed the idea with an angry wave of his hand.

Gash thought it unlikely that, after so many years, a new pest would suddenly appear and cause such havoc. There'd been no previous problems growing Earth crops on Evergreen. In fact they'd thrived.

He wondered if this sudden infestation had anything to do with the colonials' independence movement. He wouldn't be surprised if the company had one or more spies within the rebel coterie. Maybe they'd found a way to damage the crops in order to give the revolutionaries second thoughts. It would be like busting up your nose to spite your face, but he wouldn't put it past them.

His breakfast arrived, and he went to work on it, though he wasn't feeling especially hungry. The church bell sounded from up the road, and he glanced out the window. It was a gray day, and he wondered if it was going to rain. It hadn't rained in some time—a couple of months at least. It was the longest dry spell he could remember since he'd come to Evergreen.

Except for the agitated farmer, it was a quiet morning in the vill, like most Sundays were. Funday's carousing always lasted long into the night and early morning, so that by sunrise most of the timber jocks were dead to the world, lying in some flophouse, whorehouse or alley sleeping it off.

There was a small contingent of TJs who, despite their herculean debauchery of the night before, got up in time to attend religious services, which were held in the town's lone place of worship. It was a nonsectarian affair that attracted a mix of Evergreen denizens, from TJs and homesteaders to townies and company men—people who couldn't get along without a little organized supplication, even on this backwater outpost of civilization.

Kruto passed by with a trio of TJs in tow. They'd likely been rousted by the scruff of the neck and bullied into joining him. It was a Sunday morning ritual for the giant Russian, but Gash had to wonder if the pleas for forgiveness uttered by Boris Krutonov were heard, much less answered. If there was absolution to be had for a sadistic former soldier-assassin who was so psychotic even the military had renounced his services, then maybe there was hope for him. Unlike Kruto though, Gash wasn't about to pray to some unseen omnipotent being for redemption.

Any thought he might have given to matters of faith and divinity were intruded upon by Cayenne, who entered the café apparently looking for him. She grabbed an empty chair, flung it next to his small table and plopped down without invitation.

"Well, your turtle's really fucked up now," she said. "He's gone and got himself arrested."

"Eamon?"

Cayenne nodded. "Yep. Those company cocksuckers have got him locked up in their little jail."

"What for?"

"Hell, I don't know," said Cayenne. "All I heard is that he's in big trouble and they got him."

"Damn," Gash muttered under his breath and got up. "I'd better find out what's going on."

"Mind if I finish off your breakfast there?"

"Knock yourself out. If you see Ramos, tell him where I went—in case I don't come back."

Cayenne, already chewing on a link of sausage, nodded in reply.

❦ ❦ ❦

It took the better part of an hour, but Gash managed to bull his way into Administrator Oshima's office. Now he stood waiting for the administrator to make an appearance—standing because there were no chairs in the office other than the one behind the administrator's desk.

On the desk, he noted, was a sculpture, of sorts. It had originally been a length of insulated conduit, maybe an inch or so in diameter. The insulation had been cut off at both ends and numerous pieces of metal tubing exposed. The tubing was painted black and bent outward at the sculpture's base to represent the roots of a tree, while those at the top formed the branches. Thin splatters of solder created the tree's leaves. The remaining insulation had been lathered with a thick black substance that gave it the appearance of bark.

The black-and-silver artwork was eye-catching in the otherwise colorless office, and situated in a prominent place for all to see. Gash thought it an odd representation, juxtaposed as it was on this world of green. He wasn't sure what it said about the administrator.

Oshima finally stalked through the door without acknowledging his presence and went behind her desk. She was reading something off the pad she carried, and didn't look up until she had sat and set it aside.

"I remember you," she said, and her glare made any further comment unnecessary. "So, what's your business with this criminal? You're not even his supervisor." She was annoyed, and referred to her pad again. "What's this Eamon Hankala to you?"

"What's he done?" countered Gash. As he spoke, he realized he knew that name. Hankala. It was one of the names he would never forget.

Oshima balked at his audacity, and he watched her seethe. Then she seemed to reconsider.

"He broke into one of our out-buildings and was discovered attempting to gain access to secure company files. He's going to be charged, prosecuted and given a long sentence. I imagine he'll be hauling timber until he's your age," she said, her thin lips curling into a spiteful smile.

"No, he's not," said Gash.

"I beg your pardon."

"You're not going to charge him. You're going to release him and expunge any record of this incident."

"And why would I do that?" Her tone was suspicious.

"Because if you don't, then I'm going to make certain your handiwork with a whip is on-screen news back on Earth. And I know just the people who can make that happen," he lied.

A flicker of concern crossed Oshima's face before she regained control. "What makes you think that would bother me in the least?"

"I'd say a person in your position can't afford any bad publicity. I don't think the company would hesitate for a moment to replace you if they thought your appetites were bad for business. You're just another cog in their wheel, and they're not going to let it stop turning to protect *your* ass."

Gash could see her mind working, playing out various scenarios and the permutations of each. He was about to throw some more gas on the inflammatory threat when she acquiesced.

"All right. I'll release him to you."

"And erase any record of his arrest."

"Yes, yes." She sounded annoyed again. "But if there's a second such incident, I won't be as lenient," she added, to get in the final word and reassert her authority. "And I'll remember this."

He didn't bother to reply.

45

Jimiyu didn't know how high they'd gone, but he knew they'd been traveling more or less uphill since their trek began seven days ago. The higher the elevation, the thicker the morning fog and the longer it lasted. It was almost mid-day before the murk dissolved and the sunlight broke through.

As if it had been cued by the sunshine, Jimiyu heard the sound of running water. Before he managed to pinpoint the sound, the expedition came upon a small lagoon fed by a slender but soaring waterfall. The water spilling out of the butte that loomed in front of them was strikingly red.

Chanya gasped.

"The damn mountain is bleeding," Scurlock muttered.

The professor's wife stared upward, shielding her eyes from the sun's glare. "It's beautiful," she said.

Vincent nodded. "It's even redder than the river."

"There must be a high concentration of iron ore up there," said Professor Escobedo.

Harley shrugged off his pack and abruptly sat. "This is it."

"This is what?" asked McCroy.

"This is it. This is where I found that woodcarving. Somewhere around here, anyway—I think."

"You *think*?"

"Yeah, well, I'm tired, and I don't exactly remember. It was somewhere around this waterfall, I remember that."

"But there's nothing here," said Nikira.

Scurlock sneered, "Looks like a dead end."

"What do we do now?" wondered Jimiyu.

Much to his disappointment, no one suggested turning back.

"We could spread out—scan different directions," suggested Vincent.

McCroy shook his head. "No, we climb," he said.

"It's pretty steep," said the professor, gauging the rugged hill in front of them.

"It's more than likely your artifact was washed down from up there," said McCroy, his gaze following the course of the falls. "And even if we don't find anything, from that vantage we'll be able to get a good look at the surrounding area." He nudged Harley with his boot. "Let's go."

"Not me. I'm finished." Harley looked like he wasn't about to move.

McCroy kicked him just hard enough to show he meant business. "You're through when I say you're through. Now get up and get moving."

Harley glared at him, but got up.

They fell into rough formation behind McCroy and spent the rest of the day trudging up the steep, rugged incline. Their path proved to be studded with slabs of granite. Some of the rocky deposits were massive enough to force a detour.

Jimiyu watched Nikira with both admiration and loathing. His determined friend attacked the hill with tenacity, as if the farther he went the stronger he became. Jimiyu had had enough climbing to last him a lifetime. Still, he didn't complain—at least not outwardly.

On the positive side, those hairy creatures weren't following them anymore. Shortly after they'd begun the climb, they'd looked down and seen a group of the animals gathered below, sniffing and snorting. Dr. Rousch had been curious about their reactions, and mentioned later that she believed the beasts were no longer trailing them. Why they had given up she could only speculate. Whatever the reason, Jimiyu was grateful. They were so strange, so human-like in some ways, they made his skin crawl.

Now that he no longer fretted about the creatures, his mind wandered. He began thinking about how he would describe to his students what they were climbing. Was it a small mountain or simply a large foothill? What was the difference? How did you determine...?

He caught his thoughts meandering. He realized it wasn't that important a distinction. He figured if he was focusing on such inanity the fatigue must be wearing at his mind more than he realized. He shook it off and, instead, concentrated on each step.

What seemed like hours later, though was likely only one, he stepped onto the crest where, abruptly, the ground leveled off onto an expansive plateau, thick with rich, green vegetation. He staggered slightly, as much from exhaustion as the sight before him—an imperious wall of shrubbery, towering trees and tangled vines. It was a sublime tableau of nature, a jade acropolis, he thought. A crown of creation.

"It kind of takes your breath away, doesn't it?" said Professor Escobedo. "At least, it would if I had any left."

"It's like a magnificent *terazza*," his wife responded.

Nikira took three steps, stopped and held out his arms. "Look at this. This could be Eden."

The others might have thought he was speaking metaphorically, but Jimiyu knew better.

"Yeah, but man got kicked out of Eden," said McCroy, looking at Nikira, "didn't he?"

McCroy adjusted his pack and started forward. Scurlock chuckled. Nikira ignored them both and moved on. The expedition followed.

Though they were traveling more or less on level ground now, the dense foliage slowed their progress. They hadn't gone far when Max said out loud, "Where are the birds?" Jimiyu wondered what birds he was talking about. Max added, "I haven't seen a single bird since we landed on Evergreen."

"There aren't any," responded Dr. Rousch, bending down to adjust the straps of her sorrel boots. "At least, not any you'll see flying around in this region. I've only come across two bird species during my time on Evergreen—a sort of prairie chicken the locals trap and eat, and what I call a ground sparrow, a plump, stubby little thing that lives in a shallow burrow like a rodent. Both are flightless."

"No birds that fly?" inquired the professor's wife.

"Not that I've seen. I can only theorize the evolution of flying creatures on this planet was stunted due to gravitational factors." Dr. Rousch shrugged and added, "Of course, there may be other causalities as well."

"A world with trees and no birds?" Chanya shook her head as though such a thing were unnatural.

For the next half-hour or so, no one spoke. Jimiyu wondered if they were contemplating the idea of no birds, or simply too tired to talk. He guessed it was the latter. He certainly had no inclination to waste what little energy he had left on useless chatter.

Soon, McCroy had his machete out again, cutting them a path through the jungle-like growth. When he paused to rest he said, "We're not going to be able to see anything inside this salad bowl. I've got to find some higher ground. Jesper, get up that tree there and have a look."

His associate grumbled as he took off his pack, but then scurried up the tree with surprising agility. Its twisted gray boughs were broad enough and spaced far enough apart that he was able to climb easily to a point where he could stand and look out over the grove's canopy.

"There are some cliffs over that way," he called out, "about sixty degrees to the left."

By the time Scurlock scrambled down and retrieved his pack, McCroy was already cutting a new path, followed closely by his big cat and Dr. Nikira. The rest straggled along with what Jimiyu could only describe as a lack of enthusiasm. He felt it himself. They'd come so far, and seen nothing for their efforts. Happy Harley no longer knew where he was—if he ever did—and now it seemed they were wandering aimlessly, hoping they might come across something of interest. He wanted to speak out, to denounce the perpetuation of their journey as foolishness. Yet one look at Nikira, at the rigid determination on his face, was enough to keep Jimiyu silent. Some men had to recognize their own folly, or they would never see it.

Something near to him moved in the brush. Jimiyu froze momentarily and listened. He heard nothing, saw nothing, so he went on, though with heightened awareness of his surroundings. His gaze was still downcast, looking for creepy, crawly forest creatures, when McCroy called out.

"There they are."

Jimiyu looked up and saw they'd breached the thicket and emerged into a clearing of sorts. Ahead of them, still forty or fifty yards away, was a wall of reddish-yellow cliffs that grew out of the green mountainside like an ulcer. The cliffs were pocked with caves.

"They look manmade," Professor Escobedo said excitedly. "Eroded, certainly, but they have at least a rudimentary resemblance to the Anasazi cliff dwellings at Mesa Verde."

"That's nothing, look over here," McCroy suggested calmly.

They'd all been so busy staring at the cliffs they hadn't noticed the conglomeration of large rocks McCroy was inspecting. Yet, it was more than a sporadic array of stones. It was, undeniably, a structure of some sort. The huge stones had been laid together in a pattern, one upon another, forming walls and even an arch that reminded Jimiyu of the pictures he'd seen of Stonehenge. The crude structure was bearded with lichen and patches of moss so dark green as to look black.

Every member of the expedition stepped gingerly in and around the stone framework. There was a long silence, as if awe rendered them speechless. Moving closer, it was obvious to Jimiyu that much of the structure had deteriorated—the stones were pitted and cracked, and several had collapsed over the years. Or was it centuries?

"Astounding!" Professor Escobedo was the first to break the silence.

Jimiyu realized what the rough semi-circular framework made him think of.

"It's like a temple," he said, then looked immediately to Nikira. His old friend was standing in what might have once been the center of the edifice, his arms outstretched, turning slowly in place.

Nikira dropped to his knees and stared up at the early evening sky. "Great is the Lord," he said, "and most worthy of praise in the city of our God, His holy mountain."

46

Amanda idly fingered the medicine bundle hanging at her throat. Not because she believed it possessed any supernatural powers, but simply out of distraction. An uneasy astonishment crept over her as she stared at the creation that sprouted from the forest floor. There was no randomness about it, no suggestion that it could have been an accident of nature. Someone had put it there. Someone had built it long ago.

Despite its primitive structure, and the fact it was overgrown with creepers and lianas, the site inspired a certain awe. She felt it, as she was sure the others did. They'd discovered something not known to exist. What it was, exactly, she wasn't sure. Remains of a crude civilization? Or, like the hives of Mars, something more akin to the innate architectural skills of the American beaver?

It didn't really matter. What mattered was that it was here. It was astounding, and everyone felt it. No one seemed even the slightest bit put off when McCroy tried to throw cold water on their enthusiasm.

"Not much of a city," he said to Nikira.

Nikira ignored him.

"We don't know what we'll find," Professor Escobedo suggested. "This could be just a fragment of a much larger community. We won't know until we survey the entire area."

"Community?" said Harley, even more astonished than the others. "No one's ever lived out here."

"Maybe it was the Native American colonists who built this—the Washoe," suggested Max.

"Not that I ever heard of."

"These look like they were here long before anyone from Earth ever set foot on Evergreen," Amanda added.

"At first glance, I'd have to agree," the professor said.

"Judge not according to the appearance," Nikira said, looking as if he were in a world of his own, "but judge righteous judgment."

Professor Escobedo got right to work, examining the stonemasonry of the structure's foundation. His wife and son looked on while the other members of the expedition explored randomly. McCroy and Scurlock were especially diligent, searching each nook and cranny they came across. It all seemed rather chaotic to Amanda, but then, it wasn't as if the professor had a team of trained archaeologists to work with.

She could only imagine the excitement such a site held for him, yet he didn't show it. He was very serious, very businesslike. Maybe past disappointments tempered his demeanor.

Apart from the stone edifice, she noticed stacks of smaller rocks as well as partially petrified fragments of thatch, all half-buried and overgrown by weeds. Could they be the remnants of what were once smaller shelters—huts or maybe storage bins of some sort? The way the forest materials had been joined reminded her of the nests the ursu made. Could there have been a primitive civilization here at one time? Could a community of ursu have lived here after the civilization fell?

Something moved atop one of the stone arches. She was about to duck when she saw it was another of the huge lizards, like the one McCroy's cat had caught. This one was bigger—maybe five feet from head to tail. Disturbed by all the activity, it crawled slowly along the stone parapet, likely looking for a less noisy place to sun itself.

McCroy saw it, too. He glanced at Amanda with a half-smile, acknowledgment of something they'd shared, and checked the reptile again. He watched it long enough to determine it wasn't a threat then continued to reconnoiter.

Amanda wondered if what Scurlock had told her was true. Did he and McCroy really expect to find treasure in this place? Was that why they'd come? If so, she was certain they'd discover nothing but disappointment. Except for the massive stone construction, the site didn't offer much.

McCroy was right about one thing, though. It certainly didn't look like any "City of God" she could imagine. She wondered what Nikira thought. Was he disheartened, or still brimming with faith?

"Over here!" Victor Boorman called out. "Dr. Nikira, Professor, scan this!"

Professor Escobedo stopped what he was doing and ambled over to see what was so fascinating it had excited the young man. Everyone else hurried to see as well. Scurlock brushed by her in his rush. She could almost see the dollar signs in his eyes.

Boorman tore away a patch of dead creepers twining haphazardly over the stone walls to get a better look at whatever it was he'd seen beneath the tangle. Once he'd cleared a small area he stood back.

Chiseled into the rock was a pattern of engravings. Wind, rain and time had worn away at them so that most were barely discernible. Whether they were images or the symbols of some language, Amanda couldn't say, but there was no doubting what was there was the product of some kind of sentience. You didn't have to be a world-famous archaeologist to realize it. Crude stone structures were one thing, but this was something else. This was a communication from the past—even if it couldn't be read.

She wondered if everyone realized it meant that, at one time, a species of at least rudimentary intelligence existed on Evergreen—an intelligence not of Earth.

No one said anything. Like Amanda, they seemed to be wrestling with the idea of such a discovery. Everyone except Scurlock. He turned away with a grunt of disgust and went to continue looking for his treasure.

Boorman pulled away more of the dead vines, clearing a wider area. Amanda saw something else there—something larger. So did Nikira. He stepped up quickly to help Boorman, almost pushing him aside in his exuberance. When it was done, he stepped back.

Nothing could have stunned her more than what she saw carved into the rock face. Larger and more distinct than the other marks because it had been chiseled deeper, there was no doubting what it was. There, on the inner wall of the dilapidated stone edifice, was a vivid engraving matching closely in detail Nikira's artifact—his Tree of Life.

47

Cash watched the sky sprites cavort across the sunset-layered horizon as he waited for Eamon's release. Blood red and midnight blue were the colors of the evening, bold as they were ebullient. His eyes absorbed the dancing vision, but his focus was elsewhere.

Ramos's desire to enlist him into the ranks of insurgency weighed on him. The problem was, as much as he wanted to avoid involvement, the idea appealed to his inner anarchist. He'd been on Evergreen long enough to have gotten a clear picture of how the company ran roughshod over the colonists. The indentured timber jockeys might have composed their own dirges, but the homesteaders and others who'd given up everything to colonize a new world deserved better.

He certainly had no love for GMX or its methods. He didn't particularly care for Oshima's smug brand of despotism, either. He wouldn't mind rattling her cage. Still, such a course required obligation, accountability. He wanted none of that. He'd had enough of that to last a lifetime.

All of which only served to remind him of the name Oshima had used. Hankala—Eamon Hankala, she'd said. He must be related—it was too much of a coincidence. If so, then…

A marshal opened the door. Eamon emerged, looking ruffled but apparently with nothing broken. If they'd roughed him up any, the bruises didn't show.

The marshal pointed his shock stick at Gash. Gash turned as Eamon approached, and they headed down the road. When they were out of earshot of the marshal, he spoke, his gaze straight ahead.

"What the hell were you doing trying to break into the company's computer system? You were this close..." He held up two fingers an inch apart. "...to spending the rest of your life spitting bark."

"How did you do it? How you'd get me out?"

"Let's just say it was an exchange of favors." Gash stopped and looked at him like a stern parent. "Don't let it happen again, because I won't be there next time," he said, picking up the pace again. "I'm all out of favors."

Eamon followed him but didn't speak. They were far enough from Woodville's hub that the road was quiet, deserted this time of the evening. Up ahead, Gash saw the lights and heard the bustle of the town. It wouldn't be as boisterous as Funday night, but the TJs would still be out rocking the vill with vigorous intensity until first light of Riverday, when they'd drag themselves to the dock and head back to their emerald asylum.

"Thanks," Eamon finally said. "Thanks for coming after me."

"So, are you going to tell me what you were doing?"

Eamon stopped, and so did Gash.

"I was looking for a name—the name of a timber jockey. And I found it. He's here. I saw enough to confirm that before they grabbed me."

"What are you talking about? Who's here? Who are you looking for?"

"The man who killed my mother."

Black expectation bit into Gash's gut like hot steel.

"So that's why you're here on Evergreen? That's why you enlisted to be a timber jockey?"

Eamon nodded. "It happened years ago, when I was still in school. I swore I'd find him. I learned his name—I even saw a picture of him once, briefly. As soon as I was old enough, I did everything I could to find him, track him down. I finally learned he'd been sent to Evergreen as an indentured worker. Now I'm certain he's here, and I'm going to find him."

"Then what?" Gash asked, though he saw the answer in Eamon's eyes.

"Then I'm going to kill him."

"So, it's all about revenge."

Eamon looked at him with an expression that added twenty years to his boyish face. "It's about justice." He paused, and his expression changed. "It's about how I..."

He didn't finish. It sounded as if he'd been about to reveal something he kept securely locked away.

"Killing someone isn't that easy."Gash tried to sound convincing but was too caught up in his own emotions to carry it off. "If this fellow you're after is really a killer, he's not going to hesitate. You just might. If he's killed once, he could kill again."

"Thirteen," said Eamon. "My mother was one of thirteen people he killed."

A chill colder than the void of space coursed through Gash. His apprehension, his dread, solidified. Thirteen. The implication of the number immobilized him, inside and out. He gathered himself with an infusion of denial and, even though he knew the answer, asked, "What's his name?"

"Brandon." The words spat from his tongue like venom. "Paul Brandon."

It was a name Gash hadn't heard in years, except in his own mind. It was a name ripe with nightmares and malignant remorse.

"Paul, we've got a problem with a pressure equalization valve in the transfer chamber airlock."

"You sure it's not just air bubbles in the coolant line?"

"Not likely."

"All right, tell the shuttle commander to back off until we find the problem."

"He's not going to like it."

"Too bad."

"Okay, you're the duty engineer...Shuttle commander confirms a hold on docking procedures. I won't bother passing on the expletives."

"Thanks for that."

"Now what? The pressure control assembly just went offline."

"Get those passengers out of the transfer chamber and—"

"Paul, it's a micrometeorite incursion."

"Where?"

"One of the chamber's high-pressure tanks."

"Get those people out—now!"

"There's no time. That tank's going to explode. It'll depressurize the entire station. You've got to blow the transfer chamber hatch now!"

"There are thirteen people in there!"

"You've got to do it, Paul. You've got to blow it now!"

48

Staying by Luis's side, trying to help him by doing whatever she could, soon proved to be as dull as their marriage. Yet, at the same time, her husband's dedication to his work, his intense preoccupation with the tiniest detail, also endeared him to her. Filamena knew it was a contradiction. Maybe that's how love was measured, by a string of little contradictions. If you accepted them, if you were able to immerse yourself in them, that's when you knew you were truly in love.

Well, love or not, she still found the whole archaeological process tedious. They hadn't found anything even remotely exciting since they first discovered the tree-like relief cut into one of the stone slabs. Since then, there had been nothing but a wearisome collection of obscure little scratch marks, shallow depressions Luis called "pit houses" and some timeworn artifacts that may or may not have once been tools. Luis found each discovery exciting, no matter how minute or seemingly insignificant, but Filamena quickly tired of brushing the dirt away from rock fragments and mud shards as if she were dusting rare china.

She wished she'd gone off to explore the caves with Max and Dr. Rousch. She'd actually felt a twinge, seeing them go off together—her erstwhile young lover and the lanky exobiologist. Was it jealousy? How silly was that? How so unlike her. Max appeared to have conceded his obsession with her. At least, he hadn't approached her for several days, or even hinted at their past relationship. Maybe he'd grown up enough to know it was time for him to move on, to forget her.

The idea should have carried with it relief, not wistful longing. She should be glad he was directing his youthful hormones elsewhere—she *was* glad—not that she thought he'd be interested in the earnest intellectual type. Dr. Rousch was too much like his father.

Yet Luis and Max were getting along better; the enmity that had existed before appeared to be buried. They were speaking, and that was an improvement. She wondered what Luis thought about it, or if he thought about it at all.

"Luis, how is it between you and Maximo?"

He was engaged in a detailed examination of a small stone shaped roughly like a chisel.

"This could have been used to carve the petroglyphs," he said excitedly, as though he either hadn't heard or hadn't understood her question. "See how it fits in my hand just so, and how the—"

"Luis, did you hear what I said?"

He looked at her. "What, dear?"

"I asked you how things were going between you and Maximo."

"Fine, just fine," he muttered, his attention returning to the article in hand. "Maximo's fine. I'll have to show him this."

With that, he went back to work. Filamena could tell he was fixated, absorbed in concepts and concerns she couldn't share. She didn't pursue her inquiry. Instead, she put down her little brush and sat back.

She looked out over the encampment and watched as Chanya tried to get Dr. Nikira to eat something. Since they'd arrived at this place and discovered the symbol that matched his artifact, the priest had stayed pretty much to himself, kneeling at the edge of the clearing, away from the others. It looked as if he'd spent the night, and most of the day, praying. What exactly he prayed for, she had no idea. Did he really expect God to suddenly appear before him with some kind of spiritual directive?

Whatever he expected, he apparently had no time for mortal concerns. He shooed Chanya away, refusing her offering of food, and did likewise when Jimiyu tried to coerce him to sleep. Apparently, he expected his vigil to sustain him.

"Find anything interesting, Professor?"

She hadn't seen McCroy walk up. He held one of the battery-powered lamps.

"No treasure maps, if that's what you mean," she responded. "Where's your cat?"

"Boorman and the fungus-head wanted to reconnoiter the surrounding area, so I sent Jesper and Thor with them. I'm going to see what's in those caves up there."

"My son and Dr. Rousch are already up there somewhere," said Luis.

"Oh, yeah?" McCroy looked up as if he were trying to figure out which of the many caves they were in.

"Why don't you go with Mr. McCroy, dear," Luis suggested. "I'm certain you're bored with this dreary puttering of mine by now."

"Sure," said McCroy, "come on."

"All right," she replied, dusting off her hands.

She started to stand, but McCroy grabbed her arm and pulled her easily to her feet. They locked eyes for just a moment.

"Let's go," he said, turning toward the cliffs.

"Let me know if you find anything interesting," offered Luis, his attention already back on the stone implement.

It took them some time to scale the slope that made up the less precipitous side of the cliff face. When they got to the top, they rested their legs and looked around. They were high enough to see across a vast valley that stretched for miles to the south of their position; a river meandered through the center of the vale.

"Is that the same river we came down?"

"No," McCroy said, "it's running perpendicular, and it's much smaller. Probably a tributary."

"So, you know where we are?"

"I know how to get back, if that's what you mean. What this place is, or was, I have no idea." He chuckled. "It's no City of God, though, I'm sure of that much."

"What makes you so certain?"

He looked at her like she was a starry-eyed little girl. "You've seen the same thing I have. No self-respecting god I know would call this place home. A bunch of rock piles and—"

Max came running out of the cave nearest them, an ecstatic look on his face. He saw them and rushed over.

"Paintings," he said breathlessly. "There are paintings on the cave walls!"

49

He no longer felt the drag of Evergreen's gravity, but the saddle of his burden still weighed on him. His hatred for the man who killed his mother was as keen as ever, yet there was something else. He knew it was there, though he refused to acknowledge it. It had been there since her death. Try as he might, he couldn't deny it. His guilt, entombed beneath a capstone of self-incrimination, was still there.

He couldn't blame fate. He couldn't blame anyone but himself. If he'd never hacked into that computer, he wouldn't have been expelled. His mother never would have had to come get him. She never would have been boarding that shuttle. The blame was his—his and Brandon's.

Now, he'd gotten into trouble again, and Gash had come to get him. He wondered what his friend had traded for his freedom. He didn't want anyone to have to pay for his mistakes—not ever again.

He studied Gash as they feathered their paddles and their dugout canoe coasted down one of the canals that lined the flotilla of TJ City. The older man was strong, resolute but fair, and intelligent. Eamon wondered what he'd done, what had happened to him that he'd ended up here, a timber jockey on an outland world. What was his crime? Where did he fail? Was it just an ugly twist of fate that landed him here?

Eamon couldn't believe he'd done anything too terrible. He didn't kid himself he was such an excellent judge of people, but he was sure Gash wasn't that kind of person.

Maybe...maybe if he'd grown up with a father like Gash, he wouldn't have gotten into so much trouble. Maybe if he'd had a father at all, it would have been different. Maybe then his mother would still be...

"What's that?" asked Gash.

"What's what?"

"That thing around your neck you're holding on to."

He hadn't realized he grabbed hold of his medallion.

"It's something my mother gave me a long time ago. It's an engraving of Icarus. Do you know who Icarus was?"

Gash nodded.

"She gave it to me, she said, as a reminder to never fly too close to the sun—to be careful. But I never was. I never listened to her when I should have."

50

Jimiyu was the last one to reach the cave entrance. He hesitated outside the cavern's maw. He didn't like dark places, and he wasn't particularly intrigued by the unknown. However, everyone else had gone inside. Nikira and Chanya had raced up the hillside with Professor Escobedo when his son began shouting that he'd discovered something. Paintings, he said.

Jimiyu thought that was interesting, probably more so for the professor, but he didn't really want to do any more climbing. They'd been climbing for days, and he would have been just as happy to stay in camp. But Nikira hadn't been himself since they found this place. Jimiyu worried his friend's inner demons were making war on him. The conflict was apparent in the way his brow creased as he covered his face with his hands. It wasn't necessarily an attitude of prayer, as it might appear, but a sign Nikira was deep in thought.

Nikira spent more and more time rapt in that private world of his. Sometimes, Jimiyu wondered if he had his own direct line to God. No man, not even Talib "the seeker" should have such a hallowed acquaintance. He wondered, too, what would happen if God failed to respond? More than ever, he felt the need to be at his friend's side.

Everyone else, except Vincent, Scurlock and Harley, who hadn't yet returned to camp, was inside the cave. He steeled himself and forged ahead. Once inside, he took three, four steps in complete darkness, fearful his next might plunge him into some unseen abyss. He shortened his stride, reached out to feel his way through the gloom...and encountered nothing but cool air.

He was about to call out when, much to his relief, he saw a light. He hurried to catch up. Nikira and Chanya had waited for him. He was relieved to reach the bright, protective womb of their lantern glow.

The cave was much deeper than he'd guessed. He had no idea how far in they'd gone when they came upon Dr. Rousch, the professor and Max. They were holding their lights up to the cavern wall, looking at something. McCroy and the professor's wife were there too. On the face of the wall was a grouping of unmistakable illustrations.

The artwork was primitive, predominantly stick figures and outlines, like something his younger students might have drawn. However, the tableau extended some eight feet across. Its only colors were dark red and black. He couldn't be sure, but it appeared to Jimiyu that the characters portrayed were the same creatures who'd been following them—the animals Dr. Rousch called the ursu. The scene depicted a conflict of some sort.

Chanya gave voice to Jimiyu's own thoughts. "They look like the same beasts that followed us."

"*Pongoursus*," mumbled the exobiologist, as if lost in thought.

"Very likely their distant ancestors," Professor Escobedo responded.

"How old do you think these depictions are, Professor?" Nikira asked.

"I really couldn't say. Cave paintings more than thirty thousand years old have been found on Earth in southern France. Others discovered in India and China are believed by some experts to date back to the upper Paleolithic or Mesolithic, but the dating is in dispute. I can tell you these were likely created with charcoal and iron oxide-based pigments."

"Iron creates red and brown pigments," Max added. "The color doesn't fade because it's made from natural pigments, and fixed by mixing it with blood, urine or animal fat."

The professor looked at his son with both admiration and astonishment. "Where did you learn that, Maximo?"

"I had a course in art history where we studied hieroglyphics, ancient pictographs."

"My son is correct," said the professor, still staring at his son. "Even so, this art wouldn't have survived if it wasn't so deep in this cave, away from wind and water."

"It looks to me like a fight of some kind," McCroy said.

"The ursu are very territorial," said Dr. Rousch, as though she still couldn't believe her eyes. "It could be an encounter between separate communities, or maybe a dispute over ascendency between dominant males."

"I don't think so," Max said. "Look at this, the way this creature is splayed out, almost as if he's tied down. The one standing over him has something in its hand. A sharp stick, maybe. The rest are just standing around, rendered with less detail, like bystanders. I don't think anyone's fighting. I think it's a ritual sacrifice."

"You could be right," declared Professor Escobedo. There was more than a hint of fatherly pride in his voice. "That's exactly what it is."

Dr. Rousch shook her head skeptically. "Ritual sacrifice implies a belief system, faith in some supernatural power. Such belief is beyond anything the ursu are capable of."

"Anything they're capable of *now*," countered the professor. "You could say the same thing about the stone structures we discovered. For that matter, the intelligence needed to create these paintings themselves is beyond anything you've seen from the ursu you've studied, isn't it?"

"Are you saying you think the ursu depicted here actually created this?" Dr. Rousch seemed confounded by the notion.

"They do seem to be the protagonists of this art," responded Professor Escobedo. "I can only conclude they were the artists as well."

Dr. Rousch didn't respond. She simply stared at the primitive illustration.

"How well do these ursu see?" asked McCroy.

"Not that well," replied Dr. Rousch. "Their senses of hearing and smell—especially their sense of smell—are much stronger."

"Well," offered McCroy, "unless whoever painted this could see in the dark, they must have had fire, too, or they wouldn't have had enough light to create this."

Dr. Rousch and Professor Escobedo nodded agreement.

"I would say the ancestors of your ursu had a culture of some kind—a very primitive one, by the looks of it," Professor Escobedo stated. "There's no doubt they were sentient. By anyone's definition, this is symbolic behavior. They had the capability of abstraction, if not reason. I would surmise they employed vocalizations as a crude sort of language, one that surpassed the grunts and growls used by modern Earth apes."

"But that would mean they de-evolved," said Dr Rousch, "that they somehow slipped back down the evolutionary ladder."

Jimiyu had never heard of such a thing. How could something that was intelligent lose that intelligence?

"How could that be?" he heard himself asking out loud. "What could cause such a thing?

"It wouldn't take much. They were very likely just beginning to reach out, to stretch their minds. They were on the fringes of sentience, only starting to become aware," Professor Escobedo explained almost as if discussing the matter with himself, developing a theory as he went. "Maybe the entire tribe was wiped out by disease. Maybe the ursu Dr. Rousch has been studying are distant cousins who never quite took that evolutionary step—never achieved that awareness.

"Tribal warfare is another possibility. It wouldn't be the first time war has completely erased a culture. They could have been overcome by a less evolved group of near-relatives who killed off the males and interbred with the females. Some of the same genetic traits survived, but the emerging culture, the intellect, didn't."

"I have read something similar about certain dinosaur species," added Dr. Rousch. "I believe it was the troödontids that began evolving into birds then, due to environmental influences, started to de-evolve back into more saurian life forms."

"And," the professor continued, as though he'd never stopped, "though it seems unlikely, their intelligence might even have become a casualty of natural selection. Being intelligent might simply have run counter to survival. Though I can't imagine under what circumstances."

"What did they believe in?" asked Nikira, who'd remained silent all this time. Even, Jimiyu had noticed, when Dr. Rousch had made reference to a "supernatural power."

Professor Escobedo looked up from the portion of the cave painting he was studying. "What do you mean, Dr. Nikira?"

"The sacrifice, as Dr. Rousch said, implies a belief system. What was it they believed in?"

"I'd say it's this."

Max held one of the lanterns up high enough to reveal an illustration that was above the others. There, hovering over the sacrificial victim, was the same tree depicted on the artifact Happy Harley had found, the same tree design carved into the slab of stone outside—a tree with animated limbs.

"This must be their god."

It was all odd to Jimiyu. "Why would they go so deep into this cave to paint this?" he asked. "Why not simply do it outside in the light, on the stone structure where we saw the engraving of the tree?"

The professor responded, "Perhaps they did, and those works were eroded by the elements."

"Maybe this was the work of an individual, an outcast," suggested Max. "Like graffiti, something not sanctioned by the tribe."

"It could be that it was hidden away here for some reason," Dr. Rousch agreed. "Maybe they were hiding it from their god."

"No," Nikira muttered. "God created man in the likeness of God. There's no likeness of God here."

Nikira's expression was unreadable, but the rising timbre of his voice worried Jimiyu.

"No one's saying this is your god, Doctor," Professor Escobedo responded, his voice working into its lecture tone. "It's simply the representation that these creatures, for whatever reason, worshiped. Perhaps, like primitive man worshiped the sun, they worshiped the spirit of the forest. Such beliefs are common. Many trees and plants were sacred to the ancient Egyptians. The pygmies of Zaire believe God is everywhere within their sacred forest, and in parts of India, large trees were revered as the power that sustained the community. Even Shintoism, the indigenous religion of Japan, is based on god-as-mother-nature."

"No," said Nikira, his determination evident. "It makes no sense. This is His place. He led me here. This is wrong."

He turned and fled toward the cave entrance. Chanya grabbed one of the lanterns and followed.

The others were taken by surprise at the sudden shift in Nikira's demeanor. Jimiyu was not. It was what he had feared from the beginning, from the first time his old friend had set eyes on the artifact. Nikira was not only a man of resolve, he was a man of faith. Too much faith—that's what Jimiyu had always thought. Now that faith, which Nikira wore like a coat of armor, was fracturing, exposing flaws of conviction.

He saw the others looking at him, as if he could explain. How did one explain the mind of another?

"You'll have to excuse Dr. Nikira," he said. "This...all of this...is not what he envisioned."

51

The lie was clear, so he checked the lean and decided to hammer a wedge into the backcut to direct the fall. He flipped his axe and drove the wedge. The redwood splintered with a cracking sound as the tree teetered.

"Tim-berrrr!" Gash bellowed.

He leaned on his axe, waiting for the crashing thud, and contemplated the consequences of revolution. It was a good world, and he'd imagined many times making Evergreen his home after he'd put in his time. He knew it would be an even better place without the company in control. Decisions that profited the company were rarely beneficial to the welfare of the colonists. Of course, that's not to say the colonists, given the chance, wouldn't make a mess of things themselves. Rebels had a way of becoming bureaucrats once the cannons cooled. Human beings, as a species, seemed determined to constrict themselves with rules and regulations that not only spelled out what you couldn't do, but what you had to do.

Still, the idea of starting with a blank slate and building something new was tempting. Independence was a powerful word, alluring to most everyone, even if the reality of it was never as bright and shiny as the abstraction. Should he spit in the wind and join the insurgents?

The tree's violent descent and ultimate collision shattered branches and fanciful notions. If he agreed to join the rebellion, there would come a time when others would depend on him. There'd be responsibility and reckoning. The thought gave rise to a chill that swept through him like a winter wind. He wanted no part of that. He'd had enough responsibility to last a lifetime. It weighed on him like a corpse carried across his shoulders. It was a face that haunted his dreams. Her face.

> *"I've got to get up to control, so I won't be here when you leave."*
>
> *"Then come over here and give me a kiss to remember you by."*
>
> *"You're only going to be Earthside for two weeks."*
>
> *"Two weeks is a long time in a place full of rich, handsome men. You'd better remind me why I'm coming back."*
>
> *"You'd better come back. We've still got all those thank-yous to send out for the wedding gifts."*
>
> *"Don't remind me. If you'd been a brave man, you would have married me years ago, and we'd be done with all that."*
>
> *"And if you hadn't been flitting around the world to every scientific conference you could sign up for then maybe I could have corralled you sooner."*
>
> *"Okay, okay. You'd better get going, or you're going to be late for your duty shift."*
>
> *"Yeah. Have fun...but not too much."*
>
> *"Paul, I love you."*
>
> *"I love you, too, Marcy."*

A power saw roared to life over the ridge. Gash heard it grinding away at the bark, biting into the wood. The noise drowned out the shouts of the yarder crew, but in the distance he caught the sound of the *Sir Real*'s horn. Two short blasts meant it was pulling out with a new load of timber.

The limbers, Eamon among them, plodded up from where they'd finished their work downhill. The group began whacking at the felled tree. He watched them go at it—watched Eamon in particular. The kid had learned fast, and wasn't a bad worker as TJs went. Still, he was a complication Gash hadn't counted on, and didn't want to deal with. He already had enough specters haunting him. He didn't need a constant reminder.

The kid was bent on revenge, and Gash figured if he'd come this far he wasn't going to change his mind now. Sooner or later, he was going to learn the truth.

Maybe he should come right out and tell him. Get it over with instead of letting it eat at him for who knew how long. Maybe if he explained what happened, he could reason with him. It might even be cathartic. More likely it would be fatal.

52

Nikira had been alone too long; Jimiyu was concerned. His friend was seated on the ground within the stone formation Jimiyu thought of as the temple. He was in sight of the encampment, but after his outburst in the cave the others had given him his space, and had not spoken to him. Jimiyu decided it was time he imposed his company on Nikira, whether he liked it or not.

He repressed a shudder as he passed under the stone arch. Knowing what he knew now about the creatures who had lived here was unsettling. He looked at the ashlar slab sitting in the grassy center of the temple and wondered if it had once served as a sacrificial altar. He didn't let himself wonder long.

He sat next to Nikira. He didn't speak, he simply wanted to be there for his friend. He knew when Nikira was ready to talk he would. He was prepared to wait as long as it took. It turned out he didn't have to wait long.

"I know what I look like, Jimi. I know I've acted like a buffoon." Jimiyu started to object to the term, but Nikira held his hand up and went on. "Don't bother to deny it. I know what the others must think of me—what you must think. I'm not so irrational that I don't realize I was wrong. This," he said, holding his arms out, "this is not the provenance of God. I was foolish to ever believe I could find it. Foolish to think because that artifact came to me so easily that God wanted me to find it."

"Perhaps the City of God does exist...just not here," Jimiyu said, seeking to cushion his friend's fall.

"No, no, Jimi. Faith is one thing, but there comes a time when a man has to respect reality. I realize now everything they said about me was true. I'm an arrogant, vainglorious heretic, and a fool."

"I don't think you're a fool, Talib," said Jimiyu. "I think you're a man so immersed in his own convictions that sometimes he fails to lift his head above the rising waters and look around."

Nikira laughed. It wasn't a big laugh, just a chuckle, but it was the first time in a long time Jimiyu had heard such a sound come from him.

"You are truly a wise man, Jimi. A man who is not afraid to speak his mind. That is why I have always liked you."

"I thought you just liked my coffee."

"No, your coffee is awful." Nikira smiled, and Jimiyu smiled back.

The two men sat together silently for a minute. It reminded Jimiyu of the old days, when they could enjoy each other's company without the need for words. Then, one day, words became the thing his friend Talib lived for.

"You know, Jimi," Nikira said finally, "I may not have learned what I hoped, but I *have* learned one thing."

"What's that?"

"I learned that sometimes when you look deep into your soul, when you stare into that abyss that resides within you...sometimes the abyss stares back."

Jimiyu nodded, not sure what his friend meant, but knowing it was something profound.

"Will you join me in a brief prayer, Brother?"

"Certainly," Jimiyu said, closing his eyes.

"God is our refuge and our strength, an ever-present help in trouble," Nikira began. "Therefore we will not fear, though the earth give way and the mountains fall into the heart of the sea. Though its waters roar and foam and the mountains quake with their surging.

"Praise God."

"Praise God," repeated Jimiyu.

"You may return to the others now, Jimi. I'll join you shortly. After all, we wouldn't want them to think I'd gone completely off the deep end, would we?"

"No," said Jimiyu, "we wouldn't." He got up. "You won't be long?"

Nikira shook his head , so Jimiyu walked away.

He knew Nikira was putting up a front, and that his attempts at levity were simply a veil he used to cover up the magnitude of his disillusionment. He didn't doubt that, in time, Nikira would be fine. He was certain that by the time they returned to Earth he'd once again be ready to spread his doctrine and preach to converts and skeptics alike. But now...now he was bruised and battered. Now he was a man with a gaping wound in his soul.

Chanya, McCroy, Scurlock and Harley were in the camp; the rest were still exploring the caves. Chanya was cooking something, and Happy Harley was playing with a patch of grass as though mesmerized by it.

The two trackers sat together, and Jimiyu heard Scurlock grousing about something. Apparently, they'd believed the fabled "City of God" would hold some kind of treasure they could scoop up and take home with them. McCroy seemed to take the disappointment of their discovery in stride, but his associate kept grumbling about it.

"Look at this. It's a five-leaf clover," said Harley, plucking it from the ground.

"I guess it's your lucky day then, isn't it," scoffed McCroy.

"No, no," Harley replied, flinging the cloverleaf away from him. "A five-leaf clover is *bad* luck. It's not a good sign at all."

"Don't we got enough bad luck without you digging up more," carped Scurlock. "What are you doing now?"

Harley had pulled a handkerchief from his pocket, dropped an acorn in it and started tying the ends. "Tying knots in a handkerchief wards off evil. I'm putting my lucky acorn in it for good measure."

"You're loony as a gooney bird, boy," jeered Scurlock.

Harley ignored him and kept tying.

Jimiyu was about to ask Chanya what she was cooking, and suggest she prepare some for Nikira, when McCroy's big cat bounded out of the forest at a speed that was startling. The cat ran right to McCroy, almost skidding as it came up next to him. It was breathing hard and staring back into the trees from which it had emerged.

"What's wrong, Thor? What's the matter?" McCroy reached over and stroked the animal. It was alert and agitated. "Where'd you run off to?"

"He's frightened," said Chanya.

McCroy shook his head. "No, I've never seen him scared of anything. He's been around everything from elephants to earthmovers, and I've never seen him act like this."

"He does look scared," Scurlock said. "I wonder what he saw that could make him act like that."

"I don't know, but I'm not letting him loose anymore. Hand me his chain."

Jimiyu also wondered what had scared the big cat. Maybe those ape-like creatures had returned, and were out there now, watching them. He stared into the trees but saw nothing.

This place had unnerved him ever since they'd come on it. The animal's reaction only exacerbated his own feelings. His grandfather would have said this place was haunted by the spirits of its former inhabitants. Jimiyu's educated reason, his intellect, didn't allow him to believe in ghosts. Yet he conceded to himself that if any place was ever to be haunted by ghosts, then surely this place was.

53

Sundown pulled its lazy curtain over the horizon, but the sky was frantic with color. The evening's aurora swirled with passionate abandon, its frozen dance an homage to the raw beauty of nature. Amanda watched the shimmer of saffron and soft gold gradually darken into deeper, richer hues. She was moved by the orchestration of the light show, and inspired to see if she could accompany the display.

She raised the cedar flute to her lips and played, improvising as well as her meager talents allowed. As she played, she thought about what they had discovered. The stone structure, the signs of an ancient community, the caves, and the crude fresco—the existence of which alone demonstrated a sentience beyond that of any beast. The question was, were the artists the ancestors of the ursu, or a completely distinct offshoot of Evergreen's evolutionary tree?

She wondered, too, why the ursu who had been following them had given up when the expedition climbed the plateau to this ancient site. Had they simply strayed too far from their community and returned to their nests? Or was there something about this place that frightened them? She hadn't seen a single ursu since they'd been here. It could mean nothing more than there were no communities living in the vicinity.

Because her thoughts were occupied, it took her a while to realize what her ears were hearing. Not her flute—she was certain this time. What she was listening to was the descant of the wind. It wasn't her imagination, or the echo of her own play. Something was responding to the music of her flute with a tune of its own.

It was different from what she'd heard previously. There was an urgency to its tonality that wasn't there before. She stopped playing. This time, the forest song continued. She looked back from her rocky perch at those gathered around the cooking fire. No one else seemed to notice. If they heard it at all, they probably thought she was still playing.

Amanda slid off the boulder and followed the sound. She'd gone only a few dozen yards from the encampment when she found the source of the melody. She had to look closely in the fading light to see the grouping of small, sturdy plants growing out of the side of a tree. Not parasitical, she decided on close inspection, but aerophytes, deriving their sustenance directly from the air. The stalk of each growth was riddled with tiny apertures. When the wind was blowing just right, it must pass through the apertures, causing vibrations that resulted in the "music" she heard.

But why had she only heard it when she playing her flute? Was it coincidence, or had she heard it at other times but dismissed it as wind sound?

Abruptly, the plants went silent. Amanda held up her hand. She still felt a breeze, but it was faint.

"What you doing?"

Startled, she gave voice to a cry of surprise. It was Scurlock, eyeing her in that way he had that made her uncomfortable.

"Sorry. Didn't mean to scare you."

"That's okay. I was so busy concentrating...I just didn't expect anyone."

"What were you concentrating on?" he asked, stepping closer.

"Just these plants here," she said. "I've never noticed them before."

He was right behind her now. "Strange-looking, queer things. Growing right out of the tree, huh?"

"They're not actually growing out of the tree. They're just attached to the outer layer of bark."

"You sure know a lot about a lot of things, Doctor."

"Not really."

"It must be lonely for you, living all alone out here for so long. The honest truth is, you're just starved hungry for affection, aren't you?"

He reached his arms around her, grabbing her breasts and pushing up against her.

"No!" Amanda shouted, trying to extricate herself from his awkward embrace.

"Be nice, Doctor. I bet you know a lot about how to please a man, don't you? Those things doctors know."

"Let go of me!"

She wriggled in his grasp but only managed to turn enough to smell the stink of his breath and see his eyes. They seemed to bulge more than usual, and the salacious glint in them frightened her. She'd seen that look before.

She reached for his eyes, determined to gouge them, but he caught her wrists and tried to force her to the ground. Her height made it difficult for him, and she managed to retain her balance. Still, she couldn't pull free of his grip, so she kicked; and her leg found its mark on the first try. Scurlock doubled over and released his hold on her.

Her first impulse was to run away as fast as she could. Her second was to bring her knee up full force into her attacker's face. The impact knocked Scurlock to the ground. Amanda stood over him, daring him to get up. He just lay moaning, as if only semi-conscious.

She started back towards camp and ran into Mrs. Escobedo and McCroy.

"Are you all right?" asked the professor's wife. "We thought we heard you call out."

She jerked her thumb over her shoulder.

"Your man Scurlock attacked me," she told McCroy.

"Goddammit!" he responded, and took off through the brush.

Mrs. Escobedo wrapped her arms around Amanda's shoulders. "You should come sit down."

"I'm all right."

"You're shaking like a leaf, dear. Come over here, please. Here's a place to sit."

Amanda realized she *was* shaking. Post-adrenalin rush, she thought. She let the other woman guide her to a small outcropping and a flat stone where they could sit.

"Thank you, Mrs. Escobedo. I guess he scared me more than I thought."

"Call me Filamena, please."

"All right, Filamena."

Amanda hadn't had much opportunity to talk with the professor's wife during their trek. The woman stayed close to her husband most of the time, almost as if she were afraid to leave his side. Moreover, she was so unlike Amanda—poised and cultured, a classic beauty, perfectly proportioned from her long lashes and almond-shaped eyes to her wasp waist. The truth was, Filamena intimidated her. Not because Amanda had ever longed for such superficial attributes, but because such beauty reminded her of how plain she was.

"Are you sure he didn't hurt you?"

"No, no, but I think I hurt him pretty good."

"*Buono!* Serves him right. He won't try to touch you again then, will he?"

"No...I guess not."

"But you're still frightened of him, aren't you? You poor dear." Filamena put her arm around Amanda to comfort her.

"It's not that. It's not him so much. It's just that I...I was..."

"You were what?"

An old wound had reopened. A wound Amanda kept covered and never allowed anyone to see—never allowed herself to examine. But she was feeling vulnerable. Her emotions were not restrained by their usual tight controls.

"I was raped when I was younger. There were two men. I was just a teenager."

Filamena grimaced and nodded as if she understood but wasn't sure what to say. She kept her arm around Amanda and patted her arm.

"You know what the worst part is? The worst part is the feeling of powerlessness," said Amanda, staring off into the distance at the final shreds of daylight. "That's the worst part."

They were both roused by the gruff sounds of what Amanda guessed must be McCroy's voice. She couldn't make out the words, but she gathered he was having at his associate. She even heard what sounded like blows being struck. The idea of Scurlock being roughed up should have pleased her, but she didn't care one way or the other.

"They're animals."

"What?" Amanda said, not really paying attention.

"Men," explained Filamena. "They're all animals."

Still not thinking clearly, Amanda nodded. The placid scientist within her took control and she said, "We're all animals."

54

His belly full, his arms and legs weary after another long day in the timber, Eamon just wanted to sleep. Sleep was sanctuary, refuge from unrelenting malice and sullen self-doubt. All he wanted was to sleep.

He couldn't. He tried lying down, but he was restless. As tired as his body was, his mind wouldn't stop racing. Not a straight race, but a convoluted figure eight, ever-circling, impulsively zigzagging. Awash amid the jetsam of more familiar reflections, he somehow focused on Sunny. He thought about how great it had been. He tried to recall the sensations she'd conjured within him, but they'd grown vague, supplanted by other considerations. He wanted to see her again. He would, too, next time he had the chance. If he had the chance.

His body was so sore. He tried massaging a particular spot on his right bicep and, for the first time, realized how much thicker and harder his muscles were becoming. He wondered how long it would be before he was a mass of muscle like Gash.

Never particularly talkative, Gash has been unusually quiet when they climbed aboard his little flatboat. As soon as they were inside, Gash pulled out his pipe and his happy smoke. It was his routine. Night after night, he lit up and retreated into the same numbing vapors. Eamon was certain he was addicted to the stuff.

If not physically, then certainly mentally. It was the only flaw he'd seen in the man's character.

It concerned him. He wanted to ask Gash why he did it. He wanted to know what it was that pushed him to flee reality. However, Gash had told him you didn't ask a TJ about his past. The irony was that even the smoke didn't make Gash happy—at least not in the sense Eamon thought of it.

He considered trying it, but reminded himself he didn't want to risk weakening his resolve. It would be easy to do. It would be easy to let himself forget what he had to do—to give up. The idea had tempted him many times, and not just since he landed on Evergreen.

He had to stop thinking. He needed to sleep, but just closing his eyes wasn't working. Maybe if he took a drink of Gash's hooch it would make him drowsy.

He sat up and opened his eyes. Gash sat across from him, staring right at him. Eamon got up, found the bottle and took a long swig.

"Bleech! That stuff's nasty."

He put the bottle away and went back to his spot. Gash was still staring. Off in some stoned dreamland, figured Eamon.

He lay down, closed his eyes and tried to blank his mind. He tried for several minutes. It didn't work. Finally, he sat back up. Gash was still awake.

"I can't sleep," he said.

Gash nodded as if he understood. "Maybe we should talk then."

"Talk about what?"

"About how I came to Evergreen."

That caught Eamon off-guard. "Sure, if you want."

"Back then, back in the world," Gash started, "I was an engineer. I worked for the WSA."

"The World Space Agency? My mother worked for them, too."

"Yeah. Now shut up and let me get this out."

Eamon was surprised by the harshness of his tone, but kept silent.

"Anyway," Gash continued, "I was the duty engineer on the orbital space station when something went wrong. We got hit by micrometeorites all the time. The patch-and-repair system worked fine, so it wasn't usually a problem. But this one time...

"A speck of a meteorite found its way to a pressurized tank. I had to make a split-second decision. You understand? It was a life-or-death situation, and I had to decide right then, right that moment. I could jettison a single chamber or risk destroying the entire station. You don't have any idea what that's like—to have to make that decision. To issue a command that kills thirteen people."

"Thirteen?" Eamon repeated with a mounting sense of realization.

"Yes. Thirteen people died because of my decision—a decision I had to make. I didn't ask for it. I didn't want it. I wish the hell I'd never—"

"You're..." He couldn't say the name. It had eaten away at him for so long—since he first heard it. It had been engraved in searing letters across his brain. Now, his tongue couldn't give it voice.

"I'm Paul Brandon," said Gash for him. "At least I used to be Paul Brandon. He doesn't exist anymore."

He got up. He stood as if waiting for something.

Eamon couldn't move. He couldn't talk. The revelation left him stunned.

"Your mother was Dr. Joyce Hankala, wasn't she? I knew her. I knew every one of those thirteen people." He turned, stooped and stepped out of the boat shack.

Eamon still couldn't move. It was as if he couldn't comprehend what he'd heard. It ran round and round inside his head, but wouldn't stop long enough for him to send a message to his legs to function. He'd found the man he'd been looking for all these years. The man who'd killed his mother. He'd found him only to learn it was his friend. The only person on Evergreen who'd showed any concern for him. The only man he'd ever learned to respect.

And now he had to kill him.

55

When Filamena woke from her fitful night, it was long past sunrise. She'd had trouble getting to sleep, and when she finally succumbed, her dreams were invaded by large, faceless creatures that pawed her with hairy hands. They surrounded her so she couldn't escape, and chattered to each other in a language she couldn't understand.

Then, through a violet haze, one of them spoke to her in Italian, using Max's voice. In the dream, it didn't seem to matter that Max didn't speak Italian. He kept telling her over and over to "run away, run away." It was so terrifying she woke with a reflexive jerk.

Luis lay next to her, sound asleep. He always slept so well, so easily. Maybe that was the fruit of a clear conscience.

For a long time, she was afraid to go back to sleep. She couldn't get the dream out of her mind. She was afraid if she slept she might relive it. Eventually, though, her jangled nerves calmed, and she had succumbed to fatigue.

She finally woke up, much later than usual. She brushed her hair and made herself as presentable as possible, then left her tent. Luis and Max were nowhere to be seen. She assumed they were already looking for more cave paintings.

The ancient artwork had forged a new bond between father and son. Though she was glad for it, she was equally surprised at how quickly it had formed. Though their reasons differed, each found in those caves something that intrigued them, something they could share. They also seemed to have found each other.

At the same time she felt as if she'd lost Luis again—lost him to his work. He'd been so attentive, so caring during their trek, but now, since they'd discovered this place, it was as if she hardly existed. His attention, his very existence, was consumed by his work. It was the way of things with Luis. A way with which she was familiar. Yet there was no solace in familiarity.

Filamena wasn't out of her tent for long when she heard a commotion. McCroy and Dr. Nikira were arguing about something. Amanda came up to her and said, "Harley's missing. He wasn't in his tent this morning."

Filamena knew their guide wasn't one to rouse early. They'd had to roust him out of his tent almost every morning to get him going. McCroy, however, didn't seem overly concerned with the disappearance.

"He got stoned and wandered away, simple as that," he said. "He's probably out there sleeping it off somewhere."

"That may be, Mr. McCroy, but I still want you to look for him," Nikira insisted. "He may be injured and unable to return to camp."

"Fine, fine, we'll go look for him." McCroy snatched up his shotgun. "Jesper, unchain Thor and let's go find the fungus-head."

McCroy, Scurlock and the big cat went off to look for Harley, but not before Filamena noticed Scurlock sported some cuts on his face. She didn't figure Amanda had given him those.

She joined Amanda at the still-smoldering fire and poured herself some coffee. The exobiologist had tied her long chestnut hair into a bun under her hat. She was busy writing something in the Trans-Slate she carried. Filamena thought she seemed all right, considering.

"Diary?" she asked.

"No, they're notes for my study," Amanda said. "All my observations of the ursu are in here, details of various animal and plant species I've come across on Evergreen. Right now, I'm trying to get down everything we've found here. It's quite a discovery. Especially for someone in your husband's field of research."

"I'm sure it is." Filamena realized her response was less than enthusiastic, so she quickly added, "I know Luis is excited. Even Max is excited, and he...well, he and his father have never shared many interests."

"It's undoubtedly the most important extraterrestrial discovery ever. The evidence is certainly here."

"Evidence of what?" asked Filamena.

"Evidence of the first intelligent species in the galaxy outside of Earth."

"You think those creatures were really intelligent?"

Amanda closed her Trans-Slate and pursed her lips, contemplating an explanation. "Not necessarily intelligent in the way we think of a person as being intelligent. But they certainly developed an awareness that was beyond that of any species in the animal kingdom. We know they had crude forms of art, communication, construction skills—how they managed to move those giant rocks I can't imagine—and they seemed to have had a religion of sorts. At the very least a concept of the supernatural."

"I'm sure it will all cause quite a bit of commotion back on Earth."

"Are you all right?" Amanda asked.

"Yes. I didn't sleep well. Nightmares."

"Me, too," said Amanda.

A feeling of guilt stabbed Filamena. She shouldn't have dismissed Amanda's run-in with Scurlock the night before so easily. It was no wonder *she'd* had nightmares. Filamena didn't have that excuse. She was ashamed she hadn't considered the other woman's feelings.

"I was thinking of going for a walk," said Amanda. "Would you like to join me?"

"Sure, just let me—"

"Dr. Rousch!" It was Boorman, waving his arms from up on the cliff face. "Dr. Rousch!"

"What is it?" she called back.

"The professor wants your input. We've found something."

Amanda waved and replied, "Okay." She looked at Filamena. "Instead of a walk, how about a climb?"

"As if we haven't done enough of that."

241

Both women smiled, and Filamena decided the doctor must be okay. Maybe she had already put the events of the previous night behind her. If so, she was even stronger than she looked. Filamena admired that strength.

They started their climb, and a short time later joined Boorman. He led them inside one of the caves. Its entrance was much smaller than the one where they'd found the first paintings, so Filamena had to stoop for several yards until it opened up. She was thankful both Boorman and Amanda carried lanterns, because once the tunnel crooked off to the left, she could no longer see the light from the entrance.

They hiked a good distance into the cave before they found Luis. She didn't see Max, but noticed a flicker of light deeper inside the cavern, and figured that's where he was.

"Dr. Rousch," said Luis, "I wanted you to see this. You, too, Filamena."

He directed his lantern towards a recess in the cave wall, and Filamena saw a pile of bones. Not just a pile, she realized as the light bounced around, but a scattering of skeletal remains. Some of the bones were broken or half-buried, others looked recently unearthed.

"When I came across these only a few were protruding through the surface," Luis said excitedly. "So, I began to excavate. It seems to be a large deposit, deep and spread out here. The soil must be highly alkaline because the bones are partially fossilized."

"Are they human?" Filamena asked.

"No," Amanda responded, bending down to examine the find, "they're ursu, or a very close relative."

"That's what I thought," Luis said. "I wanted you to confirm. We can send a sample back to Earth, along with a specimen from the ursu you've been studying. If we can find a good DNA sample, tests will confirm if they're the same species or an offshoot."

"You haven't come across any other such accumulation, have you, Professor?" Amanda asked.

"No, I haven't. It's rather odd. From what we've seen, I don't believe these creatures actually lived in these caves—at least not for any extended period. I would speculate they used them to take shelter from storms, or maybe from their enemies—assuming they had any. However, this collection of remains makes it appear as if a group of the creatures died together in this cave."

"It looks that way," agreed Amanda. "Maybe this is where they put their sick or injured."

"Could be. Or maybe—"

"Down here!" It was Max. "I've found something down here!"

The four of them scuttled through the darkness past a couple of twists and turns before they found him. He held his light up high, as if to get a better look at something. What it was, Filamena saw, was another painting on the cave wall. She was no expert, but this one seemed more elaborate, more detailed than the other. Many of the outlined figures had been filled in, though still with little detail, and there were various shades of the red coloring. Even the proportions were more accurate.

"Incredible," said Amanda.

Luis just stared, but Filamena knew by his reaction he agreed with Amanda's assessment. She, too, found the scene depicted across the cave wall startling. She didn't need anyone to interpret it for her. The dramatic imagery made it obvious what was happening.

In its center was a group of the hairy creatures. They brandished clubs and threw stones. One of the clubs they held appeared to be on fire. All around them, surrounding them, were trees—trees with long branches snaking out, moving towards the creatures. A tree limb was shown grabbing hold of one of the creatures. Within the leaves and boughs were depictions of angry eyes that made it seem as if the trees were alive.

Her first thought was that it must be a fantasy—a nightmare some creature had paid homage to on a cave wall. It must have been a terrible dream, she thought. It certainly couldn't have been real, because what it showed was Amanda's ursu fighting against the forest itself.

56

Eamon stomped through the brush and brambles, dragging the heavy cable as he went. It snagged briefly, but he was able to yank it loose. The log had been topped, bucked and limbed, and was ready to go, but there was no gap to be found. The tree had fallen evenly, sinking into the soft loam from end to end. Chafing with irritation, he kicked it.

He didn't like being assigned to cable skidding, but then, he didn't care much for any of the jobs they gave him. At least when he was limbing he got to swing an axe. He found the chopping motion, the feel of the blade biting into the wood therapeutic. He could swing until every toxic emotion pent up inside him was consumed by fatigue. This morning, more than any other, he needed that release.

It had all seemed so easy when he began. When he set out to find his mother's killer, he never doubted what he'd do once he found him. Now, with the goal at hand, intentions previously distinct were veiled in shades of gray. There was no doubt he'd found the right man. Gash had admitted as much.

He pawed at a likely spot beneath the trunk, digging like a dog would to get under a fence.

His dilemma was that he'd come to admire the man—respect him, even. Gash had treated Eamon more than fairly, gotten him released from the company jail, and even stopped that crazy religious fanatic from castrating him. He probably owed his life to Gash.

When he'd moved enough soil he went to the other side and dug some more. After he broke through he grabbed his rigging and looped it around the log. He cinched the choker and moved to the other side.

So what if he owed Gash? He owed his mother more. Just because Gash had been nice to him didn't mean he was absolved. One didn't pay for mistakes that easily. Eamon knew that. It wouldn't be that simple for Paul Brandon to make amends. Eamon had made a promise—to himself and to his mother. He'd broken too many promises to her in the past. He wasn't going to break this one.

He need more slack on the main cable, so he pulled twice on the jerk-wire, waiting to see if the man at the haulback drum was paying attention. He pulled his gloves tight and rubbed his sore left arm. Even through his shirt sleeve he could feel the pattern of welts and bruises.

It had to be done. It didn't matter if he had personal feelings. It didn't matter if he had doubts. It was resolution he wanted. He'd waited years for it.

He pulled on the cable, found more slack and threw the bell around the log. As he did, a swarm of those pesky flies enveloped him. He swatted furiously, pointlessly, until the swarm moved on of its own accord.

"You ready there, turtle?" It was Nishikawa, the skid master, riding him again. "Let's bust a move and get it rolling."

Eamon didn't bother to reply. He tugged the jerk-wire and gave the signal to haul away. The cable pulled taut, and the log showed sign of movement. He was backing away when the rigging snapped and a length of chain whipped within a breath of his face.

He fell backwards in a belated attempt to avoid the whiplash. He got up wiping dirt from his face.

Nishikawa shook his head. "Dammit, turtle! You're supposed to double-check that rigging. You're going to end up with a mug like Gash's if you don't pay attention to what you're doing. Now grab some new rigging and get on it. You're holding up the lane."

Eamon thought the rigging was to blame. It wasn't his fault it had broken, but he knew that would just be seen as an excuse. Excuses weren't tolerated. Nobody wanted to hear excuses, they wanted results. He wouldn't allow himself any excuses, either. All that mattered was the end result.

57

"So what conclusions have you reached, Professor?" asked Nikira.

He was eating the food Chanya had prepared for him, and had even carried on a brief conversation with her, which Jimiyu knew delighted the devoted woman. Nikira seemed to take solace in her company.

Now he was engaged in a give-and-take discourse with other members of the expedition. It was as if he had put his disillusionment behind him. Jimiyu didn't think he had, not completely. Still, it was a good sign.

"I haven't reached any conclusions, Doctor, except that a primitive culture of some form once lived here," Professor Escobedo said. "How advanced they were, what they believed, I cannot say. What I need is a full dig team. I'm certain this site is a treasure trove of artifacts, artifacts that will eventually tell the story of these people."

"People?" questioned Jimiyu. "Certainly you don't think of those beasts as people?"

"You can call them people, call them beasts, call them alien beings," said the professor, "it really doesn't matter. They weren't just animals, though. They were undoubtedly aware, as sentient as our own ancestors. I'm sure Dr. Rousch agrees."

"From what we've seen, I don't know how you could deny it," Dr. Rousch replied. "I know one thing—the species that lived here was much more advanced than the ursu of today, despite the physical resemblance. The ursu I've studied use simple things they come across like rocks or branches as implements, maybe slightly reshaping a twig with their hands or mouths. However, Professor Escobedo has discovered objects that seem to show the ancient ursu used tools to make other tools. It's an important distinction."

Professor Escobedo nodded, and she went on. "I've been trying, not very successfully I must admit, to reconstruct one of the skeletons found in the cave. From what I can tell, these ursu had a more upright posture. It's likely they spent less time, if any, on all fours, unlike their descendants."

"This new pictograph you found," said Nikira, "from the way you describe it, it seems inconsistent with your initial discovery."

"In what way?"

"The first illustration suggested these creatures worshiped trees or, in a larger sense, possibly nature. Now, you find a scene showing them at war with that very same thing. It naturally begs the question: Was the forest their god or their devil?"

"Maybe it was both," said the professor's wife as she casually brushed her hair.

"Their beliefs could have changed over time," Max offered. "I've studied the artwork, and I'm certain they were painted by different artists. The techniques are different. The one we just found is more elaborate, its technique more refined. You know, for a cave painting. It's likely it was created much later than the first—maybe years or even decades."

Jimiyu could tell Nikira was engrossed by the discussion. Now that he'd accepted this was not the "City" of his faith—if he *had* accepted that—he seemed genuinely interested in the spiritual beliefs of those who had lived here. Nikira had always been resilient. Jimiyu had admired that trait in him since they were boys. Nevertheless, the man's strength of character still surprised him. He'd expected Nikira to be shattered, but though there was still a touch of lethargy about him, Jimiyu thought he was coming out of it.

"So, what are your plans now, Professor?" Nikira asked.

"I want to look around a little more then get back to Woodville as soon as possible. I plan on sending to Earth for a full team. Vincent has agreed to help fund such an endeavor. As soon as I know it's underway, we'll return here and I'll begin the dig myself."

"It's ultra-mega zapper," added Boorman, "I wouldn't miss it."

Jimiyu saw the professor's wife flash her husband a look of surprised dismay. The professor, however, didn't notice it, and she quickly recovered her poise. He'd obviously not mentioned his plans to his wife.

"Hopefully, you won't have any trouble getting clearance for such a dig," said Dr. Rousch, "the restrictions on planetary exploration being what they are."

"I can't see why they would possibly object," the professor responded.

"Maybe then," Dr. Rousch added, "I can get some assistance for my work as well—with your influential support, Professor."

"I'd be happy to do whatever I can, Doctor."

The giant lynx broke through the brush at that instant, startling those nearest. Chanya jumped to her feet, prepared to flee, before she realized it was McCroy's big cat. McCroy and Scurlock emerged right behind it. Scurlock went straight to the food, and McCroy got himself a drink before speaking.

He wiped his mouth on his sleeve and said, "No sign of Harley. All we found was this."

He held out Harley's knotted handkerchief, and as he did the acorn fell out of it. "We found some drag marks, but after that, not even a boot print. Weird, even if he was trying to cover his tracks— which I doubt."

"Maybe he just cycled back to Woodville," suggested Vincent.

"Maybe," McCroy replied, sounding unconvinced. "Either way, if Thor can't track him, he's gone."

58

Cash sat alone. He preferred it that way, and normally he didn't need a reason. Tonight he had one. He sat by himself, eating his meal away from the others because he didn't want to run into Eamon. Not yet. Not until he gave the kid a chance to think. He didn't believe time would change anything, but it gave him the opportunity to collate his own thoughts.

He actually felt a sense of relief. Admitting his identity, his past, to Eamon had lifted something that had ridden him like a parasite. It was almost as if he'd acknowledged his failing to not just a single person but to the friends and family members of each one of those thirteen people. He wasn't about to let himself off the hook that easily, but there was no disputing some fraction of his conscience had been assuaged.

"A man's fate is not necessarily his calling."

"What?"

He looked up and saw Ford. Despite his attempt to distance himself from the rest of the crew, the blind old camp cook had found him. That alone should have been a sign.

"What are you talking about, Ford?"

"Nothing. It's a just saying. You know, like the grass is always greener or a stitch in time saves nine. Though I have no idea what *that* means."

"Did you want something in particular?" Gash asked, trying to sound annoyed. He didn't do a very good job of it, because inside he was laughing. Ford, the clown prince of the non sequitur, always made him laugh.

"Nothing in particular. A little bird told me you were over here." Ford fluttered his fingers next to his ear. "So, I thought I'd come visit."

"There are no little birds on this planet, Ford. Just those fat bush chickens you rubberize in your cook pots."

"There's no call to be insulting."

"Sorry," replied Gash, though he knew the old man could take a joke, "I guess it's just my sour mood."

"Mood is what you make of it, daddy-o."

"Daddy-what?"

Ford shrugged. "I don't know. It just kind of popped out. I'll tell you what I do know. I know the dead speak to us from beyond the grave. That's what conscience is."

"What are you talking about?" Gash was taken aback. Was Ford a clown or a mind reader?

"I'm talking about my ancestors, my people, the ones who settled Evergreen. The ones whose ghosts haunt me. Who did you think I was talking about?"

"I don't know," Gash lied. He thought for a moment about what Ford had said. "Did anyone ever tell you that, for a blind man, you see pretty clearly?"

Ford shrugged. "Sometimes you have to look inside yourself to see what's inside others."

"Never thought of it that way." He stared at the old man. He'd known for a long time there was more to him than met the eye. "What you said about fate before—do you believe a man controls his own destiny?"

Ford thought about it. "I believe a man tries." Then, as if giving in to a random impulse, he danced a quick little jig. "Remember, too," he said, finishing with a soft shoe flourish. "In the world of the sighted, sometimes the blind man is king."

"Yeah," Gash laughed, "and even a blind pig finds an acorn occasionally."

Ford turned his head like he was insulted, but Gash knew it was an act.

"Well, this little piggy had better get back to his pots." Ford started to go, then his head swiveled around and his blank eyes stared at Gash. "The dead may demand justice, but their justice is not necessarily that of the living." He turned back, kept walking and kept talking. "For that matter, man shall not live by bread alone, even if he knows what side it's buttered on. The devil finds work for idle hands, but that's better than a poke in the eye with a sharp stick."

Gash watched the old gray-haired Indian saunter off, still rambling on. He marveled at how Ford moved with the surety of a man with vision. *Maybe he saw more than he knew—maybe he saw right through me.*

He realized that, somewhere between his reverie and Ford's comic relief, he'd made a decision. How he'd come to it he wasn't certain, but it was done just the same.

He picked himself up and returned to the lakefront where the other TJs were finishing their evening meal. He located Ramos, walked up to him and said, "What do you need me to do?"

59

As much as being around Luis reminded Filamena of why she'd fallen in love with him, it also refreshed her memories of being neglected. From the moment they'd discovered this site, it was as if she no longer existed. Even if she woke early enough to see him, he barely said two words to her before he was off somewhere, digging a hole or searching another cave.

She'd been especially upset when she heard him say he planned on remaining on Evergreen for a time before going back to Earth, and then returning here for what would likely be months. He hadn't bothered to discuss the matter with her first, or even tell her his plans before he told the others. He was a good man, but this expedition had only served to reinforce the fact she'd always come second to his work.

She didn't like being second. It wasn't in her nature to accept being ignored. She'd always been the center of attention growing up, more so after she'd become a woman. She could have had any man in her town she wanted. But she didn't want to stay in a small town. She wanted to see the world, to seek out adventure.

She was having an adventure now, and she was bored.

She decided to go for a walk away from the camp, away from her discontent. She hadn't seen Luis in hours. She had no idea where he was or what he was doing. The camp was empty except for Dr. Nikira and Mr. McCroy. Everyone else was off doing something, searching for ancient relics or fossils or things she couldn't have cared less about.

Nikira, while not exactly morose, had kept to himself the last few days. McCroy, on the other hand, seemed to look for any excuse to make small talk with her. She was unnerved, yet also inwardly pleased by the way he looked at her when her husband wasn't around. He never did anything overt, but his gaze drank her in the way a parched man downs a cold glass of water.

The idea of pursuing his interest was tempting enough that she'd actually considered it. Particularly after she'd failed the night before to convince Luis they should return to Earth. The discussion had grown heated, but all Luis would say was that she should go home and wait for him.

Her anger had not subsided.

So, for a brief, weak moment she'd thought about McCroy. She'd not taken the thought seriously. She'd already been down that road, and it had led to nothing but grief.

She trailed her hand through a patch of ferns as she strolled. They were dappled by striations of purple and green, one color blending to the next. It was a beautiful place, this forest world. Though not her kind of place—she preferred the bright lights and high-society parties of a big city. Yet she couldn't deny the allure of such a pristine setting.

She thought she heard something and turned around. There was movement in the bushes behind her. The notion that it was a wild animal tightened her throat. She'd been foolish to go walking off alone. Could it be more of Amanda's ursu? She didn't know if she should run or stand perfectly still. Fear forced the latter.

"Mena? Mena, where are you?"

The relief of discovering it was Max allowed her to breathe again. That was her immediate reaction. Her next was to summon up her inner guard. What was he doing here, following her?

"Mena, there you are. You shouldn't be out here alone, you know. But I'm glad you are."

She had to be strong, despite herself. The only good that had come out of this trip was that Max and Luis had grown closer over the last few days. Certainly closer than she'd ever seen them. Before, every time they'd talk, the discussion would end with an argument. Now the intrigue and mutual interest of discovery had brought them together. Max had matured in her eyes. He wasn't just the acrimonious son anymore. He was a man.

Somehow, that scared her—but not that alone. As always, she was attracted to Max, drawn by his youthful vigor and dark good looks. When he hurried to her now, and took hold of her arms, she didn't try to stop him.

"Isn't it exciting? The remnants, the art of an ancient, budding culture." He spoke rapidly, not waiting for any response. "For the first time I understand what it is my father is drawn to. It's a mystery. That's what it is. A mystery to be puzzled out. It's like a mosaic, and we have to put all the pieces in their proper places before it can be revealed."

"I'm glad you're getting along so well," she said when he finally paused.

He pulled her closer to him, and she could feel his vitality press against her.

"The only thing that's missing is you," he said, staring into her eyes. "If only we were together again, it would be perfect."

She wanted to throw her arms around him. She wanted to give in to her frustration and desire.

"If we were together again, it would destroy what you've found with your father. It would destroy *him*."

He must have felt her stiffen. Either that, or he saw the logic of what she said. He let go of her and looked away.

"I know," he said. "Don't you think I've considered that? Don't you think I've thought of what it would do to him if we told him?"

She *had* thought of it. Over the last few days, she'd been thinking more and more about admitting everything to Luis, telling him the truth about her and Max. Whether it was a way of cleansing her own guilt or just a selfish cry for attention, she couldn't decide. Several times she'd convinced herself to confess her sins no matter what the consequences. Especially last night when she was angry. But each time she'd reminded herself how well Luis and Max were getting along, and each time she remained silent.

"Go back to camp, Max," she heard herself saying. "Go be with your father."

He frowned and stepped toward her. She was certain he was going to take hold of her and kiss her. She knew, if he did, she would return the kiss with every fragment of her pent-up longing. She braced for it, her body tense.

Max stared into her eyes, and she saw his eager expression soften. She knew he'd reached a decision. He turned without saying a word and walked back the way he'd come.

A surge of conflicting emotions left Filamena limp. What she wanted, what she didn't want. She wasn't sure anymore. She wasn't sure what was true and what were just lies she told herself. No, that was a lie, too. She knew the truth. She just didn't want to accept it.

The truth was, she loved two different men in two very different ways. She loved them both...and despised herself because of it.

60

old dust blossomed in the night and fell like fiery hail. An eruption of pallid indigo evolved into quicksilver teardrops that lingered, then vanished. A volley of scarlet shook the sky, followed in rapid succession by brilliant blue and effervescent copper.

A blitz of color carpeted the firmament over TJ City. A crack of thunder trailed each burst in a recurring fusillade assault. Every explosive fount of light tinged the flotilla with an eerie pigmentation. Each was echoed by oohs and aahs and vulgar appraisals enhanced by outlawed substances.

Gash lay on the roof of his flatboat, taking it all in. It was a cool, clear night. No clouds, no fog—the perfect canvas, he thought, gazing up at the power of the fireworks display.

It was a magnificent show, no question, though in his altered state he wondered if Evergreen's auroras didn't render the exhibition superfluous. It was typical company overkill. As though Administrator Oshima, in her officious capacity, were determined to surmount the planet's innate grandeur.

The occasion was not to celebrate the landing of the first humans on Evergreen, as it had been in previous years, but to mark GMX's official founding ten years ago of the town of Woodville—now ostensibly "Redwood Springs." They'd gone all-out, that was for certain.

It was the colony's first-ever fireworks show, and most of the town, as well as many of the homesteaders from the southern valleys, lined the shore of Lake Washoe.

Their getting here had been no small endeavor. They'd traveled up Rust River while it was still day, and after the show would camp by the lake until first light. In the morning, they would return via the river as far as the rapids but would then have to disembark and walk more than six miles to town. The homesteaders would have even farther to go.

But it was an occasion—a spectacular event for such an outland colony.

Another array of explosive halos painted the heavens with amber, and Gash watched as the bright flecks, after a flickering caesura, dripped downward with the surreal slowness of honeyed ooze. Down it came, all around him, like some multi-limbed creature reaching out to seize the flotilla of humanity. For a moment, it seemed as if the photonic sludge would engulf him. His reflexes altered by happy smoke, Gash threw up his hands as if to ward off the striations of light bearing down upon him. Just as he did they vanished.

"A year from now, we'll be lighting the sky like this to mark our independence."

He sat up, startled by the intrusion. It was Shay Larimore, who, along with Ramos, had stepped aboard unnoticed. Gash looked at Ramos for an explanation.

"I told Shay you were in," Ramos said. "We wanted to talk."

"Go ahead." He lit his pipe for another hit. "Talk."

"We've been mulling over a variety of cockeyed ideas," said Larimore. "Some paper tigers want to write up a full-blown Declaration of Independence and a Constitution and then call for a work stoppage. They think the company will actually give a damn. On the other side, there's some raving cocksuckers who want to blow the fucking mill to smithereens and sodomize the marshals with their own hot rods."

"And...?" Gash encouraged when Larimore didn't continue.

"We want to sabotage the mill so it can't operate, but without too much damage so we can repair it when we're in control," Ramos said instead. "We're going to need you to ride herd on that part of the operation, and tell us how to go about it."

"That's just part of the plan," added Larimore, "but it's crucial."

Ramos cleared his throat. Behind him, Gash watched another round of skyrockets fire off from the launching barge.

"And there's some TJs who want to hear where you stand on this. They want to know you're with us."

"Well, tell them," Gash said, slipping down off the boat shack.

"They want to hear it from you."

"Since when did I become somebody?"

"Yeah, go figure," Larimore said dryly.

"You're an hombre a lot of the men trust, Gash. They figure if you're in, then maybe it makes sense for them."

"No one ever said timber jocks were too bright.

More pyrotechnics cascaded overhead.

"We're raising the curtain next Funday," Larimore announced, "after sundown."

"Your rebel army will be drunk as skunks by then," said Gash.

"Everyone who's with us knows to lay off the bug juice that night," Ramos assured him. "And those that aren't with us, well, they'll be out of it."

"Keep a pack of TJs sober on Funday? If you can do that, you just might pull off this little coup."

"When you get off the express, you'll have a few compadres with you at the mill," Ramos went on. "Have a look around, see what you can do—what you need. When the time's right, those buckaroos will dry-gulch the mill guards and stay to help you."

"Meanwhile," added Larimore, his middle finger rubbing the hair on his chin, "we'll be disarming the cocksucking marshals and having a little sit down with Administrator Oshima."

"If you're taking over, why bother disabling the mill?" asked Gash.

"To show them we mean business."

"And," Ramos added, "in case something goes wrong and we don't get to Oshima."

"Nothing's going to go wrong," Larimore assured him. "Let's go. We've got other business."

He stepped off the boat and headed down the plank. Ramos lagged behind and muttered to Gash, "Amigo, when the time comes, we're going to need you as sober as a judge, not chewing gravel. Can we count on you?"

He didn't want anyone counting on him. He didn't want any part of it. The last thing Gash needed was someone depending on him.

> *"Paul, we've got a problem with a pressure equalization valve in the transfer chamber airlock."*
>
> *"You sure it's not just air bubbles in the coolant line?"*
>
> *"Not likely."*
>
> *"All right, tell the shuttle commander to back off until we find the problem."*
>
> *"He's not going to like it."*
>
> *"Too bad."*
>
> *"Okay, you're the duty engineer...Shuttle commander confirms a hold on docking procedures. I won't bother passing on the expletives."*
>
> *"Thanks for that."*
>
> *"Now what? The pressure control assembly just went offline."*
>
> *"Get those passengers out of the transfer chamber and—"*
>
> *"Paul, it's a micrometeorite incursion."*
>
> *"Where?"*
>
> *"One of the chamber's high-pressure tanks."*
>
> *"Get those people out—now!"*
>
> *"There's no time. That tank's going to explode. It'll depressurize the entire station. You've got to blow the transfer chamber hatch now!"*
>
> *"There are thirteen people in there!"*
>
> *"You've got to do it, Paul. You've got to blow it now!"*
>
> *"Marcy...forgive me."*

Another salvo of brilliant luminance exploded overhead. The sonic vibration shook the boat.

"Well?" asked Ramos. "Can we count on you?"

He wanted to tell him to forget it. To go take a flying leap off a tall tree. To take his rebellion and shove it down the throat of someone who cared. Instead, he heard himself say, "I'll be there."

61

hrobbing thunderbolts shook the ground. The air shuddered and tree limbs rattled, yet no moisture fell. Light flared fitfully, but there was no warmth. The sky was ablaze, and then it wasn't. Amidst it all, smoke and ash wafted through treetops like silent harbingers of doom.

Silent but not disregarded.

Hysteria infected the forest. Ground sparrows huddled in their burrows, and tree lizards, roused from their nocturnal dormancy, rolled their eyes in distress. Groups of ursu woke with excited grunts, exchanging scents in an attempt to comprehend the nature of the disturbance, the degree of danger. Organisms great and small ran without direction, sought sanctuary without avail. The maelstrom assaulted their senses, spreading fear and disarray.

❧❧❧

Confusion. Stress germination. Phototropic nodes signal conflagration imminent. Bacterial network conflicted. Impulse streams erratic. Potassium imbalance noted. Alarm. Survival endangered. Root crown links threat, infestation. Response vital. Delay perilous. Root crown initiative revised, accelerated. Collective consciousness confirms immediacy. Newly synthesized di-

rectives instituted. Action confirmed. Protect. Defend. Eradicate.

62

Eamon hadn't slept well. In fact, he'd slept hardly at all. He'd spent most of the night wrestling with his conscience. He didn't know if he'd won or lost, but in the end he'd convinced himself. He knew what he had to do. Doubt didn't matter. His feelings didn't matter. What mattered was resolution.

He was wide awake when the TJs were rousted for morning chow. They grumbled and griped as they staggered off the barge where he'd sacked out. They made their way past him down the long floating plank gangway to shore, breakfast and another day of clearing timber.

Eamon wasn't hungry. Not any more than he'd been sleepy the night before. He only wanted to do what he had to do, to get it over with. He closed his eyes and gathered himself. When he opened them, more than an hour later, he realized he'd fallen asleep.

Still groggy from his unexpected lapse, he pulled on his boots and hurried across the floating planks to the dock. He jumped off the end, splashing through the shallows, bent down and threw icy lake water on his face to wash away the lethargy.

"Where the hell you been, Pretty Boy?" asked Ramos. "Grab an axe and get your turtle ass up the hill! Gash's crew needs another limber. Go on, vamoose!"

Eamon didn't bother to reply. Neither did he make any attempt to quicken his pace. He didn't care anymore if the honcho was pissed at him. After today, he wouldn't care what anyone thought. He picked up an axe, hefting it with one hand then two, getting a feel for it, seeing in his mind's eye how he'd swing it.

The timber line was a good two hundred yards up the hill, but he had no sense of the time that passed as he made the climb. His mind disconnected. His legs trudged upward, onward, but his thoughts strayed. He tried to focus only on his objective. He didn't want to falter now. He couldn't allow his purpose to flag.

Before long, he spotted Gash, chopping at one of the forest giants. A crew of limbers passed nearby, moving up the rise. Eamon didn't care. He made straight for Gash, twisting his grip around the axe handle as if he would choke the life out of it.

Gash saw him. He paused in mid-stroke and watched Eamon approach. Even as he advanced, Eamon was assailed by doubt. How was he going to overcome Gash, who was much stronger, and more experienced with an axe than he would ever be? And if he did, what would it feel like, sound like, when his blade bit into flesh and bone?

He expected Gash to take a defensive stance. The grizzled TJ certainly saw the determination on his face. Instead, Gash buried his axe in the tree and turned to face Eamon with his arms slack at his sides.

He wasn't going to put up a fight. Eamon saw it in his eyes. There was no fear in them, only weariness and resignation. Eamon slowed his approach. It was more than surrender. The look in the older man's eyes was like a plea for Eamon to put an end to his anguish.

Two paces away—two paces from that which compelled him, had consumed years of his life and sent him halfway across the galaxy—Eamon stopped. He raised his axe slowly, not certain whether he did so to bolster his resolve or give Gash a chance to run.

But he didn't run. He didn't move at all. Eamon read the look on his face. It said, *Come on kid, get it over with. Do it right.* When he hesitated and the axe in his hands drooped, he saw disappointment cross Gash's face.

Eamon was so conflicted, so focused on his intent, on willing himself to do what he had to do, he'd shut out the rest of the world. It was Gash who heard something that caused him to turn.

Eamon listened. At first, it seemed simply the racket of a busy work crew—voices calling out commands, derisive arguments and good-natured mockery. They were sounds he'd become accustomed to. Yet there was something in the timbre of the shouts that made him listen more closely. He heard belligerence...desperation.

Gash didn't hesitate. He raced uphill and disappeared over the rise just above where they stood. Eamon wavered. He was confused, as much by the shouts as by his own inadequacy. Why hadn't he gone through with it when he'd had the chance? Was he that weak? Was he that—

A scream jarred him from self-reproach. It was a fearful, wretched scream. One he couldn't imagine coming from the lips of a timber jockey, and yet...

He rushed up over the rise and stopped dead on the crest. What he saw was as horrifying as it was astounding. For several heartbeats he didn't believe his eyes. It was a scene so fantastically chaotic, he questioned whether he were truly awake.

There were at least a dozen TJs in the clearing, most covered with greenery, all struggling as if wrestling with some unseen enemy. At first, he didn't know what it was he saw. It was as if the forest had come alive and enveloped the men, consuming them. Their cries were frantic.

"Let go, goddammit—get off!"

"Help! Help me!"

"You damn..."

Those with axes and knives hacked furiously at the foliage that engulfed them. Many, though, had been caught empty-handed, and flailed helplessly. Eamon spotted Gash. He was trying to liberate Meanan, who was wrapped head-to-toe in a leafy vine. There were vines swarming everywhere. Like serpents, they slithered across the ground, coiled and constricted. Half the men stood without moving, dazed with disbelief. Eamon saw Porno Eddy pulled down and dragged away. He screamed, "No! No!" Then Gash went down.

No longer able to help Meanan, Gash struggled to free himself from the grip of the vine that had encircled his legs and toppled him. He ripped at one branch as another curled around his waist.

Eamon stood, rooted by astonishment and terror. He watched the grave struggle awestruck, frazzled by the screams. Should he race to Gash's rescue, or stand by and let his vengeance be served by this nightmarish scenario?

He was conflicted for only a moment. In that moment, he saw Kruto run to Gash's side, swinging his axe like a madman. Kruto hacked until the tendrils were severed and Gash scrambled to his feet. More vines snaked towards them, and Gash pushed Kruto back.

They were coming at Eamon now, too. He looked around. Porno Eddy and Meanan were gone. Several TJs had vanished. The few who had freed themselves were bloodied and bewildered.

"Head for the lake!" Gash yelled. "Go, go, go!"

They ran, dodging and leaping over the creeping vines. One TJ was tripped by the relentless vegetation and went sprawling. Eamon helped him up as a vine began curling about his own legs. He slashed down with his axe and cut it. The severed end continued to squirm and thrash as he ran downhill toward the lake.

63

Amanda listened. She'd been listening to the wind song for several minutes now. There was something odd about it, something different. The wind wasn't blowing particularly hard yet the sound was frenetic, its tone agitated, not at all the serene melody that had accompanied her flute.

Of course, now that she knew what it was, she was aware it wasn't actually responding to her own music. That was coincidence. She didn't have her flute now, yet she heard it whistling from among the trees. No one else seemed to—or at least, no one paid any attention.

It didn't surprise her no one heard it but her. In recent days, nature's tranquility seldom intruded upon the expedition. Instead, tension hung in the camp like dirty laundry. Filamena was standoffish, speaking little to anyone, including her husband. As cramped as it was, she remained in her tent most of the time. Dr. Nikira was equally unapproachable, though Chanya was able to engage him when she tried. Professor Escobedo was completely absorbed in his work, and his son had quit assisting him to spend more time with his Imaginator. What kind of virtual art he was creating, Amanda didn't know. He wasn't sharing it with anyone, but seemed obsessed with it. Vincent Boorman had taken Max's place, helping the professor with whatever he needed, seeming genuinely intrigued with the process of discovery.

That had left McCroy and Scurlock bored. They persistently complained and argued, attempting to convince everyone they should pack up and head back. They'd found nothing that suited their definition of treasure, and were anxious to put the disappointment behind them. It got to the point they were becoming obnoxious, particularly Scurlock, whose acrimonious stares targeted Amanda every chance he got. His bitter gaze fixated on her as if *she* were the one who had attacked *him*.

He was watching her now. What twisted schemes brooded behind those eyes of his she didn't care to know. She looked away, trying to clear her mind of such anxious thoughts, then glanced back to see if he was still watching.

He wasn't. He wasn't even standing in the same place anymore. Where had he gone so quickly? Then she heard a muffled cry and saw flailing boots in the bushes. It was the last thing she saw clearly.

Something touched her leg. She looked down. For a bewildering moment, her brain refused to accept what her eyes saw. Insinuating itself between and around her legs was one of the leafy vines. It moved as if alive. It *was* alive. Suddenly it constricted and pulled her legs out from under her. She fell, too stunned to even scream.

Her back slammed against the ground. The force knocked the wind out of her. The thick vine continued to grow around her, creeping up her thighs, sliding over her hips and stomach, slithering up toward her chest. Its thorns pricked her, but the pain was secondary to her incredulity at what was happening.

Amanda caught her breath and struggled to free herself, twisting and thrashing. The more she fought, the tighter the hold on her became. She caught glimpses of what was happening around her. The forest was alive with darting, undulating tentacles, like some nightmarish, arboreal medusa. Vines launched from trees and crawled snake-like across the ground.

She heard Chanya scream and saw Jimiyu pick up a smoking stick from the fire. He swung it back and forth, warding off the menacing vines. Chanya and Nikira cowered behind him. The vines didn't seem deterred by the waving stick until the motion fanned its embers into flame. As if sensing the fire, the encroaching plants retreated.

She heard the blast of a shotgun and twisted to see McCroy and his cat, together fighting off the tenacious vines. She couldn't tell if the man was coming to the rescue of his animal or if it was the other way around. Then she couldn't see anything.

The vines imprisoned her so her arms were pinned to her sides. The creepers yanked, and she felt herself being hauled away from the camp. She was helpless. She wanted to scream, but fear muted her. All she could do was watch the undulations of the vines as they groped along her body, reaching, searching, continually adjusting their hold on her. A tendril slid slowly around her neck. Its tip touched the medicine bundle—the one the old man in Woodville had given her.

The reaction of the vine and its tangled cohorts was swift and startling. They uncoiled as if she'd suddenly soured and retreated into the thick brush.

Amanda scrambled to her feet, exhausted from her struggles and too stupefied to run. Besides, they were everywhere. They were all around. She gathered herself and looked for her comrades. They'd learned from Jimiyu's success. Each one had picked up smoldering bits of firewood, and they were making a stand around the fire pit.

The vines grew less aggressive, and as Amanda rushed over to join the others, the leafy tentacles began slipping back into the forest. McCroy's big cat snarled. It stood next to its master, its body quaking from either fear or adrenalin.

The humans weren't any better off. They stood, trying to assimilate what had happened, too busy recovering to speak. Amanda had no words. There was no sense to be made of what they'd just seen, there was only profound horror. She could still feel the vines crawling across her skin. Her body shook involuntarily, as if to remind her she was no longer powerless—no longer in the grasp of the malevolent flora. It wasn't until she began noticing the sting of the thorn punctures that she felt like herself again.

It was McCroy who broke the silence.

"What in the nine hells of the Aztecs was that?"

No one had an answer.

"Where's Vincent?" Jimiyu asked, looking around.

"And Jesper," added McCroy. "Jesper!" he yelled as if expecting a response.

"Vincent!" called out Jimiyu.

They waited. There was no reply. Not a sound at all. The forest was silent. Even the wind was still. Except for the smoking torches in their hands and a few scattered, torn leaves, it was as if nothing had ever happened. Except that two of their number were gone.

64

"What's happening?" cried one TJ, sounding on the verge of hysteria. "What the fuck's happening?"

Gash looked over the men gathered at the lake's edge. They weren't the same hearty, audacious bunch of an hour ago. Their world had turned upside-down. Some were stricken with terror, their limbs shaking, their spirits mangled. Some were in shock; many, like Gash, were bleeding through rent clothing where thorns had gouged them. Most huddled close to the lake, as if the vast expanse of water would protect them.

He saw Ford wandering about, bewildered by all the commotion.

"What's wrong?" Ford asked when he felt Gash's hand on his shoulder. "What is it?"

Before he could answer, a TJ nearby said, as though talking to himself, "The forest—it...it just came alive and took them."

"The forest came alive?" asked Ford, then repeated it, more statement than question. "The forest came alive."

"We're okay now," Gash assured him, though there wasn't much assurance in his voice. "Stay here, Ford. I'm going to find Ramos."

As calm as he tried to sound, his thoughts were anything but. His inner self was asking the same thing as everyone else. What in the hell had happened? He would have questioned his sanity, but they weren't *all* going mad. The forest had come alive. There was nothing to explain it. There was no logic to make sense of it.

He spotted Ramos. The honcho was sitting on the ground, looking as dazed and stricken as the rest. Gash went to him.

"Ramos."

He didn't respond. He didn't give any indication he'd even heard.

"Ramos," Gash repeated, shaking him this time, "what do we do now? What's the plan?"

The honcho seemed to recognize him then. Gash helped him to his feet.

"I don't know. I don't—"

"Abominations. Blasphemous abominations," declared Kruto, lumbering over. His shirt was shredded and bloody. He was breathing heavily through angry, bloated nostrils. His sullen tone ramped ballistic. "We got to go back up there! We got to deliver our brothers from Satan's grasp!" he shouted, stripping off the remnants of his shirt.

"You're loco, Kruto," Ramos told him. "That's crazy talk."

Crazy? What was crazier than what had just happened? Of course, there were different levels of crazy. The big Russian had been one straitjacket short of a raving lunatic since the day he set foot on Evergreen. Gash didn't see present circumstances making him any saner.

Ramos was right, though. It was certain insanity to go back up into the trees. But then, who better for the job than Kruto? You had to admire him, in a twisted sort of way. And Gash wasn't about to forget Kruto had saved his life.

"Who's with me?" Kruto called out, turning to look around. His bare, hairy back revealed an impressive tattoo. Gash had seen it before. It was a scene from the Bible—Moses parting the Red Sea. "Who's with me? Who's righteous enough to take on the devil?"

"I'm telling you not to go," said Ramos. "I'm *ordering* you not to go."

Kruto stared at him. His jaw tightened, pulling his crucifix tattoo taut. He shifted the axe in his right hand to his left and pulled out his double-edged combat knife. The glare on his face issued a warning.

Ramos ignored the implied threat. He thrust his face inches from Kruto's.

"We've got no chance past the treeline. You saw that. You saw what happened up there." He backed off a single step and addressed everyone. "We've got to regroup, we've got to use our heads." He turned back to Kruto. "You'll get your chance at those devils. Right now, I want everyone off this beach and out to TJ City. We'll pull in the planks and try to stay out of reach. We'll wait for the *Sir Real* to show up for its morning haul, and then we'll catch a ride across the lake to the flume. Let's go! Let's move it! You, too, Kruto. I want everyone on the water in the next five minutes."

Kruto muttered, "His will be done, " then grudgingly joined the exodus down the shoreline.

It sounded like a plan to Gash—get to other side of the lake, catch the TJ Express to the vill, and sort it out there.

Only the *Sir Real* never showed up. They waited, and waited, until Ramos finally decided they should barricade themselves inside two of the largest sheltered barges and wait for the night to pass.

It made sense, the dark of night being the abode of the strange and terrifying. Men had taken shelter from the night since the dawn of reason. Fear and horror came in the night. Death came in the night. It was the rational move. It made sense to wait out the dark. At least, it seemed to.

Only later—much later—did Gash realize they should never have waited for the sun to rise.

65

Trauma eventually gave way to fear and panic.

"We have to get out of here. We have to leave now," urged Jimiyu, not bothering to conceal the desperation in his voice.

"God, yes, let's go," Filamena agreed.

The others concurred. Amanda still felt the sensation of those vines crawling over her, clutching her. She could feel their determined grasp, their leafy embrace constricting her arms and legs. The feeling of helplessness preyed on her. She trembled at the thought of it, while despising her weakness. She couldn't focus. All she could think of was getting away—*running* away.

"Hold on," objected McCroy, "we're not going anywhere now."

"What are you saying?" countered Jimiyu. "You're not suggesting we stay here."

McCroy looked him in the eye and said, as calm as if he were suggesting they have tea, "Yes, I am. For now, anyway. It'll be night before we can even get off this plateau. Do you want to be stumbling over all that uneven terrain in the dark?" He jerked his head, indicating the expanse outside their camp. "Those things, those plants, could be anywhere."

Jimiyu looked somewhat chastised. McCroy's point was made. The idea of traveling through the dark was unnerving. Enthusiasm for a hasty escape waned.

"What about Vincent and Mr. Scurlock?" asked Nikira. "We can't just abandon them."

McCroy countered angrily, "What would you suggest, Doctor?"

"We should...we should try to find them."

"You'd do more good saying a prayer for them. We were damn lucky those things didn't get the rest of us. I don't know why they pulled back when they did, but you should count your blessings."

"He's right, Talib," said Jimiyu, still sounding frightened. "We can't go after them. We have no idea where they are. There's nothing we can do."

The expression on Nikira's face shouted that he didn't want to accept this, yet he had no alternative to offer.

"We can't stay here," said Chanya. "They could come back."

"She's right," agreed Professor Escobedo. "We won't be any safer here than we would out there."

"We can stay in one of the caves," suggested Max.

McCroy nodded. "That's a good idea. Let's collect everything we'll need when we go and get it up into one of those caves. We'll head out at first light."

Amanda did what she could to help, but she still wasn't thinking straight. Fortunately, McCroy was. He made sure they packed only what they had to. He wanted to be certain they could make good time once they set out. He even abandoned his shotguns, calling them useless against the vines.

Professor Escobedo, however, argued that he absolutely had to bring back some of his finds. A somewhat impolite debate ensued, ending with the professor and his son adding a few archaeological items to their own packs and McCroy threatening to leave them behind if they couldn't keep up.

They chose a cave with a narrow entrance and built a fire not too far from its mouth. McCroy said it was so the smoke could vent, and for the protection the flames would give them. Despite the fire, Amanda spent the night expecting at any moment to see snaking vines creep out of the darkness. It made it difficult for her to rest—and not only her. No one slept at first. Neither did they talk much. She guessed they were afraid the sound might call the wrath of the forest down on them again.

She considered telling them it was foolish to think plants could hear, and then contemplated the idea more fully. Maybe they *could* hear, in a way. What was it that plants responded to? Light, moisture, minerals, vibrations—the vibrations of sound. It was possible this form of vegetation, whatever it was, responded to such vibrations. But how did that, or any other response, trigger an attack?

It was Max who broke the silence. "It was just like in the cave painting," he mumbled.

"What did you say, Maximo?" asked his father.

The young man had been creating something on his Imaginator. He put it down and replied, "I was just thinking how surreal it was when...when those things attacked us. It was like the scenario in the cave. The same thing must have happened to them."

Amanda nodded. Max was right. The cave painting had turned out to be a glimpse of the future as well as the past.

Huddled behind their fire, she imagined they weren't much different from the ursu who had taken refuge in these caves so many thousands of years ago. Fear had likely driven them inside, too, but it wasn't superstitious fear. It was real. It was the primal instinct to survive. No doubt the ursu didn't understand what was happening to them then, any more than she did now. She realized so many of her questions about the ancient ursu remained unanswered. Those had been superseded by new enquiries—ones concerned with their own survival.

"I was thinking how much it reminded me of the carving on the artifact," Nikira said, his stare fixed on the ground in front of him. "The ungodly way the trees seemed to come to life." He looked up at Amanda. His monotone veered sharply to emotional plea. "What in the spawn of Satan were those things, Doctor?" It was almost an accusation.

"I don't know...exactly," she replied. "I've come across vines like those before, but I've never seen any evidence they were prehensile, or that they had such rapid motive ability."

"Why would they attack us like that? What reason could they have?"

"Motive implies intelligence. Vegetable matter lacks the capacity for intellectual reasoning," she said. "A brain—at least, every type of brain we're familiar with—requires protein to grow, to function."

277

"You mean like the protein in a human body?" inquired McCroy.

Amanda knew what he was suggesting, and though she couldn't refute the grisly implications, she wasn't going to concede the point.

"The concept of intelligent plant life is science fiction. Whatever triggered the reaction was instinctual, not cognitive."

Even as she said it, Amanda remembered a theoretical paper she'd once read. It was hypothetical fancy, but it suggested that a plant's water xylem, along with "cytoplasmic streaming," could evolve into a nervous system. It also suggested, coincidently, that, as with the California redwoods, a single root ball could develop underground, living far longer than the above-ground leaves and blossoms. Within this bulbous protective case, a sort of brain could develop. That was the theory, anyway, and a far-fetched one at that. No evidence of any such encephalonic flora had ever been discovered on Earth, or anywhere else, for that matter.

Communication, the paper conjectured, could be conducted via airborne chemicals, or even bacterial messages transported by insects. Amanda had all but proven the ursu communicated with airborne chemicals—smells—but that had no bearing. Plants did not have olfactory senses. The idea of such organisms communicating in any meaningful way, barring normal responses to specific stimuli and inherent aptitude, seemed as absurd to her now as it did when she read the paper. Instinctual responses in plants were primitive even compared to insects or...

She recalled the frantic dance of the madfly. Was there a connection beyond basic biology between Evergreen's flora and other species such as the madfly? Was the dance a message itself, or did the madfly unknowingly pass on a communiqué through chemical compounds it carried from one location to another?

"I don't care what you say," asserted McCroy. "Those plants weren't acting out of any instinct. The way they came at us—it was sudden, smart, organized. They knew what they were doing."

Did they really know what they were doing? Was it instinct or forethought that guided them? Why had they taken Scurlock and young Mr. Boorman? As much as she loathed McCroy's associate for what he'd done to her, he hadn't deserved to be hauled away like so much...

So much what? What would they do with him? Amanda was still embroiled with her inner debate when fatigue overcame her and she fell asleep.

66

few timber jockeys slept that night. Gash huddled with a group that included Ramos, Cayenne and Ford. He had searched the barge for Eamon and found him sitting on the opposite side, keeping his distance. He couldn't imagine what was going through the kid's head now. Was he still bent on revenge, or had circumstances erased that notion?

Who was he kidding? It was no mere whim that had driven Eamon across the galaxy in search of his mother's killer. He wasn't likely to give up now. Gash couldn't figure out why the kid had hesitated when he'd had the chance. Maybe he didn't have the stomach for it.

No one aboard the barge talked much. For such a close-quarters assembly of normally boisterous TJs, it was eerily silent. For Ford, the quiet must have been especially deafening. No doubt the old cook realized many of them were reliving the day's events. They'd seen friends hauled off like so much cordwood by green limbs that had reached out of the forest. Even if Ford couldn't picture what he heard described, he surely sensed their need for diversion.

So, Gash wasn't surprised when Ford suddenly asked, of no one in particular, "Did I ever tell you the story of the River of Tears?"

Gash had heard the tall tale. So had Ramos and any other TJ who'd put in any time. Ramos encouraged him anyway.

"Tell us the story, Ford," he said.

"Yeah, tell us," said a TJ sitting across the deck. "I never heard that one."

"It happened long ago, when my people first landed on Evergreen. They were exploring, climbing up one side of a mountain and down the other. When they neared the bottom of one such peak they saw an enormous creature. A ragged green monster with a thousand arms, sitting in a giant nest like a mother hen.

"But it was a peaceful beast. It looked at the people with inhuman eyes but did not try to harm them. Still, the sight of it struck fear in them. They hurried to climb back up the mountain and get away from the monster. In their rush, one of them slipped and started an avalanche. Huge rocks and massive boulders rained down upon the creature. It used its many arms in an attempt to divert the rockslide, but half the mountainside had given way. Too much, even, for its many arms. It escaped the disaster, but its nest, full of its young, was crushed."

Ford told the tale with flourishes of his hands, and all the drama of a soothsayer. Gash saw that everyone in the barge was listening, whether they'd heard the story before or not. Their focus, the very atmosphere within the expansive compartment had changed.

"From atop what remained of the mountain, my people heard the anguished bellows of the creature. They saw tears pouring from its many eyes. They were tears of blood. The leviathan cried all day and all night. Realizing what they'd done, my people stayed atop the mountain and prayed to the spirits of the wind to ease the monster's suffering.

"When day came, they could see that the monster's tears had been so great they'd formed a river. Without warning, the monster ceased to cry and looked up at the men on the mountain. They feared it would now come after them, seeking retribution. Instead, it turned and stepped into the river.

"But it didn't step into the river. Its many arms stepped *onto* the river. The people watched as it walked across the bloody water, each of its thousand arms resting on the surface—not sinking below it. It is said that it traveled down the river until it came to Lake Washoe, where it sank to the bottom, never to surface again.

"My people named it Tessie after a monster of their own folklore. In the years to follow, there were sightings of Tessie's arms reaching out of the lake, searching for her young—or so my people used to say.

"So, gentlemen...and Lady Cayenne," Ford said, his tone changing abruptly, "that is the story of how the River of Tears came to be. Today you call it Rust River, but it's the same."

"What about Tessie?" called one of the timber jocks.

"Tessie remains on the lake bottom," Ford said. "She could be below us at this very moment."

There were bursts of laughter from various quarters. Grim faces relaxed. Friendly arguments concerning the reality of the story erupted. Gash figured Ford had told the perfect ghost story for men who'd been so terrorized earlier they wouldn't have recognized themselves. It broke the spell—shattered the crystal elephant in the room that no one wanted to acknowledge.

He leaned over to Ford to tell him "good job" but saw the old man anxiously clutch his neck, feeling for something.

"What's wrong, Ford? Lose something?"

"Yeah, my lucky medicine bundle."

"Didn't you give that away?"

"Yes, I guess I did. Kind of wish I had it back."

67

I t was a long way back to civilization, and Amanda knew each step would be through potentially hostile territory. McCroy led them at an accelerated pace, letting them rest when he had to but never seeming to falter himself. Even so, it was a struggle for everyone to keep up.

Thor stayed close to his master's side. The animal's head constantly swiveled one way then the other, its ears scanning for danger. It seemed confused, an emotion Amanda could relate to.

The mountainside they were descending was dotted with boulders and thickets of dry brush but little other growth. It may have been the apparent safety of the open terrain, or maybe just that their wits were returning to them, yet somewhere along the way Amanda got the impression that determination had replaced fear as the group's primary drive.

When they reached the bottom of the incline, McCroy increased his pace. As he led them into ever-thickening woods, she tried to deflect the horrific memories of the previous day. Instead of recalling those images, she wrestled with various suppositions, pondering what McCroy had said as they cowered in the cave, waiting for the night to pass. He'd called the vines "smart, organized." She had disputed him. Now, she considered the possibility he was right.

It was an alien world. What if, over the millennia, a single species of flora or an entire genus developed the capacity for cognitive thought? How would it react to the incursion of foreign entities into its world? Would its reaction be immediate, or would its concept of time be measured in epochs instead of hours? That might explain why, after so many years of human habitation, the vines had only now become aggressive.

Fanciful ideas, she thought, not based on any evidence. The scientist within her tried to reassert reason, but reason was running a distant second to bewilderment—and fear. Every tree had become an adversary, every unidentifiable growth a potential danger. They'd traveled this way before, but at the time she hadn't realized how impenetrable the woods seemed once you were deep within them. It was as if, no matter how far or how fast they went, they remained surrounded.

They'd been on the march for some time when she spotted the ursu—first one, then several. The animals were following them again, moving on a parallel course through the trees, so far off in the forest she caught only a glimpse of them now and then. She wasn't sure why, but their familiar presence reassured her.

After a while, the dread construed by her theorizing—and her more primal fears—merged into a knot in her stomach. It was past mid-day, and they'd come so far without incident she sensed their group begin to relax. Then again, it could have been fatigue and denial had simply worn down their anxiety.

"Can't we stop and rest?" begged Filamena

"Yes, please," concurred Professor Escobedo.

"I agree," Nikira said, "we need to rest before we go on."

McCroy relented. "All right, let's take ten."

"We'll never make it all the way back," said Jimiyu, more to himself than anyone else.

"We'll make it," McCroy responded with a confidence Amanda thought must be false bravado.

"It took us seven days to get here," Jimiyu complained. "We'll never last that long."

McCroy's stern gaze fell on him. "We spent half that time going in circles cause of your boy Harley. I know where we are now. And I know the shortest way back. If we double-time, it shouldn't take us more than two days."

"We can't run all the way," said Max, looking at his father and stepmother.

"Not all the way," declared McCroy. "We dogtrot, then we walk. We alternate."

"It may be difficult for some of us to keep up such a regimen," said Nikira.

"I'm not leaving anybody behind, if that's what you mean," McCroy responded. "We'll do what we can do, but everyone better move like their life depends on it, because it does."

Amanda noticed Chanya was crying. She put her hand on the woman's arm and said, "It's all right, dear. You're going to be all right."

"No, no, I wasn't thinking about myself," she replied, wiping away her tears. "I was thinking about poor Vincent. He was such a good boy."

"He was." Jimiyu nodded. "As much as I might have doubted it when we first met. Dr. Nikira was speaking to a group of young Americans, and after he was finished this wild-eyed fellow with his hair coiffed in spiked rows came up to us. I thought I was going to have to protect Dr. Nikira."

"I remember," interjected Nikira. "He was very idealistic, very enthusiastic about my theories."

"Yes," continued Jimiyu, "I was amazed that one speech was all it took to make him a believer. At the time, though, we thought he was mocking us. When he tried to hand Dr. Nikira a check for two hundred thousand dollars, I nearly slammed the door in his face. Looking at him, we had no clue to the magnitude of his family's wealth. We were certain he was having a joke at our expense."

"He believed, he really believed," Nikira added.

"Yes, and he wrote out the check just like that—on the spur of the moment. That was the Vincent we knew—always impulsive, always ready to finance whatever Dr. Nikira needed."

"His contributions made it possible for me to continue my research," said Nikira, "made it possible for us to come to Evergreen. Yet now, because he believed in me..."

McCroy stood suddenly, as if purposely cutting the conversation short. "Let's go. That's enough of a breather for now. We've got to get on the move. The longer we stay in one spot, the easier quarry we make."

"You make it sound as if we're being hunted," Professor Escobedo said, standing up and helping Filamena to her feet.

"I've never felt more hunted in my life," said McCroy, and he wasn't smiling.

They resumed their forced march, but the terrain was too uneven for them to travel very fast. When they encountered an extensive patch of the tall, large-petaled aurora blossoms growing along either side of their path, Amanda realized McCroy had already veered off the route they'd come by. She knew she would have remembered the flowers if they'd passed this way before. She hoped McCroy really did know where he was going, because she was all turned around.

Their Great White Hunter had his machete out, cutting away some scrub that had grown over their convoluted path, when spouts of seed spores began shooting from the aurora blossoms. The tufted, floating seeds startled more than harmed them. However, the air about them quickly grew clouded with fine dust. They began to cough. Professor Escobedo wheezed as if he couldn't breathe.

"It's pollen!" declared Amanda. "Cover your mouth and nose. Try not to breathe it in."

"We've got to get out of this," McCroy shouted, his hand over his face. "This way. Run!"

Nikira helped Max with his father, and they all staggered more than ran to escape the range of the aurora blossoms. Even when they'd distanced themselves from the pollen they weren't relieved of its effects. Amanda's nose ran and her eyes watered almost to the point she couldn't see where she was going. Even her breathing was labored. And she wasn't the worst off. Everyone was experiencing the same problems, the professor most of all. He was having an attack of some sort. McCroy had to call a halt so they could sit him down.

Amanda had never seen any such volatile discharge from the blossoms before. She was certain it couldn't be coincidence they just happened to be passing by. The flowers must have been responding to their presence. It had to have been a deliberate assault.

It was some time before they gathered themselves and continued their trek. When they did, there was a quiet desperation in their expressions. Amanda saw it in their eyes. She felt it in herself. Were they all wondering the same thing? Wondering *What next?*

68

They paddled towards the south shore in relative quiet and calm. Eamon wondered if any of them were thinking about Ford's monster on the lake bottom. He was. Not that he believed the tale. On the other hand, after what they'd seen, who was to say what was real and what wasn't?

He'd spent most of the night trying to sort that and other things out then fell asleep. It felt like he'd just closed his eyes when he was roused from a dream with word they were moving out. In his dream outlandishly human-like plants grabbed his mother and pulled her away from him. He ran to her rescue and cut her loose, only to discover it was Gash he had freed.

It bothered him. Why would he dream such a thing? He couldn't figure it out. He hadn't saved Gash when he had the chance. He hadn't killed him when he had the chance, either. He remembered standing, transfixed with indecision, watching as the vines pulled Gash down and wrapped around him. That's what it came down to. He'd failed to make a decision, and the recollection only stoked his guilt. It seemed no matter what he did he couldn't escape that.

It was no longer a dream he found himself in. It was a living nightmare. Who knew when he'd have the chance to avenge his mother again. What would he do if the chance arose? He wasn't sure anymore. Maybe he'd dreamed of rescuing Gash because, somewhere inside, he believed—he knew—Gash would do the same for him.

"It's the *Sir Real!*" someone called from the lead boat. "She's aground!"

As they neared the shore, Eamon saw the old steamer tilted up on one side, her starboard gunwales jammed into the beach. The mood changed perceptibly among the TJs. The hulk of the *Sir Real* reminded them of the threat they faced—of its reach and power.

They pulled their dugouts ashore with caution. There were no signs of danger...and no signs of human life. Neither the crew of the *Sir Real* nor the men from the pump station were anywhere to be seen.

"Farr, come with me," Ramos ordered. "We've got to get the pump station back online. Nishi, get aboard the *Sir Real* and collect all the charged solar packs you can find. Chaltraw, gather some of the extra axes and cut them down. Short handles are better for defense against those things. Gash, take Cayenne, Pretty Boy and a few others and get up Swank Summit. Check the flume. See if there are any survivors up there. The rest of you get that yarder operational. We've all got tickets for the TJ Express."

⟣⟢ ⟣⟢ ⟣⟢

Eamon followed Cayenne and Farr up the ladder. They were among the eight TJs Ramos had randomly picked to ride the first log down the summit. They went from the ladder to the catwalk to the shorn timber awaiting them in the chute.

He dug his cleats in and sank his grapples through the bark as deeply as he could. He pulled on them, testing their hold, and braced himself for the release.

That's when the commotion began. He heard shouts and the growl of a power saw coming to life. He twisted from his kneeling position to see what was going on.

Scores of vines emerged from the trees. At first, the timber jocks on the ground were caught off-guard, but the shock of the initial attack had worn off and they quickly defended themselves. Gash mustered a small group at the flume's base. He formed them into a crude circle. It was a smart move—it enabled them to protect each other's backs from the creeping menace.

289

Cayenne, who was hunkered on the log just ahead of Eamon, saw the attack, too. She pulled out a cleat and started to get up.

"Stay down, Cayenne!" Ramos ordered from below. To the flume master, he shouted, "Set!"

Eamon heard the flume master repeat "Set!" and the projectile they were riding began easing forward. He tightened his grip on the grapples even more, but kept his head turned to observe the conflict behind him. He couldn't see everything, but the timber jocks were holding their own. He saw the flume master drop out of sight—the catwalk had given way. Then he saw it wasn't just the catwalk. The entire flume was going down. The vines had yanked out its foundation, and it collapsed, domino-like.

The surge of destruction was headed their way, and the log was only now beginning to pick up speed. Eamon didn't think they were going to make it. The collapse was too rapid. He loosened his cleats so he could jump. But which way? He had no idea. He turned his head one way then the other. Their log was gaining speed. Then the sound of crashing timber abruptly stopped.

He looked behind him. The collapse had halted short of the section their ride was now coursing through. The first thirty yards of the flume had been destroyed, but the remainder held fast. The flow of lubricating water from the pump station had been cut off, but somehow, they were still moving, sliding along on what water was there.

The TJ Express was out of commission, and they were on the last train out. The only train out.

69

Amanda rubbed her sore calf muscles. Everyone was thankful for the break. She knew McCroy was pushing them for their own good, but even she was having trouble keeping up.

She looked into the forest. She wasn't certain how many of the ursu were out there following them, because most of the time they kept their distance. A dozen, maybe fewer—all males, from what she had seen. Occasionally, like now, when they had stopped to rest, a few of the animals ventured closer. They were curious. It was likely this particular community of ursu had never seen humans until they came across the expedition.

Amanda decided her initial observations had been correct. There were slight differences between these ursu and those she'd been studying. The coloring of their fur was definitely darker, their vocalizations more frequent, and—what interested her most—they appeared to be even more bipedal in nature than their cousins just miles away. The ursu she was familiar with moved about on both two and four legs, depending on circumstance. She wasn't certain why she thought so, but it appeared to her the creatures following them were more adapted to traveling upright.

That might signify more than tribal diversity. It might also mean there was a link between the ones that followed them and the ancient ursu of the plateau. The idea wasn't nearly as strange as the spore attack—if *attack* was the right word to describe it.

Something occurred to her. Could it be that the threat posed to them wasn't from just a single species, or even an entire genus? What if the vines were only the working limbs of something greater? What if the planet was honeycombed with a massive neural network, and the aurora blossoms were responding to commands from that network? What if it was Evergreen *itself* that was sentient?

Now she was really letting her imagination run wild. She had no evidence on which to base any such conjecture.

She turned her attention outward and saw three of the ursu creep close enough for her to get a good look. The scrutiny was mutual. She saw them sniff the air, trying to recognize the scents coming from the strange beasts that had invaded their territory. Then, abruptly, they grew alert. They froze momentarily, their noses and ears twitching, then scattered into the forest. They were frightened by something, Amanda was sure. And if they were scared, then...

McCroy's big cat suddenly let out a savage growl, and that's when she saw them. Dozens of them crawling slowly out from the underbrush. She jumped from where she'd been sitting and collided with Jimiyu, knocking him to the ground. As he fell, several of the slithering vines turned towards him.

Amanda scrambled out of harm's way. When she looked around, what she saw was a grotesque living sculpture—a fusion of man and foliage. Half their party was ensnared by the leafy predators.

She grabbed Jimiyu and tried to prevent him from being dragged away. She braced herself as he cried out—whether from fear or the bite of the vines' thorns, she didn't know. As she hunched over him, pulling with all her might, she saw the look of terror in his eyes.

McCroy was at her side almost instantly. He had his machete out, and was trying to access portions of the vines not coiled around Jimiyu. He chopped where he could, but for every one he severed another took its place. Thor stood nearby, poised on its haunches, snarling and striking the creepers with its claws, to little effect. When one of the plants grabbed hold of McCroy, the cat pounced on the offending appendage.

Even as she struggled to keep Jimiyu from being pulled from her grasp, Amanda saw the giant lynx entangled by a swarm of vines and pulled off its feet. It cried out almost forlornly. McCroy freed himself and ran to the animal's defense.

Desperation clutched Amanda. The forest creepers menaced them from all sides. There was no avenue of escape, even if she were to desert the others. She wouldn't do that—she couldn't. She tried to wrench away a vine wrapped around Jimiyu's leg and recoiled as her hand clenched on a thorn. The wound stung and began to bleed, but that wasn't even a consideration. Except it reminded her of something—being cut...healing...protecting.

She dove for her pack and frantically sorted through it until she found her jar of aloe vera. She threw the jar so that it slammed against a large rock. The brittle plastic cracked, and the gel splattered. Before she could even consider what to do next, Amanda felt a violent tug on her leg.

70

e was helpless, in the grasp of a monster he didn't comprehend. As he struggled in vain to free his arms, to grab hold of
something, anything, he saw Chanya pulled down by the same malignant tentacles that constricted him. He also saw Nikira. His old
friend stood stunned but unmolested.

Then, as Chanya was assaulted, Nikira's expression took on
life. He looked almost enraged. He ran to Chanya and attempted
to rip the vines from her with his bare hands.

Jimiyu watched the fate of his friends, powerless to help himself much less them. He was aware of Amanda's hold on him, and
of McCroy's attempts to cut him free, but their actions were a blur.
He twisted and turned in an attempt to wriggle free, to no avail.
He heard Chanya scream and saw that both she and Nikira had
become enmeshed by a legion of vines, their bodies bound and
drawn together like fetal twins.

His attention was jerked away as a vine wound around his neck
and pulled tight. He couldn't breathe. The gasping sounds he
made were barely audible over the furor of the struggle. He heard
Chanya scream again. The lack of air made him dizzy. Just before
he passed out he thought he saw one of Dr. Rousch's hairy brutes
rushing towards him.

71

er first impulse was to scream, but fear choked off the sound. Her second was to turn and run. But run where? Those things were everywhere, like tongues coming out of the forest's maw, reaching for them, groping, questing.

Before she could think, Filamena saw Luis and Max both caught up in an emerald embrace. Luis let out a squeal of surprise as he was grabbed from behind. Max's arms were pinned to his sides. The machete he'd carried lay on the ground next to him. Both men struggled to free themselves. The struggle only seemed to call forth more of the vines.

Shock seized Filamena so thoroughly she couldn't scream. She was only vaguely aware of her surroundings. The others were under assault, also. She didn't know which way to turn. She stood staring, static as marble. Her husband and her lover buckled and fell to the ground. She watched as the vines secured their holds and began dragging off the bodies—Luis one way, Max another.

They were going to die if she didn't do something. They were going to disappear into the forest like the others, never to be seen again. What could she do? There was nothing...

She grabbed up the machete then faltered. Luis or Max? Who did she save first? Was there time to save both? She made her choice, set her mind to it and began hacking at the vines with all her might.

They were resilient. It took two, three cuts of the machete to slice through a single vine. She chopped and chopped and kept on chopping. She was exhausted and near hysteria when Luis pulled the machete from her hand and wrapped his arms around her. They were both were shaking. She gathered herself enough to dare glance up from where her face was buried in Luis's shoulder and couldn't believe what she saw.

Huge creatures came charging at them—the same ones that had been following them. Their speed was frightening, and they growled angrily. Filamena screamed in terror. Luis moved in front of her protectively.

The beasts pulled up short. They didn't attack. One standing not five feet from her actually looked confused. When one of the vines slithered up its leg, the animal grabbed it and began stomping on it as if enraged. For several blurry seconds the scene, from Filamena's perspective, became surreal. It was a chaotic battle between man, beast and plant. She held on to Luis, shielding her eyes from the nightmarish tableau her mind refused to accept. For the first time in a long, long time, she prayed.

It wasn't until her awareness was jogged by an abrupt calm that she dared look up. It was over. The struggle had ended. The vines had retreated. So had the beasts that had come to their rescue. She saw one hurrying away through the trees.

She looked around for any signs of danger. She saw Amanda and Jimiyu supporting each other. McCroy was on his knees, pulling the remnants of hacked vines from around the neck of his beautiful cat. The animal didn't move. Its head hung limp.

She looked for the others, but there were no others. Dr. Nikira and Chanya were gone. And Max, where was...? The question died with the dawning of full recollection. It had been only seconds ago, a minute at most, yet she'd dismissed it from her mind, blanked it out. Now she remembered. She remembered her choice, though little of what came after.

"Max!" she screamed.

Luis pulled her back to him and held her even tighter as her body convulsed. She sobbed uncontrollably.

72

As suddenly as they had attacked, the vines withdrew. Never-theless, the timber jockeys atop Swank Summit didn't abandon their defensive postures. They weren't so sure the withdrawal wasn't a feint. They scoured the brushwood in anticipation of another assault as they caught their collective breath.

They hadn't lost anyone this time, at least as far as Gash could determine, but their only means of escape was demolished. At least the TJs riding that first log would make it to Woodville, unless the flume had been tampered with farther down the line. Either way, it wasn't likely to do them much good. He couldn't see the company riding to their rescue.

He was still trying to cope with what he'd seen. Why had the plants pulled down the flume? How could they know?

There was only one answer. This wasn't just some mindless vegetable response, some mutated freak of nature that had come out of hibernation. There was an intelligence at work. But what kind of intelligence? Apparently, one smart enough to block their retreat.

What he didn't know, and couldn't understand, was *why* the plants had attacked. Men had been on Evergreen for decades, and the timber mining had been going on for years. Why now? And if it was an intelligence, then what were the vines doing with the men they dragged away? Were they prisoners somewhere? Were they killed?

"We've got to get back to the pump station," Ramos called out. "Everyone stay close—keep it tight."

As they started down the summit Gash wondered if Ramos was thinking the same thing he was. With the TJ Express shut down, the only way back to the vill was to go upriver to the path the townies used. That meant walking through miles of dense woodland. He didn't much care for that idea. There was no way to know how prevalent the vines were. Or, for that matter, if there weren't some other danger awaiting them.

Before they were within sight of the pump station, they heard the shouts. Ramos quickened his pace, and the others followed. When the station came into view, Gash saw hundreds of creepers snaking out in all directions from the chaparral. Several TJs Ramos had stationed there were already caught up in thorny embraces. Others fought in confusion and disarray. In small groups, the timber jocks held their own; those who were caught alone were upended and hauled away.

"Let's move it, amigos!" commanded Ramos.

There was no hesitation. To a man they followed—running, sliding down the incline until they hit level ground to rush to the aid of their brethren.

"Form into circles!" yelled Ramos. "Keep your backs to each other!"

Once they congregated into groups the timber jockeys were able to ward off most of the attacks. But the vines were relentless. Chopping off the end of one might free a comrade, but it didn't kill the vine.

Amidst the chaos, Gash saw Ford standing alone near the water's edge, looking disoriented. He was about to call to him, tell him to turn around and go in the lake, when a vine darted out like a serpent's tongue and snatched him. It wrapped farther around the old man as it gradually pulled him up the shore.

Gash broke from his group and ran to help. As he did, another vine latched onto Ford's body and wove around him.

Ford wasn't making a sound when Gash reached him, and Gash's first thought was that he'd been knocked out, or worse. He stomped on one of the vines to slow its progress as he chopped at the other one. He saw Ford's eyes were open—he was conscious, but he wasn't struggling. Gash hacked off the second vine and helped Ford to his feet.

"I see them," Ford said. "I can see them."

Gash didn't know what he meant until the old man's eyes turned and focused on him.

"I can see," Ford repeated flatly, as though he were talking about the weather. "I remember."

Gash was dumbfounded. Ford had regained his sight. He'd heard the scuttlebutt that there was nothing wrong with the man's eyes, but he'd never believed it. The idea that something so traumatic had happened to him as a child that it made him blind was hard to swallow. But now...

He felt a sting on his leg, and before he could react the leg was pulled out from under him. He went down like a butchered steer. Stunned, the breath knocked out him, he looked up directly into the sun. He shielded his eyes, blinded by the glare. In the seconds it took for his eyesight to recover, he was trussed up by a clutch of vines.

He struggled as best he could, but his convulsions failed to deter the vines. The grip on his throat tightened and he choked as they dragged him off like a squirming sack of potatoes. He hadn't gone far when he heard a shrill cry. He looked up to see Ford standing over him. The old man had picked up his axe and was cutting the vines with a vengeance, shouting, "I remember you! I remember you!"

From his ground view, Gash saw more vines crawling towards them. They were going after Ford, but there was nothing he could do.

"Ford, watch—" The whip-smack of a thorny vine across his face cut the warning short.

Before he could call out again, the pull on him went slack. He rolled over. Ford had cut the vines, though he was still wrapped tight as a mummy. Gash worked to free his arms, but the severed vines still had life. The thorny cord around his neck pressed against his windpipe. He saw Ford go down, still shrieking that he remembered, still hacking with the axe.

Just as Gash freed his hands, another vine whipped out towards him. He caught it with one hand, ignoring the sting of the thorns. It wrapped around his arm like a python as he used his other hand to jerk the shorn vines from around his legs. He cast off the last of the dying creepers and wrenched the new assailant from his arm. Spotting an axe on the ground, he scooped it up and braced for the next attack.

But there was no attack. It was over. Evergreen's hostile plants had chosen to vanish back into the forest once more, taking another measure of men with them. Was that their strategy—to strike, capture what enemy they could, then withdraw?

He looked around. Ford was one of the missing. His first impulse was to run into trees and look for him. But where? There was no sign of the old man.

Kruto staggered over. He was out of breath, and his hands were bleeding. The veins in his lump of a nose throbbed.

"They got Ramos," he said. "I tried to get to him...but I couldn't. They almost got me. The filthy..."

He didn't finish.

"They got Ford, too," said Gash.

Kruto grunted with a pensive expression he had never seen on the giant's face.

Gash surveyed the survivors.

"What now?" mumbled Kruto with uncharacteristic calm.

It was a good question. Gash didn't have an answer. He knew they had to have a plan, a way to defend themselves. With the flume damaged, he doubted they'd ever make it to town now. Still, they had to try. They wouldn't last long out here. Woodville was their only chance.

73

By the time they reached the lumbermill, smoke trailed them like rocket exhaust.

Farr cried out, "We're riding the candle!"

Eamon caught a glimpse of the smoke, though he didn't see any actual flames. He was too busy holding on. It was like the old adage about rubbing two sticks together. He felt the friction beneath him. When the water in the flume ran out, he'd thought their timber missile would grind to a stop. Instead, it kept going, its momentum and the slope of the flume overcoming the abrasive resistance.

He tensed when the timber jockeys in front of him began jumping. His turn came, and he pushed off. The landing was awkward, but it didn't feel like anything was broken. He got up in time to see the log plunge into the mill's reservoir. Whatever was smoking was doused.

He followed the others in. The mill was deserted. So, it seemed at first glance, was Woodville. There was, however, evidence of a battle. Strands of cut vines were everywhere, and several buildings had collapsed where slender support beams had given way.

Apparently, the plants had invaded the town, even though it sat in a valley that had been clear-cut years ago. Eamon wondered how far their reach extended. Did they have roots? Did they grow out of the ground at will, or were they never-ending serpents, creeping, crawling wherever they wanted?

He thought about all the people in town. Surely they hadn't all been—

"Listen to that," said Cayenne.

He listened. What he heard, what they all heard, was a distant droning. It wasn't loud, but it was steady. Ahead he saw what looked like a light haze. Was it smoke? Was something burning? They approached the outskirts of the eastern end of town. Eamon couldn't see anything on fire. What was that sound?

The haze drew closer, turned blacker, and the droning became a buzzing. Before Eamon realized what it was, Farr yelled, "Madflies!"

It was a massive swarm. It blanketed a good portion of the town and was headed their way. Even as they realized what it was, it was on them. They didn't have time to react, to run.

Their attempts to knock the bugs away were as ineffectual as always. Eamon pulled his shirt up over his hat, trying to cover up; the flies were already so thick around his face he could hardly breathe. He couldn't see much, either, just enough to know that several of the TJs had dropped to the ground and were rolling around in a desperate attempt to ward off the biting flies.

"Inside!" someone hollered. "Get inside!"

Eamon followed the dimly perceived movement around him, and was soon charging through an open door. Few of the madflies followed. Most of the swarm had already moved on.

The TJs stamped and swatted at the remaining flies until they were all gone or squashed. When he was certain he was clean of the bugs, Eamon looked around. They were in Lizzie's General Store, but he didn't see the proprietor. He moved to a window. There was no sign of the swarm outside.

"Look here," said Cayenne.

She had opened the door to a back room. Eamon peered inside. There, huddled on the floor behind a desk were a man, a woman and three small children.

"It's all right," Cayenne told them. "Them bugs are gone."

The man got up. The rest of his family stayed where they were. The woman held onto her children, a boy of about nine and two younger girls, as if they might be snatched away at any moment. There was a look of desperation on her face—desperation and fear.

"McCallister," said the man, his voice uneven, "Roy McCallister." His hands shook. "I've got a farm, I mean, we...my family...we've got a farm, but those things, those plants, they destroyed our crops, drug off the livestock, attacked us. They were everywhere. All the places we passed were the same. We didn't see anyone else." At first the words poured out of him, then he slowed and said more reflectively, "I guess I got my family out faster than most. We headed for Woodville, thinking we'd be safe here. But, they were here, too. What are they?"

Cayenne shook her head. "I don't know. They're all round the lake. Where's Ms. Lizzie?"

"I don't know," said McCallister. "She wasn't here when we ran in."

"Have you seen anyone else?"

"A few people," said the homesteader, "but before we could even talk with anyone, the madflies came. We've been in here for some time. I thought they'd gone away once, but then I heard them again."

"What about the vines?" asked Eamon. "Have you seen them in town?"

The homesteader nodded. "Out the window, I saw some moving around."

"I've got to find Sunny," spoke up Farr. "She could be out there somewhere."

He started for the door.

"Hold on a minute, Farr," Cayenne said, grabbing him. "Nobody's going outside yet. If your Tina's safe somewhere, then she's safe. You running out there isn't going to help anyone. Let's wait a while, until we see what's going on."

Eamon realized he hadn't thought about the woman, Sunny, at all. There had been too much on his mind—too much happening. Farr must really care about her, whether she wanted him to or not.

"I'm not waiting," bellowed Farr, pulling his arm loose. "I'm going to find her."

Before anyone else could argue, or try to grab him, he was out the door and running up the road.

303

"Let him go, then," said Cayenne, watching out the window.

"Those things are going to get him," the homesteader told Eamon. "They got my boy—my oldest boy. We thought they were weeds. We were clearing out a patch, and they just took him."

Eamon heard the shame in the man's voice. He saw it on his face. His dignity had been shredded, his spirit broken. He'd failed to protect his son. Eamon knew now why the mother clung to her other children so possessively.

"We thought we'd be safe here in town," the homesteader mumbled.

"I doubt there's anywhere that's safe now," said Cayenne.

❧ ❧ ❧

They waited, peering out the windows for any kind of threat. They saw nothing. Nothing moved; there were no sounds. Eventually, they agreed they couldn't stay where they were forever. Of course, they had differing ideas on where they should go.

After some subdued debate, they decided to make their way to Tilley's to see if they could find Farr. The farmer and his family decided to go with them, feeling, Eamon guessed, there was some safety in numbers. He doubted it.

As they moved down the main road, they grew less cautious, and began calling out Farr's name. No one answered, and Eamon wondered where all the other people were.

When they reached Tilley's it was under siege. Vines ran up and down its outer walls and across its doors. They approached and saw more vines creeping out from between and underneath other buildings.

"Back up," shouted Cayenne. "We've got to go back."

"Look," Eamon said, spotting a trio running towards them.

It was a man and two women. The man had a satchel over his shoulder and a hand on each of the women. Eamon remembered him—the proprietor of Tahoe Tilley's. The women with him looked to be two of the working girls. One of them gripped a big meat cleaver. The other stumbled along as if in a daze.

"Larimore," Cayenne said when the party reached them, "where'd you come from?"

"We were hiding in the Pork Palace," Larimore said, breathing hard from his short dash. "Those cocksucking plants pulled down

304

the back wall of Tilley's and came swarming in. We got out just in time. They came out of nowhere and started snatching people, ripping off doors and walls. They were everywhere. The whole west end of town is overrun—overgrown. I grabbed who I could and we ran. Then the madflies—"

"Have you seen Farr?" Cayenne asked him. "You know, the little guy. He went to look for one of your Tinas—Sunny."

Larimore shook his head. "I haven't seen him. I don't know what happened to Sunny. Shit, I didn't see what happened to *anyone* else. I got out while I could."

The vines were creeping closer, moving slower than Eamon remembered from the first attack. At least, they seemed slower. Maybe it was the initial shock that had made it seem as if they were moving faster before.

Or maybe they knew there was no hurry now.

The TJ standing next to him suddenly staggered and fell to the ground. A vine snaking out from underneath the boardwalk had him around the ankle. Two timber jocks grabbed hold of him and freed him. Eamon saw more of the tenacious plants slithering closer.

"Let's go," someone cried out, "let's get out of here!"

Cayenne yelled, "To the dock!"

The homesteader picked up one of his little girls and looked for help, so Eamon grabbed the other. In loose formation, at an even dogtrot, they ran down the road. There was nothing in their way, no sign of plants waiting to waylay them.

Then, as they drew near the dock, they saw a contingent. The small group of refugees came to halt, not sure what to do next. Only a single dugout was tied to its moorings.

"We've got to get to that boat," said Cayenne. "Get back to the lake."

"Shit, what good will that do us?" responded one of the others. "Those things are everywhere."

"Larimore, when's the next ship due from Earthside?" she asked.

"Not for more than a month."

"You chuckleheads can stay here if you want," she said to no one in particular. "I'm going back with the rest of the timber jocks."

Larimore took the satchel from his shoulder and pulled something out of it. "This will blast those cocksucking weeds to hell and gone."

"What's that?" Cayenne asked before she realized what he carried. "Where'd you get that?"

"Got it from my miner friends. Been saving it for a special occasion."

She stopped him. "You can't use that thermite. You'll blow the dock and the boat to bits."

He looked disappointed, but realized she was right. He put the explosives back in the satchel.

Another TJ hefted the axe in his hand. "We'll cut our way through."

They charged ahead and cut a path to the dugout with surprisingly little resistance. There weren't as many vines in their way as Eamon had thought. As he handed the little girl to her father in the boat, though, he saw more creeping towards them.

"Over there!" shouted someone.

Eamon looked behind him. More of the tendrils were entering the river on the opposite bank. The leafy cables slithered across the surface of the water like eels. They were headed straight for them.

Cayenne untied the bowline and pushed the prow of the boat away from the dock as Eamon worked at the knots holding fast the stern. As he loosed the final loop and was about to push off he heard a cry. He looked towards the town and saw Farr running for the dock, waving his arms and calling out to them. A woman ran with him.

"We can't wait, Pretty Boy, push off! Push off!" yelled Cayenne.

"Hurry, Farr!" Eamon called.

"My God, let's go! They're coming!" shrieked the homesteaders's wife, clutching her children to her.

Eamon looked behind him. The vines crossing the river were closing in on them. If they grabbed hold of the boat, everyone was done for. Farr and the woman were too far away. He knew they couldn't reach the boat before the vines did. What could he do? He couldn't just leave them.

"Eamon, push off!"

"Let's go, Pretty boy!"

"Now! Do it now!"

The dugout rocked as if someone had stood up. The running woman slipped and fell. Farr stopped to help her, and Eamon made a decision. He let go of the dock cleat and pushed hard with his paddle. Then he closed his eyes.

"Paddle!" Cayenne commanded. "Everyone—as hard as you can!"

Before Eamon could muster his first stroke, the leading vine slid up to the gunwale of the dugout. He grabbed his axe and cut it. Ripping it off, he tossed the still-quivering piece into the river.

As they pulled away, the vines continued their pursuit, but gradually fell back. Eamon took one last look toward the dock. Farr and the woman had stopped running. They stood watching the boat as the current caught hold and it gained speed. He recognized the woman now. It was Sunny. She threw her arms around Farr and buried her face in his chest as the vines swarmed towards them. Farr stared at the boat.

Eamon couldn't look anymore. He plunged his paddle into the river and faced straight ahead. Though he could no longer see them, the image of those two abandoned people was burned into his memory forever.

74

McCroy led them straight to where he'd left the two canoes. Amanda knew they'd never have made it so far so fast without him guiding them. Which didn't excuse, in her mind, some of the ways he'd browbeaten them to keep going. She knew it was for their own good, but the man had a cruel streak in him. He was enjoying this.

He was hardest on the others. Maybe, she thought, it was because they needed it most. Jimiyu, Filamena and the professor appeared at times to just be going through the motions, as if they didn't care anymore. Amanda understood. They'd lost friends, family. That didn't seem to matter to McCroy. He stayed on them, kept them going, as if their survival was tantamount to his own. Either that, or he took it as some kind of testosterone-induced challenge.

Thus far, there had been no more attacks, and no more sightings of any ursu. After her desperate endeavor of using the aloe vera scent to trick the ursu into believing their young were in danger, the beasts had not returned. Whether their arrival had perplexed the vines or simply deflected them, she didn't know. It needn't have been either. It was possible the vines had retreated on their own timetable, as they had the first time. No doubt they'd be back. And it was unlikely the ursu would be there to save them again.

She had expected the vines to come in the night as the party took turns sleeping, exhausted from their march. If they came out of the darkness, she knew there was no chance of escape. But they hadn't come.

She'd been too preoccupied to think about it before, but as they hiked to the river she considered that the vines, like most plants, were probably diurnal. Sunlight not only nourished them but activated them. Of course, these weren't like any plants she'd ever studied. Concepts she was familiar with didn't necessarily apply.

The trek to the canoes had taken most of the day. Now, the sun was setting, and she hoped her theory was correct.

"All right," McCroy said, "let's get this one down to the river." His voice was calm, but his movements conveyed a sense of urgency.

They hauled the canoe a short distance and slipped it into the water. McCroy anchored it while they climbed aboard. When they were all settled, he stepped into the stern and pushed off with his paddle.

"We'll never make it going back upriver through those rapids," he said, as though to himself. "Not in the dark, that's for sure. We could go as far as we can, get off on the other bank and hoof it the rest of the way, but I'd rather not go back through the woods. Where does the river go, Doc?"

"It leads to Lake Washoe," Amanda told him. "That's where the timber jockey camps are."

"Downriver it is," he said, backwashing to turn the canoe as he spoke.

They each grabbed a paddle and got to work—Amanda and Professor Escobedo on one side, Filamena and Jimiyu on the other. McCroy steered them out into the center of the river and guided the boat north, towards Lake Washoe.

75

The sun slid slowly behind the mountaintops, leaving a stern, bloodshot sky in its wake. The strong easterly wind that had impeded their progress dissipated to a whisper. Eamon feathered his paddle and took a moment to rest. Ahead he saw the Twin Tits, reigning over Lake Washoe as always. No auroras came out to play along their summits, but on the northernmost tit the white vale of Snow Tree had been recast with a ruddy hue.

They were drawing closer to the pump station, and Eamon wondered what they would find. Would there be any survivors? Would they be all alone in this world of green-gone-mad? They came across a derelict section of TJ City that had gone adrift. There didn't appear to be anyone aboard the wreckage, but Cayenne insisted they stop and look. She and two other TJs climbed over to search. Eamon waited in the dugout with the others.

He tried to forget, but the memory was too strong. He couldn't erase the sight of Farr standing on the dock with Sunny, his face morphing from fear to resignation. Had Sunny recognized Eamon? Did she know it was he who had pushed away their only hope of escape? The images kept replaying in the cavities of his mind. The more he ignored them, the more they returned.

What he had done—what he'd had to do—delivered a whole new awareness. A repulsive awareness that churned and soured him. Callous destiny had left him with a bitter taste of irony.

The search turned up no one—not even any bodies. Cayenne and the two TJs slipped back into the dugout, and they silently resumed their course for the pump station.

When it came within sight, Eamon knew something was different. The place looked deserted, and the pump station was covered with...with what, he couldn't tell at first.

They kept paddling. Ten yards closer, and then another ten yards. Soon, they were close enough he could see the station was smothered with vines, hundreds of them, strung about the building like Christmas garlands.

Cayenne called for a halt. The big dugout continued to drift towards the shore.

Are they all gone, all dead? If so, where could they go now? There was nowhere left *to* go. Dread knotted his stomach.

Then the pump station door opened. A squad of timber jocks emerged, axes in hand. They called out, waving their arms frantically.

As they paddled for shore, Eamon saw Gash at the forefront of the TJs. He directed them to form a line, their backs to the water. It was a sensible move, though Eamon couldn't see any immediate threat. The vines enveloping the pump station weren't moving, and he saw no other signs of danger.

Gash looked perturbed as his companions helped to beach the dugout. "Cayenne, what are you doing back here? Why aren't you in the vill?"

Larimore answered.

"Woodville's overrun with those things. The whole town looks like that."

Gash glanced at Eamon as if for confirmation, but confirmation wasn't necessary, and he thought he saw some of Gash's steel resolve melt away.

"If the town's gone..."

"It's not just the town," spoke up the farmer, helping his family out of the dugout. "Those plants have destroyed most of our crops—ripped them out by the roots. How are we going to feed ourselves?" He didn't wait for an answer as he quickly ushered his family into the pump station.

"I think they got the mines, too," said Larimore. "Before the town was attacked, word came in that the copper mine had collapsed. I'm guessing it wasn't the only one."

Eamon looked apprehensively at the vines. There was no movement. They seemed docile—for the moment.

"It looks like the revolution's on hold," said Gash, staring at Larimore.

Larimore returned the stare with a Machiavellian glint. "Not if I can figure out how to turn this to our advantage."

Eamon didn't know what they were talking about, but the tension between the two men was unmistakable.

"Yeah," Gash replied, his voice gruff with sarcasm. "Well, right now, I'd say it's advantage Evergreen."

76

Nightfall came, lonesome with silence, its arrival bleak and desolate. Gloom's frayed blanket settled unruffled over the pump station. Outside, the enemy had tightened its cordon. More and more slithered in until the immediate area teemed with leafy tendrils, waiting. Waiting for what, Gash didn't know.

Inside, though none gave it voice, there was a sense that death was imminent. Their numbers had dwindled to fewer than two score; they'd retreated to the relative safety of the pump station when hundreds of vines crept out of the forest in the late-afternoon. The impassive plants had come at them slowly, deliberately, as if knowing there was nowhere for them to run.

Once inside, Gash watched out a window as the thorny tentacles writhed around the building, groping, searching for a means of access and settling for a snug purchase.

When Cayenne's party had shown up unexpectedly, he'd thought he'd lose more men getting them inside. The vines hadn't moved. Their leaves had barely even swayed with the breeze. He had stood outside the station, waiting for them to come, wondering what they were thinking. If they were thinking.

The news that the town had been overrun was a punch in the stomach. It didn't help matters that he'd had to tell Cayenne about Ramos and Ford. She'd been as close to them as anyone for as long as he had known her. He'd never seen Cayenne cry, and he didn't expect to now. She was too much of a man to let herself let go like that. But he knew she wanted to. *He* wanted to.

How many of the things were coiled around the pump station, he couldn't tell. He was certain, however, that anyone who stepped outside was stepping into his grave.

There was nothing to do but wait—wait and think. Too much time to think. Mostly, he thought about the last two days, and wondered why he'd been spared. He didn't understand it. Was it some cruel whim of fate, bent on nurturing his guilt, or was there some purpose to it? Did his life still have meaning?

He realized it had been two days since he'd last gotten stoned— or even felt the need to. Could a man who was so lost for so long stumble across the right path that abruptly? The irony of how precarious a thing resolve had turned out to be almost made him laugh. Adrenalin, apparently, was his new drug of choice.

Earlier in the day, before the vines had come at them again, he had kept the men busy disassembling the yarder. He'd gotten the idea to use the haulback drums as smudgepots, thinking the smoke might keep the vines at bay. His plan was to fashion litters to carry the pots along the trail to the vill. They could, of course, use torches. Gash was certain the vines would keep their distance from fire as much as any animal. But fire was just as abhorrent to a timber jockey. In a controlled area, close to the lake, a contained fire pit for cooking was one thing. The idea of men with torches wandering through the dry brush that covered most of these rain-deprived hills frightened him as much the vines themselves. It would take only a single spark to ignite an inferno.

As they worked on the yarder, he had realized that, without meaning to, he'd taken the lead. He'd marked himself the first time he opened his mouth to propose a course of action. Then Ramos was gone, and before he knew it the other timber jocks were looking to him to make decisions. It wasn't something he wanted, but what he wanted couldn't be a consideration anymore. The only thing to consider was how to keep everyone alive. There were no alternatives to necessity. He didn't have the luxury of thinking about himself, so he did what he could. Maybe that's what he was meant to do.

His maudlin preoccupation was cut short when he spotted Eamon headed towards him. Gash had avoided talking to him because he figured there was no point to it. As the kid approached, he saw the determination in his eyes—the anger. Eamon had something to say...or something to do.

He accepted the inevitable and took two steps into a vacant corner. There was little privacy to be had in the crowded pump station.

There were no preliminaries, no feigned politeness. Eamon looked him in the eye and asked, "Why'd you do it?"

"Why did I do what?" Though he knew exactly what the kid was referring to.

"Why did you do what you did on the space station?"

Gash lowered his head and sighed. He slumped. There was no missing the bitterness in Eamon's voice, but he sensed it wasn't all directed at him.

"I told you why," he said, looking back up at his accuser.

"Why didn't you at least try to save them? Why didn't..." Eamon wavered, as if he'd lost his train of thought. He turned his face away. Before he did, Gash read his pained expression. Was it a grimace of shame? Remorse?

Still looking away, Eamon went on, his words rusty with emotion. "I was the reason she was on that shuttle. It was my fault she was there." His voice fractured, becoming barely more than a whisper. He looked back at Gash. "I know it was a risk, but there must have been a chance. Why didn't you...why didn't you take that chance?"

He didn't answer right away. He didn't have an answer. Not one that would do either of them any good. It had never occurred to him Eamon had his own guilt to deal with. His quest for revenge was a mask—a bandage for a wound that continued to fester. It had been easier for the kid to funnel his guilt into hate than to live with it. Maybe now he'd admitted it, said it out loud, he could learn to cope with it. Maybe they both could.

"I wish I *had* done something different," said Gash. "I wish I could have traded my life for all of theirs. I would have done it in a heartbeat. But it wasn't just my life that was at stake. There were hundreds of others. Hundreds of lives depending on me to do what

315

I was supposed to do," he said. "I'd do anything to bring back those thirteen people. To bring back your mother. To bring back my wife. But I can't. I can't."

Eamon wavered, assimilating what he'd heard. "Your wife was there, too, waiting for the shuttle?"

Gash had no response. He'd said enough. He'd said more than he'd ever intended. He turned from Eamon and walked away.

❧ ❧ ❧

Nishikawa was staring out the window, as if straining to see through the dark. Anxiety layered the man's face. He looked tight enough to explode. Gash stepped up next to him, pretending to look outside.

"What are they doing out there?" Nishikawa asked, his voice edgy. "What are they waiting for?"

Gash responded, keeping his voice down. "Who knows? We can't worry about it. All we can do is—"

"We're not *doing* anything," blurted Nishikawa. "We need to get out of here."

Gash heard the panic swelling in his voice. He took the TJ by the shoulder and turned him so they were face-to-face. Still speaking in hushed tones he said, "We'll get out of here, Nishi. We will. We've just got to keep our heads—stay focused. We're men, we're timber jockeys, right? You with me on that?"

Nishikawa nodded in reluctant agreement before retreating to find a place away from the window to sit.

Gash peered outside. He saw enough to know the vines were still out there. He knew the glass, or the lumber construction, for that matter, wouldn't keep them out once they decided to come in. Nishikawa wasn't the only one who felt the oppressiveness of their prison. He felt it. He saw it on the faces around him. He heard it in the quiet. Never had he seen a roomful of timber jockeys so tranquil, so somber. And this time there was no Ford to bend their minds with a fanciful tale or two.

He stared outside. Something was different about the vines. Something he couldn't quite put his finger on. What was it?

It occurred to him that, once the sun had gone down, the plants had become much less active. From what he could see now, in the darkness, they were inert. Were they just waiting for a signal

316

of some sort? Waiting until desperation forced the caged animals out?

> Once upon a time ago,
> I set out on my own,
> Seeking my fame and fortune,
> Looking for my pile of dough.

Gash turned from the window to see whose rich baritone had begun the familiar tune. To his surprise, it was Kruto. He'd never known the man to have such a good singing voice, much less the frivolity to burst out in song of his own accord. But maybe it wasn't so frivolous. He'd certainly picked a good time for the "Timber Jockey's Lament."

> I fell in debt, I got locked up,
> I'm sure you've played that tune.
> Oh, Lord, cuttin' timber again."

More voices joined in, and soon every man in the room—and Cayenne, too—was singing.

> Rode in on a spaceship,
> I doubt they'll ever let me go.
> I spend my time at Tilley's,
> Downing fifteen drinks or more.
> When I run out of money,
> Tina says it's time to close.
> Oh, Lord, cuttin' timber again.

As he joined in singing, Gash thought more about the vines. Maybe they weren't waiting for them to come out. Maybe they were waiting for Aurora to rise again. It was the sun they needed. That's why they'd become inactive. It was sunlight that energized them.

If he was right, then the best time for them to strike out for the vill would be at sunset. That would give them the most time—the best chance to reach town. But did it still make sense to head for Woodville? He wasn't sure anymore. Maybe they could find some-

317

thing there to use against the vines. Maybe an herbicide or some other chemicals. In the relatively clear expanse of the town, fire could be used safely to defend themselves.

> A judge from the boss man's court,
> Sent me out this way.
> Somehow I got in trouble,
> And now I've got to pay.
> Ended up on Evergreen,
> Living on Lake Washoe.
> Oh, Lord, cuttin' timber again.

It was getting close to sunrise. If only he'd thought of it earlier. Could they survive another day? Would the vines be content to keep them cornered in the pump station? Or would they act, invigorated by the daylight?

> If I only had a dollar,
> For every tree I've felled.
> Every time I called "Timber!"
> And said "Boss, go to hell!"
> You know I'd ride a rocket,
> And back to Earth I'd go.
> Oh, Lord, cuttin' timber again.
> Oh, Lord, cuttin' timber again.

77

Fungal pockets isolated. Threat contained. Infestation controlled. Resistance minimal. Detriment ascertained. Impairment minimal. Expropriated nutrients rendered for germination. Priority to traumatic ontogenetic maturation. Nutrients routed. Synthesis ongoing. Bacterial network active. Phototropic nodes confirm onset of cycle. Nullification to resume with new cycle. Root crown, collective consciousness, concur.

78

The auroras danced their nightly jig in celebration of the coming dawn, but Filamena no longer saw the beauty in them. They served only as stark reminders of the alien world on which she found herself. A deceptively beautiful, beguiling world that had grown inhospitable and savage.

They had spent the night floating on the lake, exhausted, unsure of where to go in the dark. Though she'd rested, she hadn't slept. She didn't think anyone else had, either. Now she was doing her best to help propel the canoe along the shoreline where McCroy had steered them, but her arms were leaden, mechanical things. They continued their stroking rhythm by rote, without any guidance from her.

Her thoughts weren't on such mundane matters. They were back in the forest. With Max. The image of him ensnared by those horrible things wouldn't go away. It was there when she closed her eyes, and there when she opened them. But Max wasn't.

They should never have come here. It was *imbriggi*. They didn't belong here. This wasn't their world. It was a world of terrifying alien monsters. She hated them. Yet her hatred wasn't strong enough to overcome the flicker of rationality that whispered, *The monsters aren't the aliens, we are.*

Only the recollection of how she'd saved Luis from an equally grim fate mollified the blame she heaped upon herself. Without

320

meaning to, and with anguished regret, she thought of how now Luis would never have to know the truth—the truth of her infidelity, the truth of his own son's betrayal. That notion only burdened her with more guilt—remorse heaped upon shame.

She was so immersed in her self-degradation she didn't notice the vine until its damp leaves brushed her elbow. She looked down and saw the tentacle-like plants creeping over the side of the canoe. She screamed.

79

"Canoe!" yelled Cayenne.

Gash had relaxed almost enough to fall asleep when he heard the shout. He got to his feet and joined her at the window.

The first light of day crept over the mountains, but the lake hadn't yet begun to shimmer. He saw the canoe. It was a small one, with four—no, five—people aboard. It traveled along the shoreline, headed for the pump station.

Before he could react, the boat upended, its passengers thrown into the lake. He saw several tendrils slithering out from shore, extending into the water, and he knew what was happening.

He had only a moment to decide. Should he risk the lives of everyone inside for those five people, or leave them to the fate they likely all faced?

Gash shoved aside the desk they had used to barricade the door and said to Cayenne, "Shut the door behind me." He grabbed up two axes and was outside before anyone could say a word.

Thirty yards down the shore, the vines had hold of at least two people and were dragging them through the shallows choking and sputtering. He hacked at the stems strung down the shore—left, then right, both arms working furiously. The cut vines didn't retreat. They kept coming at him. More were awakening to the day and crawling out of the brush.

All of a sudden, he was surrounded. Not by vines, but by his fellow timber jocks. They chopped and cut and stomped. Several waded into the lake to rescue the people there. When everyone was ashore Gash called out, "Back to the station!"

The vines made a halfhearted attempt to keep them away from the door, but their movement was sluggish. Without losing a man, they made it back inside, safe—at least for the moment.

Gash surveyed the castaways. He only recognized one. It was the woman he'd met at Tilley's several weeks back—Amanda, the scientist who was studying the squats. He'd figured her for a goner, being all alone in the forest. Somehow, she'd hooked up with this odd lot—three men in their forties or fifties and a somewhat younger woman. The woman clung to one of the older men like a frightened child. Had she not been dunked in the lake, and so terrified, Gash guessed she would have been quite the looker. Her damp clothes certainly did nothing to conceal her voluptuous figure.

He could tell by the look in her eyes they'd been through some kind of hell. Even the man armed with a machete, a man who looked like he could handle himself, had a kind of vacant stare. They were exhausted, and Gash let them catch their breath before he suggested they get out of their wet clothes. Blankets and extra clothing were collected, and the two women went into a side room to change.

When they came out, Gash approached Amanda.

"Good to see you again. I didn't think I would."

"I didn't think I'd ever see anyone again," she replied.

He gestured in the direction of the lake. "I take it that wasn't your first encounter with those things."

She shook her head.

"I see you're still wearing Ford's medicine bag."

She took hold of the bag like she'd forgotten it was there. "Yes. As strange as it sounds, I think it may have saved my life. I need to thank your friend Ford. Is he...?"

It was Gash's turn to shake his head. The look on his face made it clear it was too late to thank Ford.

"So, who are your friends?" he asked.

She told him their names, and proceeded with a narration of how she'd come across them in the forest and joined their expedition. He grew intrigued by her account of what they'd discovered high in the mountains before the vines set on them. He had no idea what those ancient discoveries meant, or how they fit with what was happening now, but they were fascinating, nonetheless.

"If you can believe those cave paintings you came across, it would seem this isn't the first time the native plant life has been restless." It was a vain attempt at humor he immediately regretted.

"The same thing that happened to the ancient ursu is going to happen to us." It was the man she'd described as the archaeology professor. He was still holding on to his wife. "But why? I can't fathom why."

Amanda shook her head slightly, as if she had no answer. "Maybe the ursu began to do things that were no longer in harmony with their environment. Maybe their emerging intellect put them at odds with...with whatever is out there."

"That doesn't make much sense," said Gash.

She shrugged.

"No," replied the professor, "it does, in a way. On Earth, early man had a relatively short lifespan until he learned to protect himself, heal himself, to dominate all other species. Then he proliferated at an amazing rate—bred until he almost ran out of room. Intelligence led to that. Maybe it was the burgeoning intelligence in the ursu they feared."

"That who feared?"

"I don't know," the professor admitted. "Whoever...whatever it is that is in control of this world."

"Why now, though?" Gash responded. "I wish I knew what set it off. Why now, after so many years?"

"I've been thinking about that," said Amanda. "I don't know if it's such a sudden thing at all. What's time to a tree? What are years to a valley or decades to a mountain? Does the biosphere of a planet measure time in centuries or eons? I'm beginning to think maybe that's what we're talking about here—a planetary consciousness."

"That's crazy," said Larimore, who'd been listening along with several others. "The ground isn't alive." He stomped it with his boot for emphasis. "Dirt isn't intelligent."

"Get with it, Slick," Gash said. "These vines, the madflies, the flowers they told us about, they're not doing this on their own. There's something directing them. A brain of some kind. Hell, I don't know what it is, but whatever it is, it's intelligent."

Larimore dismissed him with a wave. "That's a load of crap," he said, and walked away.

"Can't blame him," said Gash. "It's hard to imagine something that immense, that connected."

"It makes me think of the aspen groves of Earth," Amanda replied. "In Colorado and Utah, there are hundreds of acres of aspens all growing out of the same root system. Each tree trunk is genetically identical. An entire grove is a single entity—Earth's largest living organism."

"You think there's something on Evergreen like that?"

"I think it's very possible," she said, "and I agree with you about it being intelligent. I was skeptical at first. How it functions is beyond my comprehension. It's likely a very different kind of intelligence, based on needs that are more rudimentary. But I can't even say that for certain."

"It's malevolent," said the black man who'd arrived with her. "That's what it is. It's evil."

"I don't think so, Jimiyu," Amanda responded. "Whatever it is, my guess is it's just defending itself, protecting its environment, its home, from what it perceives as invaders, just as we would protect our homes, our world."

The man had no response. His eyes were empty, his face blank. Gash wasn't even certain he'd heard what Amanda said.

"The five of you were lucky to make it this far."

"Not so lucky if you and your men hadn't been close by," she pointed out.

Gash took a look out the nearest window for any sign of activity from the vines. Nothing overt. They remained where they were, their grip on the pump station secure.

"So, now what?" asked Amanda.

He turned to her and saw she wasn't the only one looking at him for an answer. The same question was on the faces of several of his comrades.

"We wait for sundown when I hope those things are dormant. Then, we head for Woodville."

80

They had found a spot to be alone—as alone as they could be in a building packed with people. For a while, Luis just held her. She was glad for the closeness, for the security of his arms. She knew that, inside, he was trying to cope with the loss of his son. Resolutely, silently, without display of emotion, he would cope. But she knew him well enough to know the burden of grief he shouldered. She was certain he blamed himself.

Yet, when he finally spoke, it wasn't to ease his own guilt, or flaunt his remorse. It was to soothe her.

"You mustn't blame yourself, querida," he said. "You did all you could do. You saved my life."

"But, Max..." Filamena couldn't control herself. Her throat constricted, and she began to weep. Luis was so good to her, so caring. But he didn't understand the depth of her guilt. Now, more than ever, she was determined he never would.

"There was nothing else you could do," he said, stroking her hair. "There was nothing I could do. Max is gone. But we're still here. We have to go on."

Despite the sorrow that must have weighed on him beyond measure, her husband was more concerned for her state of mind than his own. It was so like Luis. It was why she loved him. She'd never loved him any more than she did at that moment. In that instant, she realized with certainty she would always love him.

81

His own wife. Gash had given the order to kill his own wife. Though the incident in Woodville had given him new perspective, Eamon couldn't imagine having to make such a decision. He couldn't imagine *living* with such a decision.

He'd been consumed by guilt and vindictiveness for so long, he never once stopped to question the reason for it. Now, huddling with the others inside the pump station, he wondered if Gash was truly the man he'd hunted—the man he'd wanted to kill. Was he the same man whose very name had caused him to seethe with hatred? He was Paul Brandon, but was he that man, that monster Eamon had fashioned from malice?

Regardless of everything he'd learned about Gash, it wasn't easy to dismiss so many bitter years, so much acrimony. The tempest had raged within him, battered his soul until there was no longer a place for forgiveness. What if he could forgive? If he forgave Gash, wouldn't he have to forgive himself as well?

He felt empty. He was depleted, drained. He didn't—

A piercing *craaack* tore through the stillness. Everyone looked up. A section of the ceiling split open. Before anyone could react, there was another awful noise as a second piece of roof was ripped from its supports. Sunlight spilled in, and dozens scrambled to escape falling debris.

There was no time to question or curse. The instant the roof pulled away, the vines streaked down through the gap. Questing, reaching, they grabbed one TJ before he could move and yanked him, swearing and shouting, up through the opening.

"Get back!" yelled Gash, rushing into the chaos. "Get back!"

There was more noise as the determined plants pulled down the station's rear wall. It collapsed, and another segment of roof broke away. Busted planks and roofing rained down on them. Eamon watched a huge support beam give way and fall. He had only an instant to react. He took one step, lunged and pushed Gash out of the way.

He hadn't moved fast enough. The beam caught him on the leg. The pain rang out from his knee as Gash helped him up.

"Can you walk?" he asked.

"I don't know," he said. "I think so."

There was no time for talk. The vines were everywhere. Timber jockeys struggled to defend themselves. Eamon looked for his axe. He couldn't find where he'd dropped it. Limping, he dodged one of the vines and tried to find a safe spot. There were no safe spots. Wave upon wave of the creepers snaked out of the surrounding trees and brush, twisting and writhing through the breach. He knew this was it. This was their last stand. There was nowhere to run to.

He found an axe on the floor just as a vine grabbed him by the ankle. He cut it with a single slash and ripped off the squirming stub. He looked around. Gash had disappeared in the chaos. The clamor of axe blades biting into wood coalesced with shouts and grunts until it was a single, tumultuous cacophony swirling around him.

The enemy, however, remained eerily mute. There was no cry of pain as his axe bit into another leafy stem, no death wail. Even as he tossed it aside there was another to take its place—and another. They were dauntless, seemingly infinite in number. Through hopelessness, Eamon fought on, revenge and guilt displaced by the desperation to endure.

A sudden explosion assaulted his ears and rocked the fragmented building's foundation. Even the vines wavered. Then another blast. Some of the vines withdrew. Others fell limp. Eamon remembered the explosives Larimore was carrying. He hurried outside the mangled structure and spotted the whoremaster reaching into his bag for more.

Gash came up on Larimore and pulled the satchel from his grasp.

"What the hell are you doing?"

"I'm blowing those cocksuckers to hell," Larimore countered.

"You moron, you're not playing your little revolutionary games now. You're going to—"

"Fire!" yelled someone just as Eamon heard the crackling and spotted the flashpoint. The blaze had caught in a thicket and was already moving uphill, voraciously consuming the dry underbrush.

"Stamp it out!" shouted Gash. "You men grab—"

Larimore caught him by the arm. "Let it burn!" he said. "Let it burn those things."

There was a moment of hesitation among the TJs. Some weren't sure what to do. From where they'd stood just seconds ago, setting the fire loose didn't seem like such a bad alternative.

Gash stood firm.

"Once those flames start up Swank Summit, there'll be no stopping it," he said, jerking loose from Larimore's grip. "Evergreen's a giant tinderbox. We let it burn, and this world won't be fit for anyone. The smoke and ash will kill us if the fire doesn't.

"Get moving!" he shouted. "Kruto, get men with shovels, anything they can find to scrape out a fireline above those flames. Keep the blaze away from the trees. Chaltraw, form a bucket brigade. Nishi, we've got to get the pump station operational. Cayenne, get some help to pull down as much of the flume mainline as you can. We're going to make a fire hose."

82

Hazard! Threat! Conflagration detected! Neural node awareness. Assessment vital! Response vital! Append-ages recalled, diverted. Root crown redirect. System-wide anxiety. Hazard! Hazard!

83

A searing ember stung her cheek. The smoke, ever-shifting with the wind, burned her eyes and lungs. Flames crackled and surged up the slope of the hill, through the scrub, creeping ever closer to the nearest redwoods. The timber jockeys had created a rough fireline that stopped the blaze in places, but for every square yard of brush they doused with water or cut away, two more were consumed and blackened. It was spreading so rapidly, Amanda didn't think they'd be able to stop it.

She and the others from the expedition ran to the lake to help with the bucket brigade, but there weren't enough containers, and the fire was burning steadily away from the lake. Each minute increased the distance the water had to be carried. The more they tried, the more she was certain they were fighting a hopeless battle.

"Get up higher! Get the stream on the fringes!"

She heard Gash's shouts over the chaotic din. He'd gotten the pump working, but it took a cadre of timber jockeys to maneuver the bulky hose, and there wasn't much power to the stream. They had one side of the burn contained, but the makeshift hose would only reach so far. How were they going to stop the flames burning out of range?

As she waited for the return of more buckets from the fireline, something down the shore caught her eye. Vines were reeling out of the treeline towards the lake. At first, she thought the motile plants were fleeing the fire, but then she realized they were thrusting themselves into the lake then receding into the forest. She watched the curious ballet for a few seconds before she realized what they were doing.

The intelligence that was Evergreen was aware of the threat. It was using its extremities in an attempt to extinguish the blaze. Still, though the vines had the strength, the amount of moisture they were able to carry on their leaves was minimal. It was like spitting into a furnace.

Amanda got an idea. What if they gave their buckets and bowls to the vines. It was a crazy notion. She knew that as soon as she thought of it. Nevertheless, she got McCroy's attention.

"Look at that," she said, pointing at the vines lashing into the lake not forty yards away. "They might do the hauling for us."

He got the idea immediately. They convinced their comrades to follow them down the beach with their containers. They stopped just short of the vines, filled their buckets and set them on the beach.

At first there was no reaction from the plants. They continued their frenzied splashing.

"They're not going for it," said McCroy. "I've got another idea."

He ran back down the shoreline, calling to a group of timber jockeys to help him. Amanda wasn't about to give up that easily. She grabbed one of the buckets and walked right into the flurry of animated vines.

"Amanda!" cried out Filamena. "Don't!"

"Watch out!" Jimiyu warned, but it was too late.

One of the tendrils slithered around her and then seemed to become aware of the water she held. It uncoiled, snatched the bucket from her and disappeared into the woods with it.

More vines reached, seeking the filled containers. Filamena stifled a scream, but the vines ignored the people, taking only the full buckets.

"Let's get more!" shouted Amanda.

As the group ran back down the beach, Amanda saw McCroy and half a dozen TJs pushing a pair of oversized canoes through the shallows of the lake. She looked at him quizzically as he passed, and he said, "Bigger buckets." She realized what he had in mind, and noticed there were five more of the big boats. She redirected several people to them. One look at the vines, and no explanation for what she wanted was necessary. They slid the dugouts into the water and down the shoreline.

It was an extraordinary sight—fantastic by anyone's imagination. A massive dugout, having been swamped by the TJs, was lifted over the glistening waters of the lake by a vigorous throng of vines and conveyed towards the burning forest as if it had been modified with the power of flight.

84

"Move the spray up the hill. Don't let it reach the trees!"
From his place on the fireline Gash shouted to the TJs manning the hastily devised firehose. Yet there was no command he could give to extend its reach. They'd stretched it as far as it would go. The flames kept running away from them, finding fresh fuel to guide the blaze's calamitous path up the mountainside.

They'd contained the southeastern rim of the burn, and the lake stood guard to the north, but it was to the west the wildfire kept shifting. If only the wind would turn the flames back towards the fireline they'd fashioned. But it was erratic, blowing one way then another. The giant yarder already burned like towering torch.

Gash's attention was on the treeline. Flames were lapping at the bases of several redwoods.

A ground fire was one thing, but he knew once the blaze reached the treetops it would spread from crown to crown and there'd be no stopping it. It would climb Swank Summit, fan across Bailey's Ridge and not stop until it reached the sea.

"Follow me!" he yelled and raced up the embankment to the threatened trees. He didn't look to see how many followed him, but he heard grunts and pounding footfalls behind him. They had to put out those flames before they ascended into the forest canopy.

The spray from the hose wouldn't help. The fire had burned out of its range. So, he rushed upwards as fast as his exhausted legs would carry him.

By the time he reached the first endangered tree and embedded his shovel into the soil at its base, the futility of his efforts was apparent. Flames crawled up the trunks of at least a half-dozen redwoods. He knew they'd never contain it now. He didn't stop, though. There was no stopping. He flung the shovel load of dirt up against the burning bark. He managed to smother some of the blaze, but the flames continued to climb. A pocket of sap exploded, scattering sparks through the branches above him.

He dug his shovel in again and stopped. He stared helplessly. It was out of control. A crown fire was imminent. In a matter of minutes, six trees would become sixty. All he could do was pull his men back and—

The ground beneath him trembled. It felt like a quake. A sharp jolt knocked him off his feet. He heard his men yelling. The soil around him churned as if it were being dredged. He couldn't regain his balance. He scrambled away on all fours until he found a stable spot to stand. The other TJs were already backing off, staring in disbelief. Gash looked up at the burning trees and saw them, one by one, begin to uproot.

He stood gawking as the tree roots pulled from the ground like a man pulling his boots from the mud. Each blazing tree teetered unsteadily before plummeting into the flames with a crackling thud, filling the air with flying embers.

His first thought was that luck had cast the flaming trees downhill into the black carnage instead of across the fireline, where they would have spread more destruction. His second was the realization that luck had nothing to do with it.

"Back on the fireline! Get back on that line!"

85

Jimiyu had to sit down, but his legs weren't up to it. He fell more than sat. He was drained, exhausted. His hands were torn and blistered. He couldn't take a breath without coughing. When he finally got the energy to raise his head, he saw he wasn't the only one who had collapsed. Most everyone he could see was on the ground, coughing, spitting. The fire was out, but no one reveled in its demise. Fatigue held sway, stifling all but the most laconic conversation.

Around them the mountainside smoldered in the first light of day, a panorama of blackened trees and burnt ground. Flecks of ash drifted in the faint breeze. Jimiyu glanced upward. He wondered if Evergreen's dazzling auroras had come out to dance with the dawn. If they had, he couldn't see them through the smoky haze.

Professor Escobedo sat nearby, his arms protectively around his wife. Her face was blank as chalk where it wasn't smeared with soot. McCroy lay propped against a stump, holding his machete. Repeatedly, monotonously, he let it fall point first into the ground. Dr. Rousch was with the fellow Gash, who seemed to be in charge. They talked quietly; he couldn't hear what they said. He didn't care to hear.

He was too tired to move his arms, but his mind was fully engaged. He thought about his old friend Talib, and about Chanya.

He tried but couldn't expunge from his memory the last image he had of them. It was horrifying, yet perversely apropos. They were together at last—at the end. The man who had denied himself everything, and the woman who wanted only him. Together forever. At least that was how he wanted to remember them.

Would God embrace his faithful servant, the Reverend Dr. Talib Kinisu Nikira? If so, would it be the god he had spent his life praying to, or would it be the tree god of Evergreen? He knew what Nikira would say. He would say they were one and the same.

A surge of movement distracted him. Dozens of men abruptly scurried down the hillside. Many picked up shovels and axes, and wheeled their tired bodies as if expecting a new onslaught. Jimiyu staggered to his feet and saw the cause of their alarm.

Several of the creepers, their bright-green leaves mottled with ash, wriggled out of the forest toward them. The plants moved slowly, like the terror that once again spread through Jimiyu.

The timber workers raised their weapons, preparing to repel another attack. One of them, a giant of a woman armed with a hand axe, sprang forward as if taking the offensive. The lead vine reared up and back like a cobra about to strike.

"Hold it!" called Gash. "Back away, Cayenne."

The woman stared at him. Her expression was defiant, but she did as he said.

"No one move," he ordered.

The men complied, and the distended vine, now joined by a swirling tangle of its brethren, returned to ground level. For what seemed like never-ending moments to Jimiyu, neither man nor plant showed any inclination to advance.

"Let me try something," Dr. Rousch suggested.

The timber man nodded, and she eased forward, approaching the vine with measured caution. Three feet from the nearest stem she squatted, dropped to her knees and timidly held out her hand. What she hoped for, Jimiyu didn't know. Did she think the thing was going to shake her hand?

The impasse persisted, but so did Dr. Rousch. She remained on her knees, unwavering, her hand out. Jimiyu began to fidget. Many of the others grew restless as well.

Then, so gradually as to be almost imperceptible, the leafy green vine drew closer. It rose from the ground and diffidently trailed its thornless tip across her open palm. It repeated the action, almost as if it were a test, and then withdrew as slowly as it had advanced.

Was it attempting to communicate? For the first time, Jimiyu let himself believe that maybe there was an intellect in control of these terrifying plants. The idea made them somehow less frightening.

Despite the doctor's theories, despite what he'd seen with his own eyes, he had thought of the malicious vines as violent freaks of nature. Only now did he allow himself to accept they could be the working limbs of an intelligence. He wished Nikira could have been there to see it. Was there a place in his friend's theology for such an aberrant lifeform? How would his faith define it? What would it tell him to do? Would he think such a discovery was more important than finding the City of God?

The vines that had gathered in the clearing began to withdraw. One of them—not the same one that had reached out to Dr. Rousch—slithered up the trunk of a tree that had been only mildly scorched in the fire. It coiled up and around, stopping when it reached an axe that had been casually imbedded in the tree. It curled about the protruding blade and across the handle. With an abrupt jerk it ripped the axe free of the tree trunk, let it hang suspended for a moment then hurled it high over their heads. The axe tumbled soundlessly through the air, end over end, flying so far Jimiyu could no longer see it through the murk. He heard a splash.

No one said anything. No one had to.

The vine unwound from the tree, slid gracefully to the ground and retreated into the forest, back into the incarnation that was Evergreen.

86

Contact viable. Impulse stream steady. Root crown assessment ongoing. Review. Reevaluation. Determination forthcoming.

AFTERWORD

It was during a trip to the Lake Tahoe home of my good friends Steve and Cecilia Vaughn that the first seeds for *Evergreen* began to germinate. They told me about some of the area's history, and I set out to research the subject. I want to thank them for their fortuitous inspiration. I also want to thank my long-time friends, readers, and editors Linda Bona and Carolyn Crow for their feedback, as well as fellow-writer Christopher Amidon. And I would be remiss if I failed to acknowledge my ever-faithful publisher and editor, Elizabeth Burton, for her work.

Another thank-you goes out to Greg Bear, David Brin, Vernor Vinge and Paul di Fillipo, not only for their inspiration, but for the time they took out of their busy schedules to read the work of a relative unknown.

This book called for quite a bit of research in a number of areas, and I want to express my gratitude to the professionals who helped me get the science right. A special thanks goes to Professor J. David Archibald, who suggested the scientific name for the ursu and gave me excellent feedback on the excerpts he read, as did Professor Michael G. Simpson and Dr. Stuart H. Hurlbert, all members of San Diego State University's biology department, as well as Ken Johnson, Emeritus Professor, SDSU. Thanks also go out to archaeologist Dr. Kathleen McSweeney of the University of

Edinburgh, Professor A.J. Timothy Jull, Senior Physics Research Scientist at the University of Arizona, Dr. Pat Abbott, a geologist at SDSU, Professor Julie Brigham-Grette of the University of Massachusetts' Department of Geosciences and Professor Calvin W. Johnson of the SDSU Physics Department who offered much advice.

Lastly, I want to acknowledge my fellow tower jockeys of the 110th MP Company, wherever they may be.

ABOUT THE AUTHOR

Journalist, satirist, novelist...BRUCE GOLDEN's career as a professional writer spans three decades and more genres than you can shake a pen at. Born, raised, and lived all of his life in San Diego, Bruce has worked for magazines and small newspapers as an editor, art director, columnist, and freelance writer. In the early '90s he moved to radio, where he worked as a news editor/writer, sports anchor, and feature/entertainment reporter. In late '90s it was on to television, where he worked as a producer for five years, earning a Golden Mike award to add to the one he picked up in radio along with several Society of Professional Journalist awards.

In all, Bruce published more than 200 articles and columns before deciding, at the turn of the century, to walk away from journalism and concentrate on his first love—writing speculative fiction. Since devoting himself to fiction, he's seen his short stories published more than sixty times in magazines and anthologies sold in seven countries. Along with numerous Honorable Mention awards for his short fiction from the Speculative Literature Foundation and L. Ron Hubbard's Writers of the Future contest, he's won Speculative Fiction Reader's 2003 Firebrand Fiction prize, was one of the authors selected for the Top International Horror 2003, and won the 2006 JJM prize for fiction. *Evergreen* is his third novel, following *Mortals All* and *Better Than Chocolate*. A collection of his short works, *Dancing with the Velvet Lizard*, is scheduled for publication by Zumaya Otherworlds in 2010.

Visit Bruce at http://goldentales.tripod.com

ABOUT THE ARTISTS

DANIELE SERRA lives in Sardinia (Italy), an island in the Mediterranean Sea. He's a graphic designer and illustrator. After studying painting, he began to experiment with various techniques and styles for his original artworks. He works with pencil and watercolors, combined using a digital process with scans of rust and dirty metals, coffee, old papers, and other unusual materials.

He has worked for various publishers, including DC Comics, Cemetery Dance, *Weird Tales Magazine* and New Page Books. A collection of his work, *Illusions*, which includes the artwork for *Evergreen* was published in May 2009 by Black Coat Press.

VALERIE TIBBS lives in central Illinois with her husband and teenaged son. She has more than fifteen years of experience in desktop publishing and more than twenty-five working with computers in general. She started a graphic design/computer company several years ago that finally started taking off recently with her foray into cover art. She has designed web graphics and marketing materials for her day job, and "several banners and such" for authors. In addition to her work with Zumaya, she has designed covers for Aspen Mountain Press, Amira Press, Freya's Bower, Wild Child Publishing, WordCrafter and several independent authors. A full portfolio can be found at http://vtibbs.wordpress.com.

Golden, Bruce   7/10

Evergreen

DATE DUE		
AUG 13		
SEP 2 8 2010		

LaVergne, TN USA
12 July 2010
189238LV00006B/8/P